D1594743

ATTEMPTED

ATTEMPTED

Love.
Lust. Lies

MELANIE BLACK

Melanie Black's ATTEMPTED Book One in a New Series

CONTENTS

Dedication   viii

Prologue   1

Remi   7

Myra   19

Stella   31

Remi   44

Michelle   50

Myra   58

Remi   64

Stella   74

Duo | Remi & Stella   84

Tom   93

Trio | Remi, Stella, & Myra   101

Trio | Remi, Stella, & Myra   111

Deceit   115

Stella   118

Manipulation   126

Myra   128

Power   134

Remi   136

Fury   146

Stella   148

Rachel   154

Pain   158

Trio | Remi, Stella, & Myra   160

Tom   166

Remi   172

Tom   182

Duo | Remi & Stella   187

Myra   193

Michelle   201

Tom   207

Witness   212

Stella   214

Michelle   220

Rachel   226

Tom   238

Trio | Remi, Stella, & Myra   244

Tom   253

Rise Again   264

Remi   266

Stella   272

Myra   279

Tom   291

Trio | Remi, Stella, & Myra   302

About The Author   305

This is dedicated to the only man that ever made me feel worthy of love, my husband, Dane.
Thank you for always supporting my dreams.

Copyright © 2022 by Melanie Black

All rights reserved. No part of this book may be reproduced in any manner whatsoever without written permission except in the case of brief quotations embodied in critical articles and reviews.

First Printing, 2022

Prologue

He loved the sound the rain made hitting his bedroom window. The mesmerizing repetition of what he interpreted as his name breaking the silence of his stone-cold bedroom as it hit the cracked and rotting rectangle one could call a window.

Tom, Tom, Tom, the raindrops fell in perfect balance with the rhythm in his head; he pretended each drop was an individual spirit that cherished him. Whispering his name, Tom, Tom, Tom; promising to stay with him through all the fear, embarrassment, betrayal, and loneliness. Tom knew these feelings better than any other. Sure, he had fleeting memories of happiness but could argue that the first sixteen years of his life had been mostly filled with disappointment and neglect.

He blamed his mother for this.

She was a tawdry person... too consumed with her next fuck and the paycheck that was sure to come with it to recognize him as a person, let alone her son.

Tom, Tom, Tom... but at the moment, none of that mattered. The comfort he felt through the rainstorm was enough to assure him that life would be better when he was on his own. An adult that only needed to answer to himself.

This was the night, he vowed he would always put his feelings and desires first. He'd never trust another person with his deepest thoughts and instead live a life shielded from the hurt that people inherently brought with them like unclaimed baggage that should have stayed abandoned at the terminal. In his mind, he made a silent bargaining plea with the darkness that consumed him-maybe it was his shadow self, maybe the Devil. Either way, a deal was struck. It's a shame that he'd lost patience and couldn't see into the near future where he would break that promise to himself.

Little did he know, he would fall head over heels in love with a young, bouncing blonde named Kim. Then again, meeting her might have been his part of the reward from the damning agreement.

Kim had it all; a beautiful smile that entranced him the first time their eyes met in math class, a bubbly personality resulting in what seemed like a million friends, big blue eyes, and even bigger boobs.

He wasn't sure which he loved more - those full, ocean-colored eyes or those voluminous breasts.... they had so much personality of their own. It was crazy to think that a person's single body part could attract more interest and attention than another person could in their entirety. But at the moment their eyes first locked, those enchanting pools were all he saw. Her pureness shined a light out through her pupils, penetrating straight through him. He swore every time she looked at him she was seeing right into his soul; reading his thoughts before he could even think them...

Some may say it was love at first sight because it wasn't too far into sophomore year that he became hers. And she, his.

They spent almost every waking moment together when they weren't being forced apart by annoying class schedules or some overbearing demands Kim's family sometimes made of her. He would hang off her shoulders in the hallways at school, laughing about some secret joke that they shared. Other times, wiping away one another's tears, trying to calm some brutal reality that was out of their control.

Kim knew more about him than he knew about himself. He understood her too, but there were always things he didn't know about Kim. Maybe if he had known more of the secrets she held, he could have saved himself and possibly her.

Kim would sneak out through her bedroom window every night and crawl through his rotting rectangle so they could spare each other the isolation that night inevitably brought. Tom's solitude was unforgivingly obvious; his mother spent her nights, evenings... hell, even afternoons, at the local bar trying to lure in another tool to first sucker punch in the cock and then in their wallet.

He wasn't very old when he first realized how and why his mother chronically entrapped men. It didn't take a neuroscientist to figure it out. What the fuckers saw was her tiny, toned body, manicured nails, bleach-blonde hair, and fake-filled lips. Those stupid enough to fall for her didn't see the toxicity that was underneath it all; like the cancerous cells that camped out on her skin and in her lungs from years of smoking and fake baking. The filth and tar collecting underneath those plastic shards she called nails. Even she didn't know about the infections that her body was housing from bad Botox injections. Then again, shouldn't you expect some kind of funk to infect your junk when you get your Botox shot up in you in a neighbor's basement in exchange for sexual favors?

It was palpable why he never felt respect or compassion for her or any of the dopes she brought home to pay the bills.

What awaited Kim at night was something that not even Tom knew about. Kim was escaping her cruel Hellmouth by sneaking out and sharing his bed. The alternative was to share *her* bed with someone else within her own family. She figured her secret sneak-outs were safe from coming to light since it would be odd for her stepfather to know she wasn't sound asleep in her room; quickly bringing the forced "relationship" to her mother's attention.

Tom didn't know a lot of things about Kim.

At the time, Tom saw her as an unadulterated outlet where he could relax and feel grounded. There was consistency in his life for the first time. He came to rely on their romance. And solely on her.

Until one day he couldn't.

It was Kim that called it quits.

Even now, he could recall every detail - like it happened yesterday.

They made it all the way to the middle of senior year. On the morning it happened, it seemed like the sun had risen extra early and was shining brighter and hotter than it ever had before. Tom remembered feeling hopeful... giddy even. Maybe a trip to the beach with Kim was due, he'd thought.

He dressed in his favorite plaid cut-off (because, yeah, it was the nineties) and shredded, white-washed jeans that were two sizes too big for him. Clothes he'd found shoved underneath the couch cushion - surely belonging to one of his mother's escapades. He'd collected a menagerie of findings; unintentional apology gifts he imagined. In his nightstand drawer, he kept abandoned watches, belts, gutted wallets, a single gold chain necklace, and next to it, a whole garbage bag full of clothes. Tom was a resourceful scab and though not quite a fashionista, he always made them work for him and his young, skinny bones.

His mom noticed, but well, didn't give a shit.

She never did about much.

Kim was standing in front of his locker when he arrived at the high school, tears filling her eyes. She wouldn't make direct eye contact with him as he approached.... right away he knew something was wrong. He assumed that there had been another fight at home, maybe another domestic between her mom and stepdad. But as he got closer to her, he didn't recognize the look of guilt on her face. No, this was something different, something new for her. His mind went to what he thought was the worst scenario possible–she had cheated on him. He sucked in his breath, and clenched it in his lungs, not allowing his eyes to release the tears that were welling up.

What came out of those beautiful rose-colored lips was not rose-colored at all.

Instead, her words stank of decaying garbage.

Tom heard her words, but his mind had stopped processing their meaning.

It was over.

She said she worried that they would grow apart since they each had been accepted into two very different colleges. For her, "home" would soon be on the west coast with the east remaining his. She further "excused" her decision by saying that if they were to stay together through their entire senior year, it would make their move to college even harder. She feared that one of them would fold and give up going to school to be with the other person.

He recalled her saying, "If we don't start spending some time apart before college and we both actually make it out to campus... we won't be able to stand on our own. I just need to know that I can do this without you."

That last sentence would stick with him for the rest of his life. Why should someone you love want to, quote, do this without you?

Memories from the past two years started reeling through his mind. Were they just a phase for Kim? Did she play him like his mother played those idiots at the bar? How could he have let himself trust her?

To say that it hurt barely scratched the surface of the crater-sized hole the disastrous exchange left. He was devastated, wrecked, shattered, and completely lost.

Just as he was entering adulthood he sensed that he had lost all connection with his own identity... what fucking timing. Even Satan couldn't be relied on; their deal was off, apparently, and Tom would be left alone to rebuild a tougher, more iron-clad version of himself.

His response to her: "Fuck off, whore." Racing past her, he broke through the school's doors that had been holding him prisoner for the past four years and ran. He didn't stop running until he crashed through his bedroom door, back at the shithole he called home.

It didn't matter that school had not even technically started; he was done as far as he was concerned. He was done for the morning... the day... the week... fuck, possibly the rest of the year.

He lost all motivation to get up in the mornings, let alone attend any classes. How was he supposed to react when, inevitably, he'd see her in the hall or in the few classes they shared? He needed time to figure out a plan and to get his head right.

And he did according to him.

The next time he "dated" a woman wasn't until graduating college with a 4.0 GPA in finance. He got his head straight alright, with a whole new outlook and goals for his life as an adult.

There were still nights when he awoke expecting to find her lying next to him; tucked into the crevices of his body like a warm blanket, shrouding his insecurities. Her essence had permanently woven itself in with his and he didn't know how to remove it without completely unraveling.

He promised himself that he would never have to feel heartache like that again, starting with his mother.

With no effort on either of their parts, he chose a life of estrangement from dear old Ma and wasn't at all devastated when he learned that she had passed away from an alcohol-related incident only a couple of months after he started his first "big boy" job.

No tears were shed and no grievance leave was taken.

Remi

Steam encompassed her naked body.

Remi was positive that the warmth of a shower's spray was a quick and satisfying way for *any* person to wake up and adjust to the idea of starting yet another day.

She had never considered herself a morning person but found with age that she enjoyed the serene stillness those first breaking hours offered. No other time of day could gift her with the same inimitable moments for her thoughts and self-discovery.

Many of her mornings started with some good old-fashioned *physical* self-discovery in that same shower... creating her own steam in between the falling droplets. After climaxing, those droplets gave her a deeper sense of a refresh than any other of her morning rituals.

But there was no time for discovery this morning. No, it was a Wednesday but not any ordinary one; today was the day that she was going to meet with a fertility specialist.

True, she had never given pregnancy a serious chance, as she had always prided herself on the high level of safety and protection she maintained in her love life. Yet, she knew that in all reality she was thirty-five and came from a long line of women that struggled with fertility. Yes, they all ended up having at least one child of their own, but most of them were much younger when they first conceived than she was now.

Remi felt split about her scheduled appointment for that afternoon. In many ways, she was excited and hopeful about the idea of creating a new little one and the life they would share. The things she could teach them, the places she could take them... Lord knows she had more than enough money to not only support them but to show them the world. She could thank her undying work ethic for that. On the other side of positive financial and emotional wealth was the question of a father. Who would be the right man? What would life be like for her kid if their dad wasn't necessarily in the picture?

But Remi's deep daddy issues melted away with the interruption of projected memories that hadn't even been made yet with her future offspring.

She saw a girl, probably around ten years old, laughing and smiling across the dining table, gently tossing her hair back. Her daughter would be quick-witted and intriguing from an early age. Remi guessed that she'd be an old soul... one with a higher intellect than many of her classmates and more mature interests like sushi, reading, and international travel.

They could start in England. Yes, perfect, start with a country that speaks English. It would be easier for a child to fully enjoy the experience and less confusing for them, right? Ooooh, or maybe she should start with a cruise to one of America's lesser-traveled states, Alaska? The exquisite beauty that Alaska holds is paramount to any other in the States. Or maybe....

"Hey babe, you ok in there? I know you appreciate your morning soak, but I'm starting to think you passed out and died in that box you call a shower. More like a coffin really... which would actually be pretty convenient if you are dead in there." The tone in his voice shared a smile that you could tell was there even without seeing him.

Oh, that voice. His voice, the one that severed her daydream, and startled her back to reality. His voice was proof enough of his existence and much of the reason why she felt emotionally confounded. He was an absolutely perfect partner for her.

When women say there are no good men left, they had clearly never met her boyfriend. Thankfully.

The two had been dating for a little over eight months, which to many, may not seem very long, but to Remi, it was a lifetime compared to her previous relationships. She saw their future together; old married, and still deeply in love with one another even on their deathbeds. It was crystal clear where *she* wanted them to go.

Ok, *crystal clear* is not a fair descriptor. She knew that her sweetheart of a boyfriend had made *it* crystal clear to her that he loved her but would never put a ring on hers or anyone else's finger.

Sure, he's afraid of marriage now, but it has only been eight months of dating- she had years to fix this.

As for children, they'd never discussed it before. She wasn't sure where he stood with kids, but could only imagine that he would see them as a lifelong commitment. And that would probably overwhelm him right now. So... yep, you guessed it; she hadn't hinted an ounce of interest in becoming a mother and he *positively* didn't know about her fertility appointment.

Remi physically shook the internal dialogue off her body and sent it down the shower drain.

"Ha, yeah I am fine. Just daydreaming I guess."

"You ever going to get a bigger shower so we can both fit in there and daydream at the same time? I love independence just as much as you do, but would love to shed some filth with you from time to time," he leaned in with a cute little sultry smirk on his face.

Oh, that face. He might look plain to anyone else, but to her, he could have been the next lonely romantic looking for love on *The Bachelor.* Any woman that got to know him would fight any other competitor tooth and nail. Hair extensions and silicon would be flying at every rose ceremony. He was quite the prize and she knew she was lucky to have him.

She should just tell him.

He would appreciate knowing.

What if he was truly excited about the idea?

She didn't know. Maybe he had always dreamt of being a dad.

But what if he's not?

What if he never wants a family of his own?

This would be way too much... she'd be way too much.

He'd just break things off with her and run as far in the other direction as he could get.

She wasn't ready to lose him, so instead, she popped her head out of the shower and said, "Maybe I should just get a bigger place altogether. You know, like a place big enough for two grown adults to live in... like *together*." Apparently, she was feeling brave enough to test the waters this morning quite brazenly...

But she regretted it as soon as it left her lips. Did she really just ask him to move in together like some whimsical, snarky shower joke?! Oh my God, what was wrong with her? Her greedy claws were losing grip in holding back her heart. It was amazing he hadn't run off already. She cringed and held her breath, listening for some sort of response. Her body grew tenser the longer the silence continued. And finally...

"Why Remi, are you asking to move in with me? I am flattered, but I don't think my place is big enough either and I just re-signed my lease," he continued with a slight stammer, "I mean; besides logistics, how would I ever get anything else done with you and your bangin' bod always around?."

"Oh God, it was just a joke," she defensively interrupted. She had to keep this calm, cool, and maybe somewhat casual?

Were they casual? Semi-serious? Serious enough to talk about having kids together?

The only thing she had to make sure not to do was wreck what they had going. Was it that hard for her to not be so needy?

In a split-second decision, Remi was more confident than ever that she'd be asking about a sperm donor. If he wasn't ready to share an address, why would she think he was ready to share DNA?

"I mean you understand, right hun? It's purely logistics, nothing personal," Tom said interrupting her thoughts again.

How could he be so perfect? She popped out of the shower, grabbed a towel, and dripped her way into her bedroom, where she found him sitting on the edge of the bed they shared only two nights a week. She wished it was more often, but he traveled so much for his job that it felt selfish to ask for more. She couldn't imagine constantly flying out and returning home to barely have a moment for herself... he was such a trooper when it came to his job. She'd remain the understanding, independent girlfriend he knew her to be, and maybe someday she'd be the one he'd come home to.

"Of course, hun. Honest- there was nothing behind it. There's no pressure coming from my end of things to move anything faster than you are comfortable with," she quickly responded. "A joke–that's all, I swear. I mean, besides the fact that I have been considering moving to a bigger place, maybe even a house."

"Really? That's kind of exciting. Where to?"

"Well, I was thinking it might be a kind of nice to get out of the city a bit. After working all day downtown, I feel like I need some kind of release from its grip, you know?"

Remi subconsciously started wringing her hands like she always did when she felt insecure.

"Actually, an old friend of mine from college just called me last week wondering if I was in the market for a roommate. She just got out of a pretty ugly marriage and an equally messy divorce and is looking for some extra income so she can keep the house. Michelle really wants her daughter to stay at the same school. With all the changes in the divorce, she thinks it would help to keep something consistent for her daughter. It sounds like she has a lot of friends in her classes and is pretty involved in after-school curricula too. I guess I didn't mention it to you because I am a little worried about the location... it's out in Newark."

She caught herself pausing there; Remi hadn't actually considered Michelle's proposal; she had hoped her prince charming and she might be closer to living together than they apparently were.

"I know. I know," she continued, "before you say anything I under-stand what that commute would look like. But I could just take the train in and use that time to, I don't know, pick up a hobby I guess. Maybe I'll become a master knitter or learn French." She half-heartedly laughed.

None of it was a lie; she was exhausted from living the life of constant motion, lights, and sounds. And she *had* always seen herself living outside of NYC with a family of her own. This would be kind of like that–just with a good friend and *their* kid. Who knew, maybe she would be expecting her own little addition sooner than later. It would be nice to have a home with a yard for her own child to play in. Her blood was rushing back and forth between her heart and her head. A real migraine maker.

He looked up at her with that toothy grin of his and said, "I think this all sounds perfect for you, babe. You won't be alone so much when I am traveling for work. No more sad girl syndrome. Plus you'd love living in a nice old row house in Newark. An adorable vintage balcony off the back to sip tea and read your gossip blogs. It will almost feel like I'm on vacation when I get to come and see you. Like staying at a cute little bed-and-breakfast."

She liked the image that was flashing through her mind minus the gossip magazines. She didn't actually read those... but how's he to know that?

And it *could* be romantic. This idea of having an old house filled to the brim with charming timepieces and character. She could just see herself cuddled up on a couch in front of a warm fireplace in the winter reading a book. Oh, how she wanted to share with him what she saw on the other half of that couch. But telling him she dreamt of him cradling her growing belly, smiling softly to himself, was probably too much.

Instead, she decided that the best response was a joke. "Yeah, we could even hire my new roomie to give us some couple's massages, cook us breakfast in bed... you know... the works. I am sure she would *love* that!" she added in a sarcastic tone.

He loved it. He touched his nose to hers and simply said, "Sounds perfect."

Welp, add that to the list of major life changes she wasn't planning on making. Moving and having a roommate should fit nicely in with an ultra-planned pregnancy that her boyfriend would know nothing about until she couldn't hide it from him anymore ...so around 5 months, she figured sardonically. Remi sighed sluggishly.

Whether she wanted to admit it or not, she'd lost a little something just then. Maybe it was the small shred of hope she felt slipping away–a piece of her that was still holding out for the perfect fairytale life. Tiara off-kilter and the kingdom crumbling, it was time to snap back to real life.

"I better start getting ready to head into the office. I don't even want to think about the stack of proposals on my desk. I think over half of them are already overdue, but getting some of these property owners to answer emails seems close to impossible." Another heave of exasperation, this time with the mere thought of the insurmountably frustrating workload ahead. "I mean, someone is interested in purchasing your property–a property you have up for sale and you don't even have enough gumption in life to respond to an email to cash in?! It's commercial real estate people, so it's like a lot of cash."

Remi sat on the bed, fighting her urge to ball up in the corner and cry. Instead, being the responsible adult that she sometimes hated that she was, she finished putting her heels on and stood to leave.

His response was just like him, cute and whimsical, "You know I hate to see you go, but I love to watch you walk away." He feigned an overly-dramatic realization with a faux dum-founded face made for the movies. "Blast, this is your apartment, though. Damn, it's me that has to get up and do the walking away though, isn't it? You see, I try to be funny but it always backfires.... I gotta start thinking these things through first," he chuckled.

She shared his smile and gave him a quick but heartfelt hug goodbye.

She didn't know the exact day when she would see him next but was already filled with anxiety knowing that she would have all this new information from her doctor's visit and wouldn't be sure how much, if any, to share with him.

Oh hell, that's not for her to worry about right now. She would leave that fear for their next encounter. Now, to get through the rest of her morning, tackle those ever-so-alluring stack of papers on her desk and survive the afternoon.

She half-heartedly convinced herself that the afternoon was going to be positively fulfilling and bring new hope.

She blew into her office like an out-of-season hurricane around 9:00 AM; hoping that no one would notice or at least not have the balls to call her out on not only being an hour late but for missing their daily team meeting. Remi figured that most of her team members bullshitted most of these daily blurbs anyway, so it was more of a waste of time than anything else.

If anyone *did* say something about her tardiness, she figured she'd retaliate with the fact that she'd been out schmoozing with the same pair of potential buyers until midnight three evenings the prior week

Even though fine dining and wine were involved, compliments of her company, it's still hard, sometimes unbearable, work. She hated stereotyping, but most of the "hard to work with clients", you know the ones that demanded kid-glove care, were rich old white men. Fogies who loved playing hard to get simply because of the pathetic sense of satisfaction they felt stealing away some poor, young, attractive woman's time.

Inflated, selfish, pompous geezers.

Surprisingly, she whipped through the infamous stack of neglected work. Feeling extremely accomplished and somehow still motivated, she used every last drop of time at her desk to rifle through and schedule new leads. It was a glorious day for progress, a mantra she had on mental auto-play that she only half-believed.

Holding onto that thought, she packed her laptop into her bag and wheeled her desk chair back to its resting place. Tomorrow is another day - another day welcomed in by an erotic steamy hot shower. But now, something for future Remi.

Deep breaths - just slow your roll and everything will be fine. Another BS monologue.

Her stilettos clicked with vigor across the pavement. Luck would have it that the specialist was only a few short blocks away from her work. Remi caught herself smiling in between gallant strides. Of course, she was nervous, but what she was feeling mostly at that moment was pure exhilaration. She had dreamt about this for so long and seeing a glimpse of light at the end of what had been an endless tunnel for her gave her a feeling that she wanted to cling to.

A brisk shiver of pure oxygen rushed up into her nostrils as soon as she stepped through those glorious (almost obnoxiously) large entrance doors. She saw her reflection in their flawlessly clear glass as she passed through and imagined herself with a full belly. About nine months full. Those stiletto clicks picked up a whole new level of confidence right then as she straightened her back and rolled her shoulders behind her. She was proud to be taking these next steps, she told herself. She'd welcome future Remi into her life with open arms and a slower heart rate.

The time had come... her turn was now.

Dr. Rybarczyk smiled warmly at her when he came into the room; there she sat wearing one of those sterile smelling, pink robes with awkward ties that no one knows how to actually use. There should be an instructional guide somewhere in this room to help navigate these bloody robes, she had thought to herself when she was getting changed.

Now she just sat there and smiled back at the doc, hoping that she didn't fuck up the robe tying too much. After all, she was there today to somehow prove her "adultness" and ability to raise another human being – fucking up robe ties would not look good for her.

She lifted her head and caught his direct gaze–he had nice eyes. He was probably like every other douchey doctor she knew; kind eyes while visiting patients, loaded wallets, and horrendous bedside manner. Dating doctors can be fun for *very short* stretches. But inevitably, their precious little egos get damaged because someone doesn't recognize them for their "outstanding work" in the medical field.

She decidedly chose not to comment about the stunning color or clearness of his eyes but simply offered a short, emotionless smile in return. She didn't want to seem cold since he would be the one helping her with her future mini so she followed up with a quick "how are you?".

A simple nod and this man was off and running full speed ahead into the vaginal talk. "So you have a hard time conceiving then?" His words were not meant to be cutting, but damn was he direct.

"Well, I am not sure. I haven't had unprotected sex in my life to know if I can, you know, get pregnant," Remi stammered out a response.

Doctor Rybarczyk's eyebrows furled. "Hm, not quite the response I was expecting. Typically, people come in and meet with me as a last resort; after they have tried *everything* that pops up on google and even sometimes on the dark web. So, can I ask why you are here if you haven't been actively trying?"

"Well, most of the females in my family have had issues conceiving, so I have some concerns. But mostly, I guess because I'm not sure that I have someone that I should be trying *with*." Those words stung. "I think I'm interested in learning more about using a donor, as well as, assessing my fertility."

"Well," he let out what seemed like a sigh of disapproval, "we can, without doubt, start things off with a pap smear to look for any red flags. As long as nothing comes back concerning, we would supply you with donor profiles to read up on. After you select the donor, we would move forward with the IUI process, which feels similar to another pap smear. Pretty simple process really–the hardest part can be just choosing whose genetics you want for your baby. It's kind of like shopping for *the* perfect human; one bad gene and your child has a birth defect- no pressure though." He giggled after that last statement.

Was that this man's idea of a joke? Jesus Christ, buddy, know your audience.

"What if it doesn't take, you know, what if I don't get pregnant? Or worse, can't get pregnant?" Remi asked, subconsciously wringing her hands raw.

"Let's not worry about things we don't know about yet. There's no reason for either of us to believe that you can't have babies, so let's just start with the first step." The doctor paused to look up over his glasses at her. More nonverbal judgment... "Now, you mentioned you weren't sure if you had someone to get pregnant with... is there a special person in your life and do they know that you are thinking about using a donor? I don't want you to feel like I'm prying, it's just that I have seen this scenario play out a few times before where the partner didn't even know that my patient was inquiring. Said patient becomes pregnant from the IUI process and the partner becomes enraged since the baby is not theirs. It can be a relationship ender, to say the least."

Obviously not. But Remi wasn't sure if she was willing to wait any longer. Her biological clock felt more like a ticking time bomb just waiting to implode, toppling her uterus to her toes.

"Yes, I *do* have a boyfriend and I *do* need to have that conversation with him. By the next time I see you, I'm sure we'll have that all worked out."

A big fat lie- even to herself. Major eye roll.

"Great. Would you want to do the pap smear now and get it out of the way?"

She might as well let him see her undercarriage and start the evaluation process. Isn't that why she was wearing that blasted robe, to begin with?

"Yeah, that'd be great," she said, reasserting her power of making *a* decision.

Thankfully, the pap took almost no time at all; after she got re-dressed, she was free to go–results would be available in her patient portal after 48-72 hours, and a follow-up appointment to be scheduled then. That was a lot of hours for her nerves to wreak havoc on the shredded skin at the bottoms of her hands.

Her cell phone rang as she was flagging down a cab. Her cheeks puffed out with the air she was holding but quickly realized it wasn't her boyfriend calling to say sweet nothings. It was her future room-mate. The word roommate danced around in her mind until the next inevitable next ring sounded.

What a daydreamer she was- truly amazing she ever got anything done during the day! She hit accept on her screen and started another kind of difficult conversation with her old friend Michelle.

"Hey, Michelle, or should I say, roomie..." Remi pushed a smile through her teeth. It'd change the inflection in her voice and she needed every extra ray of sunshine to help her get through this.

Myra

Clay | A *plastic-like material when wet, becoming coherent when dry.*
Fluid. Satiny. Vulnerable. Omnipotent.
Hard. Feral. Erectable. Raw.

Lush brown clay flowed gracefully down her arms - particles clinging to the streaming veins of water. Myra fancied herself similar to clay - fluid and open, but with concrete capabilities. And when her hands were in the mess of it, she felt like God herself; capable of creating immaculate life (sometimes recreating her own) from one of the most basic elements this earth has to offer. Like any good romance, she longed for its slippery curves when she wasn't elbows deep in it. A majestic love affair that couldn't be more organic if she tried. Downright, fucking orgasmic.

A couple of years ago, Myra found herself immersed in the potting world - bathing herself in pools of clay, swirling around to create dazzling ebbs and flows with her sleek bodice.

She fell hard and fast.

Her elemental soulmate introduces itself to her at an adult version of summer camp for the arts. Truthfully, it was more like a hippie commune, making her love it all the more. She adored *every* second of that summer. Being surrounded by original thinkers that weren't scared off by societal expectations or implied standards doled out by today's lesser impressive army of robots (also known as the majority of the US population) was an irrevocable experience. It was there that she first dipped her wanting hands into potting clay, feeling an instant connection... tied to Mother Earth and all of her beautifully bodacious cambers.

At the energetic age of twenty-eight, Myra's relationship with the arts was already a lifetime long.

Starting as early as age three, she'd been initially drawn to the language of dance and began formal training. It was her mother who quickly realized that the classes were stifling Myra's personal creativity and desire for self-expression. So instead, Myra chose interpretive dance lessons she could attend with her mom, who she had presumed at the time, were other moms at the community college. These women were followers of her mom - who had been leading a small all-female cult for the past decade. And still to this day.

Who would have guessed that shit?

Everybody. Except for Myra, that is.

As she got older, her passion for paint unfolded - a true abstract enthusiast at heart. She loved going into a new piece purely on emotion - letting her brushstrokes decide the story. These stroked stories shone and made a name for Myra among her fellow creative community members... or as she liked to call them, *her people.*

Evidently, the apple doesn't fall too far from the tree.

Her artwork had always done right by her and sold fairly easily when she needed to. Parting with them allowed her to afford the staples in life - for the most part. A few evenings a week, she *held* a separate waitressing job, but she had assured herself that it was mostly to market her art. You know spread the good word with her customers.

It wasn't until her somewhat newly found relationship with Mother Nature that inspired her most recent artistic musing - her passion for building, painting, drawing, and even decoupaging her own God-given powerhouse.

Her vagina.

Well, really more of the vulva - all those feel-good parts.

She became recognized for these "brazen" representations of the female anatomy. Some of it positive and lots negative, but whenever she was asked about her choice in the subject matter, she would always respond the same, "What can I say–I want the world to celebrate my sexuality *with* me, *not* in spite of me."

To be honest, she didn't fully know the depth of her go-to response but found that it shut people up pretty quickly... usually interrupting their thought pattern of accumulating judgments regarding her morals and assumed promiscuity. She may say "assumed promiscuity" but she knew she was well-versed sexually. It didn't embarrass her about the number of people she had been with. She admitted to being provocative in her sex life but in a non-slut-shaming way. In fact, she shared the same pride for her visual arts as she did the art she shared with others between the sheets. It was her overwhelming sensuality that spurred her inspirations onto the canvas.

Her own mother's motivation came into play here; she had always encouraged curiosity of all kinds, especially in finding and expressing ways of pleasure. For Myra's 16th birthday, her mother most elegantly wrapped a pearl-colored, iridescent, rabbit-style vibrator with a short but direct note, "Enjoy responsibly, Love Mom."

Myra's future boyfriends appreciated this. She was so in touch with how to reach her climax, that she knew all the better how to help them reach theirs. Her current partner was the most vocally grateful of them all - with body clenching ejaculation he screamed her praises - Myra's that is, not her mother's - because, well that'd be weird as shit.

His pet name for her actually originated during one of their sex-capades while climaxing, he yelled out *Pussycat*. The name stuck, so she penned one for him in return...keeping it within a 1940s mob theme, she started referring to him as her Tommy Gun.

Tommy Gun seemed different from the rest. He shared her passion for experiencing life from an elevated viewpoint while being extremely understanding and patient with her artistic process.

He was thoughtful, expressive, a little sarcastic, free-wheeling, and very generous in the bedroom.

It's not like he was super-sized or anything, but he definitely knew how to use it... EXTRAordinarily well. #eyesrollbackintoyourskull-good.

They never really talked about past sexual experiences with one another, but Myra felt safe in assuming that he had come with a lot of very pleased references–then again, she thought this of herself as well.

But fucking him was like prepping for a 10K marathon - he was a goddamn master. And she was thankful for that. Just *thinking* about his fingertips sliding into her panties gave her a full-blown lady boner.

Outwardly, they were a rather attractive couple. Myra, with her stunning auburn hair, twirling through life in exotic beaded tops and circular skirts that flowed as gently as her spirit. She was an activist fighting this country's domination of the white man through her art, spoken word, and drum circles. Yep, she even loved fucking drum circles... it doesn't get more boho than this chick.

Tommy Gun was tall, somewhat lanky, with sandy blonde hair always on his head and sometimes on his face. His beard was like an apparition; one day hanging emboldened from the lower quadrant of his face and gone the next, vanishing into thin air. Myra thought him sexiest BOTH ways.

But what she thought was the absolute sexiest thing about him was his matching passion for female rights - specifically in the workplace. One of his strongest viewpoints was that women belonged in the same world dominated for years by men–the land of employment.

"Being employed makes women much less reliant on finding and maintaining a male partner - women can be fully independent with their financial stability," he openly touted.

What he silently added in his head (never daring to breathe a word) was that keeping a woman working kept her honest. Myra would hate to hear that and would probably find this a deal-breaker. But she didn't know, so they carried on in perfect harmony.

Today Myra was picking up on a painting she had started a little over a year ago. It was one of her most challenging pieces. The smeared graphic stirred up a lot of her unresolved "daddy issues" or more like "lack of a daddy issue". Its intended use was almost a type of therapeutic aid, to fill the gaping hole in her heart. A crater that had been growing since her father left her around the same time she started dance class.

She barely had any memories of him, but the memories she had were still so clear. She could close her eyes and make out the details of his face down to the small scar he had on his left cheekbone. Her mom used to tell her that he got that scar shaving, but Myra had always thought it too large of a gash to be caused by a little razoring mishap. Instead, she'd let her imagination run wild from time to time- retelling stories of what *really* must have happened.

Some days Myra would tell herself that he was an undercover FBI agent that was found out by his biggest target; a struggle ensued- a knife was drawn from the assailant's hoodie pocket and grazed the once smooth crescent of his cheek. Years later, this assailant discovered her father's new identity, her mother and herself- threatening to take them all out... her father decided he had to leave to keep his family safe. Myra preferred this version. It was the most acceptable excuse for his absence she'd dreamt up, backfilling a little portion of that hole in her heart.

Fact or fiction, most of the time it was enough to push past some of her darkest revelations of abandonment.

But today, she was in a peaceful place, letting her brush round out the gentle curvature of her child-sized arms wrapping around the memory of her father's neck. There was no inner dialogue today. No turmoil. Her mind was somewhere else today. Envisioning her romantic date with her sweet, sweet lover that was right around the corner.

Mm-mmm, a day filled with painting, good food, chill vibes, and banging sex- what could be better than that combo?

She cleaned up her paints and covered her familiar shrine, hiding it in the back of her closet, ironically next to her secret masturbation toys. These gems were *never* to be used with a partner as not to be tainted with another person's potentially harmful aura.

Myra found her way through her studio apartment to her small but effective bathroom. Time to powder her nose and freshen up for her Tommy Gun. She admitted to calling him by his pet name more often than he called her by hers–he said that her name is intricately unique and was one of the sexiest things he learned about her within the first few moments of talking when they first met. He told her he was naturally drawn to women with unique names because their lives were typically just as unique and exciting as they were. He may not have shared at great length about his past lovers but could recite quite the laundry list of unique names at the drop of a hat, so...

He was such a poet at heart. Myra mentally gushed.

She wanted their evening to be perfect. They were going to share a fancy-schmancy catered meal together on her studio rooftop. She was by no means a cook, so catering was a considerate meal choice. Dinner under the stars filled with delish food, divine cocktails, and his devilish swagger- it would be a good send-off. He was leaving on his next venture in Santa Barbara; presenting stats and photos of our slaughtered rain forests- thanks to us humans and the global warming crisis we birthed. He had traveled to the Amazon last year to conduct his own research and was finally getting the chance to present his findings at a series of Global Ties conferences.

He was a saint of a man.

He was always putting himself out there; traveling the country to educate and protest with the best of them.

Myra always managed while he was away; of course, she would miss him, but having this time to dedicate solely to her artwork usually proved not only spiritually fulfilling but very profitable. Her bank account would thank the two of them for having such a mature relationship.

She put her waitressing skills to good use and started setting the old wooden farmhouse table that had become a permanent structure on her rooftop patio. It was a piece of art in itself with its natural weathering... sun-faded stain and a peeling topcoat of poly. Like so many elements of art, she appreciated its ruggedness and adaptability.

Where the table was located was probably her favorite part, though - sunbathing in the beautiful outdoors. Myra held a personal goal to do as much outside as possible like yoga, painting, eating, fornicating....

Earlier that summer, she had installed some cheesy paper lanterns and strings of large, bobbled lights that looked like large bits of stardust evading the inevitable blackness that consumed the last of the sunset's glow- preparing the world for its dark slumber. She liked to squint her eyes just enough to make the lit bobbles blurry; it made her imagine the chunks of stardust transforming into tiny fairies of the night sky. A romantic little nymph she was at heart. If Tommy Gun were there, he'd spar with her and jokingly edit that thought to "a romantic little nympho". He always knew how to make her laugh. And she always knew how to stroke his ego, among other things, she thought with a devious grin.

———————

He must have let himself in because before she knew it, he emerged from the staircase onto the rooftop. The smile that crept across his sun-tanned face said it all. She knew she had made it perfect for them, for their last night together- for a while at least.

He hadn't planned his exact return flight from Santa Barbara yet but had told her he planned to be out there for about four weeks.

A month without seeing that handsomely smug face. A month without hearing his earthy laughter. She knew that she would have to simply make this night count in every way possible. They would have to share enough food, laughs, feels, and fucks to get her through those lonely days to come.

"Well, aren't you a sight for sore eyes–and the spread up here is truly something else! Miss Myra, I think you have outdone yourself," he said, her dorky paper lanterns reflecting in his irises. He looked like a wizard standing there; magic in his eyes and though he wore earth-friendly second hands, a body beautifully carried with prestige and dominance. She knew he knew she wanted him right then and there.

But first... they dine.

He walked around to pull her chair out for her. He had good table manners.

He was a gentleman outside the bedroom. She secretly loved that about him.

"Thank you, kind sir," Myra snickered with her best fake British accent. "Will you be getting the car for me later as well? I may have dubious things to do in town this evening and would just hate to be without my driver as backup." She batted her long, winged eyelashes.

He smirked, eyes still glowing with stardust. She loved how they played together.

"As always, Pussycat, I'm here to serve."

Their eyes met through quiet pleasure and it felt like sparks were flying out from both of their bodies, colliding into one another, and then spiraling over the rooftop. Sheer fireworks.

"I managed to scrounge together some of your favorite foods though Tommy Gun. You mean so much to me I went to TWO different food trucks for our feast this evening. Just to please those fastidious taste buds of yours," Myra said, half-filled with sarcasm, the other half with braggery. She was proud of her efforts and she wanted to show it.

"Mmmmm, I can see something I want to eat without even moving my eyes," he stated whilst staring directly at her. He still made her blush. She was flushed with a full-on vag erection and it wasn't even five minutes into dinner yet. This night was already looking like it was going to be everything she had hoped it would be.

Synonymously, as if they shared the same brain and stomach, they dove into their plates of high-end street finds.

Another thing Myra was passionate about was her food; even though she couldn't cook much herself, she knew how to appreciate a well-implemented dish. Her taste buds could find and savor the smallest pinch of spice in a recipe. Her fallback career could easily be a food critic. But then she would probably have to study up on at least the basic elements of cooking which didn't sound all that appealing to her. She'd much rather be grateful and enjoy the talents of others in this category. Now... baking had a chance. Smoke a bowl, create art out of fondant, frosting, and other sweet treat supplies... she could dig it.

Plowing through their plates, it wasn't surprising that they finished the meal portion of their evening fairly quickly.

Her thoughtful Tommy Gun recommended they get a throw blanket and some pillows to snuggle up together under the stars.

"It's sure a beautiful night out here. I don't see a reason we should hurry back into the stagnant air conditioning when it is this perfect outside."

"I agree, one hundo–there are some throws of both kinds on the couch. Oh, and hey can you grab another bottle of wine while you are in there?" Myra shook the raised bottle with a prideful grin. "I mean let the good times keep rollin' right?!" Luckily, she had built her miniature version of a wine cellar in her kitchen pantry. One benefit of not cooking very often–you don't need to keep a ton of food on hand, leaving more room for her to stock up on alcoholic provisions.

To be clear, she was not an alcoholic. She didn't drink *that* much.

With a simple nod, he was gone, descending back down to her apartment for the goodies. Her eyes quickly surveyed the table to see if there were any remnants she would want to re-plate and bring over to what she was sure would soon be their sex blanket. That's when her eyes landed on a slip of paper lying on the chair he had been sitting on. Must have fallen out of his pocket. She glided over to pick it up and noticed that it smelled strongly of patchouli. She loved patchouli. What was this deliciously scented piece of paper?

She briskly unfolded it to find some numbers written in red ink. *145-4.* There was nothing else written on it but the handwriting was immaculate, like a loose cursive. What could those numbers mean? She liked a good mystery. But she loved knowing the facts right off the bat more, so she was quick to ask him as soon as the roof entrance door re-opened.

"Hey, babe. I think you dropped this. What do the numbers *145-4* mean?"

With a blank look, he bent to set their assumed love-making materials on the ground. He dropped his gaze down at his feet and then sheepishly lifted it back up to catch her inquiring look.

"I was hoping to keep this a surprise, but it looks like I might have just shot myself in the foot keeping it from you. That's a time frame... a proposed time frame that is," he said, returning from his crouched position.

"For what? What would you be trying to hide from me? Is it a doctor's appointment?" her tone, filled to the brim like her wineglass, only with sarcasm. "Oh my God, you caught leprosy when you were in the Amazon last year - I knew it...it explains so much," she continued teasing.

"No, no-no." He shook his head with a whispery laugh. "I was trying to get you a time slot for an open house at that new art gallery. I know how you have been itching for another showcase. I thought if you had something on the books it might give you some motivation to finish up some pots and paintings while I'm away that I *know* you have started and are *hiding from me*."

How was he so damn smart? Aware? Thoughtful?

She had at least eight different paintings started–all of them, besides her secret therapy painting, stashed behind her headboard. And there were at least three different pots ready to go over to the college for firing on top of her tomb of a fridge.

Had he seen them and just not mentioned anything earlier to spare her embarrassment? His niceties were adding up quickly. If this were a competition, he'd be running circles around her.

"Wow, babe. That's an incredibly kind gesture and I appreciate your efforts to get me refocused but I don't know if I can afford to rent that place out right now. Things have been a little tight."

"No worries hun. When I got a date secured, I was planning on footing the bill for you. I want to see you happy and be able to share your work with the world, babe. I mean, realistically, how are you going to gain more success without getting out there and having people *see* your stuff?"

"Well, fuck..." she sighed. "What a nice surprise–I feel bad. I kind of ruined it, didn't I?"

He simply shook his head no.

Inside herself, Myra was dancing around like a toddler on their birthday but didn't know how to properly express her level of excitement without feeling like an idiot. So, instead, she took him by the hand and guided him to the wall of the staircase. She playfully pushed him against it. With her mouth, she was innocently nibbling his ear, but with her hands, she was devilishly stroking him -reaching down in between his pants and briefs.

And it was on...

He seemed slightly unsure at first but gave in without too much extra effort on her part. He slid his hands beneath her velvet smooth ass cheeks that had a habit of peeking out of her tunic dresses whenever she raised both arms and lifted her up, forcing her legs to wrap around his hips.

He carried her over to that beautiful farmhouse picnic she had designed for the two of them. With one sweeping arm, he cleared the dishes to the other half of the table. While gently cradling her head, he laid her body atop the table; his hands explored further up her dress. Hooking his pinkies underneath the top of her lace panties, he drew them towards himself.... whisking them off her legs like an artist, revealing their newest and most intricate creation to a group of awed followers.

"Pink lace today, huh? Was someone expecting these to be removed this evening?" He said with a playful wink. "A bit presumptuous, don't you think? Or am I that predictable when it comes to you?"

He slid his head underneath her dress. She felt his tongue traveling up onto her. The warmth of his breath sent shivers down her spine, making her subconsciously arch her back towards the night sky.

Together they created friction for their own world... a world where nudity was the norm and clothes were optional. A world where stroking was encouraged at all times. A world where they could escape the daily grind and just lose themselves in each other. A world where you could orgasm as loudly as you wanted and as many times as you could.

And orgasm she did.

He blew his load inside of her. Claiming his territory. Knowing that she was on the pill.

Stella

Heart palpitating. Blood running warm. Perspiration cautiously runs along the outer rim of her brow, merely escaping being dissolved in her focused, penetrating eye. Air fills the chambers of her lungs - expanding to max capacity, building up to internal combustion level. Then, a sudden but controlled release, completely draining the lobes of oxygenated sustenance just to be pushed to the opposite extreme seconds later.

To say Stella is always in control is an understatement.

She is ruthless. A warrior. A true bad bitch.

She loved the way her muscles throbbed after a workout - she knew this comfortable pain was caused by tiny tears in the fibers of her muscles. Irritation was a small price to pay for what seemed to be a thousand times stronger, more resilient, and flexible body. She liked to think of her form as a vessel of resilience and resistance; her skin and bones serving as armor worn in battle.

Stella knew how far she could push before it reached a state of disrepair, and she liked to push it as close to that defining line as often as she could. Quite the powerful soldier she was becoming.

Inhaling with every lift and exhaling the inevitable release. She knew if she owned her breath she'd dominate the workout, transferring that power to her everyday life. Stella had been growing her inner sway for over the past decade - she found breathwork contributed to a calmer, unbending mind and a less "reactive personality". It's no secret that Stella had a history of anger that started fairly early in her life, but she understood her angst better through breath.

She could use that anger now. She could squash it, roll it, kick it around. It became something malleable, something she could manipulate to serve her in whatever situation she was in.

Having control over her emotions led to a life less fear-based and, what seems like almost an oxymoron, more indulgently satisfying. Rewards followed her as naturally as the sun in the sky, showering its glowing rays down on Stella. It illuminated her law career, her beautiful rehabbed row-house, and even her personal and professional encounters. Both in law and in gratification - most seemingly sexual but really rather psychological.

She didn't like to associate her "romantic relationships" as matters of the heart, but as a journey of ecstasy, uninhibited desire, and wild playdates in her exclusive pleasure den, or as it was more commonly referred to, the dungeon.

Stella's private dungeon was one of her favorite parts of her freshly remodeled row-house. It wasn't only because of its explicit layout, curious contraptions, or its overwhelmingly extensive collection of torture tools, but because she hid it from the surrounding masses. She could keep it secret, private- a secluded paradise where she could pander to her lusting playmates. Expose their deepest fears and weaknesses, arousing them through their humiliation.

Men or women- it didn't matter to her. They were equally satisfying. They both swell. They both self-lubricate. They both scream.

She got her *O* from witnessing their initial panic blossom into intricate self-loathing which, with full submission to Stella's *guidance,* transforms into a wondrously dark and unnatural creature. Society's disapproving stares have stifled a creature that was inside them all along. They peel their human bodies open from the inside out to escape their own internal bondage. They crawl out and dance in their shadows; finding exhilaration in their ravishing wickedness.

Writhing bodies contained by gags and bonds. Sometimes chains and shackles.

Sometimes a ventilated casket produced for occasions such as these.

A loud bang brought Stella back to the current time; her front door had opened and closed. That meant he had arrived and hopefully with one of her newest home reno additions. She worked from home on a more regular basis when she wasn't in the courtroom or meeting a client face to face. Surrounding herself in the solitude and comforts of her own home was much more intriguing than rushing into the sterile, cold law office where she worked in the outskirts of Newark.

She figured with the convenience of a new home workstation, aka a badass luxury L-shaped bamboo desk, she could more easily transition from her morning rituals to her hectic workday with no time lost or un-necessary added frustration from the long lines of traffic that naturally seemed to back up at the stoplights. It felt like the one million stop lights between her house and the freeway could magically summon travelers and commuters alike- ensnaring them for hours at a time. Every fucking day within the same thirty-minute window a glue-trap. Stella hadn't quite learned to temper her frustration in the realm of road rage yet, so adding a home office was her commitment to herself to not die of a massive heartache within the year.

Her current boy toy was delivering her fortress of efficiency at that very moment, and she was excited. It wasn't a cheap piece of furniture; it still needed some minor assembly, but it would be nothing like the furniture she had spent days putting together in her home five years prior... before her big home renovation project.

Since moving over to her current firm, she'd been rolling in the big bucks and chose to re-invest in herself through her personal real estate. She loved her row-house- it was made for this goddess. Realistically, Stella knew she may want to move around the country- hell, maybe the world, in her lifetime and may eventually need to list the space.

She had seen plenty of legal cases in her career where realtors, prop-erty owners, and many times banks, fought over properties in and near her neighborhood. The fact of the matter was that the community was flourishing, and its growth rate was sky-high. As a result, so were local listing prices. She wouldn't let some business tycoon take her- steal an opportunity for actual cash in her pocket.

Mama didn't raise no fool.

Over the past year or so, she'd made some major updates with plans to remodel at least one additional space every other year for the next four to six years. Then she would wait for the perfect moment when the market lay down, spread eagle, and enticed her to become one with it. She'd list the damn thing herself and would have no problem selling it within a week -she was confident of this.

She had worked hard to get where she was today and no bank, no man, no system was going to reap the benefits of her labor. If you are wondering if Stella brought this undying fighter mentality in the courtroom...the answer is yes. Every client. Every case. Every fight was to the death in her mind. She was made for this line of work; to survive, thrive, and rake the bastards over the coals. But in the end, no one could ever blow her internal light out.

A voice rang throughout her palace, "Honey, I'm home," he called out with a simple note of humor ringing in the air. "I have an enormous package for you that I think you'll like." His head popped around the doorframe; a smile planted perfectly on his face. His innuendos were both cute and extremely annoying to Stella. This was one of those annoying times, but Stella let it fly since she hoped he would put the new piece together for her and rearrange the office layout while doing it.

"Well, look at you saving the day, with your enormous package," she retorted, finding her inner comic of the evening. It killed her inside to pretend to be anything she wasn't, but she knew how to play the game, ensuring she always came out the winner. "You can bring it straight into my office and I will get you a glass of wine while you open it. Red or white?" She was assuming the sale...a tactic she had learned early in law school. It worked in almost every application of life. She used it often.

He was no fool either- he had grown savvy throughout his own life experiences. "I'll take a glass of each. What kind of food are you going to pair it with? I'm kind of in the mood for Chinese."

His ability to give it right back to her was one reason Stella was so attracted to him - he knew what she was doing one hundred percent of the time. He never called her out on it or tried to make her feel bad for manipulating most of their time together, but matched her authoritative undertone with expectations of his own. He wasn't weak like so many other playmates she hosted in her home; he already accepted his shadow-self and indulged it on the daily. With him, there was no transformation, his inner demon was not internally bound. He let his demon live life alongside him and found that much of his pleasure came from feeding his darker half. BDSM was made from, not just for, men like him.

Smirking, she agreed to order Chinese but made sure not to ask for what he wanted.

She would decide that for him. And he would like it.

After placing the food order, she reappeared in her office with two filled to the brim stemless wine glasses; a fruity sauvignon blanc in one hand and a rich woody merlot in the other.

"Delivery."

"Perfect timing. I was getting parched from all of this wrist labor. With how many screws are in this thing, I think we'll have to use a chainsaw to get it apart again," he chuckled. "My wrists must be getting weaker since I found you... I don't have to jerk myself off nearly as much. They are getting sore from all this hand screwing; you wouldn't have a drill and some bits, would you?"

Gross display of immaturity. Ugh.

"Of course, I have a drill with a complete 160-piece drill bit case. I am a woman of today, my dear, not fucking 1950."

"Well then, you don't need to get huffy, you just need to get it for me so I can save my arms from falling off. You know, if they fall off before dinner arrives, you're going to have to hand feed me and I know how much you would *love* that," he joked sarcastically.

His sarcasm made her happy, so she decided to go and look for the drill. She knew she had one, but that didn't mean she knew where it was.

Her search started back downstairs in the coat closet. Rummaging through gobs of hangers showcasing designer labels, she finally reached the back wall. Empty-handed, drill-wise, but she discovered a tiny curiosity. Attached to the closet's drywall was a little black flash drive. She reached out to pull it off the wall; the sound of Velcro crunched as it released its mounted grip. Moving it around in her hands, she found a small chrome button on the bottom next to what appeared to be a perfectly round sensor or speaker of sorts. She had never seen a jump drive like this one. Flipping it over, there was a matching chrome toggle to slide - for what purpose she did not know. It was becoming clearer to her that this was no ordinary jump drive, but what the fuck is it then? It had a USB port to connect to a computer. She evaluated her options. She could just plug it into her newly purchased MacBook and risk some kind of malware or virus. Too bad she'd left her work laptop at the firm; she'd be willing to take her chances with that outdated piece of space garbage. With how much money her firm generated, one would think they could spend a little more to not make their lawyers look like they were flying into the courts from the early '90s. These laptops were like the car phone of the 1980s... clunky and completely uncalled for. This mini gadget rolling around in her palm looked like it could do a million more things and, at a faster speed than the ancient Dell, she was sure to be a hand-me-down from another current employee.

Somewhat against her instincts, her voice floated out of her mouth, "Hey Mr. Williams, come here!" She didn't get shaken by much in this world, but whatever the hell this little black box was getting the best of her. While she waited for him to arrive, she tried to calm her racing heart with some controlled breathing. She counted her breaths, envisioned the flow following the infinity sign. She even tried holding it at the top of the inhale and then letting it out slowly...none of her old tricks worked. Her heart continued to beat out of her chest, sounding like a drum solo in a suddenly silent auditorium.

She was frightened, and she didn't like it. Fear is a loss of control. Stella didn't *do* no control. Remember, she is the Bad Bitch. She is the only person she allowed to incite fear in herself or others. But here she stood, hands trembling, barely being able to maintain her grip on the toy-sized intruder.

"Are you coming?!"

"Jesussss... Yes, I am coming! I had to crawl out from underneath that house-sized desk you got up there; I have a newfound compassion for the Wicked Witch of the East. Honestly, I was worried you were going to come upstairs with the drill and find my striped socks and black heels sticking out from underneath a collapsed 300-pound desk."

"What the fuck is this?" Stella said with her arm sticking straight out; she held it like it was a dead, rotting carcass that needed to be identified before being thrown outback.

His eyes thinned out with a curious stare. "Let me see that," he gently urged while extending his hand palm up to accept the insidious vermin. After rotating it a couple of times, he quickly retorted, "looks like a flash drive to me, where do you find it?"

"It was ATTACHED to the back of the closet wall with that Velcro strip."

"Do you think it might be one of the workers from the re-model? Maybe they forgot it here, you know, lost it or something..." his voice trailed off with what seemed like obvious disinterest to Stella.

His lack of interest infuriated her. But then she remembered she was in control of her reactions to things; an ultimate master of herself and all the baggage that was left unclaimed at her internal luggage pickup. Biting her lip had become her version of snapping a rubber band around your wrist.

She bit down hard enough until she could taste metallic hints of blood.

"I think it highly unlikely that it was an accident of any kind since it was securely placed...with FUCKING Velcro - that took effort. It couldn't have just slipped out of their pocket, slid up the wall like some demon-possessed child, with spiky spines burgeoning through its plas-tic shroud, and latch itself to the cold flat space of wall like a cocooning caterpillar," her dramatics were unintentionally peeking through her clenched limbic system.

He looked a bit uncomfortable by her swelled exaggeration and responded with a hum. You could see the gears moving in his brain; he was putting a lot of thought into it now...which, of course, made Stella happy. Her enthusiasm didn't last long because he eventually broke his silence only to suggest that she reach out to the contractor who managed her reno project to see if it might belong to him or anyone on his crew. Stella was not going to do that. That she knew right off the bat and her face showed it.

"How about this Stella; I can take this weight from you. If you send me the contact information, I will shoot the guy an email, let him know what we found, and hang onto it for you until someone retrieves it. This seems to be really affecting you so let me help."

What a douche; no. Stella wanted answers. This was no accident - she needed to know what the hell was on the damn thing and then unleash her legal hounds to hold whoever accountable. Accountable for an injustice apparently only she deemed despicable. No worries, Stella was no stricken chicken - she crushed souls in the courthouse, remember? She'd make someone pay for this.

———————

A crisp end of summer breeze rustled through the bouncing curtain of hair gracing the picture-perfect sway of Stella's back as she climbed out of her car. The omnipresent airwaves encapsulated her body; swirling all around her, above her, and even through her. Their whispers acted like magnets drawn to her unnatural polarization... a phenomenon of its own. Her aura took pleasure in slurping up those playful airwaves, letting them ripple through her, and then tacitly ensnaring them - never to be released again. Her spirit ate them up, chewing them bit by bit, stripping them of their power, and then spitting them back out along with the other unnecessary waste. Consumed, digested, and used, mimicking Stella's treatment of the others in her life.

Living in her self-made oblivion, she glanced down at her wrist to catch the time from the round, rose gold trimmed face that was hugging her slender arm with its soft white leathery straps. She had purchased the almost $1,000 sentiment as a gift to herself the past Christmas, and even wrapped it in an expensive-looking shimmering gold leaf paper. It had balanced perfectly in a row of rich pine branches protruding from her ravishing ten-foot flocked Christmas tree.

It was the first present she opened that year, even though she had been surrounded by friends and family. She had no guilt in treating herself and no embarrassment when she made a formal announcement to the gathering from whom her first gift of Christmas was from. She was sure this might have made her boyfriend (or whatever he was) feel bad, but luckily for probably both of them, he wasn't able to be there. Assuming an invitation was on his way, he proactively told her not to expect him for holidays...any of them. He had standing familiar commitments that he couldn't bring himself to break. She was fine with that, maybe even too fine with it...

The lavish, silver door handles illuminated in the morning sunshine beckoned to be pulled. Their overall girth suggested power, endurance, and the ability to standalone... if you were the person pulling them, you would have a transference of these qualities. Vibrations of justice would reverberate through your hands, a rush of energy through your limbs, following the spinal column, entering the abdomen, and menacingly dancing their way down to your feet- preparing them for fight or flight. After your consultation with one of the firm's lawyers, you would assuredly choose fight.

Stella jaunted the last stretch of the parking lot to reach them faster. She was on a mission this morning.

"Good morning Ms. Madsen, would you like me to deliver your coffee to your office this morning?" Rachel, the over-eager receptionist, asked. Rachel had learned to ask instead of assuming anything with Stella. A few months ago, she'd received a real ass reaming for interrupting a "private thought session" Stella had blacked out on her calendar. Stella didn't know or honestly care what her colleagues thought of Rachel but to her, she was a sad lowly little puppy who was always sniffing around for gratification - a pat on the head and a "good girl". Stella found Rachel's desire for accolades to do the simplest of tasks that were clearly outlined in her menial job description embarrassing. She did her best to not indulge Rachel, the droopy-eared bitch.

"No, thank you Rachel. That won't be necessary this morning, but please do direct all of my incoming calls to my voicemail," Stella retorted unkindly.

"Big case to work out this morning?!" Rachel gleamed with sincere interest. Disgusting.

"That's of no concern to you, Rachel. Please, just do as I asked." She made sure not to stick around long enough to witness the deflated Old Yeller's face. Stella stormed into her office and slammed the door behind her. She didn't have time for the office pet this morning. She couldn't afford distractions or people popping in on her. There was sleuthing to do and using the firm's computers during her scheduled office hours would probably be frowned upon. She plunked her bag on her mahogany standing desk and retreated back to the door, flipping the lock toggle into place.

The zipper on her black GG messenger bag slipped through its own metallic teeth like butter- nobody makes a bag like Gucci. The bag had been another present to herself for one of her recent birthdays. As an adult, Stella vowed to ensure they, her family that is, did not disappoint her again during the holidays. Stella grew up in a struggle... a financial, cultural, societal struggle. Well, she wasn't struggling now, was she?

Rifling through the bag's contents, she feverishly searched for the disturbingly bizarre piece of tech that had invited itself as a houseguest, shacking up in her coat closet. Her fingertips recognized the slightly rounded cap that covered the USB connector. She grabbed it, purging it from her bag like a fish caught on the end of a line, and carefully uncapped it. With a nano-second of hesitation, she plunked it into the side of her employer-provided laptop.

Subconsciously, she held her breath as the laptop searched for the newly installed device and its cryptic contents. Da-ding. It announced its successful finding of files. Ravenously, she clicked on the uploaded file. Still holding her breath as her eyes scanned the file lists... they appeared to be all audio files.

AudioRecordingJune1

AudioRecordingJune2

AudioRecordingJune3

AudioRecordingJune4

The list of dates didn't miss a day of opportunity to record whatever the fuck it was recording until it abruptly stopped at AudioRecording-September30, yesterday - the day she yanked it from the wall. She clicked the first date. She couldn't remember what the hell happened a week ago, so it would be a surprise to find what June 1 had in store for her.

It was hard to tell if the recording had started playing or not; the sound of echoey silence was all she heard for the first twenty minutes. Suddenly, she could hear a muffled clomping sound. Footsteps coming down the staircase that faced the closet doors, then a louder thump hitting what she assumed to be the entryway floor. "Shit," she heard June 1 Stella say, followed by the rustling of papers being plucked off the ground and shuffled for reorganization. Within a matter of a few silent seconds, she made out the sound of the doorknob being turned and a sudden slam. She looked at the player on the screen and right-clicked the slow-moving bar; time stamps appeared. It had been 7:37 AM on Tuesday, June 1...sounds like she was leaving for the office. Though she knew the audio file should be fairly silent for at least the next eight hours, she kept it playing, perhaps for reassurance. In the background, she could hear her washer and dryer beating her clothes into circular balls in the upstairs closet.

At around 10:30 AM, the scheduled dishwashing cycle must have kicked on because she heard the broken-down moan it had been making for the past year. It'd alarmed her in the beginning, but she'd had grown so accustomed to it she didn't even notice it anymore. Or maybe she did and instead of annoying her, it had become a therapeutic backdrop. She should really just get the damn thing fixed. She witnessed the time bar move at what seemed like a snail's pace, continuing in relentless stillness.

After about an hour of quiet, she felt her screen glaring at her, whispering, *this is a waste of time, there is nothing here Stella - Do. Your.Job.*

Stretching her neck side to side, she grabbed the mouse and fast-forwarded the day to 4:30 PM. Assuming there was no obligated social soiree that evening, she should be arriving home from work around that time. Pressing play again, she listened to the static rumble through her eardrums. She had a whole new appreciation for the description of silence being deafening. Resting her chin on her gently curled hand, she caught herself dozing off. She hadn't allowed herself to be *this* bored for some time and decided not to fight the overwhelming slumber that was taking over her eyelids, cautiously slowing her breath and her heart rate, which...

"Come on in - make yourself at home. Well, not really, but get comfortable. I'll be back down in a hot minute," Stella's voice boomed over the laptop speaker. Stella, real-life, lazily snoozing Stella, jumped with the sound of her own voice blaring through her office. Shit, shit, shit that's loud. Still coming to, she clumsily searched for the volume on her keyboard. After pressing too many incorrect buttons, caps lock, contorting the view of her screen, and almost installing an update, she got the damn thing turned down. She hit pause, held her breath as a bubble in her mouth, and listened for concerned conversations coming from her colleagues' offices. Finding relief in the hushed sounds of what sounded like client/lawyer phone meetings, she hit play.

Again, there was a brief silence until she heard her leather sofa cushion get plopped on. Who was there? Obviously, she was, but who was with her? Breaking through the stillness like a razor-sharp knife cutting through already melting ice cream, Stella's voice re-entered.

"I hope you haven't made yourself too snug while I was away," she recognized the sound of her whip cracking against the floor. "Get up. Move that fat-ass. You deserve to be locked up down in the dungeon, you filthy bitch." She heard her playmate relieve a nervous giggle. Socked footsteps clambered behind Stella's earth-pounding leather lace-ups. The basement door creaked open - Stella had left the creak for effect.

Descending footsteps knocking against the purposefully hard, stained, wooden scaffolding of a staircase. Another of her "special effects".

Stella pieced together it must have been a returning client of hers because there wasn't the new playmate interview upstairs. Typically, with fresh playmates (she referred to them as *playmates* so as not to confuse them with her legal *clients*), she'd wait to get into costume and instead sit down on the couch. Getting acquainted, discussing fantasies, fetishes, and agreeing upon a safe-word blah, blah, blah. All the legalities, paperwork, and signatures needed to get out of the way before they could start having *fun*.

She heard the basement door slam and rhythmically shut her laptop with it. That was enough for this morning. Pretty boring, really. Now, why the hell would someone, especially a stranger, put this in her home to record nothingness? It wasn't like it was in her bathroom or bedroom; you know her private quarters. That thought had never occurred to her before... there could be more of these damn things. Facepalm. She should have checked the other closets upstairs. Welp, she'd have to leave it as part of her self-assigned marching orders for that evening because she was just starting her long calendar of back-to-back client meetings.

Her search that evening wasn't a fruitful one. After hours of patting down the walls of closets and cupboards, she felt more like a TSA officer going above and beyond the call of duty in an airport security line. Stella ended the day heated; almost annoyed that she didn't find any more recorders - it had been a royal time suck. And she hated having her time wasted. She also despised feeling like a fool and with no more clues to what the fuck this cheap ass piece of tech junk was for or who put it there. Foolish was exactly how she went to bed feeling.

Remi

The overpowering odor of oil-burning exhaust rumbled through Remi's nostrils, similar to that of the splattered box truck's reverberating engine in her eardrums. The truck let out three long, low beeps to announce its reversed arrival; it was moving day and her worldly possessions were stealing the energetic limelight at the moment. This is probably why minimalists chose the lifestyles they do -*things* are an energy suck.

She felt a cocktail of conflicting emotions; she was drained from spending days thinning out and packing her belongings, nervous about having a roommate (she hadn't had one since her second year in college and back then, at least, hadn't been too keen on the idea), and yet grateful to not be alone as much as she had been. Her biggest divide ping-ponged between excitement and anxiety over the idea of a child sharing her living space. Remi loved kids - everything about them... her anxiety was more around the fear of failing at being good with children. What happens if Michelle's daughter didn't like her, or thought she was boring? Uptight? Not imaginative enough? Or, perhaps worst of all, too old? She got a hold of the self-defeating thoughts she already, without even meeting the girl, was projecting onto her and their future relationship. She would let time write the story instead of the premature tale she was dictating in her mind.

It was a good thing that Remi snapped back to reality when she did, otherwise, she would've been roadkill trapped under the back left wheel of her moving truck. She jumped to the side, closer to the curb and further from the monstrous tires. Waving at the driver and his partner, she gave a toothy grin... it hadn't been their fault that she was standing far off in another galaxy that was also their blind spot.

After slamming it into park and killing the engine, the movers hopped out of the truck, one of them returning Remi's grin with his own toothless smile. He was missing a couple of pearly whites in the front, one front and center, and the matching one directly below, but his smile still emulated the joy you could tell he sincerely carried throughout his life. The back of the truck flew open to reveal the dozens of looming box loads that lie in wait for her. She was grateful that only about half of them were going into the already well-established house, while the other half, along with her furniture pieces, would be placed in a local storage unit after the initial drop-off.

"Hello again," she said with a second smile. She was like a mid-westerner with her overzealous greetings and refusal to accept no to offered assistance. "Thanks so much. What can I help grab here?"

"No ma'am, that's our job. You payin' us, right?" She nodded silently in response. "Well then, let us earn that pay by doin' what ya hired us fer." His speech suggested that he wasn't originally an east-coaster; his dialect mimicked the sincerity and kindness of his smile.

With that, the two started moving the marked parcels into the front entryway of the red-bricked row house she now called home. Lush, green vines flowed up the front of it, appearing like a maze that followed the crevices of segments of bricks. Out in front was a small flower garden bordered with terracotta pavers and filled with rich black mulch, cutting off any opportunity a weed might have. Beautiful blue blooms shot through the mulch on dainty green stems, collared with ornate lacy leaves. She couldn't wait to smell them and wondered if it would be ok to cut a few for her new room?

Pushing past the now stacked boxes, she turned and waved good-bye to the movers from inside the door frame. The view of the outside world was nice enough, but it was the coziness of the home's interiors she couldn't wait to submerge herself within - light soft, warm, and welcoming. The walls downstairs were painted a light butter color that made Remi feel creamy herself.

She knew she would want to get as many of those boxes unpacked while Michelle was at work and her kiddo was at school, but she couldn't seem to stop her feet from moving on - exploring the house like an unclaimed wilderness. The walls were covered with stunning abstract paintings; Remi reached out to touch the canvases, realizing they were all originals, not prints. The bumps of the flowing strokes graced her fingertips and filled her with a sudden blip of energy. She pulled her hand away and examined it...she had never had that happen before. Could be her creative energies "calling" out to her, letting her know she had some stifled self-expression. Remi had just started reading about energy fields, auras, and other woo-woo things after hanging out with her friend Sam. He had seemed so cool, calm, and collected about everything in life; he really had his head on straight, you know? So... she asked him how he got that way. With a sly little grin, he said, "Come into the world of woo with me." She remembered laughing, but then he grabbed her hand and said that the first place they needed to start at was this fabulous little bookstore in Chinatown. She was still on the fence about what she believed and didn't but stifled creative juices noted regardless.

Everywhere Remi seemed to look was another piece of textural eye candy; velvet couches, rippling pottery, an exquisite mixture of cloth and metal light fixtures, macrame wall tapestries... she couldn't stop herself from spinning in a circle to take it all in as fast as her eyes would allow. For the first time in a long time, she felt like she was home.

Flashback to 1995

Remi's arms stood straight out from her the sides of her body like an airplane. Her long black hair flew around her with the self-made breeze her spin was generating. Around and around, she seemed to fly in her bedroom. Her stale peony curtains, the overflowing twin-sized pink bed, her rose-colored kid chandelier, her speckled floral wallpaper... whirring, whirring, whirring. As an eight-year-old, she felt anxious about how overstuffed her bedroom really was. There was so much in such a little space. And... so... much... pink. It was her room; she knew it but she never felt like it was really hers. She hated the color pink - she loved turquoise and dark blues - like the ocean. Her life felt like the tumultuous waves of an ocean at that very moment in time; hence, the spinning. She had done it as far back as she could remember. Whenever she felt sad, scared, or anxious, she would make her reality disappear in a blur.

"You're going to fall over from dizziness," her dad interrupted.

"I'm fine," she spat back. She was so disappointed in him... again. "Are you going to try to call her? Maybe she's hurt in the hospital or something? Or maybe there are burglars in her house and she's all tied up and stuff?!" She abruptly stopped spinning, scaring herself with the stories she had just invented. A young Remi immediately tumbled to the floor. He was right, too dizzy.

"Remi, I know when your mom doesn't show, it really hurts your feelings. I think we should talk about *that* instead of fantasizing these excuses for her." Their eyes connected. He had a sadness in his that matched that of Remi's. She went to him and let him hug her like he always did. No matter how much of a letdown she thought he was, her opinion would always change after a daddy, daughter bear-hug. Deep down, she knew she wasn't really mad at him. She was mad at her. Her mom, the no-show.

"Do you want to call your Halmoni? You know she always knows just how to cheer you up," he said, lightly pushing her shoulders back so she could witness his slow-spreading smile and comforting wink that he was known for.

Remi nodded, wiping away her alligator tears; she adored her Halmoni. She realized fairly early on in life that her father had been ultra-lucky to have such a great mom like her Halmoni must have been. Shei was a soft, whispery woman who told the best stories of adventuring knights and their warrior princess side-kicks. Her Halmoni had shared similar stories with her dad when he was growing up; always encouraging him to find an equal mate in life... not the princess stuck behind the cold stones of her own brazen, self-made tower, but the warrior goddess that rode gallantly next to him into the battle of life. Remi longed for her stories; especially at times like this. She showed a sudden burst of energized interest by running to grab the phone from the kitchen receiver, racing back with it, nearly dropping the boxy receiver, but somewhat gracefully catching it mid-air. She still wasn't smiling, but she knew she would be as soon as she heard the lyrical purr of her Halmoni.

And she was right.

It took her nearly all day to get through everything, but in all honesty, Remi took a little more time and thought about the process than she had expected to. This was a special home for her to be invited to live in, and she wanted to honor the importance of this new journey in a way that her good old buddy Sam would approve of. Amongst most of her drab need-to-haves, there were a handful of precious trinkets passed down from both her recently deceased Halmoni and her alive-and-well father. When she discovered one of these hidden gems, she brought it as close to her heart as she could manage, remember the beautiful memories it held and sent it gratitude for the love it had and continued to send her. After setting them down with the ease of a ticking time bomb she grabbed her dusting rag, wiping it as if she was cleaning the crevices of an infant's mouth after feeding.

Soon. Soon.

She had never been so sure; there was something about this house, this move, that relaxed her anxieties at her core. She could feel her lungs expanding...like *really expanding* with each breath she took. Its warmth flowed through her like an illuminated electrical current. But through her new source of calm, she couldn't quiet the voice in the back of her mind from weighing in, "he should have been a part of this."

Convincing her subconscious that her boyfriend's absence wasn't voluntary on his behalf but because he was away on yet another business trip sounded easier than it was. There had just been so many that month already...she was feeling like he was nothing but a figment of her own desperate and overzealous imagination. True, Remi had never enjoyed being alone, obviously stemming from abandonment issues caused by her vanishing apparition of a mom, so flying solo in so many areas in her life while being in a committed relationship felt unfair to her.

Unfair or not, it was definitely a trigger for all the baggage and memories she clung to from her past.

For her, the situations felt similar...the uncertainty of if and when you will see them again, not knowing where she stood or what part of the equation she held, and the darkness of perpetual solitude she felt in their absence. She thought it uncanny how the two people she felt most abandoned by in her life shared the same sea-green eyes as her. The color was almost identical to one another according to her memory. Like nature's pools waiting for her but then receding, waves crashing inward on themselves, seeming to change their mind about her... their desire for her diminished, draining the surrounding masses. Leaving her seas a tiny, waveless puddle.

She knew she needed more. From him. From life. For herself.

Michelle

Michelle's little green Volkswagen Beetle pulled alongside the chipped yellow curb; her daughter, Emmy's, middle school was vintage at that. Newark was filled with charming historical buildings that had been repurposed, re-homed, and rebuilt over the years and the charter school was no different. Emmy had started at the charter's elementary a few years back. She had flourished there both academically and socially. When Michelle and her now ex-husband had decided to move schools, they witnessed their young caterpillar come out of her intricately crafted cocoon to show the world her brilliance. Emmy had always been more on the quiet side of things- as parents, they always assumed this was Emmy's natural born personality, that she'd grow with throughout life. Again, as parents, they had some concerns about just *how* shy their daughter was. Emmy seemed fragile, easily shaken, maybe even broken a little, which at such a young age is heartbreaking for anyone to be a by-stander. Is this really who their little angel was? And if not, how could they help her?

Initially, they tried counseling, but the therapist found nothing concerning and released Emmy as an "early graduate" from talk therapy. Michelle remembered how her daughter's therapist looked at her during that last session. Judgment. Pure judgment. She was summing up Michelle and her husband with one stare, compiling mental notes and diagnoses of all the things that must be wrong with them to assume that this precious, perfectly fine little girl was the one needing professional help.

Michelle caught her gaze, which instantly softened her mind messaging from one of judgment to one of pity. Looking back at it all, Michelle now knew, or at least she told herself, that her daughter's therapist was the first one to pick up on their marital issues...even before Michelle did. Somehow, this healer in her early twenties knew more about what was happening in Michelle's life than she did. Unconsciously, her daughter was silently "acting out" because somehow this sensitive seven-year-old knew something wasn't right too. Her new school opened new doorways for Emmy- allowing her to start over, make new friends, send a different person outward into the world...one that wasn't hiding behind her parent's dueling personalities anymore.

As Emmy bounded towards the car door, Michelle created a mental snapshot of the beaming smile that had spread from one of Emmy's ears to the other.

"Hey Mom, you will never guess what we got to do today..." Emmy panted with exhilaration. "We threw eggs off the roof of the building. Well, not *just* eggs. First, me and my group had to design these cool little egg helmets to see if we could protect them from smashing when they hit the ground. Ours was so cool- it was ginormous! We had so much padding in there that when the teacher climbed on the roof and tossed it off, our egg didn't break! We were the winners... we were the only ones that didn't have their egg break. Mom, mom, I wish you could have been there...it was so fun!" The trill in her speedy story was like music to Michelle's ears.

"Baby, that sounds amazing... I wish I could have been there too and seen your egg helmet. What did you guys use for padding?"

A mischievous glint lit in Emmy's eye as she boldly announced, "maxi pads." A resourceful girl she was.

"You are a true innovator of egg safety for upcycled underwear lovers everywhere. I am proud of you, babe. I have some exciting news too. Remi moved in today, so when we get home, we are all going to have some cupcakes and chat."

Emmy looked pleased with the idea. She had been really open, excited even, about the news that they were going to have a new room-mate. Emmy missed having her dad in the house- when he was there it felt fuller. There was another voice, another laugh... Having Remi there wouldn't be the same, but it would sure help. Plus, Emmy kept mentioning the fact that her own name rhymed with Remi; it was an omen in her eyes that they were destined to like one another.

"Did you make the cupcakes, mom?" Emmy kiddingly grimaced.

"No. And watch yourself. Just because my cupcakes tasted like rocks last time doesn't mean I won't be able to figure out how to bake in the future. Now, I am also a realist and don't want to have our new roomie run out of the house with food poisoning right away either, so I did the adult thing and picked some up from Sonny's Bakery on my way here." Michelle kidded back.

Cupcakes from Sonny's Bakery were Emmy's favorite, and her wildly appreciative reaction showed it.

———————

It seems like a bond had been formed as soon as Remi opened their front door to welcome them home. Michelle witnessed her daughter and Remi lock eyes for the first time quickly sizing one another up and within a matter of seconds, relax their intensities to that of a telepathic hug. It was like an emotional scene in a movie where a young girl gets her first puppy, her first best friend. She knew that having Remi move in was going to be an amazing thing for Emmy. And herself.

Michelle gently nudged her daughter, pushing the girl past her enamored stares. "Let's get inside so we can start working on those cup-cakes. Their frosting mountains have been calling to my thighs all the way home saying 'eat me...eat me and I will stay with you forever."

"Oh my gosh, you got us cupcakes?! Well ladies, what *are* we waiting for?" Remi chirped.

All three of them sat like their own little family at the kitchen table devouring, finger-licking, frosting-smudging, and chatting for the next hour. "Holy cow, time is flying. Emmy, why don't you hop upstairs to your room and get your homework done before dinner?" Her request was met with the start of a whine but she quickly cut it off with a kind but firm, "now, please."

"She's a great kid Michelle. I can't thank you enough for having me. I think this break from the city is exactly what I need. Life is just getting too hectic there between work, the loudness of being home, and the quiet... it's strange to think that a place can be both obnoxiously loud yet deafeningly silent at the same time. Maybe it's all just *me*... but either way, I am grateful to be here with you guys. Plus, riding the train to and from work will help kill some extra time I have lying around," Remi said only half-joking.

Michelle could sense there was a deeper conversation here. One that Remi had been *needing* to have with some outside herself. So, she did what she did best... she multitasked. Grabbing the vegetables she needed cut, her favorite butcher-block cutting board, and a chef's knife, she plunked back down in her chair at the table and waved for Remi to do the same. Remi eagerly accepted the invitation and seemed to unravel right there in front of her.

She chopped and listened. Carefully. Remi shared with her that she was lonely; even though she had a boyfriend that she adored. But he was always traveling for work. It just seemed to her he was absent from a lot of important parts of her life, including conversations that they really *should* be having. "I mean if I don't feel comfortable talking with him about something as important as having a baby, should we really be together?"

That last statement shocked Michelle to interrupt her venting friend. "Whoa, are you pregnant, girl? Is he the father?"

"Not yet." Remi seemed to realize that more explanation was necessary, so she continued with the story about her visit to *the* Doctor to discuss IUI and the option of using a sperm donor.

"Hm...so let me get this straight, you want to have a child, totally get that, you feel like your maternal clock is ticking and want to go straight to IUI without even talking about any of this with your boyfriend? How do you know you can't get pregnant the good ole fashioned way... did something happen?" Michelle second-guessed her prying but knew that the best relationships were open and honest. Something she learned the hard way.

"No, nothing like that has happened- thank God." Remi flushed with a newfound discomfort with the conversation. "My family history isn't rich with successful conception stories, especially later in life babies. I guess I just have this feeling that I will need the help, so why waste time and unnecessary heartache beating around the bush?"

"Your relationship. That comes to mind." Michelle said, unintentionally sounding sharper than she wanted to. "Look, all I am saying is that there are other options out there than going straight to IUI. What I'm *not* saying is to get 'accidentally knocked up by your boyfriend, but I do think you *both* deserve to have the conversation at least. Maybe using a sperm donor will be the right path for you after all, but at least he'll have the chance to step up his game and maybe even his commitment to you. Shit, this is real tough for me to say... coming from my situation and all. But know I'm saying all this to help *you*, not him. No matter what the score is- I am team Remi all the way, girl!" Michelle paused momentarily to share one of her infamous motherly gazes. It went unreceived so she stayed on the soapbox a little longer.

"But I think the real discussion here is the one that you need to have with yourself...about whether to use a donor. I know you, deep down you want to believe he's 'the one', the prince charming you've been waiting for. But all the time you spend alone, feeling abandoned when you really shouldn't because you have someone special in your life. I know he says he travels a lot for work, but I also know you've mentioned that many times when he is away, and many times even when he isn't, he's really hard to get a hold of. Do you think it's at all possible that he is cyclically ghosting you? You know, um, avoiding your calls and texts... maybe even going as far as *making up* business trips? I'm not sayin', I'm just sayin'... because you know that's exactly what Dameon did to me and well, we all know why that was happening."

She hated having to play Devil's advocate here, but her intentions were good. She swore. Both in premise and explicitness.

Remi's face visually fell. "I guess I never thought about it. I mean, I have never had a reason to think he was lying to me. I know how I feel about him - I love him and I am pretty sure he loves me too..." Remi paused to think. What started as a blank stare rapidly evolved through *all* the emotions - fear, sadness, and a titch of anger. Her affections and intentions weren't the ones in question here. "This sounds nutty, but I'm trying to remember if I have ever heard him tell me he loves me or not. Sad that I have to think so hard about it. If I am being honest with myself, I don't think he's ever said it to me... Oh my God, I am such a fool. I have been assuming he feels the same way about me this entire time without ever hearing him say it. Dammit." Remi flung her head into her hands, keeping her eyes wide, peeking out through the webbed openings of her fingers.

"Hun, let's take a minute to breathe ok," Michelle hadn't meant to send her friend's world crashing or anything- she was just trying to raise a certain, hm, awareness. Yeah, that's the right word for it. "I know nothing about your relationship besides what you tell me. I just know from my own marital disaster of a shit storm that men can be really convincing when you are with them. Dameon had been cheating on me for two years, *two fucking years* before I finally got a clue. I couldn't have imagined that he could do that to me.... someone he took vows with to love, honor, and cherish for the rest of his days. I mean, I get it- love can fade but did he have such little respect for me - our family, our daughter, the life we built together that he couldn't have just come right out and said that he was in love with someone else. Better yet, before he had fallen for her... like *when* he realized his feelings have changed." She had derailed. Time to get this back on track Michelle. "Sorry, side tangent. I know you've always had the utmost respect for most men because your dad's truly one of the good ones. He never let you down or abandoned you - your mom did. But for a lot of us women, it has been the opposite.

You are a very trusting, empathetic, caring, loving soul, Remi. Just take care of *yourself* now, ask some hard questions, both to yourself and him. You'll be all the wiser and better for it."

Sitting in a state of shock, Remi silently nodded in response. Michelle could have expected the silence because it resembled her own not all that long ago. Realizations were hitting the home plate before the batter even took a swing. It was all on Remi's side of the field now; would she throw them out or let them try to steal another base?

"Listen, I'm here for you and always will be. It's in my nature. Just let me know when and how you want my help. I know a lot of good people in the medical industry from my job at the dental office, so if you are ever looking for a second opinion on the IUI thing just say the word. I even have someone that could probably give you some steeply discounted legal advice." Standing up, she walked over to Remi, who remained seated at the table, wide-eyed, and wrapped her arms around her shoulders. Unexpectedly, Remi turned around and went in for a full hug. This girl really needed a Mama growing up - she may not be blood, but she had plenty of practice being a mom.

"Thank you, Michelle. You're just who I needed in my life right now."

She'd hoped she hadn't taken the conversation too far... apparently, she hadn't.

Remi gently released from the embrace, sat back, and wiped her eyes. "I would love to sit down with that legal resource you mentioned. Advice of any kind is always welcome in this girl's world," Remi let out a short laugh, still transitioning from her sadness. "What's their name? Do you have their business card or something?"

Michelle smiled, "Her name is Stella. I *do* have her business card somewhere in my Mary Poppins' bag here. It'll take a hot minute to excavate it out of this tomb of wonders," she said while lifting her almost 12 lb purse to the table, "but we'll find it. It may have gum or food stuck to it, but we will find it." She was just having fun now.

"All good, just thankful for the help."

"And if it's no longer legible, I know who I can call to get her contact info again. Stella is in fact, a childhood friend of my sister's, so... we set lady, we set."

Myra

A bead of perspiration dripped from Myra's brow, somehow landing itself squarely in her focused eye. She blinked away the sting and kept her hands moving. She was in full-blow artisan mode. Tommy Gun was away on his trip to Santa Barbara, so there were no distractions for her. For a week straight she had been getting up at five AM to start the regimen she'd concocted to get her creative juices flowing. At the sound of her alarm going off, she'd roll over, grab her favorite bowl she'd bought with her beau, Swirls. She named it after the intricate airwaves that had been hand-blown into it and her branded stash of weed. Ah yes, the token toker celebrating the new day with an easy wake and bake. She wasn't what she considered to be a pot-head; she mostly smoked on days she scheduled herself to work in the large studio that dominated the majority of the tiny studio apartment. That's where she conceptualized the abstract displays of texture, form, and color that danced around her head- ping-ponging themselves between the two halves of her brain, breaking them into approachable pieces of expression.

After establishing her morning high, it was time to put the jams on... blaring whatever genre of music she was in the mood for that very second. She never committed to one genre for an entire day. Commitment was kind of a nasty thing in life. From there she would drape her favorite silk robe around her pj's and get cookin' - with paints and pottery, that is. Again... she was a disaster in the kitchen, but she had learned to work around it. She'd skip breakfast and order takeout for an early lunch. Ok, ok...she'd treat herself to some chocolate before gorging herself on an actual meal, but that was mainly to keep the munchies at bay.

Dinner was always a gamble. Sometimes it would be something nuked, sometimes a frozen entrée semi-charred on its departure from the oven, sometimes another round of takeout, or going out on the town, and sometimes nothing at all. Her favorite option was to treat herself after an exhausting day of emotional release with an outing - maybe a girl's night at some trashy dive bar- nomming on the traditional fan-favorite bar foods, or perhaps an evening out with her beau. Their date venues were always leaps and bounds above her girl-night hubs; farm-to-table, organic, gluten-free, vegan-friendly, you know, high-end hipster places. She loved these types of nights best. Tommy Gun's definition of a "nightcap" wasn't sharing something brain-buzzing together, well, not as a liquid anyway. instead, they would book-end these types of nights with semi-tantric sexual explorations. Myra never felt so connected to another human being then she did when they were coupled.

Admittedly, she could shack up with good-for-a-night any time she wanted, and truth be told, sex was always alluring for Myra so it had been hard to walk away from at least a few of the offers that had been laid out on the table. But she had always said no. She knew she had the best there was - it seemed like something customized, especially for her vagina and hopefully no one else's. She could neither confirm nor deny that last sentiment but her fingers were crossed.

Before him, she had cheated on almost *all* of her previous boy-friends, but maybe it was because she never felt like they were serious about each other. Like both parties were willing but not able. Not capable of *really* loving one another. It wasn't like this with Tommy Gun. She may never allow something shiny on her ring finger but she would consider sharing a life with him - in a non-legally binding, more nontraditional, less westernized way.

With a sigh, she freed the last droplets of thoughts about him. She would let the fact that she really missed him and his energy, evaporate outside of her body and on the tops of her brush instead, sealing her devotions into her pieces. Or was it more like camouflaging them from the world to keep them only for herself? You can't get hurt if they don't know how much they matter.

Buzzkill, major buzzkill.

She needed to get her mind back to focusing on her art. She assumed her show was right around the corner, even though she hadn't yet heard the confirmation or details from Tommy Gun. She'd texted him a couple of days ago about it; a quick response merely read "it's all set". Instinctively, Myra followed up with a message asking for the deets so could get them to her peeps. But nothing came. No response now for two-and-a-half days. She wasn't worried about him- as in his well-being and such, instead; she chose to assume goodness and settled on the idea that he was simply tied up in the project he was out there for.

An idea shot into her mind, a somewhat impulsive idea, maybe a little knee-jerky, but a fair one. She rushed to her microminiature bathroom to freshen up for a newly decided errand. This is just the thing she needed to get her groove back.

———————

The subway was hopping, as always. Myra had gotten on her train with one of her favorite songs by one of her favorite bands, Garbage, playing in her head. She silently mouthed the lyrics *I'm Only Happy When It Rains* over and over again until her ride screeched to a stop. Looking up to find her best route of exit through the crowd, she caught the eye of a little girl, probably around ten years old, that had been staring at her with what appeared to be concern. It probably *looked* like Myra was fighting for her sanity... speaking silently (singing, actually) to herself without headphones on. Come to think of it, she had even been rocking a little back and forth on the ride, jiving to the inaudible music silently blaring into her eardrums. She laughed a little to herself, probably making the situation worse because the girl hadn't yet looked away. Her little display on the train would have freaked the shit out of ten-year-old Myra, too.

She played it up a bit as she walked past her to exit the train. At the very moment that the two of them were parallel to one another, she turned and stared directly into the kid's eyes, crossed her pupils, and sputtered out a shriek. She hadn't stuck around long enough to witness the presumed "freaked as shit" petrification on the young girl's face, but jetted out the train doors.

She was such a bitch sometimes. Being a server showed her how to be one.

A fun bitch, though.

A bitch who should probably never have children.

And she wouldn't, she promised herself.

As her boots planted themselves against the concrete jungle of sidewalks, her upper body was performing a dance of sorts to push through the bustling crowds NYC was known for. The beauty of the diverse faces in the seas of people she swam through reinstilled why she loved living in the big apple. People are works of art themselves. Every dimple, wrinkle, crevice, skin texture, hairline... each an intrinsic masterpiece sharing a timeline, a story of their wearers. The lumps and folds that our clothes hide are some of nature's most exquisite sculptures, holding power behind the experiences that created them.

But perhaps the most ornate, irreplaceable, and incomparable was the female vulva. The soft curvature and feathering of its lips frame themselves around the erogenous pleasure center, showcasing our world's creator. Though she didn't want children herself, she appreciated the evolutionary nourishment it gave and on a more personal level, the transcendental sensations that stoked the flames of her creativity. Sexual energy and artistic energies are the same. The hornier, the happier she thought to herself with an inwardly devious grin.

Her legs led her around the corner and straight to the front doors of the new gallery, Expose'. Excitedly, she guided the heavy doors towards herself and stepped through them with vigor and curiosity. Two women sat chatting in velvet green upholstered mid-century modern chairs; the stunning zebra-esque wood grain on the chairs' structures was highlighted with a natural-looking varnish. Placed in between them was a multitiered milk-glass tabletop that seemed to balance on a large black Tourmaline stone, or maybe Obsidian. Whichever it was, Myra fell in love with the trendy nook right away. As for the prime display space, it was fairly typical - white bare walls. The ceilings added intrigue and a flavorful depth to it; they were open with exposed industrial-sized HVAC, but it was the color of the HVAC that caught her attention. Instead of mundane gray or muted tones of browns and blacks, it was a pearlized metallic gold and behind it a navy-blue paint making it look like a midnight sky with comets shooting across. Its contrast against the white surroundings and pops of various textured greens made the place look like a sleek, lush forest. A forest to forget yourself in. A forest to be ravished in. A forest to wander through; to get lost hiking the dirt-floored paths of sculptures and canvasses.

Twirling around the space she realized that the only other people there were the couple of chatty Cathies still seated ahead of her. Assuming they must work there she flew off in their direction. As she approached their conversation, she was struck by the dark-haired woman's eyes; their green translucence almost seemed ghastly. Myra wasn't scared, she was mesmerized. The dark-haired woman turned her head, realizing her presence; the two of their eyes met, Myra felt the stranger peering deep into her soul gathering her memories, private thoughts, pain, and fears. Though neither of them had spoken a word aloud yet, it was as if Myra had known these mysterious eyes her whole life. They reminded her of someone else. Her Tommy Gun had rich green eyes too, but nothing as piercingly perfect as this woman's pair. Sucking in a breath, Myra couldn't make herself speak. She was under a spell of sorts and was forced to wait for one of the others in the space to speak first. Someone finally did. But it was only after the green-eyed goddess nodded to her partner. The other blonde-haired, plainly brown-eyed woman turned with a slight smile on her rose-color painted lips.

"Hello, can I help you?"

Concentrating her attention on the speaker, they finally released her from entrancement. "Um, yes, hi." Myra was nervous. She was never nervous. What was happening here? "I, well, um, yeah, let's just start over," she laughed. "My name is Myra Kennett and I think I have a display reservation here with a showcase evening. I just need to know what the dates are for the show and what evening the event is scheduled for." She knew she sounded like a babbling idiot- her intro started off wobbly with the follow-up questions making her appear completely clueless and downright concerning. She knew how she must have looked...again downright concerning. Maybe she was too high? Still drunk from the night before? Get it together, girl.

The blonde's smile grew into a toothy display. "Hi, my name is Jenn and I am the gallery manager here at Expose'. Let me pull up the reservation schedule here and we will get you all squared away," she said, opening the small silver laptop that lay hidden on her lap.

After several clicks and a few mini typing sessions, she returned her attention to Myra and asked how she spelled her last name.

"K-E-N-N-E-T-T." With seemingly no control over her body or mind, Myra turned her head and opened her mouth to speak to the mysterious brunette. "Your eyes are magnetic - like watery energy fields. Do you work here too?" She involuntarily blurted. What the fuck was wrong with her? Too. Much. Weed.

The woman giggled, "Well thank you, I am flattered. I get the almond shape from my Dad's side, half Korean girl right here," she said, pointing inwardly at herself, "and I get the color from my Mom. Who is, err, was, is...? Not sure what tense to use there, but she is not Korean." She seemed anxious too. Maybe she felt the same odd connection to Myra that she had felt to her... or maybe she was your everyday basket-case. "And, no, again I'm flattered, but I don't work here... I am in commercial real estate. I helped Jenn here find and purchase this place. Remi. Remi Nash." she stuck her hand out to shake Myra's.

"Wow, well this place is pretty..."

Jenn's voice cut in. "Sorry to interrupt, Ms. Kennett, but could your reservation be under a different name, perhaps? I am not seeing any-thing under Kennett or Myra. Myra is M-Y-R-A, right?"

"Yup, that's me. Oh shit, yeah, um, the reservation could be under my boyfriend's name, Tom - Tom Williams." Remi's head popped up.

Remi

Hearing his name come from another woman's mouth cut Remi to the quick. Tom Williams was a very generic name... they *were* in NYC-an enormous city with probably hundreds of Tom Williams'. It was childish for her to assume this was *her* boyfriend; *her* Tom Williams. She physically shook the thought from her body resulting in Jenn looking up from her screen.

"Sorry, just a chill," Remi reassured the group. Dammit, Michelle for planting the idea that Tom could lie. That Tom could cheat. It was highly improbable - close to impossible... probably. Great, now her inner voice was prattling on.

"Yeah, it was actually Tommy Gun, Tom, sorry, habit, that booked the space for me. It was a surprise before he left town for work."

"Well, he sounds very thoughtful. You're lucky to have such a loving person in your life," Jenn smiled, showing her perfectly symmetrical rows of pearly whites. " Did he happen to give you *any* details about his reservation for you? I'm just having a hard time finding anything under that name, either. This is all new, so it's probably an error on our side. We will get this figured out; I promise."

Myra reached into her multi-colored, quilted messenger-style bag and pulled out a piece of paper. Remi tilted her head and stretched her neck to take a glimpse of it. It seemed like an hour had passed while Myra tried to get her fingers to unfold the damn thing. She seemed jittery to Remi, maybe this Myra woman was shook too?

Remi shamelessly realized that this, none of this, was any of her business; she had come to visit with Jenn to see how she liked the space, talk about the satisfaction survey that was going to be sent to her via email, and of course, see if Jenn had any referrals for her. But this Myra chick, her scheduling debacle, had nothing to do with her, yet she couldn't seem to break away or politely excuse herself giving Myra and Jenn the privacy they probably deserved. She wanted to know more about this woman, Myra, and her sweet, thoughtful, same-name as her beau's, partner. A partner that seemed to share the same letterhead as *her* Tom's employer. Remi's eyes bulged.

She wanted to grab the paper from Myra's hands to inspect it, but she refrained from looking like a crazy person and instead played it cool with an easy-breezy leading question.

When had the words *easy-breezy* ever been used to describe her? Never. Not even once.

"Donaldson's, huh? Is that where your boyfriend works? I have a few friends that work there too - great place, I hear."

Myra turned her attention to her. "Oh no. Um, my boyfriend is a nature activist. He studies global warming and its effects, so he travels a lot to a lot of cool places. Last year he was in the Amazon conducting a study for a few months... fascinating stuff. I couldn't be prouder of him."

"That's really neat. He must have just picked up some of Donaldson's freebies at one of their info booths or something? They *are* known for their all-encompassing presence," Remi joked. Everyone knew that Donaldson's was slowly taking over the manufacturing industry on the east coast and was, ironically enough regarding Myra's story of her boyfriend's career, a key player in the United States' pollution levels. Which, we all know, contributes to global warming. Remi didn't buy it. A real "nature activist" wouldn't even *touch paper* with Donaldson's logo on it, let alone use it to jot down loving messages to their girlfriends.

She pushed past the sudden inexplicable annoyance she was feeling and instead narrowed her eyes to scan the note, trying to make out what appeared to have been feverishly scribbled down. Myra's hand subtly shifted, fatefully, turning the note directly towards Remi. She had an unobstructed view now and she almost immediately regretted it. Her heart lept when she saw the numbers 145-4 clear as day.

She knew those numbers well.

She should. She literally *just* moved from them. Her old apartment number.

"Um, yeah, he said that 1:45-4:00 PM was the time slot for the show but never told me what day," Myra said, finally getting back to answering Jenn's question.

Jenn's face was not one that could hide its emotions well; her expressions read like an in-the-moment autobiography of her reeling thoughts. Her cheekbones sunk from the raised vexed position they had been tightly holding onto only a few seconds earlier. Her eyes narrowed a titch, and the curls of her mouth straightened mimicking an EKG machine flatlining. When she spoke it sounded as if her voice register had dropped an entire octave - her tone took on a similar depth, sounding edgy and cantankerous.

"I'm so sorry Miss," apparently Myra's name no longer mattered - she had been de-escalated to a surface-level pronoun, "but that isn't a time frame we would schedule anything for. Right now, reservable gallery times are full-day stretches, starting when we open at 10:00 AM to our closing time of 8:00 PM. Perhaps your boyfriend misunderstood... could it be that the note you're holding is about something else entirely?" Remi winced at Jen's cutting last remark. Though her curiosities made her wonder the same, she was astounded that Jenn had enough balls to suggest it to a potential client.

Myra was silent for what seemed like an eternity while Remi waited with bated breath for her response. Unlike her, Myra didn't appear to be shaken in the least. She looked more contemplative. Suddenly, Myra spoke. "Well then, I would like to reserve my showing with you now and clear up the details when Tom comes back from Santa Barbara. I am sure this is all just a huge misunderstanding and I *know* you appreciate my business, word of mouth is *so, so, so* important," Myra poignantly emphasized.

Magically, Jenn's twinkle reappeared, twisting the crooks of her mouth upwards and heightening her cheekbones once again. Remi couldn't stomach the disingenuous display that was parading itself in front of her by her previous buyer. She determined this was a great time to save herself from the inevitable reversal of Jenn's speaking voice and instead turned to her new acquaintance. Soon to be more, Remi devised. "Myra, do you have a business card or anything? I might be interested in hiring you for a custom piece in the near future. My new roommate is a passionate paint and pottery lover," Remi said directing that last part to Jenn.

Myra instinctively started rummaging through her boho-chic bag once again. "Well, I think we were destined to meet - I specialize in *both* paint and pottery," she handed Remi a light pink business card with coral italic writing- on the back was a voluptuous full-bodied flower with a vagina as its pistil.

"Great, thanks. I will be in touch." With that, Remi gave a quick nod, mouthed the words *thank you* to Jenn, and raced for the exit. Her head hurt. It was spinning outside itself, crushing through the walls of her skull and free-flying into space. What the hell just happened? Did she conjure up some kind of distorted alternative to her current reality? Were her fears coming to life - taking over innocent human bodies and guiding them to tell her worst-case scenario stories? Or maybe she was just over-dramatizing the scene that just played out; latching onto the new, tragic possibility that Michelle planted like a seed inside her spirit? No, she wasn't crazy. These weren't just her emotions claiming their territory. That, whatever *that* was, just happened.

She closed her eyes to prevent herself from collapsing from the internal spin she was in. Her esteem plummeted. At that moment at least, she shrank to the size of a measly, helpless, invisible worm. A worm that was getting vacuumed to the negative space that lies below the earth's crust. Her little worm body flailing back and forth, trying to resurface - attempting to escape the liquid outer core that was beckoning her to dive into its unforgiving warmth. Refusing to heed its calling, she wriggled herself home...no use going back to her office. She was spineless in her new form and knew that until she could transform herself again, she was void. She'd have nothing to offer anyone the rest of the day.

———————

After surviving the night's traumatic release of pent-up anxieties, past hurts, and newly found ones, Remi rose to see yet another day.

The sun's rays bounced playfully on her cheeks; scrubbing at them like a small child itching for their mother to leave her world of slumber to join them in one of their wild adventures. Remi couldn't help but smile at that. Oh, how she would love to start her morning with a babe of her own - trekking through ravenous woods to find the mystical wind whispering fairies or long-deserted islands, digging through sand dunes, and enchanted temples for treasure worthy of a king.

The sound of Emmy's sweet giggles serendipitously interrupted Remi's hopeful imagination. It was Saturday - no school for Emmy and no work for anybody. Weekends were truly like mini weekly holidays and she had every intention of making this one, one for the books.

She knew she needed answers, but she also knew she wasn't ready to have them. So, instead, she would rebuild herself from the roots up by learning to see the brilliance she brings to everything and everyone around her. And how others in her life do the same. That sweet girl downstairs with her mama were two prime examples. Remi hurriedly pulled on her favorite weekend wear - stonewashed ripped skinny jeans and her super soft black UMass hoodie. Hints of fall were in the air- Remi's favorite season to dress for. She took a few seconds to pull her hair into a messy bun and wipe some of the mascara streaks off her face (remnants from her midnight bawl sesh) and then excitedly pounded down the stairs to see the girls.

The two of them were whipping something vigorously in a coastal blue porcelain mixing bowl, grinning intensely at one another while ani- matedly chattering back and forth. The aroma of bacon and the sound of its sizzle overwhelmed Remi's senses, immediately taking her back to some of her fondest morning time memories she shared with her dad in their own little kitchen back in Boston. She had lived for mornings like those... like this. Closing her eyes, she inhaled all the warmth, all the love she felt in this space and in her heart, both back then and now. The cooking queens looked up simultaneously to greet Remi. They looked so much alike...how special it is, that mother-daughter connection. She felt a stabbing pang in her gut but decidedly ignored it. The bruises her runaway bitch of a mother left wouldn't ruin this perfectly precious moment.

"WE'RE MAKING BLUEBERRY PANCAKES AND BACON," Emmy shouted loud enough for the entire block to hear.

"Yes, we are and I think we will have enough here to feed a small army... we were hoping you might join us for breakfast. What do you think, Remi? Can we get on your social calendar this morning?" Michelle got the cutest look on her face when she kidded around... kind of like an inquisitive puppy searching out a treat you just threw.

"I think I could grab a quick bite with two dynamite ladies. I have a coffee date at 10:00 but it's just over at the Java Hut a couple of blocks from here, so I should have plenty of time."

"A Saturday morning date with Tom, I assume? Did he get back from his trip already?" Michelle inquired with some delicacy around it.

"No, actually it's not a date *date*. I'm grabbing coffee with my friend from my work - well work *building* that is. Kay, she works on the floor above me at Windsor Trust - she wanted to make the trek out here to see the neighborhood. I told her it was ok to come and see my room and all that... if that is ok with you?" She realized as she was saying it that she should have asked Michelle before inviting Kay over after coffee. But Michelle didn't seem to mind. In fact, she answered with a solid nod and said "Absolutely, we always allow friends here, don't we Emmy?"

Emmy smiled and nodded in agreement, just like her mom had. They were like twins. "Now, let's eat," the little mini screamed, running a plate of flapjacks to the table.

It was going to be a great day. Remi was looking forward to catching up with Kay; after calling in sick the rest of the day on Friday, she remembered she and Kay had planned to have lunch together. Luckily, Kay was a planner and always asked about thirty minutes prior to confirm their lunch date, giving Remi the opportunity to reschedule.

She had told Kay that there was no need for her to take the train all the way out to Newark on the weekend, that they could meet up the following week, but Kay insisted she wanted to. Kay said she hadn't been out to Newark in a while- it would give her something to do this weekend. Kay was a fashionista of sorts, which led to her condition of being a habitual shop-a-holic. But Kay didn't like to wear the current trends, she enjoyed thrifting for vintage timepieces circa the 1960s and '70s. Kay said that the warm earth tones, mustard yellows, pea-greens, and burnt oranges showcased her own God-given palette of pale skin that was still somehow rich with deep yellow undertones, golden blonde hair, and simmering blue eyes. Plus, the shameless overuse of textured variety in a single outfit made Kay feel like a walking tapestry.

During a quick walk and talk session, Kay shared she had no personal artistic skills, so wearing her expressive side was the best she could do. Remi thought she looked like a model straight out of a retro tv commercial... maybe an ad for Coca-Cola or something. But at the end of the day it was more of Kay's bubbly personality that she cared for most - true she was a bit of a gossip, the opposite of Remi, but it kept conversations lively, fun-loving, and *only* sometimes meanspirited. Whenever Kay would get going down a derogatory rabbit hole, Remi would try to change the topic; her success rate wasn't usually that great.

Remi was a pro at setting boundaries and staying assertive in her professional life. Not necessarily in her personal one, and her and Kay's friendship was tricky. It was a blur between the two worlds she so desperately had tried to keep separate.

After a more than filling breakfast with her two favorite new roomies, Remi slung her purse across her body, jammed her phone in her pocket, and gleefully shouted that she would be back that afternoon. How nice it was to have someone there with her... someone that would expect her return.... someone that was always listening on the other end of a holler. Remi was proud of the decision she half-heartedly made to move in with the mother-daughter duo...it was all really working out for the best. She just wished there weren't these gnawing insecurities about her relationship with Tom and *his* one with that woman, Myra. She made it a point not to mention any of the absurdities from the day before at breakfast - not just because it wasn't an appropriate subject for Emmy, but because Remi didn't know if she could emotionally or mentally handle another eye-opening, brain-busting, heart-wrenching discussion with Michelle.

It's not because Michelle was being unfair, or unkind, but because deep down Remi believed her...she believed it all. She just wasn't ready to say it aloud yet. If she kept her little secret buried deep in the rows of her mind, they could grow any way she liked them to without the eyes of outsiders judging their unhealthy blooms. With enough water and love, she just *knew* she could make those plants be anything she needed them to be... even if it took denying their inevitable wilt.

She dawdled a bit on her walk to the coffee shop; getting lost in her own thoughts along the way. By the time she got there, Kay was already seated in a soft corner booth with her hands warming around the sides of the stark white paper cup; its recycled paper hand protector had been slid up just barely too high, leaving a rip along its upper ridge.

Kay's pools of icy water glanced up and caught Remi's stormy seas. Kay's eyes acknowledged the pain within her own without a single audible note. Remi walked to the counter pushing out a smile of sorts and a fling of her hand that was supposed to be a wave. After getting her hot brew, she plunked herself onto the creaking vinyl pad across from Kay. Before she could even get fully settled, Kay spoke a solitary word that meant she knew too much already.

"Dish!"

"Dish, what?" Remi feigned not to know what her friend was insinuating.

"Woman, the sadness in your eyes could make me start bawling like a baby myself. You look like you just came from a funeral. Are you ok?"

"Oh, yeah I am fine. Just a little tired I guess," she lied. She was good at that when it came to covering up her feelings. She hadn't always been good at it...not when she was a kid at least. If child Remi were there she'd have come through the doors screaming and crying- forcing her disappointment onto an unwanting audience.

"Yeah...and I am the Virgin Mary. My ass you're fine," Kay decidedly changed the strength behind her voice, lessening it to a more serene, accepting one. "It will make you feel better if you talk about it. And you know I have the biggest ears on the second floor... made for eaves-dropping, breaking into safes, and special occasions such as this, " she teased. The whole breaking into *safes* thing was most probably, maybe even definitely a joke Remi assured her conscience.

"Hm ok, well then where the hell do I even start, Kay? This is a bizarre one," Remi cleared her throat and continued. "Well, I was out visiting a client yesterday and a woman came in to ask about her gallery booking..." Remi shared the rest of the story, unintentionally unraveling details she must have subconsciously absorbed; meanwhile, the display of rotating emotions on Kay's face was like a cartoon flipbook buzzing through the fingertips of a mad person. When she finished the long, uncomfortable tale, Kay's jaw dropped to sputter.

"Well, holy fuuuuuuuck! I don't know what else to say right now. Never mind, I do...what's this bitch's name? I can do some creeping on her and see what I can find for you if you want me to. This reminds me so much of the drama my ex, Ben Blank, put me through back in the day. Two timers suck ass, and so do their mistresses." Kay's reaction confirmed that she loved the drama of the situation and couldn't resist getting involved. Remi just wasn't sure if she wanted her to yet or not. "I mean, I guess it's not all this whore's fault... right? It takes two to tango, and I'd cut that dance partner's ball right the fuck off! I'd kill him!! Shoulda killed Benjamin too, for what he did to me."

Without answering her full question or giving Kay Myra's name, she told her she would think about it and let her know, then changed the subject as quickly as humanly possible. No more talk about cheating bastards, no more about Tom, Myra, or, Kay's personal trigger, Benjamin Blank.

Stella

For the next couple of days, Stella was jittery, mentally unfocused, and quiet. Quieter than she was normally; typically, her silence was calculating, but this was different. Stella was becoming a prisoner to a plague of thoughts surrounding the mystery she just *couldn't* solve. Horror story level, high-gore stories were building on top of themselves, looming over her like rolling storm clouds mounting themselves into a dangerous wall cloud. One threatening to unleash its fury as violent tornadic vortexes. There she sat like one of her own subs; exposed, tied to the legs and back of a chair with her mouth taped shut. Vulnerable. She had spent hours listening to those recordings and still couldn't discern the importance of recording her comings and goings or the sparse new client convos in her living room. There were audio recordings here and there of her and her boyfriend speaking together in hushed voices and sometimes the sound of the smacking of their entwined lips. But what good is this to someone? Also, how would they be getting the recordings off the damn thing? She realized it could connect with Wi-Fi and had Bluetooth capabilities, but she still hadn't been able to figure out a way to retrieve audio files off of it without plugging into a port. So... whichever crew member, or perhaps the supervisor himself, must have had plans to re-enter her home when she wasn't there to get the files off it. But were they planning on continually doing this after the remodeling project was over? It wasn't very smart of them to assume they could because as *soon* as they had finished up, Stella had changed her codes so they would no longer have access. Remember, she grew up in a struggle... she was not new to the idea of crime and break-ins.

One thing she *did* know was that her constant presence in the office freaked out poor little puppy dog, Rachel, even more than she already was by her. She smiled at the thought of instilling fear in the heart of someone so innocent and pure- it reminded her of her BDSM work. Seeing these pathetic little wisps connect with the unearthed pleasure they find through humiliation and complete denigration was delightful. She wondered how Rachel would hold up in her dungeon? Would she be able to let herself go enough to accept the sniveling, subordinate, little bitch she was? This is all the thought she could muster as she walked coldly past Rachel that morning - blatantly ignoring her greeting and effort to pass along a phone message that had been left with her instead of Stella's machine. Inefficient hag.

She hopped on her cell as soon as her office door closed behind her. Her boy toy was smart, not smarter than her, but maybe his fresh set of brain cells could pick up on something she hadn't. His phone rang at least four times. She held her breath, preparing herself to leave a voicemail that would entice him enough to call her back. He didn't love using his phone for anything besides apps and texting. His voice popped on the line, but it wasn't a recording...he had answered.

"Oh, hey. I thought I was going to get sent over to voicemail there for a second. I'm calling to pick your brain. Is it ripe for the taking?"

"Umm, yeah.... just a second," he sounded discombobulated. It's almost 9 AM, what the fuck was he doing?

"Oh my God, are you still in bed? Your lazy ass needs to get up and get to work. I refuse to be your sugar mama and you know it," Stella laughed, only half kidding.

"No. I am wide awake. I was just in a meeting, so I excused myself to find a quiet place to talk with you," he said a bit too snidely for Stella's taste.

"Jeez, thanks," Stella sarcastically snorted. "I have been racking both my brain and eardrums. Raking them over the coals, trying to figure out what I am listening to on that recorder and why anyone would care. I didn't find any other recorders in the house so I think it's time to serve the construction crew papers based on the one. Or would you hold out and hire someone to scope out the place even harder than me?"

" Whoa, slow your roll there. Really? I mean, don't you see you're jumping the gun on this a bit? You have no proof it was even them. I mean, I can't imagine who the hell else it could have been but if you're gonna make a case outta this, you should probably have more material to work with. It's not like they're getting back in there- you changed the door code. And not to something easy to remember either; I had to put the new one in like five fuckin' times the other night to get in," he retorted snarkily. "So yeah, I mean maybe the foreperson put it there to monitor his worker's conversations or something while they were on the job. But that's sure as shit over - in every aspect. If I were you, I would just say *fuck it, I'm going to let this go, move on with my life so I can get back to torturing people for pleasure and having great sex with my boyfriend.*" He said that last part in an imposed female voice.

"My God. Was that last part supposed to be me? Dear Lord, is that I what I sound like in that horrible head of yours?" she joked. Her mood was unintentionally lifted. He always did that for her, no matter how annoying getting there might be... she begrudgingly admitted that he was a happy annoyance. "Whatever, you're probably right. Want to come over tonight so you can start my 'moving on with my life' process? I think you said your part of it was supplying me with good sex." She loved feeling at ease enough to tease and be playful again. Not too playful... playful sounds more fun than erotic. Between the two, she would always choose the latter, she convinced herself.

They agreed on an 8 PM triste before hanging up. He was working late... again, but it didn't bother her. She liked her alone time, or at least she had before that damned thing showed up in her house. The pit in her stomach gnawed at her insides and there was only one thing to do to get it to go away.

Cords. Close to a dozen of them running the parameter of the walls, tucked above, hidden by the parallel venting. Fuck. Her instincts were right. Fuck.

Stella's hand delicately followed them back, trying to find their source. Her hand bumped against a globular-shaped hard plastic. Hoisting herself up higher with the strength of her biceps, iron-hard core, and grasping hands, she hovered her upper body above the ducting to get a birdseye perspective of the object. A small round lens popped out just above the metal HVAC shoot. It was a fucking camera.

Her first instinct was to yank the cord out in hopes of cutting live footage. The snapping sound that followed her tug sounded like what she imagined the drying veins of an animal carcass to sound like when they were pulled from it by the mouths of vultures. She shivered...grossing herself out by the thought. She wasn't an animal lover, especially not a dead animal lover.

One camera down. She followed the line of cords, repeating her acrobatic display to find another one only about ten feet away. She ripped the cords savagely and continued her search. By the time she had gone around the entire circumference of the dungeon, she felt like she could have joined the circus with her balancing act.

She looked down at the heap she had ripped out and flung to the floor- a tangled web of wires and twenty-two white, dome-shaped spies laid out in front of her. Now they were the vulnerable ones. And soon the person who put them there would be too...

Raking the pile up carelessly with her hands, she opened one of her torture trunks and threw them on top. Better keep these handy for later. A wicked flicker of delight lit her face from within. The fire inside was using her soul as a wick. She knew its flames would completely engulf her one day. But today wasn't "one day"... she didn't need to extinguish it yet. She would fan the flames. Let it burn. Let it smoke. Let it overwhelm the lungs of those closest to her. She would breathe easy because she *was* the fire. Tonight, she put their feet to it and would witness them paying for their sins.

———————

Stella had closed all the blinds and their barriers of curtains. She couldn't risk someone seeing her like this. She stood, not sat, awaiting his arrival. Whip in hand and ready for action. Tonight she would play Madam Madsen but first, she had to play sexy, flirtatious girlfriend to get him right where she wanted him. The sound of her black vinyl heel-clicking impatiently bounced off the wood floors and steely gray cabinets in the kitchen behind her. The echo was unnerving. She stopped her foot from gyrating and instead started to playfully toss the tassels of her jet-black lash. When used tenderly, its leather strings could tickle even the least sensitive of person; sometimes she used it as a tool for her clients who wanted to be tickled until they either puked or orgasmed. Some would orgasm from the feeling of puking...it was one of the more complicated fetishes, but easy enough to honor.

Faint footsteps approached the front door, interrupting Stella's tassel fondling. The sound of the entry code being punched in with tactical fingertips was the only other sound Stella could hear besides her own stable breathing.

The door opened somewhat slowly, and he called in, "Stella, you home?"

He jumped back a bit as he slowly peeked his head into the entryway of the purposefully unlit row house; her silent presence had clearly startled him.

"Shit, you scared me. Why is it so dark in here? You have all the blinds shut. From the outside, it looks like someone is dead or in mourning in here. Jesus...." he had *just* noticed that she was in full Madam gear. "Fuck, do you have a client tonight? Do they like it really dark? I can leave and come ba..." Stella interrupted him.

"No, no client tonight. Just you. A little birdie told me you have been a very naughty boy, so I thought it was time you fess up and face the consequences." She flicked the whip against her shiny black bodice. It was her favorite costume. She liked how the symmetrical tiger tattoos that followed the sides of her ribcage looked, peeking through its stencil-like cutouts. The top of it had tight, almost barb-wire-looking laces that barely kept her C cups from emerging, while the one-piece's fabric middle acted like a modern day corset with strategically placed ribbed boning.

A green hue stole the natural pinkish tones of the skin on his face. White people... their skin betrays them, showing their emotions, fears, guilts like writing on the wall, available for everyone to read. Even their enemies. Stella had always been grateful for her mocha mulatto skin - not only was it luxuriously breathtaking, but it camouflaged her own potential exposures from hungrily reading eyes around her. Now, who looked like they were going to vomit? And she hadn't even tickled him yet.

"I think you better get your ass downstairs if you know what's good for you." Her sadistic, yet sultry smile helped bring some color back into his face - showing relief, she mentally noted. There was guilt behind that structure of a so-called man. A sick fuck, really. But then again, if people openly knew about how she got her pleasure, they would probably say the same about her.

He forced out an insincere whimper and smiled at her. Apparently, he thinks this is going to be a fun game. Let's see if that changes in a hot twenty minutes. Not even. Let's check back in five minutes and wipe that smirk off his stupidly boyish mug. She followed behind him, stepping on the backs of socked heels, forcibly speeding up his trek of shame. And it starts.

"Sit," she ordered, pointing to a dog bed she had placed next to an all-black throne covered with faux diamonds. " Stay." She returned to him, smirking at him sitting in that dog bed on his haunches. She tossed him a dog treat... an actual dog treat. And he ate it like he always did. "Good boy. Up. Get in your bed." In the furthest corner across the room sat a steely metal operating table. She had picked it up from a medical supply sale that was probably meant for small, independent hospitals or third world countries or something - it worked perfectly and her clients loved it. She watched as he crawled on all fours to the table and then sprung himself upwards, landing with a thud. He unintentionally smacked his head against it and winced. Instead of asking if he was ok, she mocked him. "Fuckin' idiot. You're gonna concuss yourself with only your impatience to blame for your memory loss. Now lay all the way down, spread your feet apart, and put your arms above your head."

"What am I, under arrest?" he chided.

"Don't talk back to me," she raised her hand backward, threatening to slap the smugness right off him and his handsome face. The smile left his lips, but she could tell he was still pleased. Without another word, he did as he was told. Stella slowly walked over to the torture trunk and grabbed a wad of the cords she had ripped away from their technological mother's womb earlier. Dropping all but one on the floor next to the bed, she took the single cord and started tying his feet to the rounded stirrups that jutted out from the underbody of the cart. Those stirrups were there for patients to *willingly* place their legs in for support...he would not be given that courtesy. She'd make sure of that. She cinched the second cord down hard enough against the right second ankle that he squealed a bit.

Good. Now his hands.

Picking up another cord from the floor, she noticed it had some of its protective sheathing missing, exposing a sharp end of one of the internal wires. Perfect. She took the open-wire side first and jabbed like a miniature shank into his wrist.

"Owe, what the fuck was that?" He turned his head, noticing the cables for the first time. "Are those new? What are those? I think I prefer the cuffs, dear."

"Shut the fuck up. You don't deserve the cuffs today. Those are too easy and you haven't earned easy." She waited to continue her speech until she made sure she had his last free hand bound down to the other top leg of the bed. She couldn't have him getting up in the middle of her *talk* to him, now could she?

"You asked me if these cords are new. Yeah, sure...new to me anyway. Want to know where I got them? Right here, in my own fucking house. Right here in this very dungeon, to be specific. Yep, they were already here... waiting to be discovered and plucked out from their devious placement." Stella's eyes illustrated the pathway they once followed. And then she returned to the torture trunk, with a little more speed this time, and reappeared with an armful of the cameras. She held them three feet above his chest and then unleashed them onto him. He groaned as they pelted the cavity surrounding his heart and other vital organs. "Shall I grab the remaining fifteen? Do you want to know what all twenty-fucking-two of them feel like pounding down on you at the same time? I know you did this, you sick, lying-ass motherfucker. This dungeon wasn't even here while the remodelers were here. You're the only one with unlimited access to my house. Ballsy, dumb shit, real fuckin' ballsy." Stella was more than shouting by now...it was a demonic throaty scream escaping her mouth.

The fear in his eyes was palpable. He had never looked so frightened down in the dungeon or anywhere, at any other time, with her. She had tilted his ego off-balance; completely taken him by surprise. His mouth started moving, trying to form words, but nothing came out. He's in a literal state of shock... pathetic. At least it was in the beginning. But then his bound arms shook like they were weeping and tears started streaming down the sides of his face. His reaction was more than she could have hoped for.

Suddenly, she felt something foreign... something she hadn't felt since childhood. Concern. She was concerned about him. Without thinking, she cut through the knotted wires, strapping him to the table, and helped him sit up. From an outsider looking in, she might have looked like a nurse helping one of her patients. So compassionate, caring, sincere...where was this bullshit coming from? A thought dawned on her - she might actually love this son of a bitch. Shit. She hadn't meant for *that* to happen.

But instead of the thought halting her wanting hands, she started rubbing his back and making the universal calm noise through pursed lips, "shhh..."

He looked like a kid. He clawed at his face, trying to erase the tears, making it seem like they never happened. Like pushing the delete key until the page was void of everything that was once there. He snuffed back the remnants of his emotional storm, clearing the way for easier breathing and a more controlled conversation that was looming before the both of them. Stella hated serious talks; they reminded her of growing up in a struggle where serious talks were the norm. She remembered how they always left her stomach hurting after. She had been an anxious kid because of her family's various circumstances, but she had made sure as fuck she wouldn't grow to be an anxious woman. Her light switch flipped back in the *on* position.

"So, I'm right then, I take it. It was you... but why?"

He solemnly nodded. "It was. What are you going to do to me? You know deep down that you are the scariest, most intimidating woman I have ever met and yet I keep coming back for more... like one of your idiot clients."

Well, that was a total script flip. Not the right route for him to go with this.

"Ok wow. Well, let's put all *that* on pause. You can work on resolving all the inner problems and scars of baby boy later. Right now I want to know why...I mean what gave you the right to install cameras in my house...my dungeon -where I work *very* confidentially?!" She was shouting again, though the apparent demon possession from earlier hadn't returned.

"I just wanted to watch. I enjoy watching other people in the dungeon... I don't love being down here myself as a Submissive... I mean, I guess there are a couple of things I enjoy having done to me, but I much rather watch them being done to someone else. I know, I know, you're the DOM between the two of us, but maybe I don't want to be the Sub anymore. Maybe I want to be the DOM, which I know doesn't fly with you. So... I thought if I could live, almost vicariously through you, as the DOM, that would suffice for me and not put you...us... in an uncomfortable situation."

He was blathering now. It was a reason. Not a good one. But still a reason, nonetheless. Stella didn't know how she would respond yet. She didn't want to give any more of her pieces away to him at the moment, but she also didn't want things to end between them, either. She subconsciously narrowed her eyes at him, trying to see into his mind..searching for the truth. She was falling in love with him. She couldn't trust him. An oxymoronic set of statements, but both are accurate.

"So did you put the recorder in the entryway closet too, then?" She said, blatantly ignoring his little speech.

Offering no additional explanation, he simply replied, "Yes."

"Can you tell me why... were you getting your rocks off to the sound of silence that it was recording the majority of the time or what?"

"It was only meant for new client meetings. So I could hear what they were into, their requests from you before you took them down here. It also helped me know when you had a client so I could start watching on the cameras."

"Jesus, you are a calculating twat, aren't you?" She didn't want to say it, or show it, but she was slightly impressed by the methodical mannerisms he took in planning and executing the whole operation. She was turned *onto* a whole new side of him and, at the same time, slightly turned *on* by it.

So what, he was getting his jollies off watching...at least he's not fucking anyone else.

She glared at him with both a new appreciation and distrust.

What to do with this information... What. To. Do.

Duo | Remi & Stella

Remi's phone vibrated in her laptop bag that doubled as a purse during the workday. Before sliding her chair back into its resting place for the evening, she set her bag on top of it, reached in, and blindly swam her hand around the vastness to find the buzzing. Her phone had fallen to the bottom and was wedged underneath the power cords that always consumed more space in the bag than she liked. Grabbing it quickly so as not to miss the call, her eyes raced to read *Incoming Call From Tom*. Without thinking, she instinctively pressed the answer icon and brought it to the side of her face; for the first few seconds of the call, all she could do was breathe into the mic.

She heard rustling on the other end. The sound of his pants, no doubt rubbing together from the briskly jaunting legs that lie beneath them. She continued to listen - this call could easily be a pocket dial. She felt like an FBI agent assigned to a new high-risk, confidential national security case, but her imagination was abruptly cut off when he spoke. "Hello. Remi, are you there?"

She hesitated, briefly contemplating what might happen if she chose not to respond and instead hang up. That could lead to the end of their relationship and her chance to know the truth of what exactly was going on when they were apart. A squeak of a greeting rushed through her vocal cords and spewed out like an uncontrollable bout of sickness. "Hi." She cleared her throat before continuing. "I'm here. Sorry, I thought you might have butt-dialed me," why would she have just admitted that? Could she not keep anything from him? If she didn't get a muzzle on herself that instant, she was going to expose every fear and insecurity that had been rolling through her the past few days like a thunderstorm promising damaging, straight-line winds.

"Ha, no but that does sound like something I would do," he lightly chuckled as if he hadn't a care in the world. And maybe he didn't. "I'm back in town from my trip. I'm helping out a friend tonight but wanted to see if you were free tomorrow evening? I could meet you in the city somewhere for a bite or you could come to see my place... I can't even remember the last time you were there."

Neither could Remi - she *remembered* the fact that she'd only been there twice since they had started dating and always assumed he was being a gentleman not wanting to make her have to travel in the city at night by coming to her instead - but with his current offer that assumption seemed to go out the window.

On the other hand, she did want to see him and not for the reason one might think after her chance meeting with Myra. She had really missed him. She missed the way his cologne tingled the first time she'd breathe it in closely during their organic embrace. They were always so happy to be in each other's presence- at least it had always seemed that way.

Remi fought through the sudden sadness that was taking over her thoughts and accepted his invitation. "I would love that. I missed you a lot babe. We could grab a bite somewhere first and then head back to your place for the night if that works for you..."

"Sounds perfect, hun. Let's say Domingo's at 8 PM sharp..."

"Ok, see you then." She almost hung up, but hurriedly snuck in the three words she wanted more than anything to hear him say back to her. She promised herself if he said them, she would file this moment away in her brain, so she never had to question it again. "I love you Tom."

There was a click.

He'd hung up.

Before or after her special words, she didn't know for sure, but she was fearing the former.

The call was good, she told herself. She had plans for that evening herself... plans that didn't involve him. Plans that may never involve him. Remi had taken Michelle's advice and connected with the legal advisor that she'd referred her to... Ms. Stella Madsen. Stella's business card stuck in Remi's mind because of its almost damning appearance. If the woman's business card could intimidate her, she could only imagine how much the woman herself would... She was probably one hell of an excellent lawyer. Remi knew from their brief phone conversation through Stella's tone that she didn't take any shit. This woman meant business, and that's exactly what she needed in her life right then - assertion. That's where Remi was heading straight after work. Luckily the both of them live in Newark so she could take the train home at her regular time, stop for a change of clothes and a quick snack, and then it was only a five-minute drive to Stella's home office. She saw this as fate working in her favor.

———————————

The crisp, white, mission-style door swung open after she pressed the pearlized oblong cover of the doorbell that was held by a stenciled, and lightly studded golden shroud. It made Remi think of a crown and when she looked up and laid eyes on the woman behind the opening door, she knew she had arrived at a Queen's fortress. Stella shared a rehearsed smile at Remi and waved her in. Remi couldn't seem to take her eyes off of her... the almost whimsical flow of her naturally curly hair entranced her and her honey-hued eyes.

As Stella offered to take Remi's coat she introduced herself as blah Madsen from blah blah blah law firm. Remi's ears went deaf to the details, but her eyes picked up the slack as she continued under Stella's spell. There was so much strength, agility, and confidence radiating with every movement Stella made. Impeccable. Remi wished she could have that level of security. Or maybe it was assertiveness. Probably... definitely both. Stella's eyes lowered to meet Remi's communicating a nonverbal *"Earth to Remi"* and like the snap of the fingers breaking a hypnotic trance, Remi was back.

She caught up for the lost time by smiling and sharing her short bio at the same time. She felt like she was an actress in a toothpaste commercial...

"Thanks for seeing me Stella and on such short notice too," she saw her own hand shaking as she stuck it out, offering it to Stella. Stella noticed too.

"No need to be nervous; we aren't in a courtroom nor a bedroom. Why don't we have a seat in the living room and we can get payment settled before we dive in?" Stella had learned the hard way a handful of times that you collect your money before you give away the goods.

She showed Remi to the couch while she chose the chair sitting kitty-corner. Her majesty had taken her throne.

Remi handed Stella her credit card. "Also, towards the end of the meeting, my significant other will be coming through, but I will send him upstairs so we can continue chatting in private. I just wanted to let you know, so it doesn't take you off guard," Stella said almost sternly.

Remi shook her head in acknowledgment, packed her card away in her purse, and rested her hands in her lap. "Did you bring something you can take notes with? You are going to want to."

Remi got her cell out of her pocket, raising it in one hand as if she were a student asking for permission to use her phone during class. "Yeah, that'll work. I just ask that you don't record our conversation. For personal reasons of my own, I would just appreciate that." Stella had had enough recording devices in her life as of late; also, she was going against her contract with the firm by moonlighting legal advice... the less evidence, the better. Remi gave her a silent thumbs up and opened her notes app instead.

The conversation went off without a hitch after that, Remi wildly typing on the minute digital keyboard of her somewhat vintage Samsung; Stella spewing legal jargon and form numbers left and right... it was everything Remi had been looking for.

Until he *almost* arrived.

The pair paused their conversation when they both looked up to see him walking towards the door. It had started drizzling out. The solid, royal blue umbrella he was carrying covered the top two-thirds of his head but Remi recognized his stature. And his clothes. And the hands that held the umbrella. His neck. His chin. His lips. Her heart started beating out of her chest; she was sure that Stella could hear it.

But how did he know she was there? Did Michelle tell him?

Why was he coming there?

To join the talk - did he somehow find out about Remi's IUI plans?

How was this happening?

Remi looked up expecting to see confusion on Stella's face, but she saw expectancy. Stella knew *he* was going to be there!? Was this some kind of twisted set-up?

But then...

"Oh, sorry. Looks like my boyfriend has arrived." Stella rose with such poise and control off the couch to let him in. Stella knew he knew the door code, but it would allow her to tell him she was with a legal client - banishing him to her bedroom. Remi watched with horror as his separate life from her started unfolding right in front of her eyes. That is until he noticed her, Remi, through the window. He pivoted on his heels, retreating from the door, and took off running down the sidewalk... away from Stella. And forever away from her. Stella flung her door open with a sudden display of rage.

"TOM! TOM! Where the hell are you going?!" Stella did not know... how could she? Remi instinctively stood up and started combing the much less welcoming room with her eyes trying to locate something, anything that might prove that Stella's Tom was her Tom. She started spinning like she always did. She needed to. Around. Around. Around.

Stella's stark whites blurred into one another, making the entire row house one giant blob of nothingness. Until Remi saw it whirring through her vision as she passed the white granite fireplace. Above it hung a different type of white stone mantel, which unlovingly held the one and only dark object in the space. Remi halted mid-cycle, stood for a few seconds to still the dizziness coursing through her, and jaunted over the photo as soon as she got her bearings.

"Sorry about that. I'm not sure what got into Tom." She turned to find Remi now holding the frame, sobbing. "What are you doing? What's going on here?"

"I think you need to sit down. I think I do too. We need to have a chat about *our* boyfriend."

Stella's eyes narrowed while she silently returned to the living room with Remi, this time sitting next to her on the couch. Remi silently tapped on her phone and handed an entire folder of Tom and her smiling, smooching, and laughing together. Stella's face glowed with anger, but she said nothing. Stella silently scrolled, tapped, and tweaked her fingers out the sides to enlarge the shots. She still hadn't said anything. Unlike any lawyer Remi knew, Stella didn't ask questions. By the time she spoke, her tone held no malice nor any accusatory notes towards her. They were words against him.

"Fuck him. Fuck him to his grave. Fuck him AND his grave." Stella sunk her face into her open palms. "He's a perv, I told myself... just a perv. I didn't think he was a two-timing asshole."

"Possibly, three-timing," Remi interjected.

Stella's eyes lept from her palms with shock. "What do you mean? There's another... what a fucking prick?!" Now she was shouting.

"I think so. I ran into her at my client's art gallery. Her name is Myra Kennett," Instinctively, Remi pulled the vagina-flower business card from her bag and handed it to Stella. "I could be wrong, but she was in there looking for information on a reservation that her boyfriend, Tom - Tom Williams, had made for her. There ended up being *no* reservation for her in the time frame he had jotted down on some, according to her, random piece of paper. But the paper had Donaldson's logo on it... that is where he told he works, right?"

Stella's still assertive, on the verge of aggressive, energy had returned; she nodded yes. Remi continued telling her how the number on the page was actually her old apartment number and how she wanted to stage a visit with the artist pretending to be interested in buying a custom piece.

"Well, let's do it then. Together. I can pretend to be your roommate Michelle; she can assume that I tagged along to tell her what type of art piece I would like best as my gift of gratitude."

"Wouldn't that seem odd that you would come with me to pick out your own gift?" Remi was feeling unsure about the little plan the two were unequally concocting. There was a not-so-discreet eye roll at the end from her solitary audience member. Stella seemed to pick up on Remi's softness right off the bat and it didn't look like she was the biggest fan of it.

"People do it with engagement rings all the time. I don't think it's odd at all. It just means Michelle has particular tastes and is a woman who gets what she wants." Stella was clearly already writing fictional dialogue in her head... she was good at this. Uncomfortably so. It made Remi curious about the stains *she* might be hiding in that perfectly pristine pearl castle of hers.

"Ok, but what do we do about Tom in the meantime. I mean, he's going to know that we are onto him... that I recognized and outed him to you, right?" Remi stammered.

"Not necessarily. I mean it's not like you saw his face or anything - I never told him I had a client coming over so I mean he probably assumed the worst, but if I shot him a text right now asking if he was ok and explaining that I just finished with an advisory meeting he might think we were none-the-wiser. Actually, he will probably find it more out of character if I don't send *some* kind of snarky-ass note his way after his wild abandon."

Without waiting to hear Remi's opinion, Stella whipped her phone out. She must text a lot because her fingers raced across the screen, rabidly consuming its alphabetic sacrifices lying in wait for their opportunity to be used. For good or evil, they had no say in the matter. It appeared like Remi, they merely existed for the usery and manipulation of others.

Remi watched. Witnessing the lie that had become her life story painfully carried on. She knew, perhaps better than anyone, that deception tends to build upon itself. Every singular lie starts off as a small, almost innocent exaggeration. But then another and another form, weaving themselves together in a false unity until an overwhelmingly entangled web is all that remains for her to trace back to a prospective speck. Remi had dismantled the web that had almost completely possessed her years ago- at its center lie a venomous, toxic, eight-legged beast with enough eyes to see through a person. She was still trying to exterminate it and the hate it held inside- she knew deep down that adding to its home would only shield it more. Protected in layers upon layers of filth and denigration. She saw it all but couldn't seem to force herself to stop the lies from building onto its shelter. She wanted to know what would happen if...

"There. Sent. Now let's see if the dumb fuck believes me. I invited him back over; told him to swing by in a half-hour or so. We shall see," Stella almost appeared enthusiastic about the trap she was setting. One Remi was an accomplice of.

Against her better judgment, she heard herself almost as if she wasn't the one speaking, say, "Great. You have my cell number already from when I called to set this meeting," oh god...how this meeting had gone off on an entirely unforeseeable track. She felt like it had derailed her IUI plans along with everything else she had thought she could take comfort in. "You should probably add me to your contacts under a fake name. You just never know- maybe he goes through our phones when we aren't looking..."

Stella hadn't even told Remi about the ridiculously fucked up cameras she found in her basement but that would force her to share her Dominatrix side hustle with an almost perfect stranger. Remi would have to earn her way to knowing confidential shit like that, Stella internally decided. Externally, she gave a cheap grin, acknowledging Remi's recommendation.

Remi ominously rose from the couch and told Stella she'd be in touch after she'd arranged a meet-up with Myra and suggested she might let her know how the Tom trap played out that evening. Remi secretly hoped Stella's update would be vague, but she got the sneaking suspicion from Stella's personality that it wouldn't be. Remi swallowed the bit of vomit that had backed up in her throat. She didn't realize she was symbolically swallowing herself too... a new version of Remi had to be born - more like built. One with less emotion. Less reaction. Less guilt. Less give-a-fucks.

She slammed the door behind her and walked back out into the world. Looking at it through fresh eyes.

Tom

He whistled; the echo of the soles of his shoes against the pavement added percussion to his jovial tune. Back on his way again.

He'd made it all the way to the train station and was waiting to load himself back on like a bull going to slaughter. He was sure that they'd found out. And what do people do with their disappointment in the cattle that can no longer perform? They either get sent out to pasture or are slaughtered. Murdered. Deliciously so, but still... murdered. He'd seen a lot of this growing up; his mother would ship kid Tom off for the summer to his grandparent's farm back in the hometown that'd spat the vile woman out years ago, Jefferson, Ohio.

Even though he learned a lot about a lot those summers, they still seemed like a vacation... one spent with family that actually liked and wanted him around. The sweltering afternoons he spent conversing (one-sidedly, of course - he wasn't crazy) with the bulls over the pen were some of the fondest memories he had from his youth. And today, he felt like he earned himself a continued stay in the bullpen. Like them, he'd been mounting all the cows he could manage at one time. Unlike them, his intention was to never leave them with child. Though castration might serve his idyllic lifestyle better - he'd always hoped to remain intact. Looks like the master of the farm escapes discovery and lives another day for meaningless sex. He was so much better at this than he ever dreamt he could be.

Before the train even had a chance to get back to him he got a text from Stella.

God, women are vapid.

Even when they find fucking cameras in their home, call you out on it, and even get the satisfaction that they were right with a goddamn confession. Now, add on an inexplicable case of falling ill at their doorstep causing him to full-on run away from her... I mean how many lies will these pretentious imp fall for?

All it took for these blinded little pussy pockets were putting on some waterworks. A production of obnoxious, gag-worthy emotions that always worked. Always made them feel sorry for him and sometimes even sorry for the way *they* treated *him*. Fools that have not one iota of self-worth. Their naivety earned everything they had coming to them in their shitty, insignificant lives. Lives he knew too much about - not that he wanted to.

Someone might ask him why he didn't just have a ton of one-night stands or hire hookers if he didn't want any kind of relationship with these women? Why he couldn't care to know about the depressingly boring vats of nothingness they call their lives? To answer them, he would say, it's simple...

It's the game that I get off on. It's like a challenge to see just how far I can take it with them before they break - springs shooting out of their sides, heads steaming and spinning full-circle atop their necks, eyes glowing red... like robots malfunctioning. Oh, and by the way, I still get plenty of ass on the side from one-night stands. Their shame in the mornings is palpable... beautiful. I'm a sucker for self-hatred. One of my favorite shows to watch is some whore rolling out of my bed in the morning, looking over to find me not giving two shits, and then letting the grief and disappointment cloud over them. The disappointment is always in themselves - never in me. Nor in my performance.

Deep down he understood he was royally fucked-up, but his mother and lack of a father made him that way. His dad not being around bothered him, sure, but it didn't ruin his life like his mother tried to do. She hated him. She hated the fact that she had to take care of someone else... if that's what you could even call it. It wasn't like she'd even provided him the basic essentials in life; shelter- check he had a house to live in, albeit not a safe one. She stopped providing food for him after he turned ten years old. She told him he was old enough to chip in for groceries and threatened what she'd do to him if he burned down the house trying to operate something so plainly difficult as the stove.

Oh, she of little faith. He became a fantastic cook, but he shouldn't have had to be... that's a woman's job. He got most of his clothes as a teen from her flea-bag cunt suckers. Most of them were too disgusting to keep - the men and the clothes they left behind alike.

And she definitely didn't love him. So he chose not to love her anymore... not to love anyone anymore. Maybe not even himself, though he always promised himself he would. She had taught him well by not teaching him at all. Now Kim, his first and only actual girlfriend, taught him so much by actually showing him true betrayal. He could never, would never, forgive her - Kim. Nor his mom. Neither of them deserved it. Fucking bitches.

Jumping off his hamster wheel of thought, Tom glanced up from the sidewalk and noticed he was only a couple of houses down from hers. Raising his hands to run his finger through his hair, mussing it. He needed to look more disheveled than he remembered himself looking in the reflection he caught of himself from the back of a stop sign. Making sure he was still out of eyesight from her house, he bent down, stooping in one of the neighbor's yards, and firmly sunk his hands into the rich black soil someone had recently poured into that flowerbed. Whoever they were, had hopes that some fresh dirt would help their situation a bit. He hoped it would do the same for him.

He wriggled his fingers down deep, then lifted them, and raked them along the slightly crusted top. The powdery ash-colored proof of laborious activities sunk underneath his fingernails. He kept going until the dark shadows seen from the fronts of his nails were overly apparent. He only stopped when the pressure from the damp, caked earth hurt.

He was thankful the rain had stopped, but he was even more grateful that it *had* rained. The wet drops helped camouflage him with both the raincoat and umbrella he'd been using when he'd approached Stella's door earlier. Why was Remi at Stella's house to begin with? How did the two know each other?

Never in his years of tawdry gameplay had he hooked up with two women that knew each other. He was stepping into a whole new level of tantalizing, trauma-promising, promiscuity. He reveled in the idea of a new challenge.

Wiping his hands on the shirt she wouldn't have been able to see, he left as much evidence on himself as possible. He rubbed his palms down the sides of his cheeks and forehead. He had been a busy little digger.

Before anyone was the wiser, he stood and continued his path to the bright red door ahead. He checked the house number that ran alongside the ivy that had been cautiously climbing the chipped brick for the past fifty years. Carefully stepping over a menagerie of blue blooms, shooting up behind alternatingly stacked rows of pavers, he made his own shortcut to the doorbell. Cold and steely gray metal pushed back against his inquiring finger. The chime was a short high-pitched melody. It sounded familiar, but he couldn't recall where he'd heard it before. One slat of the cream, vinyl blind that laid safely housed in the door's adjoining sidelight, flickered open, briefly shutting just to be pried open by a pair of small, curious hands. A child's searching eyeball leered at him through the narrow opening. He slipped into Tom, nice, kid-friendly Tom, forced a smile, winked, and waved at her all at the same time. He had overacted the scene- the kid picked up on it too. She squinted her eyebrows at him in an attempt to glare at him. This kid is a riot, he thought sarcastically to himself.

After waiting too long, the door finally slid open showing only a narrow triangle of a woman's face he thankfully didn't recognize - he couldn't handle more than one unplanned reunion of *almost* strangers in a day. Their eyes locked instantly and he knew she was sizing him up.

"Hi, I'm Tom is Remi here? She should be expecting me." Or at least he assumed so since she had responded to his surprise text within a matter of seconds of hitting send. He needed to turn Stella's confused, desperate plea for his return down and test the waters with Remi. He knew Remi was one hell of a smart real estate agent, but when it came to anything to do with him- she couldn't lie to save her life! Tom was on a mission to see if Remi had recognized him earlier or not.

And if she didn't she will be fucking excited to jump his bones. He was smiling inwardly at the thought of Remi ravishing him like a starved bear cub. Licking away at him, making him glisten with her tongue, suckling his berries. He felt his pants bulge, so he had to put away the mental imagery. At least for now. The version of Remi that the world knew was an anxious, shy, uncertain, business savvy girl, but the woman that emerged in the bedroom was anything but those things. She was uninhibitedly wild, still submissive to his will, but past the surface - on a deeper level- she was one thirsty bitch. One he'd deemed worthy enough to add to his rotation of *lovers* less than a year ago. His boxers were rising again. He needed to disassemble the tent, so he tried to re-focus his attention back on the stranger that opened the door fully now and had been talking at him about Remi running out to the store or something. He didn't care what this woman had to say, he just wanted to wait for her inside like a normal human being.

"Sorry, I didn't catch your name. I apologize because I know for a fact that Remi has told me in the past, but I just got back from a business trip and have some major jet lag." He lied. Like always.

"Oh yeah, sorry, Michelle," the stranger said while pulling the door fully open with one hand and offering the other for a shake. He shook it so gently that it probably felt more like a caress. She looked like a woman who could use a little harmless flirtation. He imagined her arousal by the touch of his generously wanting fingertips against hers. Instead, she somewhat accusatory retorted, "A business trip eh... are you an excavator or something? I'm not trying to be rude but you look like you just walked off a construction site."

He couldn't stop himself from chuckling- at her, not with her, but she didn't need to know that. Women saw what they wanted to and *most* of the time they were lazy about it; never sparing an ounce of imagination of what the story *could* be, not just what was readily available.

"No, I actually got back this morning and had promised a buddy of mine that I would help him do some landscaping on his property today. Hence the dirt." He lifted both pointer fingers and aimed them in on himself like one of those cheesy *I'm that guy* shirts he hated. "We finished earlier than I thought, so I wanted to come and see my girl as soon as I could."

"Well, I know she is excited to see you... don't tell her I told you this, but she ran straight to her room when she got home and the next time I saw her she was all dolled up. That girl really likes, swears you are a good one, not like my ex, Dameon. Or most men, probably." Michelle must have realized the sting of her last statement and apologized almost instantaneously, but she didn't need to because Tom knew he was a bad guy. Most men were bad. Most *people* were bad. However, unlike most, there was a reason he had become the way he was. At the end of the day, he just didn't give two shits about anyone else to change his devious ways, so there's that...

Tom turned away from his conversation with Michelle to greet the voice he recognized as feeling shy Remi. Her demeanor seemed to change when she saw his face -she quickly transformed into hot and bothered Remi that he'd only ever seen in bed before now. She almost aggressively rushed up to him and planted her wet, full lips against his, smashing them together with a bit too much force for his taste. She must be putting on a little show for her new roomie, staking her claim on him by planting a symbolic flag of ownership.

What a bimbo.

She doesn't own him, none of them did.

He didn't even own himself; he signed off on that deal years ago, grateful to shed the skin he loathed.

She pulled away, separated their lips, grabbed his hand, and led him into the house. He noticed a smile that she gave Michelle as they passed one another in the entryway. He wasn't sure how to read it, but it looked mischievous, that much he was sure of. She announced that she was going to show Tom around and hurriedly guided him up the stairs. They were going straight to her bedroom - she *was* thirsty - parched even. She playfully pushed him on top of her bed and climbed on top of him. Pinning his arms down by the wrists, she put her face close to his... close enough to exchange the carbon dioxide slipping out of her nostrils to make room for clean air, but not close enough to kiss. He was a bit taken aback when she started whispering. Her newfound quiet didn't match the tone she had just displayed. Maybe it was because he was the only one in the audience now. He listened carefully, trying to make out what she was saying.

"Speak up doll, I can't hear you through your sexy slither voice - where did my assertive adventurer go? She was just here, I swear."

Pushing her weight against his chest, she lifted herself up and sat cross-legged on the bed next to him. She wasn't looking at him anymore... this date was going sour. Not good. He placed his finger under her chin and gently swiveled her head so their eyes met. "What did you say, kitten?" Barf, the sound of it made himself sick, but this is the character he played with her and it was time to run lines.

"Nothing. I just wanted to say that I love you."

"I missed you too." He could tell his response disappointed her. Her face said so much without her even opening her mouth- this is why he knew she could never be able to lie to him. He could read her like a book and was positive that most of the world could, too. She was a girl that showed her emotions on her sleeve and her emotions were oversized giants compared to the arms they were being flaunted on.

Sad for her.

He skipped past it to avoid getting in any deeper. Lord knows he would never say those words to anyone, even if they weren't true. It wasn't only because he despised them to this core, but if any of his agreement from his youth were to still stand with the Devil, this is the sacrifice he vowed to make to get what he wanted out of life. Which was everything.

He knew he was getting the better end of the deal - a bargain, really. He could have fortune, fame, brilliant looks, and every material possession he could dream up for the mere price of an ideal he thought to be nonexistent. So, again, sad for her.

She'd have to put up with his advances for physical connection this evening and nothing more. He was exhausted from his little run-in from earlier, so sex was the best she was going to get. And she got it. She took him in like a Robovac, sucking up an electrical cord.

He knew his secret was still safe.

Trio | Remi, Stella, & Myra

Stella

Stella walked in front of Remi, up the treacherously steep concrete steps of Myra's apartment building. It was an old textile mill that had been rejuvenated just barely enough to house a series of studios. Using old mills and warehouses for modern, on the edge of minimalistic, housing had been a growing trend over the past decade and attracted artistic types. It didn't surprise Stella a bit that a painter and potter would live there.

It just meant that Myra fit a mold. Then again, she could have already assumed that. Remi on the other hand wasn't probably savvy of these archetypes; Remi seemed naïve, aloof, and weak to her. She probably had a very cushy childhood, one where she was coddled and her relatives went goo-goo ga-ga over her. The thought made Stella nauseous. Her life was only as fabulous as it was because she had worked her ass off to get there and she cut people from her family that didn't earn their place to be there with her. Yet again, most of her white relatives had already cut *her* out the day she was born. She always dreamt that she would see one of these privileged fuckers on the opposite side of a courtroom.

She could hear Remi puffing behind her on the steps.

"Come on now. Keep going, you won't die because of a little aerobic exercise, I promise," Stella glanced back over her shoulder throwing shade at her new partner in crime. "This is exactly why I insisted we take the stairs because we humans have fallen away from moving our bodies, sitting at our desks all day and night, it's important we take the opportunities we can to move these beautiful buns," she added while pointing to her ass cheeks.

By the look on Remi's face, she knew she had embarrassed her; whether it was because she called out the fact that Remi was out of shape or because she made her look at her butt, she didn't know. If it was the latter of the two, Stella could add *prude* to the list of characteristics she had surmised about the woman-child.

Wait, was that an eye roll she saw?

Maybe there was a little spice and something not so nice to Miss Remi after all. Stella felt a sudden spark of interest in the woman-child.

Remi

Remi felt like she was drowning by the time they reached Myra's door; her lungs gasped for air, finally feeling the full extent of asthma they had diagnosed her with as a youth. She had never pushed herself physically after that. She was always too afraid that she would have an attack and she wouldn't have her inhaler with her.

As an adult, right around the same time she started college, she stopped filling her inhaler prescriptions, figuring that she was always careful enough not to overexert herself. She felt wasteful filling them like she was ripping the medication from the hands of someone with a much more severe case of the cursed disease. It also felt like a waste of her hard-earned money, which was no longer a concern, but she still hadn't invested in an inhaler since. Guess she thought she would never need it, but she sure as shit felt like she needed it right there and then.

Stella's insensitive remarks about exercise stuck in her craw more than she would have liked, but then the door swung open and an entranced Myra was standing on the other side of it. Her and Myra's eyes locked, similar to the first time they met; Remi could feel what little power she recognized within herself, consuming all that was offering itself up to her. A dizzying vibration swept through her body, extending through her limbs; from there, the energy seemed to split itself into two, with one half flowing out of the crown of her head and the under escaping through her root chakra.

Remi had learned only a bit about chakras from her friend Sam, but this was the first time she could feel the buzzing of its flow that he had tried to explain to her. It was amazing. Empowering. Rectifying. She took her power back, reabsorbing it through her pupils; she held Myra under a spell of sorts. Remi used her newfound power to push her way silently into her studio. Myra got out of her way with a look of amazement on her face.

Remi turned to see if Stella was following suit and was a bit surprised to see a similar look to that of Myra's on Stella's as well. Somewhat subconsciously Remi continued to move about the space as if she owned it or at least had been there before. Had she? She wiped away the second guessing and self-questioning...she didn't like that side of her and wanted to feel the way she did now forever.

Could she do it? Could she continue to stand in her power against anything? And anyone?

Negative.

Right then she noticed a gigantic photo canvas of Myra and Tom embracing one another half nude. Stella must have noticed it at the same time because she elbowed Remi a bit too hard in the ribs, calling her attention to it. Myra had begun talking fervently in the background- Remi wasn't listening. She couldn't yet, she couldn't because her eyes were glued to the slight shading that Tom's abdominal muscles announced in the portrait. Sickening. Even more so, they looked happy together, holding one another like they actually meant something.

Maybe they did.

Dammit, they did to Myra at least... who knew about Tom. It didn't appear that any of these women knew him at all.

Remi would get to know him... the *real him,* she vowed to herself.

Now she heard Stella speaking, abruptly cutting off their host in her own home. Remi decided it was probably a good time for her to tune in, back to the moment at hand. She had lost the momentary power she had been clinging onto so easily... she was the victim again.

"So, Remi says you paint and do pottery. She is such a sweetheart; you see she just moved in with me and my son.." *Daughter*, Remi corrected her slightly under her breath, but loud enough for Myra to hear.

"I'm sorry. Are you her roommate? I thought you said your name was Stella when you first arrived but Remi and I have been texting back and forth about a gift for her new roomie, *Michelle*." Myra was savvy to their fabricated story already. A smart little fox she was.

Soft and cunning, amber-red, quick, and filled with life... hopefully she would be able to keep herself out of the hunter's traps. Hopefully, she wouldn't get that pretty little coat of hers skinned right down to the bone for someone else to fancy.

"Uh, yeah, well let me explain..." Remi started only to find herself interrupted by Stella; who had a real bad habit of speaking over others; that won't do well for her.

"Listen, we aren't here to talk about artsy-fartsy stuff with you. I mean, don't get me wrong, I love all the vaginas on your walls and stuff- I am an alpha female too so...you know totally on board for worshipping it, showing it off... all that good shit. But the reason why we're here is actually to talk with you about something else, more like someone else you have on your walls," she said, leading with her eyes toward the two lovers' portrait.

"Tom? He's my boyfriend. Is this who it is you wanted to chat with? If so, he's out in Santa Barbara for a work thing and isn't here," she calmly redirected herself to Remi, "but you already knew that. I said it in the gallery the other day, right in front of you. Were you expecting him to be back already?" Myra recognized she was cornered. "I'm not sure what kind of trouble he may have gotten himself into, but I can assure you whatever it is, he'll figure it out with you. Tom is the best man I know and have ever met really... Do you want his phone number or something? I'm not sure when he'll be back..." Myra ripped the top sheet off from a pad of Donaldson's propaganda- identical to the one she had seen when the two first met... the one with Remi's old apartment number scrolled on it.

Before she had the chance to locate a pen in the organized mess she appeared to be comfortable living in, Remi spoke, " We don't need his phone number, we have it. We both do... because we know him... *very* well." Myra's eyes narrowed into two confused slits as she leered curiously at the two women who had barged into her place with the apparent intention to ransack her love life.

"How *well* are we talking?" The words seemed to be punctuated with an extra forced breath at their front as if Myra was trying to re-inflate something with the plug still intact. The mounting pressure seemed to be relieved, at least for the moment - someone had yanked the plug out and Myra appeared to be able to breathe again.

This time, Stella took the floor and responded with an uncharacteristic emotional word vomit, "Well enough that we can both describe his dick in great detail - down the cluster of reddish freckles he has near his ball sack," the bitterness in her voice came off as resentment towards Myra herself... that didn't change as she continued using the same manically flustered tone, "You want to sit down and exchange notes together about *our* scumbag, sex-addicted boyfriend now?" This really wasn't how Remi had envisioned this meeting going, but then again, nothing in her life seemed to be. She should have assumed she had been destined for a lifetime of disappointment and heartache - it's all she'd ever known since she came out of Satan's womb.

Flashback to 1995

Remi could count on one hand how many times she remembered seeing her mother by the time it was her eighth birthday, less than both hands by her twelfth, with no more fingers to add after that, because that's when she stopped seeing her altogether.

During her eighth year on the planet, her mother did something "very bad", as her father described it, and had to go to prison, "where other bad people went". Her dad tried to assure her that just because her mom was a bad person, that didn't make Remi bad.

But she felt like she was.

She had never told him about the secrets she kept, the dark thoughts that popped into her head when she was real mad- she'd never told anyone.

She used to be frightened by her rage, but when her imagination took over and the stories of how things ought to be started whispering in her head, she felt more accepting of it. The stories always had a happy ending for h*er*, rarely for others, but that was one of the main reasons she found them pleasing. If someone is bad or do they do bad things to hurt other people, shouldn't they be punished?

She was punished when she got in trouble with her dad - like when she got caught lying about not having any homework, he made her write an apology letter to her teacher. The letter was supposed to make Remi take ownership of the decisions she made and make her aware that her actions affected other people... when she didn't do her home-work, she was disrespecting her teacher and when she lied about it, she was disrespecting her dad. Remi understood the paradigm better than she let on - they didn't much respect her and all the feelings she was going through so why should she respect them?

Her Halmoni had always said this thing "all's fair in love and war", Remi always liked it. It made her feel powerful, justified in feeling the ways she did and, sometimes, doing *what* she did in response to how those people made her feel. Her Halmoni would understand this; she would understand the dark thoughts she cradled closely to her chest as she did with her favorite baby doll. Then again, she knew she couldn't act on most of her dark thoughts - she was too small physically for most and too small emotionally for the others. Even though she took secret delight in the stories where she hurt people back, she knew deep down that if she acted out *all* of them, she would be a bad person then too. And as she got a little older, she couldn't stomach the idea of being like her mother, even though as a younger child that's all she could have ever hoped for. That was back before the Devil went to prison for her "heinous crimes".

Sometimes after school, Remi would plop her backpack down in the center of the pink, circular shag rug in her bedroom and start spinning, encircling its borders; aiming to keep the same distance from the bag planted perfectly in the middle of her routine. To add another layer of complication to it, she would write different versions of what her mother did to get herself locked away for the "foreseeable future" in her mind. They ranged from piracy, and robbery, to cold-blooded murder. She didn't know if her mom was capable of taking another person's life, but then again, she didn't really know much about her at all. She told herself she was... capable of murder, that is. Twirling around like a tiny leaf trapped inside a tornado, she would always eventually crash to the floor with dizziness and end her thoughts with the same promise to herself... *I will not be like her. I will not be a monster.*

Myra

Myra was having a hard time digesting the pill that had been delivered to her doorstep almost an hour ago already. Time stood still while the two outsiders settled in, making themselves welcome to whatever she had to offer... her boyfriend being one of those things. What the actual fuck was going on here? She had heard Remi spew her side of the story of when they first met at Expose', but it wasn't absorbing into her brain- the words just sat there ringing in her eardrums like inaudible screeches and scratches. It took everything within her to force her emotional upset back down to her core, trying to make out the words Remi was referring to as the "clues that led me to realize it all." She needed to jump in here to clarify a few things to right herself.

"So let's rewind here for a hot minute.... you heard me say his name, a *very* plain-Jane common name, saw, what you interpreted as his handwriting on some letterhead of a place that *you* claim he works for, and are telling me that the number written down was your old apartment number.... from how long ago? Why should I believe any of this? You could easily be two jealous exes of his trying to get back at him or back with him."

Myra remembered that neither of the coupled members really shared anything about past lovers with one another, making her last statement completely feasible. She wished he was there with her right there and then to clear up this whole mess. She also wished that her first inkling that Tom was in some sort of legal trouble, or even a small claims criminal, would have been true instead. She could have dealt with that... she would have stayed by his side no matter what crime he committed, and she would have probably helped him get away with it too.

Myra watched as both Stella and Remi simultaneously pulled their phones from the bags they had brought with them... who knew what the fuck else was in those luggage-sized purses. A dark vision entered her mind and led her to believe bits and pieces of a cut-up, bloody Tom were stuffed in each.

These bitches could be murderers.

The thought made her sick to her stomach and a rush of panic flowed over her-she needed a smoke. While the two rummaged through their phones, supposedly looking for evidence to prove that their reality was everyone else's, she quietly removed herself from the living area to the kitchen where she stashed Swirls. Thank God he was already packed with something fresh and funky; thank God she had thought ahead after picking up her last dime bag. The lighter made a familiar clicking noise and a calming sensation spread over her before she'd even inhaled the green glory.

She didn't cough when smoking anymore; her toke was so stealthy the others wouldn't have probably even noticed if it hadn't been for that delicious skunky smell that inevitably filled the apartment.

Myra was no cheapskate; she only bought the good shit. No schwag bag for this girl. As if it were a smoke signal, both of the women's heads bounced up in response to the smell and gave her a judgmental look. Stella even muttered, "really, right now?" Myra had heard the bitchy comment but before she could care, she remembered these two twats were in *her* home right now, so where did they think they got off judging her and what she did?

"Listen, I don't think there is anything either of you could find on your phones that will so-called prove anything about your claims of Tom to me," Myra started, but was distracted by something shiny. A gorgeous hand-blown, pink swirl heart hung from a thick black cord around Remi's throat. She recalled Tom buying that necklace when they were at the headshop together- she would never forget that day because it was the same day Tom bought Swirls for her. She knew if it was the same one, there would be a quote stamped on the back.

Without continuing her sentiment, she moved, trancelike, over to Remi, who thought Myra had somehow fallen back under her spell-like fascination with her again as Myra reached for her neck. She held the cool glass in her hand, rubbing it along its baby smooth surface, then gently flipped it over to find what she was hoping wasn't there...

Love is gentle, Love is kind.

Her stomach twisted itself into a knot and with no warning, she turned her head just in time to spare the front of Remi's shirt from puke.

Tom had bought that with *her*. Tom had bought that not all that long ago- a matter of weeks, maybe a month at the latest. Tom said he bought that for his mom as an anniversary gift for her since his dad was no longer alive to give her one. Tom had lied. He lied to *her*. Little did she know, his lie was even larger than that - his mom was dead and his dad was a no-show.

"Did he give this to you?" she realized she was tugging on the damn thing - slightly choking one of her new foes. She slowly released it, letting the heavy wad of glass thud against Remi's collarbone. Maybe it will shatter it... maybe it will be like a fault line and shatter all of her... or somehow, magically, break both of them down to mere granules of sand.

"Yes, he did. Right before he left for his last 'work-trip'." Remi said with air quotes; obviously, she no longer believed his work trips were real and Myra was sure of the same now. Dammit, Tom.

Myra bent at her waist and visibly crumbled to her knees, sobbing. She finally knew these women were telling her the truth. She needed to pick herself back up, put the puzzle pieces back together out of the box, and stand whole again. Her mother didn't raise her to be some dependent boob of a woman. She would come back from this. She would love again. But first, she would right the so many wrongs he'd created.

Lifting herself off the floor, she silently went to the sofa on which Stella was sitting, resting her laurels. Back straight, chest puffed, tears wiped..."What's the plan, ladies? Whatever it is, multiple it times ten and count me in. This motherfucker needs to pay for what he's done to *me... us*."

Trio | Remi, Stella, & Myra

A Plan is Formed

The flames of lit candles blazed through the open airwaves in Myra's studio apartment as the three women huddled, licking each other's wounds with saltwater. The sting was so strong yet these three were hardy, independent, capable women who weren't about to let some rich white fuck get away with trashing their hearts, trust, and vaginas.

It took a good hour of swapping stories and highlighting moments each had their suspicions; mostly fabricated so as not to feel duped, but they bonded over their heartache no less. Funny how people can only grieve for so long - for Stella, that hour was more than enough to share the loss of their loved one. It was time to put their heads together and make a plan worthy enough of the crime committed.

"It makes me sick to my stomach to think in our legal system there are absolutely no consequences for men like him. For what they do to women. As long as they aren't laying a hand on you out of anger, there are no implications for them killing your spirit, putting your health at risk, and brazenly leading you to believe you are safe in their hands. Even if they do lay hands on a woman, the majority of the time, they get off scot-free. There is just no justice for crimes committed against competent women like us, or any woman, in this world. There has to be something else illegal tied to the bastard's name that sticks him behind bars because God knows hurting the livelihood, safety, and security of a woman is not *really* an offense. Not in the eyes of the law. Not in the eyes of the men that run this system... This world. Fuck 'em." It was clear that both Remi and Myra had been sucked in and entranced with Stella's rant. The wheels were turning in the trio's heads, but it was Remi that had the first gear fall into place.

"So we connect Tom to something illegal," Remi stated matter-of-factly.

" I don't think there's much for us to go off of here. I run full background checks on every guy I date and Tom Williams looks like a saint on paper." Stella had no hesitation in sharing her near cavity-search of Tom. "No tax evasion, no assault charges, no theft, or known drug issues. He's a fully employed, white-collared white man with a clean record of legal health. So, I don't think we'll have anything to 'charge him with'. Unless there's something either of you knows about, what else can we do?"

Myra chimed in, somewhat quietly at first, "I feel like what he did makes me question who I am. Like, how could I have been so dumb and so willing to ignore some of the most obvious lies? How did I let myself betray everything that I knew to be watchful of because of this trust he made me think I could have in him? Am I really that vapid?" Myra watched as the others shook their heads "no" but continued, "No, really... I have no idea how I got this way. Love drunk and naïve enough to want to be 'owned' like a fucking object by another person. It's never been who I am until him. I guess the best way to put it is I feel like I've had my identity completely ripped away from me."

Once again, Remi's gears clicked away as she broke in, "Ok, so let's rip his away from him then. Let's make him go through having his identity completely deleted from society and make him the one without a name to live off of. Like killing him off on paper. No more home, no more job, no more money in the bank. Tom Williams no longer exists because..."

"...he died?" Stella asked the question, completely enveloped by the idea. "Killing someone off legally is fairly easy to do if you have access to the right forms and know all the legalities ahead of time. Lucky for us, I am that person. Unlucky for us, Tom's not actually dead, so he's a walking, talking body with a whole storyline of accusations to make and God knows how many other 'relationships' that can vouch for his health. The chance of us taking the fall for this is higher since he's completely able and in his right to talk and make all the claims he'd want. We'd have to somehow plant a seed of doubt in the court's eyes preemptively to discourage him from striking back. Any ideas?"

"I repeat, tie his name back to something illegal. If Tom Williams is dead on paper but this body is up and walking around, who the fuck is he then? A con that stole the identity of a poor soul named Tom Williams. A con artist that has been getting away with something as close to murder when the man whose identity he's been sharing actually dies. We see his obituary and know that he is gone - none of us knowing he's fully alive and well, operating under his legal name once again. Solves two issues with one story. And I can almost guarantee that none of the other hoes, sorry forgot who I was talking to, women, he's having relations with could neither confirm nor deny his stolen identity. We'd make it look so convincing on paper that none of the others would believe a word he'd say. If there are others, that is." Remi felt like a goddamn genius.

"Hm, that actually might work. Did you know Tom has had minor plastic surgery on his face? He actually showed me the before and after photos of it. He looks similar, but could easily be pegged as two different people. So what would his real, fake name be then?"

It was Myra's turn to make an artistic suggestion. "How about something close and generic like Tom Johnson?"

"I think that is a little too close and a little too generic. It feels fake." Stella retorted.

"As a favor to a friend of mine, what about the name Benjamin? Benjamin Blank. Of course, she'd never know anything about it, but I would. And I feel like I would be doing the world a favor, too." Remi suggested.

"Sure, that works. So how do we want to proceed with a list of duties, then?" Stella continued in her normal bobby-business harshness.

"Well, I know he's nowhere to be seen on social media- which actually helps us, but I have quite the local following on my artist fan page and could start implying that the boyfriend that those that know me know I had but never actually saw me with had been diagnosed with a terminal illness... cancer? He passed suddenly. And recently. Tom told me he was going to pay for me to show some of my pieces at Expose and I think I should hold him to that. It'd be a great place to show some art created around the death of the man I loved. You know, finally opening up about the heartbreak and grief I went through. Another way to say, the Tom Williams we knew is dead." Myra seemed pleased with her idea while the others agreed to let her have her moment of glory.

"Ok, well I will take on all the legal aspects of killing the 'real' Tom Williams off and creating a phony existence and life for Benjamin Blank. Remi, I am going to make you Power of Attorney as Tom's 'official' girlfriend; I cannot have my name linked to him in any way if it's my credentials tied to these forms. I may have a way to work around that, but it could get hairy. It's better to play this safe than be sorry. Remi, since you're in real estate, I want you to deal with everything housing. Get in contact with Tom's landlord and discuss a last-minute vacancy due to illness. As POA, you will also be in charge of depleting funds while I verify and ensure there is no' next of kin' for Tom. As far as I know, his mom was the only one around and he told me she died, but I will make sure that is true and let you know when to move shit around."

Myra's eyes welled with tears as she realized another lie, remembering that Tom had told her the necklace around Remi's neck was for his mother. And she's dead? What the actual fuck is wrong with this dude?

"Myra, your role is killing Tom off socially and as for our sweet boy's employer, well, I think things will unravel just the way we need them to. Just think, in a matter of a few weeks, our little lover will have nothing to his name, including his name. Actually, yes, a name. Benjamin Blank, professional Identity Thief - a crime worthy of doing time"

Deceit

Lies, Lies, Go Away
Please don't come another day,
My Daddy wants to come and play
From him, I try to run astray
Lies, Lies, go away
Please don't come another day
My Mommy says he's here to stay
I wish here I didn't have to lay
Pain, Pain, go away...

Seeing you for who you truly are... more like a *what,* you truly are... should make my stomach churn, but it doesn't because I already knew. I have known it at my core, but now I am just like you. A cunning, seductive, elusive Devil that slips in and out of the folds; twisting ourselves into the fibers of the shrouds we use to hide our true selves in, devouring them from within.

That's right, you're a good boy. You're doing what you're meant to by eating us all out, smacking your lips to get the full taste, and then digesting our innocence. It's what you were designed to do... use and abuse.

But my dear, you're not the only one on this beautifully fucked-up planet of ours that was bred for such mannerisms.

Tsk, tsk, tsk.

Shame on you for believing you were.

Deception lies in the eyes of the beholder... or is it perception? It's both and you know it... we both know it and deep down you want it that way. You may not be fully aware of it yet, but you will be. Your sultry misleadings aren't just missteps of yore that have been eroding your soul, dear one...that's too plain of a story. And I know you no longer like plain. You want exotic, erotic, torturous beauty that lies only on the surface but you're in for a surprise because I am all of those things both internally *and* externally. You just don't know it yet since you've flipped your eyes inward on yourself, blinded by the obviousness that lurks around you. We may be shadowed and even a little disfigured, but that will only be more intriguing for a sick fuck like you. You like the distortion, the pain I wear, my scars... you want to lick them off me, spread them around with your tongue, and create more of them with your name stamped on them... branding all of us.

I want to be branded by you.

I was.

I am.

But I haven't soldered mine into *your* flesh yet.

The smell of burning skin will get you off, I just know it.

Torment is what you're into, right?

Well then, step a little closer and I will get my irons hot for you and your precious nut sack.

A matching pair, one for each ball.

You're gonna love it.

It might seem like you have been a naughtier boy than usual, but not to me. You lie to everyone around you, even yourself. But you can't lie to me, Tom, not really. I accepted your double-dealing lifestyle and instead choose to soak in each lie as if it were true. I choose my own reality because *your perception is your reality;* truth is, I accept my pious virtues and will spit them back out, regurgitating them all over your constrained body. You're gonna love it. You're gonna love the vengeance I take and receive, for all the *truths* you have been telling me and so many others.

See, like you, I was bred for this too... you just don't know that yet. But you will. You will. And in the end, I will make sure my trademarks are out flailing in the wind for the world to see who you belong to now and forever.

Get your balls out because they're going to burn.

From one fraud to another.

Stella

Stella rolled over into a puddle of her own sweat. The nightmares from her youth had returned. She could only guess that her love triangle fiasco was to blame for their resurrection; she hadn't had them since, well, the last time she did something bad.

Real bad.

Not like the everyday aggression she enjoyed wearing, toting it around and slinging at those that deserved or, sometimes *needed* it the most. Some people benefit from being on the receiving end of offense; it teaches them to stand up for themselves, to grow a fuckin' pair of their own. Without balls in this world... you're never going to make it. White men have been proving that for centuries.

No, it wasn't this type of badassery she was methodically referring to, nor was it the bad she brought to clients in her dungeon or even in her personal boudoir. It was evil... an evil that was fueled by hate, rejection, loneliness, and a soul-consuming passion for retribution. She had acted on it once in her youth; its results were disastrously satisfying. Yet, she knew it wasn't something she could make a habit of. Instead, she vowed to God she'd starve her edacious dark side by never doing it or anything like it again... but here she was doing it again. And she was dripping with anticipation. Thirsty for it, like a stranded demon in a desert.

The nightmares were the same as they used to be, Stella watched herself plunging repeatedly and becoming engulfed by the rings encapsulating the pits of Hell. In her dream she could hear the screams escaping her scorching body and smell the skin roasting in the blaze, peeling back like the layers of an onion away from her musculoskeletal system.

When she was a kid, Heaven and Hell and the ways you got to them were ingrained in her through both the church and the backside of her Mama's hand. Stella was a curiously naughty child but never did much more than your average attention-seeking, slightly bored kid, but her ma had felt differently. With every bout of "talk back", every eye roll, or hands-on the hips stance, Stella's face met the underside of her mother's mitt.

She'd never forget the unforgiving sting of those giant palms nor the red streaks her twisted, arthritic fingers left behind like a receipt from the transaction. A visual reminder of what was to come the next time she'd let herself "become a little bitch." Her mama truly believed it was demonic possession that led to Stella's naughtiness and apparently, she felt the best way to purify her was to slap Satan out. In her heart of hearts, she wished her mama was there to slap him out of her head right now. But she knew that wasn't possible... and it had everything to do with the bad she'd done so many years ago.

Did she regret it? Not one bit. It needed to be done just like this did. And so it will be... She'd have to just wait and see if her soul came out intact after the saga was over and Tom was gone.

The library didn't open until nine o'clock that morning so deciding that it made little sense to drive all the way into her office for a mere hour of work she decided to put her recently constructed home office to use. Setting her laptop down on the cold, sleek, all-wood desktop reminded her of him and the night he'd put it together for her. The night that the lies started... they didn't really *start* that night - she knew that now, but it *was* the night that started their demise. Feeling sad for a brief moment, she shook it off like a wet dog coming in out of the rain. She needed to remember that she'd liked him, but didn't love him. Those other women did - pathetic really, but then again if it weren't for them they wouldn't be ensuing this grand scheme and then Stella would feel sad because she knew deep down she'd enjoy watching him disappear. Not just because of who he was or what he'd done but because she'd been waiting for the right time to break her vow of innocence and do it all again. Her hour of focus went out the window. She couldn't seem to settle her brain. She was becoming obsessed with the plan... again.

One hour of "work" from home and she'd be in front of one of the library's computers to start phase I of the dirty threesome's revenge plan.

―――――――

Using a library computer under a new, fake account was Remi's idea and it was a smart one. Stella needed to eliminate as much tracing back to her as possible, knowing she'd never be able to eliminate *all* traces since she'd be using her name to make the changes. But at least this way it was more likely to stay hidden from her employer. She was risking a lot... she knew that. She could lose her job or worse, be disbarred, but she was already risking those two things by moonlighting, giving legal advisory meetings with people she knew would never become a client of hers. It was clearly outside her contract and if someone at the firm found out, well that'd be the end of the line for her. At *that* firm.

She knew as long as she kept her law license, she could always work her way into another. Just like she had worked the librarian over to give her a library card without having an ID. A couple of bats of her eyelashes and a sleek, come hither and fuck me grin that could entice the Devil himself into buying what she was selling was all it took.

Desperate idiot.

Another nerdy white guy thinking with his virgin pecker. True, she'd chosen a fake name, but it was still a familiar name... she took a gamble that they wouldn't be flagged as already in the system. And they weren't, not even when Stella gave the twat their address... their *real* address. Apparently, they read very little.. that explained so much. What kind of psychopath doesn't have a library card for God's sake - there's no expectation to use it, but it takes a completely moronic lunatic not to have one. Tsk, tsk, tsk... their loss was her fortunate identity-thieving gain.

She sat and started logging into at least half a dozen accounts... it wasn't hard to kill Tom off in a legal sense. Just time-consuming. But there was a definite order of operations here... first things first - Remi becomes Tom's Power of attorney since his recent cancer diagnosis. Shit, stage four cancer- brain cancer, fucks his cognitive abilities sideways, making him incapable of his own decisions. So sad to hear that he is deteriorating so quickly. A slow, wicked smile spread across her chiseled honey brown cheekbones.

Poor, dying Tom has no next of kin or remaining family members, so it only makes sense that his girlfriend, life partner really, would be the one to "take care" of him through the end stages of his life. Poor fucker. Remi's loaded herself, so she's not even in it for money-just to sip the dripping sap of sweet but bitter, sticky redemption.

Before typing to fill in the form blanks, a moment's curiosity struck Stella. What were the odds that the person's name she'd just used for the library also had credentials to access the same forms she was looking at? Probably fairly good since so many of her colleagues still preferred working off paper and couldn't scrounge up enough strength to print anything out themselves. Old, pathetic sad sacks. It would only make sense they'd have a happy helper get them the forms they needed, right? Stella backed out of her profile and clicked on the firm's logo to view the list of employees. There she was. All Stella needed was the password. And for a generic account for someone who didn't actually practice law, it would probably be something simple. Something stupidly simple. Like the name of the law firm.

Cha-ching, Mama was in. And now Stella was fully incognito. Try and trace any of this back to me. I have my shit covered.

Stella spent the next hour starting the paper trail necessary for Tom's official death and the resurrection of Benjamin Blank - which ended up being a much more common name than she'd had expected. Everything was going fairly smooth with miscellaneous oddities here and there, like the fact that there was no "father" listed or signed by on Tom's original birth certificate, but that would all be rearranged anyway, so that's neither here nor there. And not really an issue to start with anyway- that happens a lot these days. It almost happened to Stella herself if her granddaddy hadn't dragged her father's sorry ass to the hospital to sign.

One more click of the submit button, and onto the next application- she will need to get a copy of Tom's digital signature, but she thinks she knows just the gal to help her with this. Anything for an old family friend... right?

She pulled her newly purchased burner phone from her Black GG and pulled up her new bestie, aka Remi's jaded, man-hating room- mate, Michelle. See, after meeting Tom for the first time the other day, when the jackass ditched their plans and hiked over to Remi's instead, Michelle recognized him and later told Remi that he was a patient at the dentist's office where she works. Where she handles all the patient files and the individual paperwork that, of course, has client signatures all over them. Patient files that then get scanned into their digital files to be used for special occasions such as this and... well, tooth extractions and shit.

Stella remembered her high school friend's little sister Michelle well. They grew up in the same neighborhood and their parents were good friends with one another. They were cut from the same cloth. A stained rag filled with gaping holes where there should have been securely entwined fibers there to support and comfort.

Stella knew her trauma because it was also hers.

Michelle was always getting herself into trouble through her own poor decisions back in the day; she must have maintained the natural attraction for it since she apparently married a cheating, lying pain in the ass named Dameon.

For a brief second, she realized she was in a similar sad-ass boat as Michelle, but the pang quickly faded when she reminded herself she hadn't been stupid enough to marry Tom or any other asshole. Marriage was for suckers.

Hey, long time, no chat. I enjoyed meeting with your friend Remi - what a brave young woman to go forward with living the life and having the family she has always wanted without having some lazy bastard lying on her couch. Great gal, I really enjoyed helping you both out. Up to return the favor? It's a little hairy, but I think you might like the overall purpose of it...

———————

Stella's car door slammed harder than she had intended it to, startling her. It was probably to be expected that she'd feel jumpier from now on - she'd have to conceal that, or it'd be a dead giveaway to anyone that even remotely knew her. Reasserting her bad bitch self, she straightened the front of her suit coat, grabbed her bag, and headed in to restart her workday once again. She glimpsed the back of a bobbing blonde head as she gripped the door handle of the building. Probably someone's client shooting the breeze with Rachel, the hound dog, while they waited. Their loud jabber could probably be heard all the way to fucking Mars, Stella imagined the two chatty Cathie's as green goblin-like extraterrestrials in heels. She caught herself chuckling and so did they.

The pair of probably twenty-somethings turned their heads in her direction and for the first time, Rachel glared at Stella as if she had interrupted something vitally important. Rachel must have realized how exposed she had made herself and was quick-on-the-draw for a recovery. There's that slobbery almost salacious smile we all know and hate. She was such a desperate, minuscule bitch... a walking advertisement of her own lack of confidence. Rachel would probably give out blowjobs to anyone who said they would be her friend at the office...at least that's what her pathetic puppy-dog stares said to Stella.

Fuckin' fleabag bimbo.

Stella pressed on as much of a convincing smile as she could manage, only because there was someone else in the room. Someone she didn't know but decided it was her right to. Walking straight up to the sunny-headed nit-wit she shoved her mit out in front, gesturing for an exchange of hands.

"I'm Stella, one of the defense lawyers here. And you are?"

"Oh jeez, hi. I'm Kay, I'm a friend... oh gosh can we call ourselves that?" She paused, then accepted a nod of permission granted from Rachel before continuing. "I'm a *new* friend of Rachel's. We met this morning at the coffee shop across the street. We were both sucking down our morning dose of caffeine and she caught me *inhaling* one of their blueberry scones. She's got an eye for sweet treats this one here..." the Kay lady said pointing to Rachel and giggling. Rachel joined in and the two of them sounded like gaggling geese. Stella wanted to press her hands over her ears and block their cackles from rupturing her pristine eardrums. God, these two were made for each other. She hated them both. But before she turned to leave, she caught a shared look between the two that spoke volumes... how had she never noticed before? Rachel *liked* women. Rachel was a lesbian. Rachel *probably* wanted inside Stella's pants-maybe that's why she was always such a kiss-ass to her...She had always assumed she was that way with everyone in the office. Well, this changed things. A bit. Not much. She still hated her. Her and this Kay loser.

"We were just setting a time and place to meet for lunch if you'd like to join us," Kay said, clearly without running it past her new bestie first. Rachel shot her daggers...a nonverbal message saying that she'd hoped they'd be alone together. How sickening. Holding the rising vomit back in her throat, Stella shook her head no and said, "thanks for the offer, but I am *sure* I have something better to do." It was cold. It was rude.

Stella turned, making her hair spin, flirtatiously in the air. Now that she knew Rachel's sexual preferences, she might as well have some fun with it. She knew she could be a cock-tease, but she had never tried to be taint-tease...

It must have worked because when Rachel came back from her lunch date, she showed up in Stella's office and told her she knew about her side hustle. Stella didn't know how to respond at first, no one else in the office knew about her evening whips and chains gig.. so how did she find out about it? And what did she *think* was she going to do with that information?

It was much to her surprise when Rachel requested to set up a *meeting* with her at her *home office*. First, she's a lesbo and now she comes to her, basically begging for sexual brutality... Stella had been wrong. Rachel was no dog. She was a horny closet-freak with an itch that she wanted Stella to scratch.

Stella narrowed her eyes and said, "Ok, but this stays between us."

Of course, it would. Stella had set up a preemptive defense when she'd used Rachel Dobbs' identity to create all those legal forms and under her favorite new library card account, too.

Manipulation

It's raining, it's pouring
The puppet strings are soaring
They say only what they're fed
And climb back inside your bed
But you won't wake in the morning

Sex dribbles off you like melting butter on the tops of hot crisp kernels yearning to swim in your pools of cum. You love the way women tense their private parts when you're around like they're trying to pleasure themselves with a self-induced, hands-free orgasm by holding their breath and pussy muscles at the same time.

You sense it, sniffing it out like a bloodhound on a trail of something rotting and delicious in the woods.

Keep following your nose, dirty dog, it's going to lead you down a path that makes you forget where you are. But don't worry, even though you'll be lost, un-fucking-believably lost, you'll never forget *who* you are... I'll never let you. You're a bastard by every definition of the word. Bastards don't win the game, Tom. You may have won some races and you're gonna feel like you win some in the near future, but by the end of it all, you'll be nothing but a dickless corpse.

Well, hopefully dickless. I'm working on that as we speak.

You're not the only one with people skills, you know. I have been feeding and watering mine for a couple of decades now and I must say, unlike you, I'm really getting good at not fucking my way into any and all relationships.

I made some new friends recently. I think you know most of them *personally,* but I won't get into the details- they'll just bore you. But I do think we'll stay friends for a while, at least while I'm holding their strings; after that, I'll most likely have to cut them off and let them crawl back to whatever light they can still see at the end of this semi-suicidal mission.

I'm not concerned about the other girls - they seem gritty.

At least one of them should survive their guilt.

Fingers fucking crossed for them.

Until then, we plan things *together,* but you know me... I'm always in charge, even when I pretend not to be. I make the calls. The hard decisions. I've made more of them than you know dear one... all the times you haven't been there for me, well, I made some calls because *someone* had to, I don't think you're gonna like the ones I've been making lately though. A bad day for little Tommy Gun is what they all lead to.

A.Bad. Deadly. Day.

You probably think you held *my* strings for a hot minute, but then you took out the longest, most jagged dagger you could scrounge up and sliced me down the middle with it. You thought I'd bleed out without the strings being attached... without us being attached, but you were wrong, pet, you were wrong. I didn't even bleed out when they ripped her from the inside.

You can't kill the already dead; especially when she never got the chance to live in the first place.

Myra

Little clay fingerprints danced themselves onto almost every sur-rounding surface in Myra's studio the past few days. She'd been busy; too busy to wash her hands in between every spin around the potting table. Too busy to wash the evidence away. She'd get to it - she'd have to because Tommy Gun... fuck, she needed to stop calling him that, was coming over later. Myra didn't want him to get too curious about any-thing; she needed to pay for her show at Expose' before he could know *anything* about her recent work. And to do that, she was going to have to transform herself into a sly little minx. She was a good pretender. Myra'd been acting a part for as long as she could remember, so she wasn't afraid of lying to him like had been with her. Creep deserved it.

She had a lot of work to do... a lot to prepare for her upcoming gallery debut. The show had a new theme, so she had to start from scratch; her hands dove in and out, around, and down, lacing her fingers to make intricate rolls and folds in the multiple vases she was making for her largest installment.

She planned to call it *Deathbed*. Each carefully crafted, unique clay vase would hold bunched displays of wildflowers... all sent from those who loved him most. Flowers were supposed to symbolize empathy, compassion, care during times like this but Myra, though a firm believer in visual messaging because well, duh, she *is* an artist, never agreed with their presumed sentiment. Anyone could pick flowers from the earth, plunk them in an old, recycled jelly jar and some water and say that meant something deeper. Like they *really* went out of their way, outside the scope of normal, above and beyond, to yank some stinking weeds from a dirt patch. Not the case. It took hardly any time and almost just as little thought.

Fuck the pansies...literally. In all realness, it was mother Nature that deserved credit for the little joy they might bring to the untrained eye... Not some dope.

It wasn't the plan they had agreed upon that made her empty inside; it was the ruminating on the fact that he'd been lying to her this *entire* time. What a scam he pulled... a full-on phony relationship was one thing, but posing as a nature advocate was another. He fucking lied about it all... his concern about global warming, his appreciation for gender equality, all the casework and environmental projects he'd been hired to do. Only a psycho would do that; he was probably becoming a legend in his own mind from his lies. It was actually pretty sad; this man was literally lost in his own life because of his insurmountable pack of lies. He believed them all - she knew it in her heart of hearts.

Before she could start second-guessing the role she was to play in his demise, she toked down a bowl of cheap, shitty weed (she needed to start a savings account for the reality check that was coming after their little ploy) and grabbed some spray bottles. Time to slip into Myra, the domesticated bitch.

At least she'd be high for it. Barely.

She encircled herself with a wreath of dusting spray and went to town, scrubbing away the sins they'd left behind... sins that were mostly his now. Myra felt like an angel compared to him, and she was no fucking angel. This must have been a bit like how her mother felt when her dad disappeared... there had to be secrets he'd been hiding. Another woman, another family, another life - probably yes to all three. Myra watched as her dish-gloved hands turned into her mother's; she felt an ache in her back as she leaned over the coffee table and the ache traveled to the heart, leaving her body as tears. It wasn't her crying; she felt her mother's rage. She felt her pain, exploitation, and grief... for the first time she empathized, truly empathized with her mother - experiencing firsthand the heartache that comes from the deceptions of a lover. She and her mother were living parallel lives that *very* moment- the two of them had merged into the same being. Myra finally understood and accepted that what she was about to do with these two other women wasn't only for them, but it was for her mom, too. For every woman who'd suffered. She would do it... everything she agreed to with no shame, with no guilt. Instead, she would do it, "kill" him off from the world around him, with pride.

Ignoring the last puddle of spray that had settled atop a side table, Myra tossed the bottle into the kitchen sink, decidedly re-prioritizing how she was to spend the next hour before the villain's arrival.

She needed to crawl out of her skin for a while and try on a different costume of sorts. She rifled through her armoire, searching for a slippery, sensual vixen to come flying out at her. And there it was, gliding towards her - a backless red dress that hugged her curves as tight as the gloved hand that was going to be examining Tom's prostate later. Disrobing, she stepped into the mini, basically painting it on. No panties. No bra. She needed him to have every distraction in the world tonight. Nipples and ass cheeks are extremely distracting, she smirked to herself as she twirled in front of the full-length mirror. Tonight wasn't about mystery... tonight was about getting what she wanted, and she knew exactly what that was.

His credit card.

———

Tom was the metal rod and Myra was the overpowered magnet, the two connecting through centrifugal force as soon as he walked through her doorway. She hated to admit it, but she felt happy to see him, almost as if there was this giant boulder lifted off her chest, making room for her lungs to expand and her heart to beat again. Seeing him was like a breath of fresh air, but she knew it shouldn't have been. She knew she had to hate him. She knew what she had to do to him... that *is* what they had planned the evening for from the beginning, wasn't it? Of course, it was.

As their bodies entwined she walked him backward, her lips locked with his and her eyes only open wide enough for her to guide them to her king-sized mattress where she planned to get what he came there for and pick his pockets at the same time.

Two birds...one stone.

Their bodies rolled, tumbling like a pair of twitterpated socks in a dryer. During one of the brief seconds that Myra was on top of the love heap, she slid her hands down the sides of his pants suggesting that she wanted them off then seductively snuck the fingertips of her left hand into his coordinating back pocket just far enough to grab the tip of his wallet. With it in hand she made a dramatic roll, flinging herself across the other side of the bed, quickly shoving the wallet underneath her mattress. She'd need that later. What she needed now was to feel him inside of her, caressing her with its bulbous mushroom head. She knew it was wrong to get intimate with him after knowing what she knew but she didn't care... she'd put that all out of her mind to enjoy the moment... possibly their last time together-*together* but then he had to go and ruin it.

"Fuck me like you mean it. Like I'm the only person on the planet that matters to you."

You gotta be kidding? Who the hell does this guy think he is asking this from her... From anybody. Like he's fucking the *only* person who matters to him, her ass. No one mattered to him - he was fucking everyone in the world; it's not a crime to be sexually active, promiscuous even, but to lead someone to believe that they are your one and only was just plain wrong. Hurtful. Shameful. It was no secret that Myra had always been an advocate for sexual exploration and expression, but they were more than just a good romp in the sheets. They were partners, best friends... at least she'd thought so.

She shivered and instinctually pushed him off of her. She was overwhelmed with the realization of why her mother encouraged and supported all things sex... she'd been hurt by a man and accepted a new reality - one where she found fulfillment by loving herself enough to take affection freely without loving her partner in exchange. Love took trust and she'd been burnt by that before - now they both had.

Myra tried to force herself to re-engage, give herself the same permission as her mother did to just simply enjoy this trade for exactly what it was...a good bang. But no matter how hard she tried to overrule the undermining thoughts in the back of her brain, she couldn't. She just couldn't. Perhaps because it was *him*.. the one that jaded her like her father was to her mother. As far as she knew, her mom had never re-connected with her dad or let him have any second chances in the sack. And this was exactly why- they meant too much and they destroyed that with lies, greed, and almost hateful selfishness.

No, she wouldn't. She couldn't allow herself to climb back aboard the Tom train. Instead, she rolled herself off the bed, stared at the wall to recollect herself, and slipped back into actress mode.

"So sorry," she said, flipping her head around while covering both her boobs with her hands. She could still lie to him, but she found a new sense of shy awkwardness around him. He wasn't her lover or even a one-night-stand... he was an enemy. "I forgot to take my birth control while you were away so better safe than sorry. No whammies...am I right?!" Pushing out what felt like the world's most insincere grin and a flirtatious hair flip. Tom didn't seem to notice its insincerity and instead offered to run out and get a box of condoms.

"Oh shit, no. I come from a long line of Fertile Myrtles'. Every woman I know of in my family got pregnant when using one. Plus, they just make me feel like I am getting a pap smear... you know, a gloved finger shoved up there... not sexy." She had been redressing herself while giving her little speech. None of what she had just said was true-not even in the slightest, but it convinced him. Selfish prick couldn't handle having a kid... it'd mean he would have to think of someone else from time to time. That was something he couldn't, wouldn't, do... that had become abundantly clear. Myra had never envisioned herself with kids either, but for a separate set of reasons- none of which were his business any longer.

Speaking of business, it was time to get down to it... she got what she needed from him; time to kick the bastard out before he notices his wallet is missing. A bout of fake tummy troubles a few moments after they'd left the bed had him fleeing out of her building and down the sidewalk faster than she could make it back to the lifted wallet only a few feet away from her.

Out of sight, out of earshot, out of the wallet you come, Mr. Mastercard. She rubbed her fingers over the embossed numbers- this card was ancient...she checked the expiration date. It looks like she had stolen it in the nick of time... Christmas. She had three months with her new plastic boyfriend; just long enough to get what she really wanted from Santa that year.

Power

Ring around the liar
Things will get much dire
There's no need to glower
I've got all the power
Ashes, Ashes
You all found down

Tommy boy, bitter, tiny-dick, Tommy boy... you think you have it all.
No, what you think is that you have us *all* fooled into believing the
atrocities you bought for the price of your worthless, measly soul. Your
dick might be tiny but your brain isn't- you have just enough shit
zapping around up there to know your value. Which is, of course,
nothing. Soon, it will be a sackless, dead, nothing - with no soul left to
float around us in the afterlife. That's right, you won't even have the
power to haunt any of us for what we did, more like what *I* did... am
doing right now without you knowing. With none of them knowing
that *I* am the puppet master, the only one strong enough to do what
needs to be done to permanently delete you.

   Strength equates directly to power, you know that, asshole? I bet
you didn't...otherwise you would have been upping your inner-
strength game and learned to love yourself instead of masking it with
all of us. We are an illusion you created to make yourself feel important
and in control for once. Sad little Tommy Boy crying in the corner
because he felt out of control of his life; unloved, invisible... yadda,
yadda, yadda. Poor me baby bitch serum, you have been feeding your-

self your entire life. If you could have just wised up and realized you weren't a victim, not an *actual* victim, maybe you could have been somebody. But see, you didn't and now you *are* a victim. An actual victim. My victim.

You know what twat boy? I don't think there's a way out of this for you. There's power in numbers.

Fact: you are alone.

You think you're not, but you are.

Fact: We have each other... its numbers- sheer numbers. I'd like to say our plan isn't personal, but it is.

One hundred fucking percent personal.

You know there's a saying around that too, "the power of personal". I have to laugh. I'm so fucking witty; it rips me up inside. It seems *I* do truly have it all - but I want more. So I think I'll take the little shards of everything you have left.

If you only knew Tom, and I guess if you weren't on the receiving end of it... you'd be laughing and loving it all. I promise. I know you would because I devised *all* of it from inside your head.

You think no one knows you, but I do.

I have a front-row seat looking out from behind those pools of piss you call eyes.

I see what you see.

I know what you know; the difference is I don't think what you think.

Your thoughts are pathetically desperate. Mommy didn't love you enough, so now you have to shit on everyone else that actually might.

You fucked yourself... you really did.

You're actually lucky I am around to help you pull the plug.

Your bark is worse than your bite, so let me sink those teeth down a bit harder into the power cords and... yank... Electrocution.

And you're dead. You're welcome, douche.

Remi

Remi's morning felt like a tidal wave hovering above her, waiting for the least opportune time to drop down for a bite of her backside. It hadn't dropped yet, but she already felt like she was drowning. Being a power of attorney and essentially stealing someone's assets was a lot more work than she imagined, and she wasn't even operating "Mission Killjoy" alone, as most criminals would be. Oh, Jesus, she was a criminal now. She'd not thought of it that way yet, but now that she had, she felt like throwing up in her wastebasket. Possibly from the mere thought of her treachery, but more likely because she'd also just finished her first round of IUI that morning. The hormones were already feeling a bit crazy inside her, but that was to be expected. Remi's office phone rang, interrupting her bile backup, she lifted the receiver and answered in the most professional voice she could manage; "Remi Nash speaking."

"Well, good morning, aren't you just a cloud of sunshine?! With a greeting like that I think I am warranted in asking if you're ok," the chipper voice at the end of the line belonged to her building buddy, Kay. "You around to grab a cup of coffee this morning? I'd ask for a lunch but I am just crazy busy with meetings this afternoon."

Coffee sounded like the perfect escape Remi needed from the guilt she had been packing on so far since her new POA rights had officially kicked in. "Lady, it's like you can read my mind. Meet you outside, in front of the doors in ten?"

"Sounds perfect. It also sounds like it's a 'my treat' kind of day, so no need to bring your wallet. I got you." Kay was always a bright and shiny bubble, and today Remi was more grateful than ever for her friend's cheery disposition. She only wished she could feel that light and carefree herself. Though a blob of darkness surrounded her, she reminded herself of the secret that'd just been implanted between her legs. Clutching them together in fear of losing the seed she imagined already taking root inside her once-rotting innards, she stood to leave. She wouldn't be alone in this world forever - at whatever cost it took, she'd not be alone.

Remi couldn't shake the feeling that everyone in the coffee shop was staring at her, as if they all *knew* what she was becoming and ALL of her secrets. Was it that obvious she was conforming to the social norms of a psychopath? Convincing herself she couldn't be a medically diagnosable psycho she turned her attention back to Kay, who was just coming back from the counter, steaming hot brews in both of her hands. She couldn't help but notice the plain pearl that graced Kay's wedding ring finger.

"Whoa, well hello there pretty pearly-thing. Is there something you'd like to share?" Remi knew Kay and her boyfriend, Doug, were getting serious, but she had heard no mention of an engagement from Kay. Kay wasn't the type of girl to keep a secret, let alone one of this size. She was the type of girl who made the world her oyster, her bestie, and she would have climbed to the top of NYC to share news like this.

Kay's face flushed a little in embarrassment. "Nope, no news. Besides that, it's a fraud. I started wearing it because I am so sick of guys trying to pick me up; especially the weird-ass new hire we brought on a couple of weeks ago. The guy is incorrigible. Everyone else in the office, besides him that is, knows it's just a space keeper, but it seems to help deter Playdough playboy's advances. "

"God, I'm sorry to hear about this. Nobody should have to be harassed at work- well anywhere, really. Have you mentioned it to HR at all?"

"No, I've been mentioning it to Doug though, trying to get him to realize that he needs to put a proper ring on my finger and stop dragging out the inevitable. He wants kids, but he also knows that I won't give him any until we're married, so.... the ball's in his court, really."

"Can I ask why you want to be married first? Just curious, no judgment." Remi hadn't shared her plans of going through IUI, using a sperm donor, any of it, so she felt like she'd get an honest opinion from her.

"I guess I have just seen too many kids born out of wedlock usually end up with only one parent, and then grow up feeling like they weren't important enough for the people that should love them the most to stick around. It's too heart-wrenching. Honestly, deep down I don't think Doug would ever do that, you know, abandon our kid, but if he were to, I'd want to make it the hardest, most expensive decision. Divorce costs a lot of moola and I think I've shared this with you before, but Doug is a cheapskate so... it's a great little insurance policy I have written for myself and future family."

Remi got a sour taste in her mouth; Kay's viewpoint and method behind getting married and starting a family with the one person she supposedly loved more than anyone else in the world sounded like one giant trap. Trap someone into staying in a marriage with kids and the threat of a wallet-gouging-styled divorce. That mindset might work for Kay, but it couldn't be further from what Remi wanted from life. She smiled in response, knowing that nothing good could come out of her mouth in response, so a lone smile would have to suffice. And it did.

Almost as quickly as the topic had floated into the conversation, Kay fluttered to another, leaving it trailing in a discolored dust storm. Kay wanted to know everything about *her*. Remi hesitantly shared her story of heartbreak. The one where the main character gets pulverized by the villainous, two-faced prince... leaving her for the bedsides of real princesses that unconsciously lie, vulnerable, in wait for him to forage through their souls - breaking everything he touches. Remi surprised herself when she flat out said she was going to get back at him but quickly stopped herself from going into detail. She felt like a monster even saying what she did out loud; she could only imagine what Kay'd think of her if she'd shared too much. It is a murky, slippery slope to becoming the villain in her own story. Remi knew she'd have to keep her balance and walk the fine line with pristine footing.

Of course, Kay wanted to pry- this was big, exciting made-for-tv, shit. Remi couldn't blame her for wanting more of the action-packed, dramatic details. But she couldn't. She wouldn't. So they said walked back to their building and said their goodbyes at the elevator doors. The doors squealed shut behind Remi, closing hers off from the world around her. Her finger reached out, but instead of pressing her floor number, she illuminated each one of the round buttons - a proven way to get it stuck. It lurched to start its rise and then heaved to an abrupt stop... she was finally alone now. She reached up and covered the camera with her scarf. There, now she was truly alone. Instinctually, she let her guard down, making way for the pressure behind her eyes to surge through the invisible dam that had been holding them there for as long as she could remember. She knew she'd have to rebuild it, but for now, she needed to be broken.

The clock in her office ticked and tocked its way through the afternoon until 3:00 finally came. Starting another step in the plan, she claimed to be visiting another of her current clients that had recently closed on their property, excusing herself from her office earlier than normal. It was a complete lie. She'd stop by after she'd taken Tom's wallet over to the post office to secure his new P.O. Box. It was a little sad, really. Tom had been in a tizzy about losing his wallet and apparently had contacted all three of them, claiming to have lost it at each of their places. Confirming that one another had told them they hadn't seen it, it left them wondering how many others he contacted making the same claim. It couldn't just be the *three* of them. But it *would* be the three of them to avenge every woman he'd ever wronged.

Hijacking his mail was one of the necessary, but boring steps in making that happen. At the core of everything, she knew her role in the plan was vital in making the other steps work, but it just didn't feel like enough.

Even though it made her stomach feel like a washer on spin cycle, she wanted, craved even, to hurt him in unmentionable ways. In her dreams, she saw herself holding the hammer above his writhing body, rich purple-black blood pouring out from behind those once sea-green eyes. Those damn eyes. They had tricked her. She had trusted them and they used her and her good graces.

Devils like him didn't deserve pure pools like his; her mother had them, too. Maybe she should have seen this as a warning sign that he too would be capable and willing to destroy her. As for her own pair of onlookers, they were a darker, richer hue. More like the teal-colored fluorescent anemones that lie beneath their seas, waiting patiently as it silently stalks its prey. Taking in the world while fooling the floaters all around them until their next meal swam close enough. Then they would consume. And she would devour him whole, she decided.

Flashback to Senior Year

Senior year was the roughest one yet for Remi; halfway through, her father and she hopped on a plane to say their goodbyes to an old and dying Halmoni. Her hero, the only person she felt proud to consider family, was leaving this plain for the next. She'd be lost without her, but she knew it was unreasonable, and even a bit immature, to be mad at her sweet Halmoni for dying... no one could control death. Not even suicidal people. She firmly believed that those that were drawn to taking their own lives had reason to because of beliefs they just couldn't control.

Accepting Halmoni's end-of-life transition was the most loving thing he could do for the person who loved her most. Holding the frail, wrinkled hand that swam in its own loose skin, she watched as her sweet, brave little Halmoni closed her eyes and drew her last breath. She kissed her forehead and said a prayer for peace above her, knowing that the woman's spirit could still hear her even though it had been freed from its human form. Remi felt a piece of herself die alongside her that day- a chunk had been ripped out from her wholeness, exposing a gaping hole that would attract parasites as soon as in the weeks to come when her mother was released from prison.

The monster had gotten out on a legal technicality of some kind. After throwing away almost ten years of her life behind bars, her mother somehow hired a high-profile lawyer who studied her trial. He was the one to discover the loophole; her get-out-of-jail-free card, and the start of her own demise. It wasn't Remi's responsibility to forgive and forget all the heartache and pain the bitch had caused her. The years of negligence couldn't be undone - commonsense- but her mom didn't have any of that and assumed she could just waltz into her life as if she'd been there the entire time. Yeah, fucking right, lady.

It started with unwanted home visits. They made Remi physically ill to the point where her father finally stepped in and demanded these little unplanned drop-ins stop. There was an argument about it. Her mom got mad, raised her voice, and then something crashed against the wall. Remi was upstairs hiding underneath her bed's comforter; she gently hummed one of the songs her Halmoni had sung to her as a young girl while she pressed her pointer fingers into her eardrums. She would have to be deaf to not hear the shattering glass and the yelp from her father as it apparently whizzed past his head. She removed her fingers to hear him say, "You're going back; one phone call from me right now letting them know you are breaking your parole by being here and acting in a threatening, violent manner... you'll go back. Leave. Leave now, Melanie, before it's too late."

She left. Then the insistent phone calls started - straight to Remi's cell number. Remi never did figure out how she got her phone number, but then again, it must not have been all that important to her because she never asked, even when she had the perfect opportunity to.

One day she answered. One day, she agreed to meet her Mom. One day, the parasites took over, gnawing away enough of the real Remi to take the lead. They met at her favorite coffee shop. The fragrant black java beans could be smelled brewing from blocks away, but the aroma was best when you passed through the red brick building's doors. That's when a sugar rush fled up your nostrils from the lovingly baked sweets that filled the visible wall ovens at all times. Remi's favorite table was ready and waiting for her every time she came in. That day, the one when she met her mom, she chose a different and unique spot, so as not to taint her secret haven with the evil that was about to unfold.

Her mother was late. Shocking. Over fifteen minutes had passed over their scheduled meet up and Remi was just standing to leave the shop, coffee in hand, when the small bell above the door rang. Coming through the doors was a bedraggled version of the woman that'd given birth to her. She looked homeless; probably because she was. Getting out of prison for a violent crime was hard on people's living and working arrangements. Remi heard about it all during their scheduled whine session- she also heard every excuse in the book about why she'd become the person she was. Remi tuned her out and instead focused her eyes on the coffee she's purchased. She knew she needed to find out what *she* actually needed to know before it started kicking in. She'd have twenty minutes if she was lucky.

Interrupting mid-babble, "I need to know what you did that landed you in prison?" Remi blurted.

Her mother looked shocked, almost wounded, that she'd been cut off with such a staggering question. "Well, sweetie.."

"Don't fucking call me sweetie."

"Ok, well then, Remi, what I did is in the past. I'm not that person anymore..."

"You're always that person. You always will be. You can't just decide to be somebody else one day- it doesn't work like that."

"See, if I believe that, then I don't know how I'll rebuild my life - survive this and move on. You know that Remi, I know you do. "

"No, I don't know. I'm not a criminal like you. But I *do* know you better than you think I do and I can promise you this, there's no new life for you. You can't come back from this or anything else you've done. You'll never be forgiven, it'll never be forgotten, and you'll rot the rest of your life way in the sewage you made out of your life. Hard to believe that I could know you so well without you *really* being there for me, isn't it? Now, just answer the fucking question...what did you do?"

Tears welled behind her mother's sociopathic eyes. She was only feeling sorry for herself- she'd made her entire existence out of being a victim, and this was just another time that poor little Melanie got trapped in her own broom closet.

"I got high, robbed a bank, and I um... I... I didn't mean to, you have to know that Remi... I shot someone that tried to get in my way of leaving. It was a headshot wound. They died. I went to prison for the robbery and murder. They didn't seem to care about the drugs in my system at the time... priorities, right?!" she choked out a sick, perverted giggle. There's the sociopath Remi knew and hated.

"Great," Remi spouted sarcastically, "Next question. Why did you have me? Why didn't you just get an abortion or something if you never really wanted me?"

No matter how much emotional prep Remi had done for this meeting, nothing could have prepared her for the answer she was given. "I couldn't afford one and I wasn't going to kill myself trying to do it alone. I was desperate. Not dumb. I knew that there were other ways I could make you nonexistent. I took the easier way out, the safer one, for both of us really. I mean, yes, leaving you was shitty- but killing you before you were even born would have been worse, right? In the end, I made the better choice and now I am choosing to have a relationship with you and right some wrongs from our past together."

"You sick cunt, you can't right the wrongs *you* did to *me*. Hearing you defend your actions and praise the choices you made for being better than the murderous alternative... seriously, fuck you. And just so you know, I didn't meet you here today to try to 'rebuild' anything with you. I came here to confirm what I guess I already knew and say good-bye forever. So, goodbye forever. And in case you're wondering, I don't forgive you and promise that I never will. So *don't* rest in peace."

She stood to leave and didn't even glance over her shoulder to see her mother's face one last time.

Felony Melanie's body was found on the sidewalk about half a mile away from the coffee shop. Her skull must have bounced off the pavement pretty hard on the way down since it was fractured in three places. It was the perfect place to die. There were witnesses all around to assure police officers she folded down to the ground all by herself. The drugs in her system explained everything. She was, after all, a recovering drug addict.

Remi knew she'd done right by society and her mother's inevitable future victims by dosing her coffee with a lethal amount of ketamine. Poor old felony Melanie fell off the wagon and landed in a coffin.

She'd be lucky if she got a funeral.

Dear Mr. Davis (or current landlord of building 205, Lennox Ave),

My name is Remi Nash and I am writing to you on behalf of Tom Williams regarding his lease for apartment #135. It pains me to inform you that Tom has been diagnosed with terminal cancer; his life expectancy is unknown, but we are all hoping for the best.

Since Tom has no living relatives, he made me, his girlfriend, his Power of Attorney. Sadly, he is failing rather quickly - the illness has been affecting his cognitive abilities and memory mostly, but we assume there will be physical atrophy coming.

I wanted to make you aware of this because he could literally die at any moment, and in that case, we would need to square up the details within his lease. Can you get back to me? I'd appreciate going over his contract with you and settling what needs to be done before he's gone.

It seems that through all this, someone has made a grab at his identity as well - thinking they will be able to cash in on disability checks, no doubt. We are working with the authorities and a law firm to clear up this mess but are trying to make Tom's last days here on earth as pleasant and peaceful as they can be for him. I do request that you communicate with me directly, as not to upset him - I am not sure which he is having a harder time handling, his prognosis, or the identity theft.

I have attached my documentation proving POA and look forward to speaking with you soon.

We are all praying for Tom. But, as we all know, prayers can only do so much.

Fury

Row, Row, Row your boat
Away before you scream
Merrily, Merrily, Merrily, Merrily
Your life I will redeem

They say there's no wrath like that of a woman and Jesus Christ, and man are they right?!

When men sit down to plan vengeance against their wrong-doer, they let their precious egos get in the way, blinding them from obvious flaws in their schemes.

Men and their quick to anger personalities; it's a disservice to their long game. Their internal flame lights like a candle wick soaked in gasoline but is extinguished by the fingers of a sharp-witted woman just as quickly as it was ignited. A simple, methodical gesture steals their light and squelches whatever tactics remained in their pea-sized brains.

Now, women, we use slow-burning hate to fan the flames, allowing our passionate fury to spread and eventually engulf our offenders along with anyone else that gets in our way.

We're thinkers *and* feelers.

We may leave a battle or two bloodied and broken but that's what bandages are for.

We strap our pain back down and rebury it within our bodies- nurturing it so it can grow from a sliver of hatred to full-blown fury. And it grows and grows with the world being non-the-wiser. When the time is right, no, fucking perfect, that's when we unleash our wrath, showering hurt down on the heads of those that deserve it until they are gone.

Dead.

How delightful would it be to have enough power to erase you from the past, the present, and the future? But sadly, that's not how souls work.

Yes, I promise you, by the end of this war, you will be dead Tom but your soul will not be. So, the question I guess I have to ask myself is, what will I do when you're gone and my mission is complete?

You probably think I'll still be hung up on you? Crying myself to sleep over what we did, *I* did, to you. But we all know you never really were there. You were a performer in a play you call your life - never thinking things all the way through or considering that nature always provides consequences for your actions. Think again, motherfucker - I am the one that owns your soul when you leave this earth. You should have chosen more wisely dear boy. Instead, you fucked with the Devil's daughter and now you get my horns - like a weiner jabbed through a skewer roasting, burning, melting over the flames.

I am the one that will hold you accountable.

I am the one that will deliver you to Hell.

I am the one that will hold you there until you don't matter anymore.

I am Satan's right-hand woman.

You are nothing.

Stella

Organizing someone's demise was much more time-consuming than Stella'd realized. Balancing all the secret operatives while managing her workload, still fitting in a few subs in the evenings, and maintaining an insincere relationship with her *boyfriend* Tom was overwhelming. Even with that being said, she was rather excited for her new submissive to show for her initial rendezvous that night. Rachel, the sad little lesbian bitch from work, had just about invited herself over for a taste and Stella planned to dish it out by the ladle.

She found one of her newer bodysuits and strapped herself in. Instead of dressing in the traditional all-black, she wanted to jazz things up a bit for her newcomer. This suit was a rich wine color with black leather straps lacing their way up, zig-zagging itself into a modern-day corset. When she ordered it, she found the most divine coordinating stockings to throw under a pair of leather heeled boots; their color was almost identical to that of the suit's but they had an almost iridescent metallic sheen to them. They were fucking hot riding her thighs like a futuristic DOM bot. Her makeup would fit the theme of the evening. Heavy eyes with a fabulous set of fan-styled feather lashes and dark brown lippy. Stella could have been a professional make-up artist if that'd been enough for her - instead she took pride in styling her DOM get-ups and made loads of money as a lawyer. Fuck being poor.

Her newly painted face was still drying when her doorbell rang.

She's early. Thirsty bitch.

Stella took the time to clear her bathroom counter of any evidence that she had been applying a whole other person, swiftly scooping intricately shaped bottles, shimmers, and glimmers into a well-loved rectangular basket that lived below her sink; hidden behind two beautifully crafted wooden doors. She caught one last glimpse of herself in the mirror before ascending through the hall, floating down the stairs like a weightless ghost. She was stealthy... a silent hunter, even in her heeled bitch kickers. One final hair toss before she slid the door open just wide enough to confirm the eyes of her new spank baby sub.

On the other side of the door stood those desperately needy puppy dog eyes she knew so well. Rachel had arrived. Stepping behind the door, she pulled it open as a nonverbal invitation for her to enter. Rachel walked through the doorway, her eyes spanned Stella's home, greedily taking it all in as she entered. Rachel hadn't even turned to say hello to her host yet- she seemed stunned by the simple elegance and high-end touches Stella surrounded herself with. Stella recognized that Rachel might feel a little envious; seeing what being a lawyer can mean- the lifestyle you can afford. She couldn't imagine Rachel made much in her measly servitude at the law firm. She also assumed, fairly she thought, that Rachel was unattached so her income was her one and only source. Suddenly, as if Rachel had just remembered that it wasn't her home and she was not alone, she turned to Stella, a fake smile already planted in place before her head could swivel full turn.

"You have a remarkable home, I just lo... wow, you are dressed... sheesh, you look different from the Stella I work with. I'm sorry if that sounded rude. I didn't mean it to be. It's just that I wasn't expecting... I mean, it's *your* home. I'm glad you're comfortable... I'm just gonna shut up now." she paused, sucked some new air into her lungs, and continued in a breathy whisper, "I love your home. It's very glamorous."

Stella was a bit confused by Rachel's reaction; was this not what she was expecting. This must truly be her first time working with a DOM, so to be fair - which is something Stella didn't like to do often, sad little Rachel probably didn't know what to expect. Stella would have to just take the lead, like usual, and show *her* what the expectations were to be. Then again was that not her role as the DOM? She fluttered her winged lashes and slipped back into the not-so-over-reaching character she was about to play.

"Yes, I'm sure you do like it here. It's perfect. I think everyone would like it here. Now, for the basement...well bad, sad, worthless little Rachel... I don't think, no- I *know*, not everyone would like it down there. What's down there was imagined and built especially for people like you and me.. you're going to fucking love it. Want to see it before we get started with the formalities?"

Again, Rachel looked confused and this time a little frightened. Perfect.

Stella took Rachel's fingertips in her own and slowly guided her to the door towards the back of the ominous black ascending staircase. At first, she sensed resistance but felt it release and loosen as they got about halfway there. Stella saw from her peripheral vision Rachel was mentally wandering again, daydreaming about the endless possibilities Stella must have with her outrageous financial status. Stella didn't think she looked as jealous this time; instead, there was a purity behind her gaze, almost like the wonderment of a kid in a candy store. One that had loads of cash in their pocket and could buy anything and everything their little heart desired.

The staged creak of the dungeon door brought Rachel back to the current moment and the fear in her eyes reappeared. Stella flicked the light switch and the faux flickering red undertone lightbulbs blinked on, barely illuminating the steep steps. Stella loved the level of detail she had put into it all. You know what they say, *the Devil's in the details;* a mischievous, sultry grin flashed in Rachel's direction all on its own. Sometimes Madam Madsen took over completely, pushing the inhabitant out of its vessel, making it their home for the next hour of playtime. Madam Madsen was in full control now and Stella had no choice but to do her bidding.

The sound of the pair's footsteps echoed off the cold concrete underneath their plodding soles and bounced off the midnight black painted sheetrock that sealed the space off, trapping its guest in and locking intruders out. Tom had helped her paint the dungeon - helped, as in painting the entire thing for her. At the time, he'd said he found painting relaxing, but he seemed anything but relaxed when doing it. Thinking of him being in this space, *her* space, seemed like a violation. He himself was a violation- a vulgar disfigurement of nature. She was a Queen- perhaps a wicked one, but still a Queen, nonetheless.

Their feet landed at the bottom of the stairs, giving Rachel her first opportunity to see the entire scope of the BDSM space. Her eyes transformed into two giant olives balancing on the front side of her skin. A tiny gasp left her barely parted lips- she looked as if she might have been literally biting her tongue, but Stella could neither confirm nor deny it. Rachel seemed to search for her words, traveling inside that bulbous brain of hers, rummaging around it with a dimly lit flashlight, but nothing came. So Stella took the lead- again.

"So, as you can see. My side gig has been doing well- I've grown this dungeon tenfold just over the past two years. There are more people like you and me in the world than you may realize Rach. I can call you that for short, right? Rach? Well, I guess we'll get to that when we discuss your safe words and boundaries... that is unless you don't have or want either of those things." Stella licked her lips as if her lippy had a sweet cherry syrup added to it. She let her eyes dart over in Rachel's direction for dramatic effect... or perhaps not. Perhaps it was how Madam Madsen wanted to look at her and she was being fully controlled by the character once again. Regardless of the motive, Rachel was being her authentic self, a scared, puzzled, lost twat of a woman-child.

"Um, well, Stella... this is just so much more than what I was expecting. I don't know what to say. I thought when we set this meeting up... well, I actually had something else in mind..." Rachel stopped herself and Stella could see the rusty wheels trying to turn. She was thinking hard, and it was taking for-fucking-ever. Stella didn't have the time or patience for second thoughts.

"I completely understand, it can be overwhelming your first time. I think the best thing we can do is to head back upstairs in a space you're more comfortable in, to discuss what kind of working relationship you'd like between us." Rachel gave a silent nod in agreement. She still looked shocked as shit, but at least she was agreeable. "Before we go though, I think we need to slip this on to get you in the mood." Stella drew her hand outwards to a near-invisible inset shelving system directly above Rachel's head. Rachel visibly and audibly held her breath as Stella reached across her new Sub on tippy-toes, making sure the tips of her breasts grazed Rachel's face. She quickly withdrew her arm, her elbow threatening to contact the top of Rachel's naturally slumped shoulder. A shiny metal tag glinted in the dim red glow; Stella moved towards Rachel's throat, who in response ducked away from her. Her defenses were raised- she was going to put up a fight. Stella liked fighters.

"Just something pretty for my newest pet. Don't shy away and be a nasty dog. I don't know if you deserve this anymore... if you want it, get on your knees and beg for it," Stella demanded in her best Madam Madsen voice.

To somewhat *both* of their surprises, Rachel slowly lowered herself to all fours, lifted her chin up to make pleading eyes with her DOM, and started a whiny whimper that didn't sound all that different from her speaking voice, Stella surmised. Accepting the little bitch's plea, she reached down and roughly clasped the tagged collar around her. She yanked the tag, gruffly guiding her pet to stand and follow... Rachel clearly had laid her fight down and was all about obedience now. Boring AF. Stella had hoped for a bit more struggle than this but what the fuck ever, she was getting her jollies and pay either way.

Back upstairs, hand still holding the choker leash, she brought the two of them to her living room sofa. "Sit, girl, sit." Rachel plunked her ass down quickly on the cushion beneath her and sat silently, waiting for the next direction to be given.

"Now, let's talk about what you want out of this relationship. I will ask the questions and you will answer when, and only when, I tell you to. Understood?"

"Yes."

"Yes, what?" Stella barked.

"Yes, Ma'am."

"You call me Madam Madsen. Got it?" Rachel nodded. "Before we start, you need to sign a confidentiality agreement stating that what we do stays between us on both of our ends." Stella shoved a pen into her Sub's hands and threw the three-sheet stapled agreement in front of her. Carefully, Rachel grabbed the packet and appeared to read it... a waste of fucking time. Jesus Christ, is *this* bitch the lawyer or what? Rachel seemed to have picked up on Stella's frustration and changed her in-depth novel read to a quick skim of the front page only. She flipped it to the signature line and scribbled an illegible blob. Bitch writes like she has paws too.

Rachel

She did it. She signed and had no idea what it was she was agreeing to. Then again, she had no idea that *this* was the type of meeting Stella had thought she was referring to. A little birdie had told her that Stella was side-slinging legal advice outside of the firm... besides the contract she had just been forced to sign, there didn't seem to be anything else legal about her current situation. But what could she do... she couldn't correct Stella- nobody did that and lived to tell the tale. So, instead, she did what she thought was best... not anger the beast that is Ms. Stella Madsen and go with it. Rachel did a mental gulp... all of it.

Never in her life would she have imagined herself getting into a predicament like the one she was in... never in her life could she have thought she was going to be submissive in some BDSM production. Of course, she liked to think of herself as the leading lady in her life, like almost everyone else on the planet, but she would have been just fine playing a supporting character in this one-act nightmare. Too late Rachel, you signed off and have held your tongue for too long- if you say something now you'll only perpetuate her lowly opinion of you and never build rapport with the monster woman. Her front teeth clenched down further, breaking through the surface of her tongue. The familiar metallic taste of blood overwhelmed her senses.

"Madam Madsen, Could I bother you for a glass of water?"

Stella stiffly turned and pointed at the kitchen sink and replied with sheer steeliness in her voice, "There's the sink pup, fill your own bowl."

Rachel felt her eyes flutter to the ground. "Thanks," she mumbled, sliding off the sofa. There, next to the sink, as advertised, was a dog dish. What an asshole... does she make all of her *clients* drink from these or is it just because of her opinion of her- *the annoyingly needy office bitch that they let run free and shit all over the carpets?* Stella might have thought Rachel didn't hear her verbal diarrhea, but she did. She heard everything that went on in that office...that's just *one* perk of having access to each of their phone lines. Rachel knew more about her coworkers than some of their life partners did, like who was having an affair with a married man, who had a twenty-one-year-old side piece, and who had lost their life savings with a single bad bet. Gambling addiction was the worst, and she'd know since she was a closet gambler in recovery herself. Stella was the only nut she hadn't cracked so far; she was always using her cell phone in her office, so Rachel didn't get many eaves-dropping opportunities. Plus, Stella was working remotely more and more- how was she ever supposed to get on her good side if she couldn't learn anything about her? Well, there's a silver lining when she needed it most... like it or not, she was surely learning a lot about her mysterious, crab-ass of a co-worker right there and then. And this... this she could never have guessed.

Stella and she discussed the terms of the arrangement and even agreed upon "Cuticles" as a safe word. Why cuticles, she had no clue... she'd been too busy watching Stella's moist lips move up and down to recognize the words they were forming. They looked like two dark slugs underling her slender, almost skeletal nose... looks like Ms. Madsen got a nose job back in the day. Interesting, what else on her was fake besides her slimy smile and unabashed confidence? Rachel had decidedly admit-ted to Stella that she was very into being tickled. A moment of honesty here and there might lead to moments of minor enjoyment, she thought to herself. With the couch chat wrapped up, they were trudging their way back down the stairs and Stella was back in full DOM mode again, pulling her by the choker and giving orders that demanded obedience. Rachel had learned to be good at taking orders. Most of the time, she preferred them over having to dole them out. Maybe she truly was a sub, and this was the wake-up call she needed...

———————

What happened in the dungeon stayed in the dungeon - she fully understood the purpose behind Stella's statement now that she had survived it. Ok, *enjoyed* it. Rachel knew she left a completely different person than the pure and unsullied, naïve shroud of a child that had first arrived. It's almost like she'd finally discovered herself, her body, and the pent-up sexuality she'd hidden beneath some unrealistic virtues of what perfect looked like. *A* perfectly precious innocent had been walking around in her newfound body, acting as if her own pleasure and desires didn't matter, let alone acknowledging that she had a clitoris that needed tending to. No, together they forever changed her- her transformation into womanhood was complete. Sure, had been scared, shy even, at first, but after a few minutes playing the role of the wanting and willing Sub, she could feel her once heavily armored walls collapsing, leaving dust clouds as they crumbled. It was the end of Rachel's reign within her and the start of a new Leader's... same name, a whole new game.

Being submissive wasn't a weakness at all. It was about having the strength to allow yourself to be vulnerable in order to get what you wanted at your core. And for Rachel, it was the first time she had let go - had loosened her mind, and the damming morals she'd thought were so deeply engrained they could never have been ripped away at the seams. There had never been a big enough hook to shred her tightly wound ways before; she found her source of freedom that day- it wasn't in the form of a hook, but in a pair of leather straps and a vibrator the size of a handheld vacuum. That beautiful handheld machine stroked and sucked the chastity right out of her, slurping up the evidence of her orgasm along the way. She was quick to realize that the toy was not *actually* a vacuum as her own warm slippery slid down the insides of her legs as she stood to exit. The heat between her legs, the juice spilling out of her were both new sensations, but nothing could top those mounting screams that had regurgitated from somewhere deeper than her vagina.

Rachel Dobbs - you can be sexual; you just can't be into women.

Pain

I have no words to stick you with
No silly rhymes to wordmsith
Just hatred in my heart for you
No tune to whistle this poem to

Most would think I'd have no pain watching you suffer at the hands of those that "loved" you after what you've done to me and, well, the rest of us. But, sadly, there *is* a pain in seeing you suffer - only because it didn't need to be this way. We could have been happy if only you would have just let us... But you didn't. You had to lie and connive, trick and treat us until the game became apparent and you were the only one enjoying yourself.

Selfish bastard.

My stomach flips inside out still every time I see you and I hate myself for it. You're a shit. You truly are, and the fact that it even somewhat pains me to make you suffer makes me one too. Oh, to a much lesser degree, my dear, don't misread the room. You're still the motherfucker in here and you *will* pay for your sins. We all do in the end - your repayment will *be* your end... big difference, fuck head.

The glimpses of sadness I feel in witnessing your demise dissipate quickly. No need to worry, I am not getting soft on you. Never have and never will. Holding you accountable is something you used to respect about me but now, I'm not so sure you are going to care much for it.

You haven't started squirming yet, but something tells me you should get that ass a-wriggling because the show is about to start. Those heavy red curtains have been drawn to the sides revealing a naked, bound, and bloody version of you, Tom.

You're ugly. You are now, at least.

Pounding a mallet down onto your face, smashing your cheekbones in, mushing that rubbery mask you call skin around with its cold, bulbous head. Sounds of bones snapping, cracking, popping in your skull under the weight sing like a church choir in a special, private ceremony made just for me and you to share.

You scream soprano and I will laugh baritone.

Making harmony together, finally, in your death. I'll rejoin the unison when I meet my maker and soul taker; when the lapping flames of Hell's fiery ring find me- we will sing together in agony for all eternity, my love. The way we were meant to all along.

But it's not *my* charred throat that will be leaking and spurting now. It's your special time and I wouldn't dare steal that limelight away from you as you stole it away from me. You never even thought to ask. You never cared enough to consider that others could be hurting as much or more than you. Instead, you assumed the worst about me- that I was dumb, easily fooled, and too damaged to seek revenge.

Well, you know what they say about assuming... and yes, you came out looking like the ass in this story.

A big, flappy, white, shit-stained ass presenting its hole for penetration.

You'll get fucked...don't you worry- it's a scalding sword that seeks you out.

So lube up, bitch.

Trio | Remi, Stella, & Myra

The three spiteful women congregated around Myra's kitchen island, silently searching one another's eyes for approval of the deeds they had been acting upon. Unintentionally, the trio found themselves clothed in all black; Stella glittering with lavish accessories, a midnight dress flowing over Myra's curves tied at the waist with a simple jute rope-like one you'd tie a noose with, and Remi looking like a female specter of Johnny Cash. Laptops, tablets, and cell phones lie across the countertop like a menagerie of miniature robots resting silently in their tech graves. But they didn't come here to die; no, they arrived for combat- as the weapons replacing the wands that belonged in this moody brood of witch's hands. God knows their perfectly manicured nails had been clicking and dragging across those screens endlessly the past few days preparing for their lover's exit from the world around them- well on paper, that is. No one had the intention of *actually* killing him- they just wanted him to disappear in every other way possible. He'd lose it all without giving him the satisfaction of the easy-out that something like death brings a sinner. At least, that's what some of them were telling themselves.

Myra made the first move, breaking the frozen frigidity that had swept over her studio, holding them under an imaginary spell by sliding her cell across the marble surface to the others, a bright white screen screaming out to be read by the pair.

"Well, I have a few more pieces to erect, but these are what I have so far for the show. It's probably not my best work, but to be fair, I have never had to push out so much in such a short amount of time before, so... I guess."

Stella reached for the phone first, beating Remi to the punch, but held it in a manner that they could both witness the stunning display of Myra's deeper inhibitions held in the narrow parameters of her phone. Little clay vases filled with different shades of velvety red flowers enveloped an old antique hospital bed. Above it, suspended from the air hung an abstract painting. A solid black pit with what appeared to be ashes lying around its opening encircled camo-colored swirls of morbidity. Myra had unintentionally depicted the pit of Hell perfectly. She did what she always had and let her brush do the talking for her subconscious and out poured the burning pit for worthless, defiled souls. Myra, herself, couldn't quite grasp how she felt about it but she recognized her instability and inner turmoil showcased in those strokes. Pain that she knew would come out in her art in time. It was fitting that of which she suppressed most would come out just in time for payback, at least one of those that had wronged her would feel her wrath. While her father might never see it, hear it, taste it, smell it - this piece of shit would.

Remi spoke first. "Wow, Myra. I can't believe that something without words can be so powerful. You encapsulated it all... everything I am feeling inside and all I am wishing for our dearest Tom. What's your process? How did you design something so torturously beautiful in our tiny little time window here?" Remi's sincere awe oozed from every pore in her body- Stella's eyes rolled. Hard.

"She's an artist Remi- this is what she does for a living- it's literally what she does all day for money," Stella moved her eyes to meet Myra's. Was she looking for approval or forgiveness here? She'd receive neither from Myra- that was for damn sure.

"Actually, art is not like your typical working industry. It's not necessarily always planned or even executed in an organized fashion, but I guess you can't expect everyone to understand that, even if they *are* highly educated and hold a fancy law degree." Myra paused and turned her head away from the target of her aggression and towards sweet, kind Remi instead. "I paint what I feel, sometimes without knowing I am feeling it. I literally let the paints decide what colors are used and trust the brush to guide my hands to where it needs to be." She gave a sideways stare back over to Stella hoping to interpret even the smallest amount of offense taken by the drama queen. She saw a smirk of approval spread across Stella's lips. Stone-cold Stella was a sadist, Myra thought to herself. "He's as good as dead on social media as well. I have been sharing all kinds of sob stories about his illness taking him from me- I even boosted a few of the posts on my professional creator page on Facebook... over ten thousand people alone have seen those. I've even seen a couple of my friends and a handful of my followers repost and share my 'heart-wrenching news'. Morbidity sure makes for a good advertisement," Myra chuckled, "I think there are over five hundred people that have said they plan to attend my art show so... I guess you could say I've been holding up my end of the deal. Where are you ladies at with your assignments?" It was so out of character for Myra to be little Miss Bobby-Business; she was usually the free-flowing, hippie-dippy peace-keeping love maker, but it appeared she was liking her new assertive side.

Remi jumped in; she was more than ready to give those fried nerves a break and release some of her guilt and anxiety through a powerful verbal letting. "Well, thanks to both of you, everything is ready and waiting for Tom's official 'final breath' at the funeral home. His landlord has been more than accommodating to work with and even sent a stunning sympathy bouquet to my office. Apparently, he'd run into Tom in his apartment's mailroom the other day and reported back to me that Tom was looking quite pale and fragile- he'd stayed the course of our understanding and said nothing more than a cordial greeting to him. In which, Tom responded with a bewildered look... his inability to see anyone but himself is playing into our plan. Can you say self-sabotage?" Neither of her fellow conspirers answered her but Stella looked thoroughly amused and Myra appeared to be listening - that was the best Remi could ask for before returning to her spiel. "Being his power of attorney has a ton of perks like I got to decide which non-profit to donate a sum of his money to... I chose a local domestic abuse shelter. I hope that's all ok with you guys," Remi's confidence went on a momentary hiatus. "I probably should have conferred with the two of you before making the last call on that. There will be plenty of money left over to split among us..."

Finally, some kind of reaction. A response from the two audience members. Stella's eyes got wide while Myra opened her mouth to speak. "Honestly Remi, ALL of his money could go to charity for all I care. I don't think I want anything to do with his filthy cash. I see a very profitable future for myself thanks to the publicity his death is giving me - that's enough for me. I vote to donate it all."

Almost in unison with Myra, Stella's head nodded in agreement. "It's actually in our best interest to donate it entirely to deter nosy eyeballs from looking in our direction if someone comes out of this believing Tom, the 'real' Tom, is still alive," Stella smirked at her own foresight. She was pure genius in her own eyes- this was more than apparent to Remi and Myra; the only difference was that Remi took Stella's forceful personality in stride, whereas Myra always looked like she was going to be physically ill after hearing Stella speak. But Remi's brain wasn't computing the dynamics of the trio's relationship at the moment; all she could think about was how beneficial those extra funds would be for her to pay for her IUI procedure since she hadn't actually donated any of his funds. And God, if she did have to resort to IVF- it could cover the whole damn procedure. It was such a good plan and honestly, Remi didn't owe either of these two imposters anything. Including the truth. If Remi wanted to be a *good* mother, she'd have to start thinking and acting like one now... even if that meant telling a few white lies.

"Ok, easy enough. I will change the dollar amount on the donation form and that'll be taken care of. Stella, you double-checked into the possibility of living relatives, right?"

Stella's unspoken reaction to the question made it known that she was annoyed by even being asked it. "Of course, that was one of the first things I did." Insert characteristic eye roll here. "His mom died a few years back, no father's signature on the birth certificate or legal traces of adoption throughout his life, no siblings, both known grandparents are deceased and his late mother was an only child. This dude was truly alone in this world- well, look at me using past tense like he truly is dead," Stella gloated. "Everything is legally set for his death; it's very helpful that one of us has POA so that in the event of his passing we can easily cut things off like cell phones, email accounts. He will be so busted when he shows up alive and well to work the day after the funeral... his boss being shown the obituary and all by some anonymous source. But what happens if he believes Tom or I guess Benjamin Blank, over the obit?"

"Of course, we are going to cash in on using a photo of Tom *before* his cosmetic surgery so as long as his boss isn't a complete moron he'll recognize the facial differences AND there's the whole work-up of lies we are going to benefit from... Plus, I think I may have a possible alternative solution but I'm still working out the details. " Remi's voice trailed off. The beginning of that statement had started with a level of sincere confidence but quickly dwindled to an uncertain murky muddle. In her mind, she was certain that the other's red flags were being raised that very moment. To be fair, hers had been flying high throughout from the get-go. But again, to her astonishment, the other two didn't seem triggered in the least and just nodded with a passive acceptance of her inconspicuous offer. And apparently, that feeling of ease and utter trust in one another continued to flow through them because Stella declared that everything was "looking good" and "right on track" so that they could dismiss themselves from their bleak little meeting of the minds.

Myra couldn't help Remi and Stella out of her apartment door fast enough.

Myra's mouth formed a kind of frumpy line as she spewed more positive affirmations their way upon their exit... Remi knew the girl was doing the same things she was... lying to herself to make what they were doing seem permissible. Myra, however, would be able to release her faux front in the next few moments, whereas Remi would need to keep hold for a few more hours. She'd save face until the pills were back, hidden away at the house.

They'd need to be carefully stored because a smart little girl shared her space and curiosity was what killed the cat. Remi intended to kill a man, not an innocent little girl.

Careful placement Remi. Careful placement.

Tom

Tom woke to gasp for air; the nightmares had returned. He hadn't had them since college- well, the early days in college, before his reunion. So much had changed in his life since then, but something familiar always seemed to creep back into his brain like a poisonous black widow spider. Thoughts and memories he had hoped would have diminished by then. Lord knows, he'd been with enough women since her to help eliminate her... the feeling of her backside pressed into his front as they spooned, the soft aroma of lilacs that danced along the pores of her velvet skin, the little dimples that popped at the corner of her smile, and those full round breasts. Those were perfect, always had been, and he could only believe they still were. At least they were in his imagination. But that was the heart of the problem right there; he wasn't supposed to be imagining her anymore. He had worked so hard to stop it from happening- perhaps this was part of the cursed consequence of his deal with the Devil. He thought he'd been pretty clear about his expectations back then; yet, in all reality, he'd only be a kid when made it so there was plenty of room for error. Or at least misremembering.

He let himself toss and turn, rumpling his already mangled bed-sheets a moment longer before he pushed his body into a standing position. His hands hurt, his lower back ached, and the muscles in his thighs were locked up - this must be what getting old is like, he thought to himself. Through all the aches and pains, he knew that at least his heart would never break again. He wouldn't allow it to; hence, his adopted free-wheeling lifestyle chalked full of fun anti-romantic romps and meaningless banter. Once in a while, he innately helped one of his girls more than he probably should have... like putting together a piece of furniture or mowing a lawn. He wasn't trying to play the boyfriend role; if he could fully control it he'd be the straight-up simple-minded, sex-driven tool that most young flits and twits were attracted to, as unbeknownst to them, short-term relationship material. But something inside him was still whipped - held by the chains of what could have been. It's not like he still yearned for a lifelong partner; he *did* stop himself when he realized he was overdoing it but so many times it wasn't until after the good deed" that he recognized his own self-betrayal. The pressure to stay committed to only himself and his happiness plan was real, sometimes too real to handle. These were the times he sort of "went off the grid" for a while. He'd lie low; only going back and forth between work and home, turning off incoming calls and messages, and just taking a beat. It was exhausting pretending all the time. It was exhausting acting like he was *theirs*. It was exhausting keeping his end of the deal. All in all, it was exhausting just being him.

As he stood there alongside his masterful, king-size bed, he felt the urge to scratch away at his inner turmoil. Claws still recoiled, he bent in half at the waist instead. He knew he'd never be able to itch his painfully depressive scratches so he might as well work on working the tightness out of his muscles. There's nothing a good morning routine couldn't fix; most days he felt like he was forcing himself through it but he always felt cured after the regimen. After a few more toe touches, he did some gentle yoga to keep limber and then went to draw the heavy black velvet curtains open - letting enough light in to blind a mouse. Tom paused a moment to enjoy his witty thought and then continued to his oversized all-glass shower. Growing up how where he did, he'd never have imagined that he would ever have a home like the one he'd made for himself. His apartment bulged at the seams with his expensive taste that he'd paid for with his hard-earned cash; nothing stolen, nothing borrowed here. After years of wearing the secondhand rags of his mother's pathetic drunkard "boyfriends," he made a promise to himself that he would never again accept anything secondhand in his life again. And he'd done well keeping it.

A perfect ratio of suds to water wrapped around his slightly chiseled body- he'd never been *really* ripped but what he had worked for him. He watched as a pair of tiny bubbles slid down the front side of his chest and landed squarely atop his penis. There they sat, like two legs mounted on a fleshy saddle completely unscathed from the showerhead's brutal sprays. Oddly enough, they seemed peaceful...trusting and secure in their exposed location. Tom grabbed the hosed shower head, removing it from its fixture, and blasted the bubble bastards off. Too clingy.

Feeling refreshed, he jetted out of the shower doors like there was a fire hot on his trail, igniting a rhythm for the day. And to amp up that rhythm, he ordered Alexa to play some jams on his wireless speaker system he had installed in each room...just another part of his morning regimen. Music always helped him set the mood for a successful swagger and today would be no different; wake up, make mad money at work, booty call, bedtime... fit some gourmet meals in there and some frivolous flirting and he had another bomb-ass day of the week. See what denial of depression could do?

He had a pep in his step as he locked up his apartment and jaunted down to the mailroom - it'd been a while since he's checked it so he was expecting a flood of crap mailers and bills that would come due soon. But when he popped the miniature door open, there was nothing. Nada. Zilch. Not even the residue of years of shuffled papers lay on the metal bottom. It was so clean in there you could eat off it. Flipping the door shut, he checked the box number again, matching it with the one he had scrolled on his key tag.

"Nice to have a helper, isn't it?"

Tom whirled around to find an elderly woman that apparently lived in his building, watching his confusion implode into a low-level panic.

"I'm sorry, what?"

"It's nice having a helper... my girl gets my mail every day for me, too. She also helps me write the checks for the bills - I haven't had a late payment since I hired her. I still like to take a daily walk down here just to double-check that she remembers to grab it but haven't caught her missing a day yet." The old bitty shrugged and giggled at the same time. "Guess I'm just a little bored. You know, boredom is the leading cause of snoopiness. I sure am that." This time, she let out a full-bellied guffaw. "What agency did you go through for your girl?"

"I'm sorry, what girl? I am not sure what who you're referring to."

"Oh shit, there I went, confusing you. Didn't mean to upset you. Just glad to see you out and about - us lepers need to stick together." Her deep throaty laugh changed direction as she turned her walker to guide her exit of the mailroom and thankfully, from Tom's life. What in the fuck was that crazy old broad talking about? Where the fuck was his mail? He'd put a call out to his landlord when he got to the office; he had already wasted too much on the matter and thanks to that senile skeleton, he'd be late to work.

Another day, another dollar. Now it's time to make a girl holler.

Stella had texted him earlier to let him know that she'd be getting home after he got there, so to just let himself in. She was going on her weekly 10-mile bike ride, something she'd never been able to convince him to join.

Letting himself into the bright airy model home, he plopped down on the couch only to find a pair of handcuffs jamming their way up his ass. He hopped up to find a little spread of DOM tools on the cushion. Seemingly, he was in for a treat that evening; Stella never brought toys up from the basement for her clients... only for him. A whole new sensation of excitement swept over him - instant boner-making material here.

She announced her return by shoving the door open with just enough force to make a deliberate pop against the neighboring wall - Stella loved making an entrance. Tom subconsciously jumped with the bang, followed by a sensation of needle pricks throughout his groin.

He adored her angst against the world, it brought him to the thralls of unspeakable pleasure. And *she* thrived on the power she assumed over a man that she had tied up and gagged in her Kink Cage (that's what Tom privately liked to refer to the dungeon as.) This may seem super fucked up to some, but with men, she got her shits and giggles from being a true masochist to her core.

"What the fuck are you doing still upstairs? You know where you are supposed to be... are you going to disobey the house rule again?" Stella glared sternly while shaming him.

"No disrespect was meant, madam. I slipped up and forgot. Please forgive me..." he said, smoothly slipping into his character for this role play. Mad mama... one of his favorites.

"I don't understand why your ass is still sitting on that couch like a rotting vegetable. Get up and get downstairs - now!" Stella demanded.

"Yes, Madam Madsen." As he passed her, his eyes looked deep into hers; they were sparkling with anticipation. He loved being a naughty boy.

He continued his march to the basement, head hung low, his dick flying high.

Tom reached the top step of the basement and saw Stella pushing him down them. He'd seen her mind teetering on the edge of reality and insanity before and now it was making him lose it. His imagination ran wild on his own edge of vengeance and violence.

Stella stopped abruptly as if she could read his mind and was afraid of what she saw.

"Are you still coming, mama?" he asked with the purest sense of child-like innocence.

"Yup, just get down those damn stairs before I lose interest," Stella said with a dramatic sigh. Of course, this was just for show because inside she wanted to run down those steps as fast as a coyote chasing after a fat little jackrabbit. She was hungry for it... thirsty as fuck.

She continued to follow him down the stairs, making sure to leave enough distance between their two descending bodies to emphasize her dominance. It was like a dance of sorts where she was leading her powerless partner further down into a secret lair below the ball-room. No twirling was involved though, just a governing female and careful footing.

Tom sensed something was different. Stella's orgasm at the end of his torture sesh came from no helpful fingers or that penetrating penis of his. She did it all on her own and seemingly without even touching herself. Obviously, she liked what she saw. Tom sat up with a sensation of supreme sexuality about himself and how his throbbing cock must look. Stella remained in the same stance she had taken when she started their private rendezvous - she was feeling something else.

Pure hatred.

And that made her hot.

Remi

Friday afternoons were typically Remi's favorite part of the work-week; her imagination used to run wild with plans she had in the making and big ideas she'd shoot to achieve... mostly life experiences. Growing up in a single-parent household had many time challenges and necessary hurdles for her father- he never got to spend the time that he wanted and she needed with her on the weekends. There was always looming yardwork, frustrating home repairs that inevitably came from having to live in a house a single income could afford, and of course, all the week-long errands that stacked up. Remi recalled enjoying the fun "trips" to the grocery store, the gas station, and her favorite - The Liquor Hut (they always offered her a heaping bucket of safety suckers to pick from at the cash register). These outings were the most time she got to spend with her pops, and looking back, he truly did his best to make them fun for her. As a pre-teen, she might not have appreciated all the extra effort, but she sure as hell did now. Now, or at least in recent history, she'd made sure that she could dedicate one hundred percent of her weekends to doing things she *wanted* to do. She'd done everything from as low-key to parties in the park to more adventurous finds like skydiving.

It was fair to say she wouldn't be jumping out of any planes this weekend, more like plummeting off the propeller and crashing to the earth in shredded, bloody shards.

She hated having to do this... become this person again.

Even though it was temporary and easily controlled, she feared at her core that it wouldn't behave so well forever. Someday, that person could become permanent.

She just needed to make this the last time- make Tom the last of them.

He had asked her to come out to his place that Saturday and, as always, promised a good time, not only in the sheets, but he had mentioned something about trying something new and crafty together. He had said it was a surprise when she pressed for details with forced enthusiasm and a fake smile on her lips. A person can tell if you're smiling when you talk. Remi had learned that from the many prison calls from her mom. Something a person shouldn't have to learn that way or that young.

This weekend wasn't supposed to be filled with smiles and laughter. This weekend was meant for murder.

Even pretending to have a good time together would make her in-sides go flippy-floppy when it was time to dose the bastard.

Sharing sunshiny lies and gut-felt guffaws would turn Remi's guilt up full blast.

She'd push past it, she assured herself. She had to.

———

Saturday morning came like a bat out of Hell. Remi woke in a puddle of her own sweat; her sleep had been filled with nightmares, all telling a different story around the same premise... her soul burning for all of eternity for the lives she had taken.

She had never been so grateful for the innocence of a child finding her when it did - Emmy came tumbling through her bedroom door, acting as if she was sneaking up on an assumed to be slumbering Remi. Remi played along until the sweet girl got close enough for her to grab, rolling her into the bed alongside her. Emmy giggled all the while, pretending she was a ninja princess warrior being taken captive by her arch-nemesis, Captain Crook.

Remi had heard all about Captain Crook before she'd even moved in with the pair; Michelle had laughed all the way through the story years ago when they'd met up for some lunch. Michelle had been bubbling over with Mommy pride on cuteness patrol when she shared Emmy had become obsessed with the Disney version of Peter Pan but, as most small kids, had a hard time pronouncing the character's names. Peter Pan was no challenge to the sweet babe but Captain Hook was understood to be Captain Crook- Michelle beamed with the idea that she wasn't going to correct Emmy- she thought it was a better, more accurate name for a pirate. Obviously, Emmy was old enough now to know that wasn't his name but played it off instead that he was a figment of her creative imagination - he had never been tied to Peter Pan but was instead a friend she conjured up to play with up in her room. Captain Crook had come in handy throughout the divorce; becoming a genuine friend to the poor kid when she needed one the most. And today, Captain Crook became a genuine friend to Remi, too.

The two tumbled around until Emmy suddenly stopped to announce that it was time to get some breakfast. Inner peace stopped, and the panic returned in Remi's voice when she responded with "You go ahead, I can't today. I have some plans I need to take care of."

Racing out of the room, apparently not affected too much by Remi's dismissal, Emmy left her to the thoughts and fears she'd been trying to escape only moments before. Unsticking herself from the mental torture, she hopped out of bed to greet the day with a shower, a fresh find from her closet (something she hadn't worn in ages), and a mask of makeup. The more concealer the better- she'd protect her true self from the evils that were about to ensue... understanding a masked face could lead to saving face. And hopefully, soul.

———————

Her heels echoed against the sterile concrete steps of Tom's apartment building. Technically, she was walking the fire escape route to his floor - a slower route to delay the inevitable. Their clicking morphed into a rich beat that hosted voluminous strings of harmony in her mind. Remi had found comfort in music, both audible and in her head, for as long as she could remember. The overtures started wheeling through her mind the day her mom disappeared for the first time. Meditation. Peace. A forged path towards healing. Lord knows she would need a good round of therapy after all this.

She sucked in her breath and clenched it in her belly as she pulled the door open to Tom's hall towards her, barely forcing her feet forward and through it. She was almost halfway down the empty hall when she heard a door creak open and a head pop out. It was him. He was too excited to see her to stay behind closed doors. Remi reminded herself that this was to be no longer considered sweet, but sickening. He was a horny tool of a boy that used her for her body...wanting nothing else and giving barely more than the bare minimum. It took her heart being completely shattered for her to realize what a selfish, non-committal, game player he'd been throughout the tenure of their "relationship". A sweeping balance of esteem and rage reignited the darkness that she'd been trying to delay from all but consuming her. She felt one hundred percent confident in her decision to kill the bastard once and for all.

A degrading cat-call interrupted her thoughts, but not her unwavering stare.

"Well, aren't you a sight for sore eyes? Hurry up and get in here.. my arms much rather be holding you instead of this heavy ass door." A smile lit his face, illuminating the tiny dimples hunkered down in his five o'clock shadow. Remi's body was on autopilot; she was surprised and happy at the same time that she could maintain her speed. She wouldn't be following any commands of his or anyone else's anymore. Instead, she fixed her eyes on her target and felt the corners of her mouth curl up in the corners. Strange, it was a sincere smile but not hers... she could feel its cunning, almost seductive nature bleeding through her lips. Her hand automatically rose to them to ensure there was no true gush of blood, but instinctively wiped the grin right off her face. Tom needed to know she wasn't too wrapped around him and that two could play his game.

Today, she would dominate. Overpower. Overtake.

Today, he would be the soft little doughy-eyed doll. Submissive. Still. Dead.

"Well, hello yourself, handsome. It must have been longer than I thought- I see you've decided to grow your beard out again? Looks like it's coming in nicely," she added an unexpected wink. "You look like a double agent- or maybe I'll be sleeping with someone other than my boyfriend tonight - a bearded stranger I met at the bar." The sultry side of things was definitely a first for her, but it seemed to pour from her like an over-filled pitcher. Tom looked shocked by her enthusiasm and sudden grasp of her sexuality. He played right into it like putty rolling around in her hands.

"I see someone is feeling feisty... now get in here so we can do something about it," he pushed the door wider for her as she finally approached it. As she skulked through it she made direct eye contact with him. Her eyes bore into his. She stared so hard for so long she could almost see the insecurities he'd buried below. Showing his obvious discomfort, he looked away and pretended to cough. Just a tickle, he would claim. Another lie. And another reason to believe that nothing he said was believable. Her eyes wandered first to his living room walls, then the furniture, and the floors. Now knowing what he did, what he was capable of, it was like she was seeing his space for the first time. Subconsciously, she was playing detective; looking for clues that should have given it all away. But she found nothing. Truly nothing. Everything was so impersonal there... blank... sanitized. She'd never noticed just how blah the space was, or how closely he emulated it. There was nothing that said anything about who he was, what he liked, or the things he cared about in his home. Could it be part of his lifestyle, or was it because there was nothing there to show? Did Tom not have any interests, passions, or hobbies? Could he have played a character, more like multiple characters, for so long that *he* didn't really exist anymore? A sense of sadness came over her... if it were the latter, she could almost relate to that. No, not this guy. You have nothing in common with this piece of shit. A mischievous grin curled through the corners of her mouth once again as she licked her bottom lip and presented it for a brief introductory hello. The kiss was passionless- short but anything but sweet. It was automated. Unstimulating. She was going to need him to step up his game a bit if he was going to have any chance of getting one last lay. His boner wouldn't be the only thing stiff on him in, oh say about an hour from then.

Who was she kidding? Satan would be this bastard's final lay... fucking him up the ass until his soul ruptured into millions of shards of ash and glass mixed together. Ruptured into oblivion.

Tom turned to her with a phony look of interest in his eyes as he asked how things had been going for her with her new living arrangement. She zipped her lips tightly together and nodded her head in a silent positive manner. He hadn't earned the right to know anything more about her personal life or the people of value in it... except maybe one. Contemplating whether she'd share *that* story with him while he was fighting back the toxic foam and vomit was not something she took lightly. She'd never told anyone before. Originally, she thought it might be freeing to ease the heavy darkness and pangs of guilt she felt from time to time by getting it off her chest. And who better to tell her darkest secret to than a dying man? Someone that would literally be forced to take it to their grave?

Evidently, her nonverbal nonanswer sufficed his lack of curiosity because he swiftly moved on to the next topic... his raging hard-on. Remi felt her eyes roll but caught it in time to turn it into something a bit more seductive. Grabbing his hand, she led him to the sofa; this was new for the two of them. They'd never fucked on the couch before. Well, she was sure he had with at least one of his *many* other gal pals. But never with her. Touching, rubbing, and spilling into one another in a different setting might serve as closure for herself later on- she'd be able to separate her fond memories of what she'd once believed was love-making from the murder scene that lie in wait. Subconsciously, she'd decided that she was going to push all this out of her mind after he died- everything that had come to light about him... them... herself over the past few weeks. Instead, she would return to a life of being a devastated widow of sorts, swearing off a future of affection or a long-lasting lifetime of love. She'd mourn his death the rest of her life because, well, it was the only way to come out of this with some ounce of her purity intact.

She felt her hands graze his collarbone as they streamed down the lengths of his arms, returning to the tops of his shoulders. She shoved him. Down onto the couch. A look of surprise came to his face. For a moment, Remi thought she recognized a look of fear but it passed as quickly as it was noticed. It was important to her, and only her, that she kept full eye contact with him throughout the entire experience. She wanted to make sure that he knew she'd seen him and when his last breaths danced along his trachea, he'd remember those eyes... her eyes. Realizing that she was gathering the last bits of life from him to seal the final chapter of shit-ass life. Her mind whirred with exhilaration; feeling intoxicated by the morbid imagery- she was looking him dead in the eyes, but she wasn't seeing him anymore. She saw his corpse. She saw her hands rip his pant zipper open, felt her fingers grab at the snake protruding from underneath. She saw those same fingers yank it to the surface- her surface. Her legs were already parted as she straddled him. Almost as if it was no longer connected to his body, she took no concern over the amount of vigor or use of strength in shoving it up into her body. She saw herself pumping. Sweat plunged from her forehead, raining down onto him. She shifted just enough, so it fell directly into his eyes. stinging them with the salty grime of Remi's day. She ignored his complaints and instead rode hard and fast, listening to her own heartbeat pounding out of her chest. Her quick shallow breaths. She raised her head and hands towards the ceiling, finally breaking eye contact. Finally reaching orgasm. It was the biggest and best she'd ever had...no thanks to Tom. He lies under her looking like a run-over bird. Eyes bulging, mouth set in confused disgust, looking almost lifeless... and the best part was- she hadn't even poisoned him yet. Just wait buddy, the real fun is just beginning for you. She climbed down from her mount and stretched as if she had just had the best fuck she'd ever had because she had. She turned to look back at him. He still looked shocked. Uncontrollable laughter purged through her mouth, stinging the surrounding airwaves. Tom didn't know how to react at first but when he realized her cackling wasn't ending anytime soon, he joined in. He joined the raving lunacy out of sheer social pressure and the stabbing bits of awkwardness Remi was shooting out, masking all other energy in the room.

"Well, I think I worked up quite the appetite," Remi said while biting her bottom lip. She had been viciously naughty again... the darkness was creeping over her- spreading like an infectious disease. Maybe this time she'd decide she liked it and didn't want to find the cure. Maybe this time she'd let herself go too far out into the pitch-black murky waters, knowing she'd never be able to swim back to shore. The idea made the translucent remainder of her sanity shudder; it was trying to convince her she'd drowned out that far. Instead, she tossed her hair, slid her pants back over her velvety-sleek legs, and left the room. No shirt. No bra. Men could do it- why couldn't she? Tom's eyes surveyed her from head to toe. He was liking the shiny new version of "his" girl - singular, that's a laugh!

"So where's the grub? What are you feeling up for?" This was a much more familiar conversation for the two of them to have during one of their evenings "out". Remi's eyes glinted with a fierceness that neither of them had seen before. Something told Tom that he needed to get on the ball ASAP. He reached for his phone to let her know that they'd be ordering in, "lady's choice". The words seemed to stumble from his jaw like a drunkard falling down the last cracked concrete steps at the bar on his way to the next.

"Chinese it is," she added a smile- all the better to calm those little raw nerves of his. Such a sensitive predator he was and fucking predict-able too. Remi knew before she'd even left for his place that he'd have no plans for food, let alone any other form of entertainment besides sex. There was nothing new to try together. All lies and this time it was ok. No, perfect. It gave her plenty of time to plan out his final meal...something with a short lifespan, even shorter than his. Seeing him die wanting, starving for more out of life was everything she could hope for and Chinese food was notoriously known for not sticking with a person for very long. It was symbolic. Little did he know she was ordering a little extra for herself in part to celebrate his departure, but she was also now eating for two so one could say it was also to celebrate the new life growing inside her.

She grabbed his phone out of his hands to place the order; he reached out in obvious discomfort, trying to stop her, but her ears rejected his annoying whimpers and whines. What a baby. Not my baby, she thought happily to herself. She had secrets racing around that big beautiful brain of hers. A silent smile wriggled its way from the ominous spirit that was consuming her and planted itself satisfactorily on her face.

Tom didn't seem to notice, but he did. He knew that something had bitten his once innocent little nymph; he assumed she was going to share some exciting news with him that evening. News that would make her confidence soar- like a promotion at work or maybe an entirely new opportunity out of town? Maybe that this whole long-distance thing wasn't working? That'd be amazing. He'd be one hundred percent off the hook with *this* chick. They'd cordially agree to go their separate ways...he'd pick up a new Wednesday night girl and all would be right with the world again. His train of thought was utterly annihilated when he overheard Remi trying to order an entire restaurant worth of food. Were they having guests over?

"Ok, thanks so much," Remi ended her order, hung up, and immediately handed the cell back to Tom. She had no interest in what other tragic stories the device must have been bursting with and wanted to get the cursed piece of toxicity out of her possession as quickly as possible. "They will be here in about twenty minutes to a half-hour," she reported back.

"Jesus, even with all that food?! They must be slower tonight to put together an order like that so quickly. Is *all* that just for us or are others coming?"

Remi couldn't stop herself from laughing. "The way you said that sounded like you were wondering if aliens were joining us. You are too funny!"

"Well... are there aliens, humans, bears, dinosaurs coming to eat that feast you just ordered with us?"

"Nope. Just thought we deserved a little extra tonight- well, at least I do," she showed her perfectly straight, toothy grin.

"I knew something was up. You seem a little different; excited maybe?"

"Yes, and yes. I have some great news to share with you, but I want to make sure the timing is perfect, so you will just have to wait until after supper." Fire erupted in her pupils, spreading the darkness further towards the rims, until her eyes looked like two giant black holes.

Tom

Tsk, tsk, tsk Remi, you should know better than to butter me up before *bad* news. It will not change anything. Tom was sure that his assumptions were right about Miss Remi's career opportunity and his fingers were triple crossed that there was a relocation in the near future for her. Was their mid-evening romp goodbye sex, or I'm looking for commitment sex?

He could feel the gears clunking around, trying to devise a response. How gentle would he have to be with her so she didn't go completely bat-shit on him? He'd had that happen a handful of times, but it was never more than he could handle. Sometimes he had to rip his mask off and show his true colors; like a snake shedding its skin to show the ugliness for a week or two. In all actuality, he enjoyed freeing his sarcastic, sadistic. A self-centered version - like he was unleashing a dog to run off into the woods to play and hunt freely. He always came back with some kind of chew toy- never fresh kill, but a prize at least. He kept his mouth and hands clean- bloodless and pure- being the good boy he had trained himself to pretend to be. Disembodying varmints wasn't his style unless he someday needed it to be.

The two of them sat silently in the same room, eyes penetrating a hole into the fifty-five-inch hanging on the wall; one of their favorite re-runs, *Medium,* was on. Remi seemed fully enthralled by it, even though the sad little sack of emotions had probably already seen the same episode a hundred times. For him, it was a comfortingly dull background noise while his mind reeled through his upcoming agenda. It took calm to realize he'd double-booked himself that upcoming Thursday evening.

He'd told both Myra and Stella that they'd get together... one thinking he was about to leave on another of his planet-saving adventures out west whilst the other had invited him to some yuppy black-tie wine-tasting bullshit. Weighing out his options, he quickly devised that even though the lay with Stella would be better, the chances of him getting any were slim since they would be out at one of her hoity-toity "friend's" houses. On the other hand, Myra would be sooooo sad to see him go again. She was sure to jump his bones at first sight. Welp, that decision was a lot easier than he thought it would be. Without hesitation, he slipped his phone out of the pant pocket and texted Stella the sad news of a death in the family. He'd have to go to the wake and funeral later that week and *just* wouldn't make it back in time for the *fun* evening they had planned to spend together. Such a shame, the sarcasm echoed through the tunnels of his own ears, making him laugh out loud. Remi's head snapped in his direction. "What's so funny? That guy just killed himself?"

"Oh, nothing. I guess I just found the humor in how poorly some of these scripts are written," he racked his brain trying to recall the details from the last time he saw that episode. "It's just so obvious that he didn't *really* commit suicide -I mean, he wouldn't. His life on the show looked pretty amazing. He seemed happy... nothing that would lead someone to off themselves. So apparent that the show's script is trying to lead you down a road of assumption; thinking that this is every viewer's first rodeo with these thirty-minute brain drains."

The look on Remi's face could have scared the stripes off a skunk. She seemed genuinely pissed about his unimpressive opinion. "Suicide is not so black and white, Tom. Just because someone appears to be content, or even happy, or we, as self-consumed third parties, think they *should* be happy with what they got means jack shit. Suicide happens to all kinds of people." Remi raised her eyes to meet Tom's. They drilled through him- they'd been doing that since she got there. "Murder happens to all kinds of people too- keep that in mind." What the fuck was that? A threat? Or was it just her turn to word vomit all over *him*? Brushing it off, he figured it was the latter and with good timing too, because his apartment buzzer started shaking the strained silence only seconds later. A great way to change the subject. Maybe Remi would go bat-shit on him... time to get some food in that woman's angry mouth and shut her up.

Before he could get off the couch to answer the buzz, Remi had already pressed the button, granting building access, and was racing to the door like it was a fucking marathon. This bitch is HUNGRY.

She ripped the goodies from the delivery guy's hands and then gave one of the sincerest and familiar smiles Tom had seen come from those typically shy and naïve lips of hers. "I'll dish up," she said in a sing-song voice, and off to the kitchen she jaunted. Tom hadn't ever seen this side of her before... he wasn't sure it was a good look for her. Nope, he decided hastily. It wasn't just ill-suited- it made her more annoying than the norm. Get through dinner, fain a stomach bug, and kick the bitch out. Done. He smirked to himself as he walked stoically back to the couch, waiting to be served by the night's wench. And there she came, swerving his plate downwards towards his crotch, acting like she might spill it all over him. He caught it with ease and she giggled in return. Then he saw her mounded plate - the food disparity between the two was unreal. If she wants to get a fat ass before we break up that's her choice- another unpleasant look for her, but soon to be, not his problem.

He scarfed his supper down and awaited her "good" news. He watched her, waiting. She seemed to be glowing - not with happiness or excitement, per se. Physically fucking glowing. A green hue was radiating from her form, encompassing her like the shine radiating from a gemstone. And there were two. Two of her waving around like a bad television signal. He pressed his eyelids together and rubbed his fingers over their backside but when he opened them the situation had only worsened. She was sitting on the floor in front of him; closer was not better. "What's wrong?" he heard her say, but he didn't see her mouth move. It stayed in a straight taught line until it suddenly curled up in the corners. He closed his eyes again trying to erase the wicked phony smile from his mind and straighten out his vision. He kept them closed.

It seemed easier to listen to that way. He felt her hand reach for the backsides of his arms.

"Here, let's get you up. Can you stand?" Without him knowing it, feeling it, sensing it he stood. Tom felt like he was flying across the floorboards. He couldn't feel the hardness underneath his feet. He couldn't feel the bends of arches, ankles, or joints that must have been on autopilot as she directed him to who the hell knows where. He could only assume she was getting him to his room where he could stretch out and sleep off whatever the fuck was going on with him.

There was a thud. It echoed in his eardrums. He could no longer tell if his eyes were open or closed, but there was a tie-dye oblong that pulsated in tune with the echo. The hypnotic, colorful layers would widen with the loudest portion of the thud on repeat and become almost invisible when it quieted. He couldn't get it to stop. He realized his hands were pressed tightly against his ears when he felt Remi softly remove them.

"There, there. Everything is ok now - we got you somewhere we can all be a little more comfortable with. I am so glad you could walk. I don't think I would have been able to carry you; especially not in my condition." Her voice sent shooting pains down his spinal column and made his forehead feel like a thousand miniature machines bulldozed it. Remaining conscious was all he was managing to do, and he was struggling to maintain *that*. "We did this together; just the two of us. Me and the baby that is. Such good news, right? That's what I wanted to tell you, I'm pregnant Tom. I get to be a Mom after all this and you get to die knowing that you might have had a child in this crazy, cruel world. That's the other thing- I'm not sure if it's yours or not." she paused only long enough to laugh at the duplicitous situation and how well she was killing two birds with one stone. "So surprise. I made it happen. Just like how I made this happen. I went rogue, Tom. None of the others knows that I'm doing this. And shit, it feels good to make a decision again. You know, a *real* decision. A life-altering, spirit-crushing, mountain of a choice that will only lead to my happiness and your demise."

Tom heard all of it. Most of it was distorted, but he still heard it. He had also realized by the growing numbness in his tailbone that he was not lying, or even sitting on his bed. Tom was nowhere near his room- he was seated on a cold, hard concrete floor and the only place he knew that had that type of flooring in his apartment was the hidden storage closet behind the walls of his oversized luxury bathroom. He'd give his left testicle to be anywhere else but that closet; he knew it was the only place in probably the entire building that he might go undiscovered. His ears started buzzing and the sound of Remi's voice slowly melted away, as if the constant hum had cooked it into whatever the hell it was she was baking up.

He slipped into a slumber. The Devil hadn't come to collect him so he knew he couldn't be dead. At least not yet.

Duo | Remi & Stella

A Call for Help

The panic in Remi's voice was undeniable. She'd gone off script, Stella was sure of it. It was too early in the conversation to know how, necessarily, but the breathy gasps and uncontrolled sobs on the other end of the line promised nothing good for the trio.

"Whoa, slow your roll. Breathe and then speak Remi." It was a good thing that the sad sap of a twig wasn't in the same room as her - there was no way Remi could have avoided the exaggerated eye roll that regurgitated from Stella's core.

"I just... I jus.. well, I did something, and it's not working. He's.. he's... Jesus Christ, what have I done..."

"I don't think Jesus Christ has anything to do with the three of us right now and I'm assuming he's got nothing to do with whatever you just did either...so I wouldn't be askin' him for any insights or favors."

Remi could hear Stella's smugness vibrating through the speaker. She cautiously set her phone down, closed her eyes as she rose to a sloppy standing position, spread her arms out wide to the sides, and set to spinning. On every trip around the whirl, she could momentarily hear Stella's angry voice get more and more panicked. Shit, she should freak out right about now. They were so close to getting everything buttoned up on Tom's "death" and she let her temper get the better of her- throwing a fucking monkey wrench into the whole damn operation. They'd kill her. Yup, that's what they would do. At least if she was dead she wouldn't be the one serving time... the other two were edgier, smarter,

187

a little more innately wicked than her. They'd get away with homicide. Hers and any others that might eventually be pinned on them. Remi halted the spin and faced reality. Squatting down, she lifted the phone back to her mouth and whispered, "You still there?"

"Yes, you crazy bitch, I'm still here. Where the fuck did you go and what the fuck have you done?"

Stella didn't give her a moment's chance to answer before she asked the big, dirty question, "Is he dead Remi? Did you kill him... like, *really, really* kill him?"

"Not exactly." Remi paused. "He just won't die. I mean, I think I gave him enough and all he's doing is frothing at the mouth and murmuring in the closet. I think he might even be sleeping... What do I do?"

"The thought never occurred to you that this might happen before you made such a stupid, uneducated call here? I mean, fuck, Remi; we wanted order to be restored in our world. Justice. Not to spend the rest of our lives in prison." It was Stella's turn to pause. "Did you go into this not willing to have to finish him off? A backup plan? The way I see it, we have two choices here. One, we revive him and then blackmail the shit out of him. Or two, you're going to need to do it another way - ALONE. I am not getting blood on my hands and I'm sure Myra would say the same here, so.... what's it gonna be? How dedicated to your dumbfuckery, are you?"

"Oh my God Stella. What are we talking about here... like sawing him up and burying him? I am not the type to own a gun, so that's not even an option. I just wanted him to slip out of his body forever. You know, quietly disappear."

"And what exactly was your plan for afterward? What were you going to do with the body? *Those* don't just disappear, you know?!"

"Well, I was going to leave it and have people assume he offed himself after his crazy cancer diagnosis. I thought it was just crazy enough to fit with our equally fucked legal manslaughter plan..." Remi heard herself trailing off even though her mind was still going a thousand miles a minute and she knew she could keep spewing for the next hour if Stella were to let her. She wouldn't, and she knew it. And yet, Stella's silence just sat there like an awkward fourteen-year-old playing wallflower at the middle school dance... hands shoved in pockets, eyes completely diverted from anything else with a pulse, and an incongruent boner slowly bumping up on his hand from the other side of the cotton pocket liner.

"I just got done texting with Myra; she's getting her shoes on now on her way over and I am already out the door. Just don't do ANYTHING until we get there; think you can manage that?" Welp that explained the uncharacteristic silent treatment from the BDSM Bad Bitch - it couldn't have been a moment of personal growth... she should have figured that much, Remi thought, berating herself for being so fucking naïve all the time. People are who they are- they don't change no matter how much you hope for, beg for, or need them to.

Remi knew she was a lot more capable than Stella might think, like re-writing the trio's entire plan in one deadly evening. Remi had been there before - just with a higher success rate. She felt the darkness spread from her chest into her limbs as she threw the phone and punched another "blah" elemental pillow on Tom's sofa. She was angry with the way Stella doubted her, but she was *pissed* with herself for failing in the first place.

Flashback to Sophomore Year

Seeing her frailness firsthand, wounded her. Remi's eyes traced down the sides of her wrinkled arms. They were two thin branches with taught, sun-damaged skin stretched just far enough over the bones peeking out at the hinges. On each, there was a single ball-like protrusion located where a full bicep would typically be. Her mother was looking like a scarred-up female version of Popeye; one that was addicted to just about everything besides spinach. Her pupils barely moved as her irises surveyed the remains of who was supposed to have been her mother. Remi liked to think that God had mistakenly assigned Felony Melanie to be her parent. A simple mix-up of papers in the intake and out-take office (which of course, was completely constructed out of clouds because fuck, she was still a kid, right?).

In her youth, she felt down to her core that God would have never set her up for failure by giving her such a horrendous excuse of a being to be the one person that should have mattered most to her. The one person that Remi was supposed to learn from and relate to in her older years. The one person that should have had her back with every school-yard bully she faced, every boy that made her feel like the dirt beneath his shoes, and every man that Remi would clobber off the face of the planet. But now she was older and wiser. She could easily wade through the ocean of lies that her father, the church, and shit, even her teachers had tried to construct in the basement of her bones. Each fallacy deemed suitable for a young, impressionable, up-and-coming young lady who should want what everyone else has. A well-fed, well-mannered family back at the immaculate home she would inevitably keep along with working full-time as a Physician's Assistant or Nursing Manager, two dogs, two kids, plenty of cash in the bank, and a permanent smile tattooed above her perfectly pointy single chin.

Fuck them - she was sixteen now and had figured a lot of shit out on her own... the hard way. And now she stared at the empty pit of a person across the bulletproof glass and reluctantly picked the phone receiver up. The face on the other side was unchanging. No smile. No look of excitement. No love. Just a robotic response to reciprocating in conversation by lifting her own receiver.

"Hi, Melanie. I see you're down a few more pounds. No newbies to haze- no one to steal food from? Or is it a new flow of drugs that's keepin' you trim?" The bitterness that dribbled down her chin as she spoke even took her by surprise.

She watched as her mother's eyes slowly rolled from one side to another. A slow, sadistic smirk grazed across her upper lip for a brief, fleeting moment. The sullen stare returned and she opened her mouth to speak- never a comprehendible response, always a random fact. Remi had gotten accustomed to seeing her mom stoned out of her mind. Her brain could barely function when she was sober from all the burn-out she'd caused over the years, but when she was high, nothing clicked mentally or emotionally. So, Melanie would resolve to little bits of "intrigue" she'd learned from some prison library book that was originally made to teach toddlers. Today it was birds; specifically, blue jays.

"Did you know blue jays are an aggressive species? They kick the other birds out of their nests and take them as their own... They will actually attack and kill songbirds, chasing them out of neighborhoods and in your very own backyard. To get songbirds to return, you must first resolve the issue and exterminate your blue jay population." Her eyes stared straight forward towards Remi, but they weren't looking at her by any means. "Even nature has its thieves... murderers... it's the fucking way of the world. Natural. Humans are so afraid to admit what is true to our core... every living thing's core. So fucking afraid. Don't judge, lest you will be judged."

Her eyes moved ever so slightly and she saw Remi... really saw her. Remi felt herself freeze, eyes locked with hers. Remi saw a flicker of light in her mother's irises and then they went dark... darker than she's ever seen. Melanie's eyes were a sea-glass green, but when the flare passed through they deepened to a rich chestnut brown. This wasn't even her mother. This person, this woman, this sick fuck was an imposter posing to be her mother. It wasn't possible for her mother to change the color of her eyes behind bars, where supplies are limited and guards are always watching. This couldn't be Felony Melanie... this *had* to have been someone else. But then there it was her wicked, wench-like cackle. It came from deep in her throat, bubbling its way to the surface like a toxic brew spilling over its cauldron. You couldn't fake that. No one could mimic that, no matter how good of an actor.

"See, I taught you something, my pet. I *can* teach you things even if they aren't things you *want* to know, you'll be better off knowing them. Other mothers coo and caw over every stupid, unimportant thing their offspring does, building false esteem that won't get them anywhere in their life. Even if this is all you learn from me, know that it's what you *actually* need to know to survive and fight through the filth. People are animals too. We follow the same laws of nature... laws of stalking, hunting, killing for survival."

Remi nodded and paused only a couple of seconds before she silently hung up her end of the line. This would be her last visit to her mother in prison. She was more unwell than she realized. She also made more sense than Remi'd like to admit. Years later, she would use this very ideology to eradicate the speaker of these very words.

They say the apple doesn't fall from the tree - but what happens when the tree gets poisoned by its own apple?

Fucking redemption.

Myra

Myra had never been good with blood, so she was hoping she would not have to come into contact with any. It actually had nothing to do with the fact that it was the main human life source, like oil to a car, but more of the violence she automatically associated with it. There were a few, blurry memories of her early childhood where she could recall her father coming home with blood splatters on the fronts of his clothes, chasing up his neckline and finding a final blotting point near his ears. Recalling these images as an older child, made her think of a man kneeling down, headfirst into an oscillating sprinkler, like the one she loved running through at her Grandma's in the hot summer months of Tennessee. But this sprinkler was spraying blood from its tiny, nodules, coating the man from the neck up. Every time the image would end on a freeze-frame of him looking up from the mist, staring right at her - inevitably she'd mouth the word "daddy" silently into the air. She knew it was just a conjecture of what once was, but it haunted her all the same.

The headlights of her mini cooper shined into the deafening darkness within the almost post-apocalyptic-level empty parking ramp. She rarely drove; in fact, most of her friends probably didn't even know she had a car, including Tom. For living in a city that never sleeps, Myra had always found a way to get around easily enough. Then again, she wasn't one of those people that was dead-set on much, including leaving her studio. So if she found a cab, great. Can't catch the train, she'd get to it the next day. But when someone calls you with news of an attempted homicide- one that might have your name attached to it- well, there was no waiting for that. She felt like a frightened little kindergartner trying to remember how to operate the only car she'd ever had. She toddled away at the steering wheel and plunged its four wheels into the darkest spots she could. She'd meditate on the situation later - she'd need to release the inevitable guilt she was already planning on putting more toxic sludge into the already polluted air, but for now, she'd focus on not drawing attention to herself. Pulling her hoodie up first over her ears and then after tucking her curly mange inside she firmly gripped the top and ripped it over the top of her head. Though she was tempted, she didn't pull the drawstrings to fully cover her fiery identifier. Only a murderous madwoman would do that and murderous madwomen attracted a lot of skeptical and overly interested stares.

Slamming the door a bit harder than intended, she hopped down the stairs of the parking ramp, openly avoiding the almost promised security cameras of the dingy gray elevators she knew all too well.

She was inside Tom's building. She'd made it. Kinda.

Her finger stood poised over the visitor button... one press to enter. Tom's dying on the floor of his storage closet, and Remi's been advised not to touch anything else in there- why would Myra want to stick her neat little fingerprint on the call button for forensics to find later on? She knew she'd been there *numerous* times before and she also *knew* that late-night CSI shows weren't one hundred percent accurate. She was torn between the two- her natural instincts and that of what a fictional TV drama taught her. There were a lot of unknowns... too many of them. By the grace of whatever God existed, someone came flying out the door, spooking Myra, but not long enough to make her miss her opportunity for unidentified entry. Her freshly painted jade fingernails slid behind the slamming solid panel in perfect time and pushed it open just wide enough for her slender hips to launch through it.

Remi was sitting outside Tom's apartment, repeatedly rubbing the tops of her thighs with her palms as she rested her laurels on the steely gray hallway carpet. Myra instinctively reached down without looking her in the face, grabbed her hand, yanking her into a standing position, and did everything she could to not physically shove her back inside the secret security of the apartment's walls.

"Dude, what are you thinking? You can't just be sitting out there looking like a scared little bird that just pushed its non-flying siblings out of the nest! You gotta get a hold of yourself because our ventures together are far from over," Myra said while glimpsing that intrinsic sparkle she'd seen in Remi's eyes back at the art gallery. Myra knew she wasn't *just* there to revive a dying man but to save a life almost fully lost. She could sense the deep hurts and anger that resounded within her new friend and could relate. Myra decided to help this poor soul back to the light when these other shenanigans were done and over.

Remi watched her own feet as they guided their guest to her little closet of horrors. Myra had thought she'd understood the gravity of the situation, but now standing over the top of a barely conscious, mouth-frothing, and mostly inanimate Tom, she panicked. Her left hand slid down into the correlating hoodie pocket and reappeared holding a tightly wrapped joint.

"Myra, he's already stoned out of his mind... I don't think pot is going to bring him back to us," Remi said in a half-shocked, half-scolding manner.

"Oh, well, aren't you just the homicidal pharmacist?" Myra retorted sarcastically. She could still be sarcastic, even if she wanted to help the little fallen angel. " It's not for him- it's for me."

Myra lit the end and toked it like it was the last breath she was ever going to suck through her lungs. Automatically, the hand holding it shot out towards Remi as a peace offering, but Remi just nodded her head no and instead returned to the comfort of a nervous whimper.

"Ok, deep breath, Remi. The first thing we got to do is get the shit, all of it, out of him. So I hope he had a light meal because everything, and I mean *everything* that went in that pie hole the past twenty-four hours, is coming back out." Remi watched with childlike curiosity as Myra's hand disappeared into the other hoodie pocket; this time re-appearing with a full bottle of ipecac.

The crackle in Myra's knees as she bent down to administer was audibly louder than anything else in the apartment but was still lost in the voices and shrieks that filled both women's heads. Myra parted

Tom's lips almost lovingly and poured the Ipecac straight down. A finger and thumb traveled up from his mouth and clamped the sides of his nose firmly together. Remi quietly gasped and Myra lifted her head just far enough to catch sight of her partner in crime's eyes. Fear. All she saw was fear. Pure impenetrable fear.

"It's ok Remi, I just need him to swallow it, that's all." And like magic, Tom glugged the vomit inducer down trying to make room for premeditated mouth breathing. There was no need since Myra released his nose and rolled him to his side.

It took only a matter of minutes before the retching started. Loud, traumatic retching. Chunks of undigested chicken, strings of onions, and celery from the Chow Mein spewed out of his mouth like a fire hydrant that had been cracked open. Myra looked down at the pile that was accumulating and saw bits of blood throughout the vile mixture.

"He's going to be extremely dehydrated after this- we will need to get as much water in him as we can if we want him to pull through. Know anybody that has access to IV equipment?" Myra highly doubted a positive response, so her mind went to imagining a homemade remedy when it was interrupted.

"Actually, I think I might," Remi's hands were beat red from the constant ringing she had been giving them. "This is going to complicate things, isn't it?"

"Probably, yeah, definitely will. How much do you trust this person?"

"A fair amount, I'd say. Do I have to tell them *everything*?" Remi waited with bated breath for an answer she was hoping to find acceptable.

"I don't think you should but you're going to have to come up with some pretty unbelievable backstory and quickly... he's slipped back out of consciousness already so we need him to get hooked up asap. I think if you can get the supplies here I could figure out how to put it in." Myra knew how to be delicate and patient with her hands- potting demanded that. And sticking a needle and tubes into someone's bloodstream would too.

Remi silently nodded and then vanished out of the closet and around the corner with her phone in hand. Myra returned her attention to the man she almost thought she loved. His oxygen path returned through his nose, making his breathing sound much less labored. Instinctively, she reached for his hand and still held it, knowing what he'd done and who he was. Her thumb caressed the backside of his palm, and her mouth opened to whisper calming thoughts to him. "Everything is going to be ok. We are going to get you all taken care of and put back together. You're going to live through this... not on paper, but in body and spirit. Just hang in..."

"Shut the fuck up, you bitch. All you do is talk and talk and talk and talk... no one cares what you..." His stoned mumbles trickled away at the end. His voice was low and his words almost inaudible, but Myra heard them. She heard them perfectly. She dropped his hand and went to stand.

"I'll make sure you survive this and then you can rot. Got it. Rot. For all eternity, you asshole." Wiping the tears away from the bottoms of her lids, she turned to leave when his hand grabbed her by the ankle.

"Who's there? Who is this? Where am I? I can't see anything! Are my eyes open?" Cutting through his drug-induced stupor, Tom was regaining some cognitive and physical abilities. Myra stood there silently, not knowing how or if she should respond. As if she'd had a revelation, she stooped down with her mouth next to his ear and said, "I am not really here and neither are you. You're dreaming of Hell... and when you finally get to open your awakened eyes, you'll realize... you're still there. You live there now." Myra pulled back and away, noticing that Tom's eyes were, in fact, open as she stood and left the closet, closing the door softly behind her.

Remi was sitting on the all-leather sectional stone still. Myra walked over to her, anxious to hear the news about the IV supplies. She knew from the bottom of her everything that he wouldn't make it without it. It was easy to read Remi's face, something had happened on her phone call.

"Well..." Myra said, opening the doorway for conversation.

"I told her everything, and she's on her way here now."

The brazen confession stunned Myra. "So this person knows everything as in what, exactly? Who are they, and are they coming to help with the equipment?"

"Yes."

"Yes, is not enough of an answer here, Remi. You are going to have to divulge a little more info than that."

"I'm sorry. I'm so sorry." Remi's voice trailed off. It was apparent that her mind was not in the same room as her body. It was more than likely racing around in a getaway car, fleeing manically from the crime scene she'd just created.

"Earth to Remi; I am really going to need those details if I am going to stay here and put my shit on the line, you know?"

"Yeah, um, sorry. Her name is Michelle. She's my roommate. She works at a dentist's office and can get the stuff we need. I told her that I found out he was cheating on me and I tried to poison him."

"And she said..." Myra sure as shit hoped it wasn't *ok, great. I will tell the authorities.*

"She said she understood and was on her way." Remi's spirit finally floated back into her body, regaining full human-like capacities. It was short-lived. The doorway to the apartment and big, bad, and bodacious Stella stepped into the room, silently slamming the apartment door shut. How does one do it silently? They tense their shoulder blades and wind up like they're going to be throwing the opening pitch at a Major League Baseball game and swing the door fast and furiously towards the jam while maintaining full control of it. The two women who had been huddled on the sofa jumped to their feet in response like little tin soldiers responding to their General that had just entered.

"Why the hell are you two over here? Why aren't you guys with our 'patient'?" Stella emphasized the last word with air quotes. Her hair matched the look in her bugging eyes...crazed.

Remi was visibly relieved when Myra took the baton and spoke up, "Tom is doing ok, we got some Ipecac in him and he's already spewed his guts out in there. He's going to be extremely dehydrated but Remi jumped on the horn and has some IV equipment on its way here as we speak." Myra stopped short when she saw the undeniable flare of rage sweep the entirety of Major Madsen's face. "So... we have everything under control here," Myra added at half the volume.

"Um, so, how the hell are you getting that IV stuff here? Does someone else know what's going on?"

Remi knew it was her turn to speak up, but she couldn't seem to force the words over the hoarseness that took over her vocal cords. She pushed past it. She had to. "Yeah, so I guess now would be a good time to sit down and make sure we're all on the same page."

"Jesus, Remi I think you should have had this conversation before you tried to *actually* kill him- as far as my memory goes back, I can't recall us ever being on the homicide page. Am I crazy too or is it just you?" Stella squawked sharply.

Myra's arms encircled the two others and lead them back to the sectional. "Come on Stella, give the girl some credit here...better late than never right? I mean, it's not totally off the wall here that one of us would crack and take things into our own hands a bit further than the other two agreed upon..."

"I think murder is a thousand, no a million miles past a 'bit further. Eliminating Tom's identity is already a ginormous endeavor but it's one that ALL three of us talked about and agreed upon. We all went into this understanding the risks and possible legal ramifications we would be under if we were to get caught. But NONE of us agreed to potentially serve a life sentence in prison for murder. I take this extremely personally Myra- an attack on our futures- and if you don't see that, girl, I will pray for your ass to get some sense in that obviously stoned head of yours."

Myra rolled her eyes. She didn't feel the same way about it and that was a good thing for Miss Remi Nash. She knew she needed the others to help her get through this; being lost between good and evil - light and dark- she realized she was relying heavily on these two strangers to see her out of the shitstorm.

The trio sat in dead silence with only the occasional sound of a puking Tom in the background until finally the strength returned to Remi's gullet and her mouth started forming the story of what she'd done - to first, Tom and now, to her dear friend Michelle.

Michelle

Michelle pressed the little phone icon to end the conversation with a very shaken Remi.

She'd inadvertently created a killer... another scorned woman who hadn't loved her partner as long as she had Dameon. Not long enough to stop herself from erasing him from the planet. No matter how much she hated Dameon for what he did and what he continued to do with Emmy, she could never hurt him. Even if she said she wanted to. There was not a mean bone in her body, not an authentic one anyway. Michelle owned the fact that she grew her own mean bone inside of Remi by planting the initial seed of doubt. So. Much. Guilt.

There was no time to waste. Michelle brushed her shame and blame blob aside, pulled her boots on, grabbed her car keys, and ran out the door. It was a blessing that it was Dameon's week to have Emmy, so she needn't worry about staying secretive or returning to the house by a certain time. Her game plan was to get in and out as fast as she could, trying not to forget any of the pieces she might need. The entire drive over to the dental clinic, she visualized where each piece was kept- imagining herself running through the different supply cupboards, ripping them apart, and then trying to stuff everything back into its exact last location. Don't go so quick that you leave a little crime scene behind yourself, Michelle.

Once physically arriving, she proved her eidetic memory acutely accurate and was flying back to her car door in less than ten minutes. Gently enough, she placed her bulging bag of stolen (let's say borrowed...it sounds so much better) medical supplies in her back seat and put the keys back in the ignition. The car's engine shuttered and killed. NOT FUCKING RIGHT NOW CAR! Another turn of the key, another disabled attempt by her go-go green Beetle. She knew investing in new tires for this metal heap wasn't a smart choice. COME ON YOU RUSTY SACK OF SH... third time's a charm. The Volkswagen was purring now and Michelle was grateful she'd replaced the tires once again. She typed Tom's address wildly into her phone's GPS and was off, leaving a cloud of smoke behind her hanging tailpipe.

The sound of the buzzer made the three women leap from the cushions; on the other side of that door stood their lifeline. The *only* other person who could and *would* ever know about Remi's big mistake and yes, even the pay-back plot. This was the conclusion it led them to; both Stella and Myra felt like their hands had been forced into an unwanted witness... more like an accomplice. Remi shouldn't have veered so far off from the plan, but wishing doesn't change decisions already made. They were in this together and now a fourth person was joining the circle of accountability.

Stella's eyes darted in Remi's direction-she'd assumed since it was Remi's friend at the door that she'd be the one jumping up to let them in, but.... nope. Another futile disappointment comes from the weak woman-child. Stella released an audible huff, pushing her toned legs up and forward to retrieve their highly anticipated guest. Myra and Remi silently waited for Stella's return with Michelle. Whispers echoed across the stagnant, pale walls bouncing back and forth, one to another like a high-action tennis match. The hushed voices seemed to take longer than Myra felt comfortable with, so she slid herself over to the newcomer to interject and interrupt any private shenanigans that might go on between the two. Myra deep down, felt like she shouldn't trust Stella further than she could throw her... and by the looks of those bounded biceps and toned tush, she couldn't lift one of Stella's legs, let alone her whole body.

Moments later, the three of them were passing right in front of a disassociated Remi, still seated, still lost in thought. Michelle lovingly extended her hand toward her roommate and mouthed the words, "you ok?". Remi slowly nodded her head and joined the rest in the now-overcrowded closet. Tom's position had changed very little since she'd seen him last. He was laying in an almost crouching position; his abdomen twisted and his legs hunched under him like a tiger who'd fallen asleep mid-pounce. Remi knew she should have felt bad for what she did to him- the good side of her, anyway. But she just didn't. The fear, the anger, the sadness she was experiencing was because she'd failed her mission and she didn't even understand why. Unbeknownst to the others- it had worked the last time. It had been enough to take *her* out. To remove *her* from this earthly plane. To disintegrate the lifetime of heartache that awful bitch caused her. But she'd made a mistake some-where along the way, and *that* was the most upsetting part. Michelle's commands interrupted Remi's trance.

"Ok, I've seen Dr. Anderson do this a million times so I feel pretty confident that I'll be able to get this IV going, but I am not guarantee-ing it on the first try. Or at all. Are you all aware that if I mess this up there can be some pretty serious complications or even fatality? There can be air bub..."

"Uh yeah, I think we are all past the point of understanding that there is a good chance that he's going to die from something that took place here. Am I right in assuming that we are willing to try this in the slight chance it will save his sorry ass and keep us out of prison?" The ugly head of impatience was showing itself in Miss Stella. It fit with her personality so well that no one seemed taken aback; especially not Michelle. Michelle was an old family friend of Stella and her sister's... true she hadn't seen the over-bearing prima donna, sadist since they were teenagers, but like much else in life, Stella hadn't changed a whole lot over the years. In Michelle's eyes, she was still the same power-hungry, completely capable, competent, vamp that she'd met over thirty years ago.

Michelle scanned the other two's faces for objections, but none were found, so she went to work.

One hundred percent from memory.

Michelle felt like she had everything from her fingers and toes to her pubic hairs crossed. She might have almost ruined her friend's life, but now was her chance to save it. She had to do it- she had to resurrect the lying little sack of shit lying helplessly in front of her. Not because she really wanted to give him more chances to steal women's dignity, but because a prisoner Remi would be a dead Remi. Michelle had known her roomie for a long time now so she could easily forecast what other inmates would do and *get away with*. Her hands grabbed, tightened, pinched, pulled, tied, and snapped until she had a fully functioning IV bag injecting fluids straight into the con's arm.

"Can someone go to the coat closet and grab me a hanger?" Michelle's eyes searched the space for possible resources; she was going to need to keep her drip constant so as to not encourage any unwanted air bubbles into Tom's vein. She spied a medium-sized box that was long and narrow. Perfect to rest his arm on. "Stella, reach up there and grab that box, will you?"

With much displeasure, Stella responded by grabbing said box and handing it off to Michelle. Lifting the arm with the IV tube, she placed the box carefully below his elbow and forearm and dusted it off with her hand before lowering his arm on top of it. As she brushed the dust away, she saw some very feminine scroll on the top. *Kim and Tom's Memory Shit.* Hmm, interesting. Remi returned with the coat hanger she'd asked for and helped lace the IV bag through its top hook.

"Where did you want to hang this?" Remi asked, seeming a little more inside herself again.

"Here, let's put something in the doorway to prop it open, and then we just hang it over the top of the door." Remi and Michelle were beginning to work together like oil and popcorn. Something was finally clicking back for her dear friend. Remi meant more to her than she could ever know - a Mama Hen looking after her littlest chick. The chick that never grew. The chick that got lost in the hay who had only started pecking her way to the sunlight before the Mama Hen accidentally sat on it- almost suffocating it to death. Luckily for them both, Mama Hen moved her feathered rump out of the way just in time.

After about an hour of staring at Tom, watching to ensure that the IV drip was getting into his system, the four of them felt safe in leaving the closet for a more comfortable conversation space. Myra led the way down the hall *away* from the living room, *away* from the kitchen, and into familiar territory for the two other Tom toys... his bedroom. Stella and Remi exchanged a questioning look with one another, but neither opened their mouth to expel curiosities. Once inside, Myra shut the door and stood in front of them like she was about to give a business presentation at some public forum.

"This has been a lot ladies... for ALL of us, and I think we need to reconnect with the Universe a bit before we go back out there. I figured this was a space where we all would have been 'active' with Tom- somewhere we've all been betrayed, so having a cleanse in this space just feels right. Thoughts? Feelings?"

Myra was the only one in the group that Michelle didn't already know, but she was learning quickly what type she was. Myra was an open book- a flowy wu-wu type, so she didn't make it necessarily very hard for others to get to know her. Bet she gets hurt *a lot*, Michelle thought to herself. To Michelle's surprise, Remi was the first to chime in.

"Yeah, I mean you are probably completely accurate in saying that we have all, looking back now, essentially been defiled here, but I am not sure what universe you're getting at and what we are supposed to do in here." Remi hadn't and wouldn't share with the others that she'd fucked Tom only an hour before calling them. She'd purposefully chosen *not* to do it in this room to protect her own mental stability down the road.

"I think all of us, you, Remi, Stella, and myself, could use some sort of release from Tom. I mean, I guess what I am trying to say is that it has almost felt like we are under his spell, and now that we are symbolically killing him and physically saving his life at the same time I think we're all going to need a little closure- a little peace after all this..."

"And maybe for Kim too whoever the hell that is..."Michelle word vomited. The heads whipping in her direction insisted on an explanation. "The box I put under Tom's IV arm had a woman's name on it, Kim. It said 'Kim and Tom's memory shit' on it, so maybe you all can talk to the gods or outer space...aliens, whatever you're planning on doing for this Kim gal too. She's probably another one..." Michelle wished she hadn't mentioned the name on the box because the reaction from the others was a fairly unbalanced combination of anger, excitement, and stunned frustration.

"Come on, ladies- we figured there had to be more of us out there." Stella sounded a little pompous in her presumptuous tone.

"Yeah, but we have a *name*." Myra chimed in.

"And she has a box," Remi added. "Do *we* have boxes?"

The trio raced towards the doorknob; Michelle dove onto the mattress to get out of the manic women's way. There she goes, opening her big dumb mouth-making more monsters. She waited for the stampede to pass before she stood to follow.

By the time Michelle joined them, it was apparent she was late to the party. Tom was awake and staring straight at them, eyes unmoving, deep heavy breaths plummeting from stretched nostrils, and a slow whimpering moan.

Who's there? I think I need medical attention. Can you help me? Please... I can't see anything, but I can hear you in here with me. Who are you? Where am I? Why can't I open my eyes?

Ah, if only Tom knew he hadn't said these words aloud. If only he would accept that he couldn't yet...

Tom

His chest was rising and falling, he could hear his heart pounding; tiny beads of sweat had formed around the parameters of his face. With each exhale, another beadlet released hold from its wrinkled mothership and rolled down the sides and front of his face. Some would seep into the corners of his eyes, others would splash over the thing hedging of eyelashes straight into his irises. The inescapable darkness had him believing his eyes were shut tight, maybe even taped shut- that would have explained why he couldn't see anything but exploding stars shooting across an internal midnight sky. But the stinging- the salt from his perspiration penetrating the outer layer of his eyeballs let him know his eyes were open- vulnerable to his own elements.

He couldn't see around the shaded screen that must be covering them. Whoever did this to him, whatever *this* was, must have been blindfolded and bound. The ties must be tight on his wrists because he couldn't even feel his hands anymore... full blood loss - that sounds serious. Permanently serious. He knew he needed to break free, but without being about to see or move his upper limbs, he could only rely on his legs, but even those didn't feel useful yet.

They always say when one of your senses is out of commission, the others will become stronger. His sense of smell was never that great, so he knew he would be fully relying on his auditory abilities. At first, he heard nothing... too much nothing. He thought he might actually be dead, but then he realized Hell wouldn't be this quiet, nor would the Devil. His eardrums lurched forward as if they were leaning outside his ears to listen... he could make out the sound of muffled voices-higher-pitched voices. A woman's voice. More like multiple women's voices. He listened intently, trying to figure out how many there were.

One, two, was that one the same as the first, or was it a separate person?

Three?

Five?

It felt impossible to make patterns out of the varying pitches and speaking rhythms, yet he knew he had to. In fact, it was the *only* thing he could do at the moment. Then he heard *her* voice; quiet, meek-sounding but stronger with words, she felt more confident in saying things like *sell, commitment,* and even when she said the word *apartment.* It was Remi. He knew Remi was there.

Then again, hadn't she already been there? They were having dinner together- and then...what? Eating a massive amount of Chinese food was the last thing he could recall- then it was completely blank from there. Literally and figuratively.

Remi couldn't have done something to him. She was an anxious dreamer, a giver not a taker, the most emotionally needy out of the host of women he was currently seeing. Desperate, but capable of hurting him? No way; she had no backbone, and if it weren't for him and whatever relationship she imagined them having, she probably wouldn't even be a successful realtor. In fact, he'd always thought she embellished details from her job to make it sound busier, more fulfilling, and financially rewarding than it really was.

Her problem wasn't malevolence. It was sweetness... she was too sweet. But if it wasn't her that did this to him, then who the fuck was it?

Just then, he heard a pair of socked feet coming towards him, then a pair of barefoot ones, and finally a set of booted heels. Three women. His assumption that one was Remi was confirmed as she addressed him directly:

"Well, I see someone's awake," Remi said in a taunting tone. Tom remembered something had been different, *off*, with Remi before and during dinner.

Shit, yeah, now it was coming back to him, in pieces, but it was coming back to him. She was going to tell him some big, exciting news but not until after they ate their dinner...he could picture her kneeling over him while he was lying there. She was saying something to him but he couldn't hear her words; her hollow mouth was moving but he couldn't even read her lips.

Tom shifted his weight as much as he could manage. He was getting nervous... what if Remi *had* done something to him? Focusing all of his brain strength on moving his upper lip first and then his lower, he managed to push out a somewhat understandable, "what happened?" No matter how hard he tried, nothing more would leave the parched crack in his face.

"Hmm, let's see here. We fucked, we ate, and you almost died. What more do you need to know?" Remi's crassness shocked everyone in the room including herself; she hadn't intended for the others to know about the pre-homicidal sex she had engaged in with Sir Thomas. Too late now.

Tom couldn't see her but he could feel her stare penetrating through him.

"Am I dead?" A sentence, a full sentence- hallej-fucking-luah.

"Sadly, no."

Her response shook him at his core. She did it. She DID do this to him. Just when you think you know someone, they go and surprise you. Attempt to murder you...

There was more. The bitch had more to say. "I am not sure if you can remember the last thing we talked about before everything probably went VERY dark for you but in the slight chance you do...don't worry, it has nothing to do with you."

Ok, sounds great, whatever that means, you crazy fucking cunt, is exactly what he was saying to her in his head when he mumbled, "mmmk."

A small rush of blood was coming back into his hands. They felt tingly. Numb and tingly, but the fact that he could feel anything was a good sign. Pushing all the energy he could gather, he focused it on trying to lift his left thumb. It lifted. He lifted it. He did it. And now give me a little wiggle...just enough to know that I can. He could feel the tip of his thumb bumping first against his thigh and then on the other side, against something he presumed was wood.

And that's how it's done, folks. That's how you become the master of your mind and body; once you master your own, you can master other peoples' too. He's gotten into Remi's head at one point; now he just needed to get back in through a different entrance. The wheels started turning while he subconsciously uttered the words, "who's all there?"

There were a few seconds of pause. "Well, there's me, the Wicked Witch of the South, then there's the Wicked Witch of the North, and the East, and the West all here in one room just for you. Doesn't that make you feel special, you lying sack of shit?"

So she knew. Well, she knew something...some stuff. What stuff? Did it matter at this point? Probably not- he'd been wrong about Remi- she was a bat-shitter and he didn't bow out in time to prevent this little scene.

"Hm, sounds like a party. Let me see you all." That amount of words exhausted him, but he needed to get the rest of his request out. "Take the blindfold off so I can see what the bitches look like." No doubt they were some desperate and sad side-kicks Remi had picked up from work, or maybe even that annoying roommate of hers. He knew he didn't like her the first time he met her.

"Love to help you out with that, but there's no blindfold to take off. You're looking right at us." Remi had never realized just how exasperating he was- unless that is, he wasn't really pulling her chain and he actually couldn't see them. To test it out, she turned and waved Myra over to join her. The boho beauty slid down next to her on the hard concrete pad; Remi reached across her, grabbing Myra's right hand and placing it in Tom's left hand.

"Tom, can you feel my hand in yours?" Remi asked, testing the waters.

"Yeah, I can feel your cold and clammy claws. I hear you, I feel you, for fuck's sake I can even smell you, but I can't see you. What the fuck do you have over my eyes you fucking psycho bitch?! Untie it, scrape it off, remove the helmet...whatever it is just get it off me and I will contemplate not going to the cops with all this but you have to do it NOW!" Panic overwhelmed him; he got the notion Remi was telling him the truth, and he was indeed not blindfolded... just blind.

Remi and Myra sucked air into their lungs in unison, somehow maintaining the act of being singular. Their eyes met, and they both realized that Tom was, for once, being honest when he said he couldn't see them.

The two women's unspoken telepathy seemed to continue as Remi's eyes widened... she did it. Well... kind of. She hadn't been strong enough, brave enough, or acutely accurate enough to kill the bastard, but she *had* stolen something remarkable from him. And perhaps forcing him to live a life without one of his most consequential and necessary senses was more desirable for Remi to observe. He would have been...could have been just gone - dead and delivered to whatever fate awaited him. Remi was sure there was nothing pleasant waiting for Tom at the pearly gates, but death *would* have been an easy way out of it all for him. She'd never thought about it that way before. Tom losing his sight seemed deliciously worthy of his crimes - along with having his entire life known to society erased. What a welcome twist to the plot. She caught herself grinning at Myra. Myra looked frightened in return.

Myra knew she wasn't dealing with the person she assumed Remi to be. Myra knew she was dealing with a monster - one she shared commonalities with. One she didn't know how to evade. Things were changing quickly for the trio- now quartet. The players were switching instruments, personalities, and gleaning their once shiny, bright, clean souls for replacements that have come as blackened fragments, matted with tar and shards of broken glass.

Myra knew.

Witness

Locked away and in danger
Cold concrete for your bed
The little Lord Jesus
Can't save your fucked head
The light and the faces
You shall never see
Blinded for life
You'd be dead if it'd been me

Watching you through this dreadful process has been nothing but a joy for me and baby. Our souls may be very far apart right now, but we do feel one another - we have a bond that can never be broken. Oh, I wish you could have met her, but I am afraid, for your sake, since you still have a pulse, you won't be anytime soon. And just know dear, when the dark days ahead are too much for even an unearthly scathing savage like yourself, you won't be able to commiserate with her. It won't be me keeping her from you- you made that bed and now you have to live in it. Oh, the fun family time you are gonna miss. Sad for you, really. Actually, I'm not sad- we're not- not one bit.

Seeing the void in those stormy seas implanted where eyes could have remained is something new I will have to get used to. I was always hiding my true self from you, but now I can roam freely. I know you can never know me again unless I choose that for you. So many things in your life will be decided on the basis of *if I choose to* from here on out. You probably think me a wretch. I am not- I swear. I am the big bad wolf that mows the wretches down in my jaws, devours every limb, every organ, every last ounce of meat on their hanging bones. And then I throw the calcified remains into a heap to become the prey of the beasts that lie in wait in the tree's shadows. The moon shines enough light to lead them to a blind sack of shit like yourself. Your eyes will have already been plucked out, but I'm sure they will appreciate the bits of tendon and natural sinew that come from your sun-dried veins.

The best part of your ravaged remains is the heart that was left behind still beating. Pumping and pulsating; searching for blood that's no longer there to fuel it. There's nothing left for it to fuel- its purpose has been uninhabited and soon I will tear it to shreds too, so it withers in a million tiny torn pieces of rubbery muscle. More bait; a million little bargaining chips all for me and the Devil to divvy up and decide who gets what.

I know what I want, but I'll never tell *you*. Even if I do so choose to let you know me again in your life. Chances are slim, but Tommy boy, miracles do happen every day. Maybe I can still be your miracle. But even then, if it were to happen, there has to be something that I hold near and dear to my heart for the day that I get to die. And my wish is just the secret I know I need to keep.

Tough day for you.

Phenomenal viewing party for me and babe.

See you around...well, I guess I'll be seeing you around and you can just try to guess who is in the room with you.

Stella

While the two idiots were chatting up Mr. Stevie Wonder over there, Stella was going to use her time a little more wisely. She took her heels off and tip-toed behind the pathetic floor squatters, looking around for more boxes with bitchs' names on them.

If this Kim person got one, Stella was going to be goddamned if she didn't get one too... who the fuck was this little Kim anyway?

Obviously, she was another one of Tom's sexual acquisitions, but why the box? Was it something Kim herself had put together because she was one of *those* girls? You know, the stage five clinger that thinks the only thing you need in your life is to see her beautiful smile every moment of every day so they gift you dozens of framed photos of themselves, hoping you will put three or four in every room of your house.

Stella gagged.

There were plenty of these high-level leeches out there; she'd experienced a few back in her day- some men, some women. But always people she met on the job. Both of them. Like any sex worker, it's one of the biggest risks you run into in the industry- the obsessive stalker who truly believes you were meant to be together because you see, understand, and accept their saddest versions and have them leaving feeling fully acceptable, capable of love and being loved, normals when in all reality it's just an exchange. A business deal between a professional and some desperately haggard bag that needs to have their fetishes and esteem reassured and harmonized through pain and humiliation. Absolutely, Stella enjoyed it- that's what made her a DOM; if she didn't enjoy it, she would feel like a cheap, angry hooker that only heel stomped ball sacks behind alleys. But she *always* knew her role, and that was to rip down for them to repair- not to claim sincere emotional connections.

In her mind, Kim being a psycho stalker was the only reasonable explanation for why she'd have a box there with her name on it and no one else did. If Tom were the one making these memorabilia coffins, she'd have one. There was so much a person would want to remember about her - her body, her wild and wide scope of behaviors in the boudoir, her insane wealth, her argumentative abilities that rocked the courtrooms... her box would be the biggest if Tom were making these. But since she couldn't find any others, she knew Tom wasn't the crafty culprit. He was just another lying, greedy, man-baby that got off on lying to women. Using them and discarding them for another haram hire.

She wondered how being blind would affect his little dating game. If he couldn't see a woman to judge her, how would he decide who was worthy of a romp?

And would anyone *want* to?

Would he trust another person enough to not expect to be dosed again?

Almost murdered?

There was no doubt in Stella's mind that Tom had been with enough women through the years to navigate his way around the female form without being able to see it. He'd probably be a master at that- but would a woman *want* him to? And if they did, would it be out of pity?

Tom Williams Gets only Pity Fucks From Here on out. Now that'd be a headline she'd read the rest of the article for.

Stella directed herself stage left and found her way back to Tom's bedroom where Myra had led the women right before they charged the closet for a little detective work... then the others got distracted by a not-so-peeping Tom blah, blah, blah. Stella wanted to give his room a shakedown without the others knowing.

By the sound of it, they hadn't caught her drift and were still fucking with Tom's mind while trying to repair his vision or something stupid. Her feet pranced automatically over to Tom's dresser. Ripping open each drawer as if the wood rectangles had been gasping for oxygen, she rifled first through a pile of nothing but hideous tie-dye and loud rasta ware she'd never in her life seen Tom wear; nothing interesting besides an old hand-blown multicolored marijuana bowl. Resin covered the bottom of its basin and reeked like old, used skunk ass.

Next.

This drawer had nothing but mundane-looking polos and cargo shorts, the third was boxers, briefs, socks, pajama pants... again nothing too impressive.

When Stella went to pull the fourth and last drawer at the bottom near the dresser's base, there was some resistance. Leaning down, she could see there was something jammed between the top of the drawer and the top of its slides. Stella tried to shimmy her hand into the opening but no matter how hard she tried, she couldn't noodle her arm in far enough to grab it. She leaned down further, scooped her hair back with one hand, and narrowed her eyes into focused eagle eyes, hoping to see more detail of the mystery protrusion. It was definitely a book of sorts, thicker, with an almost padded-looking top cover- more like a photo album or scrapbook. *What secrets do you hold, you prickly motherfucker? Come to Auntie Stella and I won't rip you to shreds while getting you out because I AM going to get you out one way or another.*

Anyone or anything that tested Madam Madsen was a fool; whether they started out knowing it or not, they always left with it stamped on their foreheads. Scarred for life.

Stella whirled around to scope something out that might act as a thinner, more flexible extension to her velvet smooth arm, but nothing caught her eye. Probably something in the kitchen...off she snuck down the hall, but this time she was discovered. Michelle was strolling straight towards her, hands on hips and lips pursed like a shaming mother entering a room of arguing kids. Stella remembered this side, the only side really, of Michelle.

Growing up, Michelle was always playing *Mother Dearest* with all the neighborhood kids. She was the most mature six-year-old to this day Stella has ever met. Michelle was seriously never a kid herself; she was always watching, always cooking, cleaning, and caring for all the boo-boos. There wasn't a wrong that didn't get corrected by little miss Mama Michelle back in the day and it appeared not much had changed.

Stella wasn't afraid of her... never had been, but she also knew that Michelle was a force to be reckoned with herself. And... Michelle had connections. This was part of the reason Stella wasn't overly surprised to see her aging, oblong face in Tom's apartment doorway. Remi made a mess and Mama Michelle was there to clean it up. Honestly, whether or not Remi would have called her, Michelle would have found out what was going on. Again, the woman had connections- none of which Stella knew, but that didn't mean they didn't exist. Michelle would have been a part of this, regardless, because she and Remi were friends. Stella and Remi were not. Not really.... and Michelle sensed it. A girl can leave the hood, but the hood never really leaves the girl and they always become the most dangerous, insatiable women.

Leaders. Boss Bitches. Man-eaters.

Though with her meek lifestyle and low-income assistant job, Michelle was still a Bad Bitch. She was like the Godfather- essentially knowing enough people to get a job done and done right. If it wasn't, Mama Michelle was going to have to follow up herself. She'd feel like shit about it later, but she knew what she'd have to do it. She was a lady who got shit done and people out of the way. Remi didn't know any of this- Stella was sure of that. But Remi would find that out quickly and hopefully. For her own sake, she was a fast learner.

Michelle said nothing as Stella brushed past her, acting as if there was nothing to be talked about, no questions that needed to be asked from either of them. Stella knew she was done snooping around; Michelle had sniffed out her scent and would shut down any further detective work as the alpha bloodhound. Instead, Stella marched back into the closet to round up the troops. The fucker was going to live. Yup, he was blind. There wasn't much they could discuss or figure out while they were still on his turf- now that he was conscience again.

Disguising her voice with a fairly impressive French accent in an entirely different octave made the others second guess their eyes and ears at the same time. "Ladies, a word with you all out in the hallway please." Stella was never that polite; it was an excellent cover. Tom would have never guessed she was present for this shit show with those elite mannerisms and eloquence...well, that and the phony-ass accent she just threw.

Stella lovingly maintained her new French persona while the group discussed the next steps in the hall. After a bit of back and forth, Stella got her way, like she knew she would. They were leaving. After moving him, that is.

The three agreed it would be completely careless to leave him at the scene of the crime (the puke-covered, medical tube-infested closet that had started out so clean). Stella and Myra were on moving duty while Remi was supposed to clean up the mess she made. It was only fair that the stupid bitch should have to do the gross part since it's her fault they were even in this, to begin with.

Even with her arms tucked tightly below Tom's damp underarms and Myra on foot duty, Stella caught Michelle leaping to Remi's rescue, mop in hand. Their relationship was getting to be gross. Stella was all for backing and supporting your fellow female but this Mama bird, pet worm, bullshit was disturbing as fuck. Pushing out one of her signature eye rolls, she and Myra turned Tom around the corner of his bedroom, lifted him up, and plopped him down on top of his bed.

Tom let out a noise. Clearly, he wasn't expecting the human body toss but seemed appreciative once he realized he was lying in the comforts of his own bedroom.

"Don't get too comfortable," Stella hissed, losing her French accent at the moment. Tom's face went blank and Stella could see the cogs in this head-turning. he was trying to identify her. She'd been close to blowing it. Some might say she *did*, but she knew it wasn't enough to blow her cover. She was just fine with Remi being the only one taking the wrap on this... in all fairness, it *was* ALL her fault.

Myra spent way too much time taking the blankets out from underneath him and placing them a little too lovingly over the top of his balmy body. Stella watched as Myra went to his dresser and switched the old-fashioned AM/FM radio on. Fucking A- this bitch was going way out of the way to make this asshat feel at ease. Slipping back into Frenchie, Stella squelched the hippie's *good vibes*, "Ok, I think that is plenty of extras for him... not so sure he's deserving of anything more than a good smack in the face. Time to go." Myra silently nodded and unapologetically left Tom for dead.

With tubes packed and all the skeletons back in the closet, the four of them were off. And they were heading over to Michelle's and Remi's. Stella had insisted that using Michelle's home was a safer choice; since *she* technically had no relational connection to Tom if curious minds were to snoop. The others deemed any advice to be sound advice if it came from the mouth of a lawyer, praised Stella for her good thinking and quick wit. Stella gladly accepted the accolades even if they were under false pretenses. All of it. With Remi being Michelle's roommate, and Tom knowing all too well that it was Remi at fault for his blindness, Stella's inner genius helped her compartmentalize the situation and future retaliations. Keeping her name out of his mouth was her only intent. Her *only* care. Save herself. Fuck the rest.

Michelle

They were all sitting in *her* living room. The same living room that her sweet little Emmy snuggled up and watched movies in. The same living room where that same amazing daughter and she would play board games on Friday nights. The same living room where Emmy and her friends had sleepovers. And now it was the same living room that would someday be ripped away from her- just like her family would be.

She was going to get caught for her aiding and abetting these future felons; she could feel it in her gut, but there was no way out now. At least not one she could see very clearly and trust you me, endless story-lines were running through her head trying to escape yet another bad decision she'd made.

She should have never answered Remi's call, she should have just remained focused on having a Mom's weekend by herself with no one else relying on her. She was always letting people, maybe even leading them to, lean on her. Her shoulders were only so wide and as she got older, they were shrinking. Michelle should have known better. She should have never let Remi move in. She should have never let anyone move in; no matter how well you think you know someone, you'll never *really* know them enough to have them around your kids. And yet, here they sat. Here they talked...all speaking at the same time. Michelle's ears hurt. She caught herself holding them with the insides of her hands.

No one else noticed. No one else cared.

Remi was trying to speak now, but the others just kept chattering over the top of her; swimming over the top and drowning her entirely. Michelle lowered her hands from her ears and tried to make out what

Remi was trying to say. It was a whisper now...the volume at which Remi was speaking. She could see her friend disappearing into herself. Michelle's hand shot out in Remi's direction, causing her friend to look down at it and instinctively take it in hers.

"I think Remi is trying to say something," Michelle's voice boomed over the sea of distressed chatter. Both Myra and Stella stopped talking abruptly and turned their attention to Remi who in response squeezed her eyes shut and parted her lips to speak.

At first, Remi sounded like a mouse who'd been caught by its tail in a trap, but as she continued, the others heard her confidence and strength regenerating. She was coming back into herself and beyond anything she'd ever let anyone else see- well, anyone she wasn't about to kill. Not even Michelle had heard Remi speak like this before. Michelle thought it inspired and comparatively empowering.

"I think I owe you all an apology for dragging you into my mistake...my mistake being not finishing the asshole off. I am sorry to you all, but not about *what* I did. I don't feel sorry for myself and I will never feel sorry for Tom. He could have died. He should be dead, not blind. Incidentally, he's being given another chance granted against my will but he should feel lucky that all he is is blind. Underneath his shitty bag of rotting skin lies a pulse. A heartbeat. He could never see it but he can still feel it and he owes me for that. He owes all of us for that," Remi raised her hand when she saw Myra shifting uncomfortably in her seat, lips pursed and on the verge of speaking out. Remi'd finally gotten the floor and she wasn't about to step off of it so quickly there was a lot she still had to say.

"I understand that you guys are concerned about Tom knowing who was all there and I want to congratulate you all on your stealthy efforts to keep your identities hidden. Really, you all did a remarkable job with it- hats off to you, Stella, for that uncanny accent you pulled out of your ass at the last minute. I'd ask where you learned to act like that but I think A Day in the Life of Ms. Stella Madsen *is a* consistent rehearsal."

A fire raged through Stella's eyes, burning every tree down in its fury. Remi continued by throwing some water on the flames. "You know, being a lawyer and all. I mean, you must represent guilty people from time to time, but you have to do what you have to do in order to win their case. You *are* getting paid with the presumption of winning, and sometimes that takes a little role-playing, doesn't it?" Remi didn't pause long enough to let Stella answer.

"So, my apologies are limited to only the three of you for asking for help. Next time I will have enough balls to complete the task myself."

Sideways glances shot throughout the room from one woman to another. There would be a next time? Would it be another attempt on Tom's life or who the hell else was on her list?

Michelle made a mental note to stay on her roomie's good side even though she knew their bond was deeper than anyone else's in the room. They were ride or die in Michelle's mind. The rest of them...well they could be next. She just didn't know any other backstories other than the ones Remi might have shared with her in passing.

With an elongated silence, Myra assumed safely that Remi was finished with her soapbox speech of *sorry, not sorry.* "So, I think we really need to discuss what the game plan is for here on out. I mean, as far as I understand we have everything finalized in killing Tom on paper am I right there?" Myra's eyes surveyed the room and accounted for all heads nodding- besides Michelle's, who had just learned a summarized version of the original trio's plan on the SOS call from Remi mere hours ago.

"Ok, well that mission is accomplished. So now what? What I guess I am trying to say is that the majority of us weren't planning on actually hurting a hair on Tom's head- just fucking his life up for a bit. Making it hard for him to continue life as he knew it. But now... well, things are a bit different." Myra was trying to keep her cool even though her brain was telling her she need a smoke and a toke to keep this cool, calm and collected charade up for much longer. "Do we just leave him there, fending for himself? Does one of us help him with the basics to keep him eating, breathing, etc.?"

"Well, if we do, *do* something to help him get back on his feet - just a little nudge to get him in an upright position. I think it should be short-term, like a week or two at most, and I don't think it should be one of us. It's too risky." Stella said in her most authoritative court-room voice.

A hyper-awareness scattered amongst the women as they unani-mously nodded- even Michelle, who was unsure how much of this con-versation she was really a part of. After giving it a little more thought, she decided to quietly excuse herself from it. She was never really a member of this little tae-on-tae and she didn't need to get herself in any deeper than she already had... she *was* the only one there that had a kid-she had the most at stake.

Nothing would get between her and her baby. She knew it, felt it, tasted it. Her role was primarily mother, then friend to criminals. Of course, it was Stella that called out her exit. Michelle ignored the assumed backhanded comment and kept walking.

At the edge of the entryway, Michelle climbed the bright white wooden staircase while grasping the railing harder than she was used to. She knew she was holding on for her own life. She wasn't sure what heaps of trouble she'd just allowed herself to become a part of but she needed an exit. She needed a redo. She needed her Emmy.

Flop. Her body sank down into her little girl's all-pink ruffle comforter. Michelle sucked her daughter's scent in sharply, pulling the young flowery aroma through both nostrils at the same time. Memories came rushing back when she brought her bundle home from the hos-pital. It was pure magic; her warm, soft and fuzzy sprite cooed in her arms. She remembered she couldn't have felt happier; more excited for that next stage in her life. Motherhood.

But now flowing back with the happiness Michelle recalled the look on her now ex-husband's face- he was concerned, rigid, uncaring, cold. He was posturing himself exactly the same way she now knew he did when the two of them were in a room alone together- him holding his secret affair close to his chest and her begging for more affection.

Shit. Dameon had been cheating on her when she was pregnant too, wasn't he? It was less of a question than it was a crystal clear epiphany. The anger welled up in her chest; the pain, hurt, and frustration were there starting all over again. She took another long inhale into the comforter. She and Emmy had appropriately named them "the magic blankets" because they magically comforted others with their pillowy poof, the texture of the tenderly stitched seams, and perfect cotton-blend fabric currently caressing her cheeks as she turned her head from left to right, rubbing it all in.

The shock of her epiphany was fading; dimming. She felt like *she* was dimming since it all began. He had stolen her light, her inner freedom to feel good in her own skin. He had never loved her. Not even when she grew that beautiful baby inside of her. *Their* beautiful baby- the one they made together out of what Michelle had once thought was love. It was all an act- the entire time.

Why did he even marry her if he never planned on committing wholly?

Did the answer even matter to her anymore?

Probably not but her heart ached to know it. Then, with a slow blink of her eyes, it dawned on her that these emotions were the exact ones the three ladies sitting below her in her very own living room were feeling. She was a part of their trio more than anyone had realized.

She would help them. Smartly, but she would help them.

Little did Michelle know, the trio was discussing connections and how to best use them to get out of their sticky little situation. Luckily, Michelle's name stayed out of the other woman's mouth as a possible aid for Tom. However, Stella was quick to offer up a boring office bitch she'd recently gotten to know on a much more personal level. One she had a bit of control over, a piece of personal identity, and a shameful secret she could work with.

Resident brown noser and Lassie, Rachel Dobbs.

Time to call her client and schedule their next playdate.

But this time enough would be to emotionally blackmail a bitch into doing them all a favor. One she'd most likely never understand the implications of.

But that's why people bring mutts to a dogfight... too stupid to know what they're doing is wrong.

Michelle was no mutt; she was a purebred pitbull. She just needed to remember her training.

Rachel

The vibration in her pants pocket sang along with the one she was diddling herself with. People need stuff at the least convenient times. And she was always their go-to; the one they trusted would do their bidding because they knew all too well that she wanted to make a name for herself.

It was working. She knew it because just the other day Dale from the office called her by her actual name. He knew it, he didn't call her Stacy this time. He forgot again later that afternoon, but Rachel was starting to realize that senility might be the cause of Dale's forgetfulness. Another poorly aging man in her life; she should feel worse than she did, but deep down she knew that the fewer of them there were, the more opportunity for young females like herself.

Unable to refocus her mind on her clit, she threw her vibrator down with a frustrated sigh and reached for the phone that had buzzed itself out of her pocket. Releasing one last blast of breath, she planted the biggest grin on her face she could manage. The biggest *anyone* could humanly manage. She heard once that the person on the other end of the phone can tell if you're smiling because the upward curl automatically changes the inflection in your voice. "Good morning, you've reached Miss Rachel Dobbs." Her cheeks were already on fire, but she kept the Joker painted on her face.

"Rachel, Stella Madsen here. Madam Madsen to be specific. I wanted to catch you before you headed into the office- I figured you'd be a bit more open to discuss setting up your next playdate with me outside of the firm."

To be honest, Rachel was floored that *Ms.* Stella Madsen, the baddest bitch in the office, was calling *her* for another rendezvous. And so soon too. The chin-splitting smile turned genuine as she was genuinely pleased. Maybe following her instincts to a lesbian office relationship *was* the way she was going to get to that next pay grade. Her mother's voice floated to the front of her mind:

> *You know it's wrong to be gay- you don't really like other women. You just think they are pretty; that's normal because women are pretty, dear. And men are handsome. Just because you think one of these two things about someone doesn't mean you want to sleep with them...especially if they have the same parts as you. You would burn for eternity if you even try it once with another woman. And then I would roll in my grave forever, knowing you would never meet me on the otherside. You'd be stuck with all the rejects, homos, and minorities down with Satan. Not my baby. I won't allow that to happen to my baby.*

Her mother was always "looking out" for her when she was alive. Rachel could only hope that her last little experience in Stella's dungeon hadn't counted against her- it wasn't really lesbian sex. It wasn't sex at all, to be truthful. There was no penetration, so it couldn't have been. Her hands started picking the sides of her thumbs. She *knew* better than to sell her soul to get to the top, but she was just *so* close- it was hard not biting off the last chunk even when it was marked POISON.

But what if she was enjoying it all a little too much? Does that mean she truly is a lesbian? She couldn't be. Not possible. She rejected that idea from the bottom of her soul, crossed her heart, and swore never to be a dike.

"Hi, yes, talking about these kinds of things outside of the office *is* a lot easier for me. I am not sure that there will be a next time though. I am wondering if my first experience was the one and only I needed to, you know, get back in touch with myself or whatever. I mean, don't get me wrong, I most definitely enjoyed myself and have left it feeling so much more aware of myself but blah, blah, blah," this is where Stella stopped listening on the other end of the line. Stella was no fan of rejection or just the word *no*. So with no further consideration, she stopped the trickle of lies and inefficient chatter with her commanding DOM voice.

"Now, now Rachel. Let's not get ahead of ourselves here...it *is* your tendency to over-promise and under-perform, which is exactly what you're trying to do here. You are cutting yourself off and expecting the one session to provide you with enough satisfaction for a lifetime. You know better than anyone else, your mother, and probably God himself, that you are one broken little girl inside that tight sweater vest and those black riding pants."

Rachel's ears perked as her mind wandered instantaneously; so Stella had noticed her outfit yesterday. One point for Rachel, she thought giddily to herself. Her thoughtful outfit choices were home runs- that's what she took from this segment of the conversation.

Stella was prying every bit of detail she had stored in her almost eidetic memory- the multiple framed photos of Rachel and who she assumed was her mother, the prayer beads underneath her keyboard, and the crucifix she wore daily around her miniaturized, pixie-sculpted neck.

"You have been up to something lately. I know it, you know it, and the Devil knows it, Rachel. We see it all even when you don't think there's any way we could be watching. It's time to repent and reconnect with your pure being. So I *expect* to see you in my dungeon this evening at 6:00 pm sharp. Don't be late, it's your salvation at risk." A hard click echoed at the end of the line. Stella had physically hung a phone up; a sound Rachel hadn't heard since she was a young child speaking with her mom over her foster family's phone. She cringed, remembering the intermittent stints she was in foster care- her Mom was in psych wards from time to time and there wasn't anyone else willing to care for Rachel in her mother's absence. She loved her though, her mother, she had to have. Mothers *have* to love their children otherwise, God wouldn't allow them to bear children, to begin with.

A racing mind that mimicked her heartbeat was not the way Rachel had planned or liked to start her day. She was feeling unsure, a little edgy, and definitely anxious. She was between a tight space and a rock now... she couldn't say no to Stella- that would be professional suicide, but saying yes had its own damning implications.

What if her mother could see everything she was up to; what if she knew everything like the thoughts she has when she sees Stella bending over to retrieve a fallen sticky note at work? Or what if her Mom knew she got wet the first time she laid eyes on her new friend, Kay, at the coffee shop or how her nipples hardened when Kay accidentally grazed her breast while reaching for her latte?

She was sunk if souls could read minds and see through walls, well, undergarments in her case. She had tried to push those urges down for years. Feeling something romantic for another woman was wrong... she didn't want to believe that, but she was afraid of what would happen if she didn't. Taking the risk to be happy in this short, less meaningful lifetime wasn't worth risking a blissful eternal life. It just wasn't. She just couldn't.

Rachel couldn't face going to work that day either, so for the first time in her three years of employment at the firm, she marred her perfect attendance streak by calling in sick. The most complicated part of the process wasn't working up the nerve to call but figuring out *who* to call... they usually all called the reception line to report an absence. So... she reported it to herself by phone to maintain consistency, but then sent out an office-wide email.

No one responded to it. Not even Stella.

———————

Cold, smooth steel pounded back against her fist; there was a slight drizzle hanging in the air. Her stomach lurched as she heard footsteps approaching from the other side. Rachel was suddenly much more appreciative of her earlier insights to hold off on eating until after her "playdate". Last time she could hold the vomit in the back of her throat until she got home, but she didn't know if she'd always be that lucky.

Stella's air of expectancy staunchly greeted her as the door swung open. It did not surprise her to see her in the least; not even though she'd been out of the office all day because of a completely made-up illness that she probably went into too much detail about in her email. Then again, maybe Stella never read it- nobody responded, so maybe nobody read it.

"Wasn't sure you'd still come since you had some version of typhoid today," Stella retorted sardonically. She'd obviously read the email and, just as equally obvious, didn't believe a word of it. Rachel started dwelling on it; worrying that others read it and knew she was lying as well until Stella shattered her internal dialogue with an announcement. "Come on in. We want to get started right away since there is going to be a twist in today's activities." Rachel searched Stella's face for any kind of insight into what that twist might be, but there was nothing. Truly, honestly, nothing- just a blank void where they should have been at least a remnant of a passing emotion. She didn't know how she could do it- but then again, she supposed that came within the whole being a sadist territory. Rachel realized at that very moment she'd never be a dominant person; she was a good faker, pretender if you will, but she didn't and would never have the capability of showing nothing...

"Ok, sounds good. Let me just take my shoes off here..."

"No need, you're going to want those on today. I am glad to see my assumption that you'd be wearing heels was correct. That's perfect, fucking perfect!" Stella's eyes briefly lit with amusement in herself. "It's gonna be sooooo much more of a challenge this way."

A very confused Rachel followed a very vague Stella down the basement steps into what Rachel liked to think of as the sex lab. Yes, dungeon was accurate for most likely everyone else that shared the space with Madam Madsen, but not her. This whole thing was like one large experiment in her mind. One where she could test the waters in pools she'd never been allowed to swim in. Her quaint floral heels tick, tick, ticked against the floors; their rhythm turned and twisted into a melody fitting for the presumed next scene.

Stella turned back to make sure her Sub was following her the way she should be; she reached out, taking Rachel by the wrist and leading her to what she could only guess was the surprise twist she'd been warned about. Looming ahead was a sterile, black and white treadmill - a newer, high-end model with a digital screen showing a petite, overly muscular blond yapping away at an invisible audience. Her voice was rather invisible too, as Stella had her on mute.

"Damn woman never shuts up; it's better this way," Stella said while pointing to the fact that the woman was forced to play on silent. Another subordinate in the room for Stella to humiliate and belittle. Fascinating just how well the whole damn thing worked. "We're going to get your heart rate up *before* we even begin. I think it will help you reach orgasm a lot faster, and I want to know just how fast you can run in those heels." Stella pulled a miniature whip from behind her back and snapped it at the back of Rachel's heels. "Let's get those pumps pumping and those ankles bleeding. Hop up and start running."

Rachel did as she was told. She was unsure about the process and whether it really would help her with her waning o-face, but she knew better than speak up in life. Her mother taught her as much:

Do as you're told and you will be told to do things you actually enjoy doing someday, my sweet girl. The sooner you learn that the less I have to hurt you. The less we all will have to.

She imagined her legs blurring into a pair of wheels. It took a minute or two to get used to running with your foot in a tight, elevated angle, but she got the hang of it - she was rocking at it even. But then there was another added element that threw her a loop- more like a stumble. Stella was wrapping her neck with a spiked collar and attached a long leather leash to the end. The cunt was walking her dog... Rachel being the dog. This really pissed her off - she was seething inside while trying to maintain her perfect smile on the outside. She hated the fact that Stella referred to her as a dog at work, but bringing it into their client, DOM relationship was going too far.

And then she felt it. She was wet, both in her mouth and in her panties. There was only one other time in her life where she had foamed at the mouth - it was during one of her destructive foster stays. The dad wasn't a fan of little girls, he would tell her, but he wasn't a fan of anything that walked and talked and had a vagina. He had pushed her against her foster brother's bedroom wall because he thought she'd stolen something out of his eldest son's bedside drawer. He told her he *knew* she'd taken it- it was a natural instinct for unloved brats like her- self- and he was done asking nicely for her to give it back. At her age, it wasn't likely that she'd even know what the missing item was- she did, but that was beside the point. She hadn't taken it because... ew, gross. What in the world would she want with a fleshlight?

As for the slip and slide down below- that seemed to happen at the least convenient of times. The moments where it made little sense, ideologically or morally. No matter how many times she told her body to stop, it never listened. Nobody took herself seriously; apparently, not even her own loins.

Stella's hiss slithered through a backdoor and got first into her ear-drums, then into her mind. "Bark, bitch. Bark."

A throaty, mid-sized bark flew from her gyrating jawline. She looked around the room expecting to see an actual dog in the room with her, but then the yapping came again and she recognized the hideousness was coming from her. She was the epitome of pathetic. The metallic points encircling her collar dove into the front of her throat. Stella was pulling on the leash... hard. "Shut up, bitch. Shut the fuck up. You bark ONLY when I tell you to." More dribble between her legs.

Time seemed to seize and everything seemed to go black, well light blue actually. Rachel had never *seen* color, and only a color, before. She'd heard of people literally seeing red when they get mad; she'd never experienced it herself, not red, nor any other color. But it was happening now, and it was like a time warp. Anything that might have happened in her blue haze wasn't anything she could control and most likely didn't want to.

The next thing she knew, she was sitting up on the operation-like table buttoning the top buttons of her shirt. Stella was nowhere to be seen, and she felt light- like she was floating on a cloud of light. Hopping down from the tabletop, she turned and immediately jumped. Stella had moved a lounge chair from her upstairs living room to the basement and was sitting directly behind where she'd been lying only moments ago. She was a massive, cushiony roadblock securing the pathway from unwanted travel.

"Did I scare you, dear?" Madam Madsen's tone had dropped into a mothering one. It almost held an ounce of concern, or at least forced concern, in it.

"Yes, actually. You scared the shit out of me." Rachel hardly ever swore, but it seemed to flow so freely now. "When the hell did you find time to move that chair down here, and how did you do it by yourself?"

"I'm a lot stronger than I look. I can lift almost three times my weight, which is also a lot heavier than I look too. I am tall- so I can get away with having a full-sized rack, ass, and hips. As for when I moved it while you were orgasming..." Stella's mouth curled into a Tresher Cat grin and her eyes sparkled with pride.

"That can't be possible. That would have taken you at least eight to ten minutes to move that by yourself down those stairs, no matter *how* buff you are."

"Yup, that sounds about right. You have a good sense of time, dear."

"Yeah, fucking right. I'm young, but I wasn't born yesterday. I have never heard of *anyone* orgasming for that long- it's gotta be like world record status if it were true."

"No, it's actually not the world record. Not even close actually, but we can keep working you in that direction. How do you feel, you little sinner, you?" Stella seemed to know all the right buttons to push with her. She didn't hate it like she knew she should.

"I think I might have actually blacked out there for a bit. Refresh my memory of what all went down, will you?" Ms. Dobbs was feeling very much like a Miss at the moment. It was one hundred percent necessary that she return to some kind of formality in her life so she could reset some expectations for their new little relationship. Fully committing to the submissive role was work, even for her.

"I don't think it was technically a black-out. I mean, a medical professional would straighten you right out by educating you on the *true* meaning and implications of using that term. It can be quite dangerous for someone in my field to hear those words after 'sharing time together', if you get my drift." Stella found the defensive easily; secondhand to her natural state, really.

Rachel stared back blankly at her in sheer confusion. She did not get the drift, she didn't even see the drift, but apparently, she was stepping further and further into it the longer they spoke. Stella had fully left the body of Madam Madsen and was fully dressed in full-blown lawyer persona. "It sounds rapey, Rachel. And almost on the verge of accusatory. Neither of which makes me feel comfortable. Does saying those things make you feel better? Excusing yourself from the shame and fucked up guilt you feel about enjoying it all? Who pounded these sex-hating, self-loathing, body-shaming notions into that pea brain of yours? Is that why you are the way you are in the office?"

Whoa, what the actual fuck...Stella had come unhinged and was teetering on the edge of psycho with Rachel. She shifted in her mismanaged anxiety; uncrossing her legs, slouching at the waist, arms hanging uselessly at her sides like a used-up, rag doll. Leaving her power stance behind, she felt her actual feelings for the first time since she could remember. All of them came flooding back. Fear of failure, abandonment, disappointment, and disappointing others. Shame filled her to the brim until it leaked over the edges and poured down the sides of her invisible walls - spilling all over the floor, her tears flooding the gray concrete below her. Her uncontrollable sadness, the pools of salty-wasted waters, reminded her of the scene from Disney's animated *Alice in Wonderland*. It had been her favorite as a child; it gave her hope because you could escape from your life, your circumstances, your family (or lack of one) through a world you create of your own. It only took seeing the film one or two times before she vowed to her five-year-old safe that she too would one day do what Alice did. And she'd be all the better for it.

But she'd forgotten that promise, that hope for herself as she got older. When did she give up on herself and let her mother take full control again? How old was she when she stopped fighting for herself - the soul that was wavering behind her tired bones? And why was she just realizing that the life she was pushing so hard to get was the one she was *told* she should have? The one she *should* want.

Rachel hated being a pit bull dressed over in florals- hiding like a wolf in sheep's clothing to steal the next inch ahead in the road. She wanted none of this shit. She wanted to be a nurse; a caring, compassionate mother-figure guiding her adopted children of any age back to health. She knew she could never handle children of her own- she never wanted to be tied down by anything so whiny and unappreciative, but acknowledging her deep desire to be needed and valued by others.... well nursing would have fit all of those pegs for her. Now she is standing, half-dressed, mascara running down the sides of her cheeks, staining the shoulders of her favorite floral tunic. What a mess. Just like her entire life.

"I'm so sorry Stella, that's not at all what I was trying to imply. In fact, it's probably better if I don't know the details. Knowing my stupidity, I would probably ruminate on how dirty and bad this makes me feel as a person. I know, before you say anything, I know none of that is true but you're right about another thing... you're right about a lot of things, actually.... it was my mother who taught me to hate my body and its natural urges. All of them." Rachel's eyes shot to the ground with that last statement. She had been blocking so many of those urges over the years- never allowing herself to feel good with the types of people she naturally did. What a waste of time- what a burden she has been to the world, her colleagues, and herself.

"Well, I think you should know that you told me to finger you. So I did. You squirted. Sprayed across the room. That's when the screaming started. At first, I thought you might be in pain so I pulled out but you yelled at me to put it back in. So I did," Rachel's eyes refilled stock, and alligator tears came a-rolling out again. "Jesus Christ, Rachel. You gave me permission to take care of you and you liked it. So. Fucking. What?"

Rachel sniffed the snot that was threatening to peek its ugly head out from the bottom of her nostrils back, shooting it all the way to the back of her throat. She coughed and cleared her eyes enough to open them. She could barely face the idea of making eye contact with Stella, but she lifted her head and muttered, "Does this prove everything I have always feared? Am I a lesbian?"

The air split open with laughter. Rachel had never heard Stella cackle before- this was yet another side to the Rubik's Cube that was Madam Madsen. "Of fucking course not. A hand is a hand girl- I am pretty sure if any pair of fingers that know what they're doing down there could do it for you."

"But, there are other things that happen... like the work up to it all." Rachel felt embarrassed by her lack of vocabulary for the content of which they were speaking. She was starting to feel her walls rebuilding from imaginary straight to brick. She knew she'd have to talk quickly before they closed back around her.

"Like the fact that you are interested in women? Or maybe the one about them turning you on? Now those things may lend more to lesbianism, but you still could be bi..." The glint in Stella's eyes as she made these suggestions to Rachel was just another reminder that she *liked* getting her goat with suggestions. But Rachel needed someone to do it- to bring her back out from the center of the mortared blocks. So she let her.

"Yes. I started having these feelings...attractions to women when I was a pre-teen, but my mother told me it was unGodly, unnatural, and heathehenistic. I agreed with her, still do, but I know I can't continue living this life the way I have in this body anymore. I need my mindset to change- reverse itself to how it used to be when I was younger. But the only thing I have ever used to reset my thoughts is repentance... if I don't have that anymore, what do I have to help me through accepting this new...no, not new, *real*, version of myself?"

A slow smile spread across Stella's soft succulent lips- she was the real wolf in sheep's clothing here. Stella was the badass version of Little Red Riding Hood where she is the Big Bad Wolf that ate her Grandma right up and then went straight to those plump little piggies' homes and blew them all over with her rage. Stella had slipped her red cloak back on in the past five minutes, ready to share the secret of her angst with one of her least favorite people in the world... Rachel, the oh-so-annoying Goldilocks.

"You can still get to personal freedom through repenting- it's just a new kind of sin you are asking for forgiveness for. Luckily for you, I have the perfect opportunity for you.... it involves helping another that has lost himself along the way. He's delusional, blind, and probably dying - he needs help caring for himself and figuring out how to become his next version...kind of like you. I think you could learn a lot about yourself by serving as his part-time caretaker for the next couple of weeks. He needs your help and frankly, girl, you need this chance to unfuck yourself up."

It was perfect. Rachel's tears disappeared. Exuberance. Lightness. It was time to get the details, so she could get started.

Tom

They had left him there; used, abused, almost murdered, and now abandoned. That fucking bitch will rot for this. Remi, a closet sociopath, was out free, loose, wild in the world after she'd just stolen his light. Sure, he had a heartbeat and all the movement to his limbs had returned, but his eyes... those didn't seem to be making a comeback. How was he supposed to live as he knew it without his sight? His job... fucking impossible. Driving... never again. His playtime...game over. The whole goddamn console felt broken without his eyes. Most of what he enjoyed about sex was visual; his dick slamming against some tight, toned thing.

Faces didn't really matter to him after her; only the neck down from then on. Those bouncing blues took a piece of his soul from him; he'd never give another human being the chance to do the same again. All the eyes were just portals to pain, plotting their next takeover. They were lonely, desperate; overwhelmingly, pathetic. It took practice to alter the natural path his eyes instinctively wanted to take when meeting someone, anyone, for the first time. If he could avoid direct eye contact during the first "per-chance" meeting, he maintained self-ownership, like a wild animal refusing to be broken.

Perhaps losing his sight would free him from the reins he'd been holding onto more as of late. No chance to be sucked in. No chance for them to create an internal dialogue about the "story" he was telling them with *his* eyes. These stories usually started differently from one another depending on how the two of them had met, but they always ended the same... happily ever after.

Yeah, fucking right- there was no such thing; especially not with the train wrecks he targeted.

They were almost always guaranteed drama, but such easy prey. He had mastered that category of unmarriables. But now with his handicap why not shoot higher? If he could get away with it. The next realm of women was much more emotionally stable and usually a little less needy... not as hot as the crazies, but fuck, if he couldn't see them anymore, what did it matter?

But first, before any more hoes, he'd need to get out of his bed, figure out what to wear, and get to work and do it all without being able to see. Anything. Nothing. He was a persistent bastard; if anyone could pull this blind shit off and well, he could.

Sitting up in his bed without assistance was something the persistent bastard would need to accomplish first. He'd lost of lot of muscle strength. What the fuck had Remi given him?

Whatever it was, she had to have planted it down deep in that Chinese food- deeper than the layers of fake wonton bites, water chestnuts, and MSG. He hadn't tasted foul play, but was that even possible? Did poison even have a taste? Admittedly, he was a blackened, damned soul, but even he hadn't stooped to the level of poison before, so he hadn't the slightest clue how the shit was supposed to taste. He realized he might have been better off dabbling in it now, but woulda, coulda, shoulda... he just needed to get out of that goddamn bed.

"Hello?" A young, intimidated-sounding voice chimed into Tom's ears. Was he imagining it? Was it the poison messing with his brain still? Nope, not likely because there she was again.

"Tom? My name is Rachel, and I was told you might require some help this morning. Can I come in?"

Sure, why the hell not? Oops, he'd said that inside his head...now to open his mouth and say it aloud.

"Yeah, I don't know who you are or what service you're with, but come the fuck on in." The sores in his throat pulsated as he raised his voice. That hurt. His head did too. He hadn't noticed until he'd spoken outside himself that he had a splitting headache. The sound of old-school windbreakers swooshing their way into his room filled his eardrums, and the pictures started drawing themselves inside his mind; behind those closed-off visionary ventricles, there was an imagination the size of Texas. He'd always had it but rarely used it as an adult...

Isolation was over. Time to dust off the mold and mildew and give her a good shine. Secretly, he hated he was smiling at the stranger; seduction had become second nature, and even now, blind, unaware of what was happening and whom with, he couldn't turn off his magnetic desires to first charm, then overtake. What if she was complete fuggo-chances were high that she was; especially if she was a paid caregiver. The only good-looking nurses were in the movies and those pretending to be ones for Halloween. He forced his lips to uncurl and managed to attain what he assumed looked like a more serious, concerned, pained face. There, that felt like a better fit for both himself and the situation he'd been forced into.

He heard the swishing pants stop abruptly and in its place felt a hand reach out and lay flat upon his forehead. "You don't feel feverish, but would you mind if I took your temp anyway, just to be sure?" The stranger had a sweetness to her voice; he could hear that now that she was sitting next to him.

"Orally or anally? Yes to either," He cringed at his own inability to turn it off. Just try to be a fraction of everything you know you are capable of. "I'm just kidding. Just tell me when to open my mouth and when to close it. I'm not sure where you come from or if they told you I recently lost one hundred percent of my sight, but that's what the fuck's happening here today." His irritation with Remi was returning to a full boil. He could feel the steam rising from his belly but swallowed it back. He needed any help he could get and barking at whoever this person was would not get him any closer to getting back to work and his *real-life* (whatever was salvageable anyway).

With no sign of laughter, Rachel simply replied, "Now," and shoved the thermometer in. This Tom guy was a piece of work. Stella was right that senility wasn't a good look on him. Like most older males, they get brazenly crude when their mind leaves them. She was quick to realize that this douche was no exception. Three beeps cut into her thoughts," 98.6- perfect temp. Can you remember what your name is today?"

What the fuck was wrong with this chick- he was blind, not dumb. "Yeah, I think I still know who I am."

"And that would be..."

"Tom Williams. I am a thirty-four-year-old Caucasian male born to a complete waste of breath of a mother and an invisible father." Why was he opening up to this woman? Was the trauma affecting him already? Was it triggering him into some kind of sick weakling that couldn't filter himself anymore?

"Sorry, no. You aren't Tom Williams today, Benjamin. I know Tom is someone you like to escape into being, but you are Benjamin Blank, and I am here because you are very sick. I owe my boss...er... friend a favor and this is what she asked me to do for you."

"Who's your boss, friend, lady boss person...whatever? Who are they and who the fuck is Benjamin?"

"Oh, well, I'm not supposed to release that type of information -who hired me, that is. All you need to know is that there is someone that loves you a great deal out there and what's to make sure you are being taken care of the next couple of weeks until someone more permanent can be assigned to you or you pass..."

"Pass? Pass what? What did that fucking bitch put inside me to make me this way? You know *she*, your fucking boss lady, did this to me. Remi Nash did *this* to me! Feeling like a saint anymore, are you?" Tom couldn't believe the nerve of this gal. First, she comes in and doesn't even give him the slightest giggle for his good humor, then she tells him he doesn't know he is, and that she isn't allowed to divulge who hired her?! Another day, another cunt bag.

"Well, I can honestly say I do not know who a Remi Nash is sir, she's not the person who hired me. I assure you the person who did cares about so much and wishes they could be here themselves but just couldn't take the time off work. Now, as for who Benjamin Blank is- that's you. You, Benjamin, are thirty-six years old and I was told born and raised in Los Angeles. You have no siblings but had two wonderful, loving parents that were lost too soon in an automobile accident. Does any of this sound familiar yet? And it's ok if it doesn't Benjamin- we have all week together to jog that memory of yours. And I'm a fantastic runner."

What a horrible fucking joke- great, a girl with a dry sense of humor, no innate ability to listen, and frankly, it seemed like spiraling esteem. The bitch almost seemed to whisper whenever she started speaking to him. He wasn't a baby who needed soothing, or a confused, senile old man that needed his ego patted- he was a victim of attempted murder that kept his pulse but lost his most appreciated senses.

"Nope. None of that is correct. In fact, I don't think you're even in the right place- I don't have anyone that loves me immensely or would be here to take care of me themselves or whatever bullshit you think you know about the relationship the person that hired you and I supposedly have. My name is Tom Williams, I work for Donaldson in the city- have for about eight years, and was born and raised outside of Detroit Michigan, and I have no one that truly loves me- because well, no one truly *knows* me." Shit, that all felt awful to say aloud but also somewhat freeing. For the first time in a long time, he was being honest with someone other than himself. He probably couldn't give two shits about her in return, but that was beside the point.

"Hm, well you do look a *little* like him, I guess," this crazy lunatic Rachel was an insane mad-woman. What had she just said to him? "I mean, I found this old LinkedIn picture of a Tom Williams that worked at Macy's as a business analyst- there's definitely a resemblance, but you are clearly *not* him."

"Oh yeah, and why do you say that? Is it because his nose is fatter than mine? I got a nose job a year ago and never updated my profile picture."

"Yeah, that and your cheekbones are completely different than his. And... it looks like his lips are a different shape and size than yours." Rachel responded without putting too much thought into the potential of starting an all-out argument with the guy.

"Again, just a little facial reconfigure I did a while back. All plastic surgery. Nothing more than that- it's me. Look at our eyes- they'll be the same." Tom had her there, he just knew it. But his heart sank with what she told him next.

"Benjamin, you're cross-eyed. It's close to impossible to imagine what they'd look like if they weren't, like this Tom guys. I get it, there are a lot of similarities in the looks category, but you can't be Tom Williams, you just can't be..."

"And why the fuck is that? Because whatever fucking poison that bitch gave me snapped my eye muscles? Because you can't even imagine what I would look like by your definition of 'normal'? Because...be- cause... what?!" Spit was flying from his bottom lip; this only happened when he was losing the last strands of control over himself. It hadn't happened since college- since the day he'd seen her last. The day she thought she could just jump back in and have a re-do- like he was some kind of toy that could be bought, played with, thrown away, and recycled into the very same little toy to start the cycle over again with.

"No, Benjamin. It's because Tom Williams is dead. I found his obituary online; he died pretty recently too..."

Trio | Remi, Stella, & Myra

Meet-Up with Sam Feeler,
The Miraculous Healer

The beautifully bright and always effervescent Sam Feeler hurried the lovelies into his home, making them all feel as welcome in their current condition as physically possible. Meeting with Sam was Myra's idea, even though he was Remi's friend. Myra had heard about Sam Feeler, the miraculous healer, through a grapevine of both artists and addicts. A LOT of her friends were his biggest fan; praising his other-worldly abilities to read energies, find their broken roots, and uproot them out of the ground long enough to let new oxygen in to heal their soiled wounds. Amazing shit really... Myra couldn't have been more exhilarated when she found out that Remi was one of his best gal pals. Not something Myra, or probably any other person on the same planet of these two oddly paired amigos, would have been able to guess. But whatever and wherever the bond between the two of them- the Universe was blessing them in its own unique and intricate way.

As Remi passed Sam at the doorframe to his highly unkempt, loud, and eccentric apartment, their eyes latched onto one another, with Sam consuming the bits of indigestibles Remi's were feverously releasing. No spoken words were necessary here; Sam knew he was going up against something much larger with a mountainous shadow enshroud-ing all of his friends' natural light. He could sense through her that she was struggling to keep hold of the one last morsel of goodness she'd been able to save after what seemed to be an excruciating twenty-four hours. Whatever had happened- it was fresh, filthy, and threatening to completely envelop Remi.

Once in the sitting circle, he'd mapped out with laps of red wall paint he had left over from painting his prayer room. He instructed them all to take a seat with a simple nod of his head. His arms spread out to his sides in a silent greeting- his hands shook, the vibrations slithering up his arms, straight to his chest where they hovered over his heart. They were all heartbroken- everyone in the room but him. A flash of light filled his eyes temporarily blinding him... that was something new. Not knowing what it meant, he decidedly proceeded with caution, figuring to keep the short-lived flare to himself until the moment was right to ask the question. It wasn't until everyone was seated and had stopped their nervous fidgeting that Sam proceeded.

"So, I recognize my good friend Miss Remi here. I believe you are Myra," Sam said looking to the left of Remi in the circle of trust he had, unknowingly to the women, formed. Myra's red hair bobbled slightly with a shake of acknowledgment. "And you must be Stella." Sam's eyes glided all the way to the right, passing over Remi, who was seated in the middle of the trio. Why was he not surprised that his good ole' buddy Miss Insecure would be the glue holding these two *very* different entities together? Sam simply watched and read the energy that was flashing through Stella at the speed of light. There were so many colors and so much confusion in their direction. They seemed lost, misman-aged, anxious, and overwhelmingly chaotic. And there was a *lot* of red-which meant anger in most cases. There was no doubt Stella was a fierce one- a genuine force to be reckoned with. Her domineering energy was swallowing the room. He felt threatened, but he couldn't let *her* know that, or she'd run wildly away with it the power he essentially just handed her.

"So, ladies. I understand there has been some recent trauma in all of your lives- I get the feeling that the pain happened when separated from one another. Am I correct in that?" The trio nodded silently. "Remi, I feel you're struggling between the light and the dark right now- over half your energy is dancing in the darkness while the remaining light seems to be wavering in the wind like a torn and tattered flag of surrender. What war are you fighting? Your soul is being badly battered? I get the instinct that you might need to sit the next few rounds out..."

Sam didn't mean to let his personal relationship and interest seep in so much as he did here. But Remi and he were bonded; first as friends and now for the rest of eternity as parents. You didn't think Sam would say no to Remi when she asked *him* to be the donor for her IUI did you? Not a chance. Sam loves Remi for all that she was and everything she would be as a Mom... now clarifying if these feelings were romantic or not was a whole other web to traipse through.

"Well, that's not an option for her. She's already dropped the ball and now I'm the one cleaning up her mess, so sitting out or, whatever you want to think of it as, is off the table." Stella snapped. Sam saw her irritable aura rising to the top of the hologram image whenever his eyes scanned even a foot away from her. He himself needed to retreat from attack, apparently. He would tread more lightly and refocus his feelings onto Myra- a much calmer, more secure artistic type.

There's a lot to like about this one... mostly light, artistic, free-flowing vibes here, but there definitely were some kinks in her camber, probably resulting in uncharacteristic depression from time to time and most definitely walls prohibiting full creative potential. Without having too much hidden below the surface he knew Myra was somebody that could be trusted to be honest and up-front with just about anyone on this and any other plane.

"Myra, how are you feeling about everything? Of course, I know nothing more than what you shared with me when setting this little tae-on-tae up, but I'd like to know how you're recovering from the stress of the situation?"

Sam had only been told the bare minimum- the three women discovered that they were all dating the same white dude with a perfect smile, ghastly facial hair that came and went with the wind apparently, and the clearest green eyes. Without meeting this Tom fella, Sam would say the way the ladies described him that he could have been the stereotypical all-white wearing, polo popping, chummy jerk-off that could be found in any and every country club in the US.

Handsome? Sure.

Of any depth or stimulating intellectualism? No.

It was extremely difficult to quiet his inner voice that scolded the women for getting into it with any male that fit this description - besides typically being the same brand of bland, they were usually oversexed horndogs that couldn't stay committed to save their lives. But, Sam wasn't there to judge, nor did he want to, so he pushed these thoughts to the furthest corner of his mind trying to evade them. He realized Myra had already started answering the question he'd forgotten that he'd asked.

Don't be a tool yourself Sam and get out of your own thoughts- this woman is opening up to you. And did she ever...

"I guess what I'm trying to say is that I'm struggling more than I initially thought I would when we first discovered that Tom had been two, well actually, three-timing us. It could be more- we're the only other ones we *know* about but that obviously doesn't mean there couldn't be more of us out there. For me, the hardest part of it all is letting go of the idea that he actually cared for me. I feel like a fool, really. A used-up wench that let her heartstrings puppeteer her around instead of letting her brain do the operating for her. I've never really trusted love and always kind of doubted that it existed...with Tom we were getting so close; my root system was transforming before me and I got tricked. Taken advantage of...completely used. Like all of us," Myra said, looking at the other two female love triangle participants.

"Most of these ideals came from my childhood when my dad just didn't come home one day. He just disappeared, never to be heard from by neither myself nor my mother again. For years, I've told myself various horror stories of something crazy happening to him that prevented him from coming home to us- usually some badass or heroic tale where he'd been trying to protect his family by not returning. You know, like some stupid idea where he didn't want to lead gangsters back to his family so they wouldn't slit our throats or some shit." Myra paused. Out of her purse, she casually raised a rolled joint to her lips and lit the bottom, holding her inhale long enough for the sensation to take over her thoughts maker and heart center. This was all very hard for her to say. Everyone in the room knew that. *Almost* everyone sympathized with her.

"Tom was just so perfect. He was everything my dad hadn't been. He cared about the planet and his own personal carbon footprint. He supported women in their fight for equal pay - I mean, our souls sang in unison at some of those rallies. We were so in-tune. Now knowing it was all a lie- all fake- I think I could hate him if I allowed myself to. What a fucking mastermind really... to have orchestrated this whole separate identity, and for what? Just to have sex with me? For another notch in his belt? How demented do you have to be or maybe, how unhappy in your own skin? That took a lot of planning, prepping, researching, and acting... where does this guy from? What kind of life did he have before all of us that made him this way?

Shit, now I'm starting to almost feel sorry for the bastard and with all the challenges he's facing now. Part of me wishes we could take it all back and undo what we did- but there's not really a way to do it without getting caught. I mean, I know because I did some deep Googling at the college's law library and well, after chatting with Stella for a bit, I am convinced. A TRUE believer that the BAND-AID has already been ripped off so there's no way to prevent the sting now."

Myra looked up about to take another toke when she realized the shocked and disappointed glares coming from both sides of her.

She had said too much.

More than Sam had been made privy of and there was no going back on that either. What could she say, she was an artist? Creative types are known to be well-connected with their emotions and are rarely afraid to express them- that was the whole meaning behind the purpose of art. Why they hadn't cut her off when she had clearly climbed the stairs to the diving board before she jumped off was a mystery... one she'd have to think about later when she wasn't stoned. Things were too confusing, even blurry for her at the moment. Another puff would help intensify the fog and save her from those incriminating stares.

"I think Myra has shared some incorrect statements here. Fake news, if you will? Though I really appreciate your opening up to the group Myra, I think we need to get things back on track a little with the whole reason we came to you in the first place. Sam, as you can imagine, there's a lot of heartaches here in this little group and we need your help getting some of the bad ju-ju off our chests and out of our minds. I know you help all types of people. Is there a prayer or something you can say or do to help clear our energies?" Remi nervously chimed in.

Sam was not in the least surprised about Myra's blatant honesty or even Remi's anxious cover-up. What he was a bit surprised by was Remi's lack of faith in him and the work he did.

Remi and Sam have been friends for years and over those years he'd prided himself on his ability to share his passion and education in quantum physics. She'd always taken an interest, which didn't guarantee buy-in, he knew that, but Remi had at least used to be open-minded to it all. She was different now- she had been changing over the past year, he'd seen it but never dare say anything.

Now an alien sat inside the cross-legged corpse of what used to be his most trusted friend. She was gone. Vanished and the alien holding the reins from inside her was ugly. Dark, loathsome, vengeful. Ugly. He had to help her but he wasn't sure how yet. Or if there was still time to. But if they were going to raise a child together, he'd have to ensure his other half wasn't fighting for the Devil himself, which was the current inkling he was getting from Remi's slanderous negativity.

"Yeah, sure Remi. The best way to get to the other side of this is through it. So that's what we need to do here today - we need to go through emotions, thoughts, fears, all the above in order to release some of the negative energies for ones that are more loving, self-accepting, forgiving, and overall much more in balance with your being. Balance is everything in nature - with animals, mother nature, and humans alike... it's all about striking a balance in our chi's. Think about it like this, we want our energetic inputs to match our outputs and vice versa."

"That sounds poetic, but I don't think we are all as open to sharing our feelings as Myra is." Remi somewhat clapped back at Sam. "I guess I can only speak for myself, though. Stella, are you comfortable divulging everything that has gone on the past few months with Sam, a complete stranger to you?"

"Nope, I'm good, really. I wasn't even on board in coming here. I don't have any sins to admit- I didn't kill anyone or try to." What the fuck was wrong with Stella's filter today? All of their filters? Was Remi the only one thinking straight? Boy, that would be a complete one-eighty from the transgressions a few days back.

The thickening tensions in the room were getting Samari sword deep. Everyone seemed to say a little more than they planned to, but that's what happened when people were around him. Sam was an Empath, so folks naturally and sometimes inexplicably opened up to him. He was usually fine with it, especially if it was in the proper setting like the four of them were then, but his comfort level was slipping by the minute. He was picking up more than he wanted to know and it wasn't all just from what was being said right in front of him. He could see, hear it, taste it; it was so palpable he almost thought he could touch it. Something grim had happened here- *with* these women, not to them. He heard their voiced pains of distrust and abandonment, but what he felt was how they'd let their hatred boil up and over- burning everyone and everything in its path. Sam needed to stay out of the way or he too would come up marred for life.

"Understood. Don't agree. But understood. You're the boss...all of you and whatever you're willing to say and do is your choice. Just know that every choice you make in life has an innate consequence. Not all consequences are bad, but those that follow careless scheming to avenge the heart usually are. It may seem like the victor has the last laugh and lives on in a 'happily ever after' scenario, but that couldn't be further from the truth. Those that assert themselves in the business of the natural order of things suffer at the same end as their victim. So, remember before you make any frank decisions about your devastating love lives, think about what it may feel like standing at the podium and taking the oath at your trial. A trial that could bury you for the rest of your life if you choose incorrectly."

Sam looked up just in time to see Remi infamously wringing her tired hands and one of Stella's presumed go-to defenses... the dreaded, powerless eye-roll. He'd hit a note with them; now what they did with it was completely in their hands.

As Myra laid her fatty down and opened her mouth to speak again, Remi fiercely interrupted. "Ok, well, I don't think there's anything you can *really* do here to help us. As always, I appreciate you and our friendship, but I think we got as far as can go here today. Ladies..." Remi stood and held out her hand as if reaching for a young child needing guidance to safely cross the road. The other two silently followed suit, neither of them accepting the outward hand but stood to exit, anyway.

"Well, thank you ladies for coming by. I hope after you have some time to put thought into what was said here today, it sinks in a little deeper and means a little more because old friends and newfound friends alike, you all mean a great deal to me."

Sam walked them to the door. Then out of it.

After closing it behind his guests, he sunk to the ground with a searing pain in his head. When he opened his eyes, he saw nothing but the blackness behind his own eye sockets. What had they done to that man? What was someone or something trying to tell him?

And then, with his eyes still open wide and the blackness floating around him, he saw it. A bound man on the floor of a storage closet somewhere. He was leaning to one side and then rocking over to vomit on the other. He was weeping. He was afraid. He was alive- barely. She had done this to him. This man must be Tom.

His friend was falling deep inside the ravines of Hell and he was realizing this wasn't her first time. She'd been sucked into the shadow world before- he saw that now. The image of Tom slithered away and was replaced with a young Remi spinning and sobbing in circles in an all-pink bedroom; slowly she faded into a young woman who stood looking over a woman's lifeless body on a sidewalk.

Remi was a killer.

She had killed once before and she'd tried again.

Sam felt sick to his stomach; his vision had returned, but his strength to overcome had not.

Tom

That Rachel girl had been coming over the past few days helping Tom get his bearings around his apartment- in constant darkness. She was nice enough; some days nicer than others. On the off days, her demeanor was different, she was rougher with him and spoke only when spoken to. He figured something was bothering her, but he didn't care enough to ask. He had his own problems - too fucking many of them for him to pry into some sad little girl's world that mattered nothing to him. All he wanted to do was get back to his normal life with a routine of work, eat, fuck, sleep, while making Remi pay for her sins.

Rachel arrived at her usual time of 8:30 AM... how did he know? Well, because that first day she'd been there, she'd set up an hourly alarm with a coordinating chime. The clock was meant for blind people like him or old, hard-of-hearing fuckers that were more senile than they were breathing.

At eight o'clock, there would be eight chimes followed by a beep so that he knew it was AM, not PM... PM had no beep after it, just the chimes. He heard her slam her bags down harder than she usually did on the living room coffee table. She must be having a bad day again.

Oh goody.

He'd like to say that he didn't need her, but in all reality, he was getting nervous about the idea of him *not* having her assistance by the week's end. His fears were interrupted by an overly charged sigh coming from the corner of his bedroom. Rachel was in there now with him; ready to help him into the shower, no doubt.

"Good morning Rachel. How are you today?" A formality he felt he should ask, though he couldn't care less about the response.

"You can stop the formalities now- I know you don't give two shakes of a rat's ass about my answer to that question." she snapped back. Rachel had never called Tom out on his insincerities, nor was she apt to swear at him. She must really be pissed today. Tom decided it was best to keep his mouth shut since he was still rather reliant on her. Instead, he forced a cheesy grin on his face and silently worked his body to what he felt to be the edge of the bed.

"Shower time then, I assume." With that, Tom undressed, holding his dirty sleepwear in an outstretched hand for Rachel to launder.

"Oh, no you don't, mister, not anymore," Tom frantically started redressing in his clothes, feeling suddenly very ashamed of his assumed nudity. He could feel after a few quick seconds that he'd been trying to put his underwear over his head- what a laugh he must be to her.

But why the hell did he care? Her tone? The change in her demeanor. Did that make him care all of a sudden?

"No, no. You can get undressed. You're right about it being shower time, but I am not taking your dirties from you anymore to clean. You can set them to the right of your bed. I moved your laundry basket there for you to put your soiled clothes in. You will need to learn to use the washer and dryer on your own by feel. I put some brail on the knobs so eventually, when you learn to read it, you can know what your booping and bopping."

Tom continued removing his clothes while pondering the differences he was sensing in his helper, Miss Rachel, that morning. She wasn't using words he'd ever heard her say, well not at least over the past four or five days and her voice sounded edgy, almost on the verge of tears. It was heavier. She felt heavier altogether.

"Understandable, Rachel," he said her name to confirm that it was really her. She didn't correct him or say anything different, so onward to the shower, he marched...more like groping the walls towards. He was starting to get a step count down for about how far away things were, his kingsize bed being the epicenter of his internal map. His hands glided over the tops of furniture and along the walls to reassure his path. He felt the door frame and took a sharp left. He suddenly felt the cool tiles of his bathroom floor beneath the soles of his feet as his toes gripped their way over to the open-stall shower. He'd never been so grateful for his modern taste; his finishings were spacious, open, and symmetrical...all things that helped a blind person get along.

The only downside to his mod deco was the sharp corners on *every-thing*. And all the glass. He was surprised with the fact that he hadn't concussed himself yet on any of those damn right angles or cracked his entire head open. Those angles had come in handy for fucking. Always having a place to put a leg up or balance someone or something on them.

He could feel his penis lifting slightly with the memories that were playing in his mind like a porno on the big screen. A hand, her hand, grabbed it... hard. He could feel the warmth of her breath on his cheek as she leaned in and whispered directly to him, "You're one sick fuck. Better take better care of who you let see you hard- it's not all that flattering on any man but you especially." She released her clutch on his junk and slithered backward away from him.

The way she spoke to him was so hateful; like she knew him and had a reason to be. Could it be Stella, the sadist he'd gotten himself entangled with? No, there's no way.

One, there's no way she'd have figured out his multi-player game; two- she probably wouldn't care or at least have any hard feelings about it if she *did* find out.

That's one great thing about sadists. Most of them aren't that interested in commitment, nor do they typically stay monogamous to only one person. And three- this chick sounded nothing like the throaty ex-smoker he assumed Stella to have been. Then again, Rachel's voice varied from day to day it seemed, but never to the depths and vibrato of that of Madam Madsen- now that was a woman who demanded a presence when she spoke. Her tone was always sharp, pitch slightly low with the slightest hint of a rasp at the back of her throat, but it was the natural sway of attitude and ear-suckling charisma that made her stand apart from any other voice he'd ever heard.

On her good days, Rachel seemed almost airborne she was so light. But on her not-so-good days, she was thicker, curvier, and more demanding. The overall voice was similar but there was a distinct difference that Tom had picked up over the past few visits: happy-go-lucky Rachel had a slight lisp when she said her s's and rude (also apparently crude) Rachel didn't. He continued to take notes as he felt his way into the shower, remembering to sidestep around the plastic toy box he kept handy for both his solo and partnered sexcascrubs - he hosted many a week, shit sometimes multiple a day. That little box of joy wouldn't go to waste; he assured himself that he'd be erect and humping again any day now.

Originally, he thought his first time back on the horse might be with Rachel but after her little comment, he was less sure about that. He scoped out both hot and cold water knobs, turning them into the on position. Feeling the water without seeing it was an entirely new sensation. Shocking at first but after both body and water temps met in the middle to find a comfortable balance, it was like he was experiencing a waterfall for the first time. He could feel every single drop pummel his skin separately and follow its sinking path along his body until it fell into the gurgling drain below.

Had it always sounded like that? Like a tornado whirling, collecting the day's dirt (in this case, almost a week's worth)? The daily details that usually get stuck in the muck and then left out for their defenses were much more mesmerizing than he could have ever imagined. As he poured the liquid body wash onto his hands, the same brand he'd been using for a decade probably, he could smell the hints of lavender it had always advertised but he'd never smelt before. The minute scrubbing beads felt like giants sanding gown the dead skin cells.

Everything was new. Everything felt, tasted, smelt, and sounded distinctly larger and more or less abstract. Was he having a stroke or was this sensory overload? Was it only going to be momentary, or would it last forever? He secretly hoped for the latter. It'd at least give him something to look forward to.

"Time to wrap it up in there. You still need to brush your teeth and get dressed so you can get into the office." Rachel's hand must have jabbed itself in between his torso and the shower because the therapeutic droplets abruptly halted. Even his pipes were shocked by how sudden the change was as they groaned, lurching back to their dehydrated state.

Tom silently vowed to them they'd never again get so dry, that he'd be back again tomorrow and the day after that and the one after that until... well, he died. He wasn't planning on going anywhere. Perhaps overconfident, but he *was* making stellar headway in this whole new world of being a blind man.

He was a master of his perception, which he knew firsthand was what became anyone and everyone's reality, so if he envisioned himself as a successful visionless chick magnet.

He was feeling good. But that, like his overindulgent shower, came to an abrupt halt when he made his way into the office.

———————

Rachel had gone with him for his first time back on the subway. She not-so-gently guided Tom through the process of putting more money on his MetroCard without the help of the booth attendant, how to fight through the crowds with his cane and locate the train doors, where to stand as a handicap, and of course, to be hyper-aware of the muffled overhead announcements.

Being able to push his eardrums past all the other bustling sounds and commotion in order to even hear the speaker, let alone understand what they were saying, was the most challenging of all the tasks. He'd missed his stop multiple times when he no longer had Rachel there to physically maneuver him around onboarding patrons and tugging him through it all for his departure. His head ached; he had never been so grateful to hear his footsteps against the freshly laid, smooth concrete sidewalk that led him directly to those familiar and friendly Donaldson doors.

Reaching into his back pocket, he retrieved the steely gray, genuine leather wallet he'd gifted himself a few weeks back and held it up to the digital card reader.

Access denied.

Let's try that again.

Access denied.

As he went to raise the cowhide coin purse to the reader again, a voice came over the speaker.

"I will buzz you in manually and meet you at the front reception desk. Thank you." Not a voice Tom had ever heard before; he made it a habit to avoid security officers, pigs on bikes, or porking around in cars whenever he could. It's not like he had a record or anything but his Mom and friends growing up sure as shit did so, needless to say, he had plenty of forced interaction with them throughout the years. He'd never met a cop he liked, let alone respected. He forced an enthusiastic grin on his face, waiting with bated breath for the d-bag to "greet him" at reception.

"Hi there sir, my name is Officer Dandy. I hope I am not offending you in any way but I think you might be trying to access the incorrect building. I see your cane and understand you are vision impaired, is that correct?" The security officer was shouting as he spoke with kit gloves.

This guy *knew* Tom was blind, not deaf, right?

Unfortunately for the *officer,* an offended Tom bit his tongue and nodded in response. "Ok well, sir, this is Donaldson's. So again, I think you're in the wrong place, so I will assist you back outside to your lady friend for you to figure out where it is you need to be, ok?"

What a fucking pompous, presumptuous asshat this guy was... assuming Tom was deaf, dumb, and blind because there was no way possible a blind man could work in such a prestigious place. Boy, was this fucker in for a treat when he learned that Tom not only worked there but was high enough up that he could probably have his sad-sack fired.

"No, thank you. My name is Tom Williams, and I have worked here for almost a decade now." Tom reached for his wallet once again and flung it open for the dumb shit to see.

"Hm. Well then, that's interesting. We haven't had those doors act up in years. Do you work for Lloyd or Barry up there?"

Tom was brimming with the words I-told-you-so inside but gave a one-word answer- that's all this guy deserved from him. "Lloyd."

After a terse phone call, Lloyd was standing in front of Tom in the lobby within a matter of minutes. Though Tom couldn't see him standing there, he recognized the stale scent of aging body oils and cheap whiskey. Lloyd was an eccentric oldie that enjoyed his top-shelf liquors almost as much as his extramarital affairs.

"Oh hi, Lloyd. I'm so glad you came down here to straighten this guy out," Tom's right hand lept forward to offer a shake of gratitude.

"Hello, Mr. Williams," Lloyd's voice was taught with an unnecessary mass of professionalism. "I think you need to do some 'straightening out' on your end as well. Thank you, Officer Dandy, for your vigilance, but I will take Mr. Williams to my office from here. You can let that young woman standing outside the doors know that she'll want to wait there for about fifteen minutes longer."

Tom felt Lloyd's handgrip the underside of his upper arm, guiding him to the elevator, no doubt. Tom also felt very confused- why was Lloyd calling him by his last name, and why was Rachel supposed to wait outside for him? He understood he had some explaining to do about his unannounced absence the past week, but he assumed that once his boss saw his current state, it would be water under the bridge. But everyone needs to *talk* about everything these days... Too much self-awareness, mindless and meaningless chatter. But he'd jump through Lloyd's hoops and maybe even get some sympathy gifts out of the ordeal.

Lloyd's hand released its grip as he gently pushed Tom into a familiar oversized office chair. Tom had spent hours sitting in that same chair yucking it up with the old bastard; he'd grown to know almost every stitch in its slightly stained, red upholstery and, without seeing, could warn the next guy of all the lumps in the back cushion and where they would feel them on their bodies the next day.

"Tom, I am a little unsure where to start here. There's been a lot of changes since I saw you last... I think it's been a little over a week since I've, any of us, heard from you. We tried calling, but the calls didn't seem to go through. For God's sake, I had my secretary call all the hospitals to see if you were laying half-dead in one. I almost sent her to your apartment to check on you, but I called your landlord instead. At least he could tell me you were sick... like really sick. So then I was confused if you were so sick... Why weren't you in a hospital somewhere? Why hadn't you called or emailed? Your landlord gave me the contact info for your girlfriend... of which I had *no* idea you had, to get an ETA. And that's where I learned Tom Williams was dead.

Well, then I started feeling that horrible guilt a person gets when they feel like they've been a shit. Here you were so ill, never said a word of it, *any* of it, and went off and died all by your lonesome. I stand corrected, with your life partner at your side. But then a fax came through, with your name but a different *you* attached to it. The paper was the official death notice for Tom Williams, but the photo was of somebody else. Well, now what?

I hired a P.I. is now what. And they found you living with a woman, Miss Rachel Dobbs, the woman outside the doors waiting for you right now. And she told me your real name was Benjamin Blank. She'd never heard of Tom Williams. Funny thing, my guy ran your info, and lo and behold you are NOT Tom Williams, Tom Williams *is* dead. You are Benjamin fucking Blank."

Lloyd paused.

Without being able to see his facial expression, Tom was unsure if he was allowing him to interject there or if he was pausing for dramatic effect.

Nope, drunkard Lloyd was back on his nonsensical bat-shit soapbox again.

"Of course, I was curious now. I googled Benjamin Blank, and I found little... no social media accounts, no LinkedIn, not a trace of you.

But for Tom Williams, there was an outdated LinkedIn with a similar-looking mug staring back at me - NOT you but close. Oh, and of course, page upon page of obituaries. Tom, Benjamin, whoever the fuck you are... I saw your obit, Tom Williams', that is. You are a very convincible Tom Williams, Benjamin, but you can't trick a mastermind. There are obvious differences physically...one being that Mr. Tom Williams of New York, New York- originally from Detroit, Michigan, is dead as a doornail. How the fuck did you do it? Why? Never mind, I don't want to get caught up in your bullshit, which I am sure the courts will already get my name entwined in it in the near future, anyway. "

Tom's heart was audibly pounding out of his chest; he was sure that if he could see, it would have visibly jumped from the carcass that was trying its damndest to restrain it. This couldn't be happening. The panic started bubbling up through his windpipes and wouldn't subside until he let it out, and when he did, it came out in the form of a scream.

"I can't seem to wrap my head around it all...you are either a criminal that stole someone else's identity for God knows how long, have a secret almost fiancé, and/or are terminally ill or are terminally faking-it... I don't know whether to even believe that the cane you brought with you today serves a purpose."

The room got still as the dead once again and Tom took it it was his time to speak- stand up for his character and deny it all because, well, it was *all* a lie... most of it anyway. He felt a short wave of air brush past his face. His head jerked back in response to the invisible attempt.

"Jesus Christ, you moved. You saw that. You're not even blind... you're faking that too. You poor, sad, piece of shit. What story did you come up with to explain this new 'phenomena'?"

Ok, that was it. He'd let Lloyd talk enough. It was his turn now. Tom's turn, not Benjamin Blank's, Tom's. He opened his mouth to argue facts when he felt two very strong, large hands grab both sides of him, this time lifting him up out of the chair. The way he was being pushed forward let Tom know that he was being *seen out* by two burly men.

"The nicest way for me to end things with you here at Donaldson's is to tell you to leave and never come back. If I see even a hair on your head pass the threshold of his building, I'll turn you into whatever agency that's out there looking for you and press charges. You will have not a dime to live on and will more than likely rot the rest of your life away behind bars, so... my advice to you, take this nicety and get the fuck out of my face."

And Tom was walking.

More like being wheeled out on the rolling balls his feet had melted into. His cane drug against the cheap carpeted floors as he shrieked and shouted his way through the building. This might be the last time he'd be there, and he needed his presence to be known. They'd regret this.

Once they found out they'd been played by some little red riding bitch and none of it was true - he'd sue the pants off them. He'd come back as CEO and fire all the fuckers that didn't believe him. As for Remi, she was as good as dead now. He was going to kill her for this. But first, he needed her to undo whatever the hell she did to make him "alive" again- then she'd lose hers. He'd cut her head off. No, he was would strangle her with a nine-iron. No, he'd trade her life to the Devil so he could get his soul back. Whatever the final decision- the cunt would pay now and for eternity.

He strode home as best he could, barely in one piece, emotionally and mentally ruined, blind, and unemployed. At least he had Rachel there to help him home. That is until he discovered there was no home to return to anymore.

While he and Rachel had been away, Remi, his landlord, and he could only assume a crew of movers had taken all of his belongings.

Removed. Missing. Gone forever.

And the only way he knew this was because his apartment door was still propped open; according to Rachel, the only thing there was a small toolbox filled with screwdrivers and wrenches and his old door handle. The locks had officially been changed, and he was officially homeless.

He remembered back to his shower early that morning, realizing the promise he'd made to his water pipes didn't even last a day.

And neither would Remi. He would make sure of it. Assuming his landlord would believe nothing of his story, similar to his old boss, he'd make the two white old tight assholes pay too. Everyone, except dear Mr. Benjamin Blank, his new identity.

Rise Again

Tom, Tom, he can't see
A little blind bat threatening to fly at me
Sad, sad, is what he is
A homeless beggar he's meant to be

Watching you through all of this is hysterical; better than anything on television these days. Now, what would I call it, if your life were a show?

Torturing Tom, Tom's Travesty, Days that Ended your Life, The Bitches that Broke You...so many options... how will this sweet little brain of mine choose? Or maybe I don't have to. I'll make one of the others do it. They like to put on their big girl pants and think they're making calls from time to time. I've seen them do it firsthand.

Remember all the whispering back at your apartment; oh shit, you probably don't because you were slowly dying. Too bad really. You missed a lot of good conversation amongst them. They say you never can know everything about a person, but these chicks were unloading the dirty dishes the other day- you would have learned so much about all of theirs, *our*, true colors.

We are all the same... at the core. Really, we are. All equally fucked in the head and tormented at heart; some of us just wear it better than others. Like your painting pottery pussy, Myra, she doesn't let her dark side out enough to play. Why the hell else do you think she holds that racked brain to the canvas on the daily? She's trying to crack her brains open and spill them out into the open where she no longer feels the necessity to hide. Her crazy, her hatred, her shadow is just buried beneath layers of pastel oils and dried-out bristles hardening around her organs- creeping in like a cancer.

That's what all this does to a person you know- makes them sick. It's best to release your pain out in the world to share its burden. *Better out than in,* that saying works for so many things in life. God, I am hysterical- just like you. Stronger, better looking, more intelligent, but we are equally funny.

You're welcome for giving you that.

You don't deserve the niceties, but it *is* time someone started telling the truth. And Jesus, there will be so much truth slamming your pea-sized everything against the ground you won't be able to stand. Nope, there's no "it" after that last sentence. You will bear it but you won't be able to physically sustain it. Not after I am done having my way with the entire goddamn nightmare you wrote for us. Just because you weave a tale doesn't mean you're a talented author. You're shit. Shit at life. Shit on the street. Shit that even the hungriest of dogs won't eat.

I see you slouching on the side of your bed, head hanging like a used condom lazily slung over the crossbars of a metal headboard. Defeated? No, I know you're just over there stewing- cooking up some asinine concoction for revenge. You won't win. Not against me. I see you. I hear you. At all times, or at least I did before I kicked you out of your home. Hours upon hours of footage, I have. And hours upon hours I have spent watching it, trying to stop myself from underestimating your ability to charm the pants off anyone. Pussies behind skirts, pussies tucked up and away from soft cotton seams, ones that are pushed down and stuffed into joggers... old pussies, young pussies, fat and thin pussies, brown, white, purple, and blue pussies too. You're the fucking Dr. Seuss of vaginas over there.

But that will change now. I guarantee it one way or my way.

We'll see which side you fall from-both are gonna singe a little, but one will burn you straight through.

Ashes to ashes.

Remi

Remi's nerves were fried. She couldn't keep hold of the pen in her hands long enough to finish drafting one of her client's offers for purchase. The deal needed to close by the end of the day but the way things were going; she was unsure if she'd manage.

She couldn't sit still in her desk chair, so she tried standing and working, well that was way too inviting to pace and who can write and walk at the same time? Not this girl. She needed to focus. Be present where she was and remove herself from Tom's closet. Eyes closed, eyes open... it didn't matter. All she'd been able to see since the whole charade was that POS crumpled up on the floor of his storage closet and she only wished he wasn't still breathing.

She *was* turning into a monster; whether or not she wanted to accept it, it was happening faster than she could have ever imagined. Even Sam was concerned about her. He didn't come out and say it directly, but his voice was drowning in worry when he called her the night before. He wanted her to come over to chat one on one about her situation; you know, the one she hadn't really wanted to get him involved in to begin with. But too late- Sam had a gift... not one she recognized for its full potential, but she *did* understand that *the something different about him* was enough. Apparently more than enough this time.

He not only saw right through her at their group gathering the other day but was inside her mind. He knew more than what he was letting on and knowing that made Remi want to accept his invite if only to guarantee his silence. But there sat the text; open on her cell phone screen and not responded to.

The ring of her office phone made her jump ten feet in the air. She needed to get a grasp over her anxiety. What a fuck up she was. If only she'd finished the job- there wouldn't be any loose ends or wagging tongues to worry about.

Remi had never been so happy to hear her good-time gal Kay's voice on the other end of the line. Her timing was always almost perfect; that sweetheart of a chick seemed to know when she needed a break or at least a distraction from herself.

Kay had a contagious exuberance of positivity that rubbed off on even the grumpiest of assholes. Today was no different as Kay chimed, "coffee?" into the receiver. Remi gracefully accepted and agreed to meet on the lower level of their building in fifteen. Not waiting a second longer in that stagnant think tank, she'd allow herself to float facedown again later, Remi was out the door- slamming it behind her. Her office neighbors all peeked out their doors to see what the ruckus was.

Slamming was outside of Remi's character.

Or at least it had been.

———————

When Kay finally joined her, she felt like linking arms with her gal pal and frolicking across the street for their usual favorite cup of joe but her arms reached out and wrapped around Kay bringing her in for a deep, long hug instead. Kay seemed a bit taken aback when Remi finally let her go but shared no complaints. Surprisingly, Kay beamed from ear to ear and said, "well, hello to you too girly. I am happy to see you as well!" And like a twinge of fire flashing at the bottom of a thinning pan, they were off - escaping to a sanctuary.

Soon enough, the two were cozied in a corner booth bantering about office mishaps and strange personalities they would never engage with outside of work.

"It feels so forced when I have to talk with Ed in accounting... he's such a pain in my ass. I know I don't cover it up well either... my discomfort... but he seems to be the only one not picking up on it. Everyone, like *everyone*, else up there, can tell how I feel about having to interact with him...which of course makes me feel a little guilty but... Jesus, Remi, am I a bad person? I hear myself talking over here and I am hearing how I might be a bad person. Do you think this is why Doug won't propose? Do you think he sees me as bad- evil-vain? I mean, I told him about Ed when he first started- you know about him hitting on me and everything but then he seemed to get annoyed by the topic so I went into a mean mode. Like instead of telling Doug what Ed had done that day, I'd just started talking mad shit- like making fun of Ed's looks and flakiness. Blah, Blah Blah. And now I'm worried that Doug thinks bad of me... oh, shit I feel like horse crap now."

Remi hated seeing her big-hearted friend so down on herself; she'd never met Doug, but he sounded like a dick. She followed her instinct... make her friend feel better about herself by making Remi's own character out as questionable.

"Girl, you are nothing but lovely. Light and lovely. You're literally the furthest thing from dark or ugly or evil or whatever. Trust me, you don't have a mean bone in your body - not really. You could never hurt a fly, let alone try to kill Ed or anything."

"Whoa, shit, I wasn't going that far with it!" Kays' surprise was obvious, but that didn't stop Remi. In fact, it excited her. Exhilarated her because she could shock people with her reacquainted inner demon- it made her anxieties melt away, replaced by pride.

So, what did she do? She took it too far...

"Yeah, I mean, I think Ed probably has something coming to him for basically being a rapist. Or at least contemplating being one. There are people you can hire to send a message, you know if you're too afraid to do it yourself. And of course, you are. You are still pure. Whole. Just you- there's nobody else inside that brain of yours trying to split you in two. But there are people, Kay, people like me out there that have very few qualms about blowing up a life. Or ending one."

Now it was time for Remi to be surprised; she'd expected to witness a continued state of shock on her friend's face but Kay was smirking. Kay was almost smiling after all that.

Remi felt the need to step it up again to get her friend back where she wanted her. "Don't believe that I have it in me? Well, you remember Tom, right? The one that I thought was cheating on me with that Myra girl? Yup, he was and with at least one other too; her name's Stella. The three of us killed him off on paper- he has nothing. Nowhere to live, no job, no access to the little money he has left in his bank account- N.O.T.H.I.N.G. And with the way he looks now, I don't think he'll be charming anyone's pants off."

Kay appeared to be latched onto the storyline; she slid forward on her bench seat as if she was watching her favorite daytime soap- scooching closer to the screen, making sure not to miss a drop of drama.

"Holy fuck, Remi. You are such a badass. To say you took manners into your own hands would be playing the whole sitch down. No, you fucking created a gang of mercenaries to take the asshole out. I never doubted you had it in you Remi, I want you to know that." Kay's eyes flashed a whole new look of respect and appreciation at her friend, the bad bitch soldieress. "So what did you to his looks?"

Remi felt pressed. Flattened.

She was giving away way too much... her basket was almost completely empty now whereas, only a few minutes ago, it had been filled to the brim with glistening gems. Secret jewels that had belonged to her and few others. It was too late to take it all back now- she couldn't just say she was kidding and change the subject. She'd have to finish what she started with Kay, understanding she was putting mounds of unpredictable hope in her friend from the offices upstairs.

"I desecrated the things that made him. Besides them, he was a slightly above-average preppy businessman with the same goddamn black suit and tie like all the rest. Same slicked to one side haircut, same brawny smile, same sun-kissed skin tone as every other rich white male in his thirties-down to identical frown lines. But these... they were like nothing most people have ever seen. Besides me. My mother had them too. And I got the mud-infested swamp-style version of them; no clarity, no truths can be waded through mine. Then again, it only looks like there is a certain depth to wade through in theirs- in all truth, they're nothing but a green-screen illuminating a projection of whatever you want to see in them."

The confused look on Kay's face let Remi know she'd lost her on the path she'd seemed to travel down. There were people in this world who desired, needed, bluntness...Kay was one of them.

"His eyes. I fucked up his eyes. How they look and how they work, more like don't work. Now he looks like a homeless soothsayer that had been living at the beach for the past few years until someone died and left him, a stranger that told a fortune to some lonely, gullible old fuck one time, a bunch of money. He is a blind sheep following the herds in his shiny Amedeo Testoni shoes, just hoping nobody robs him on the train to work. He deserves it. All of it. And you know what, Kay? I thought I'd feel guilty about it and maybe for a few ounces of a millisecond I did, but I don't anymore. Where remorse once stood, there is nothing left but a gaping black hole- null and void of emotion of any kind- it's growing and I think I *like* that. For once in my life, I'm not constantly second-guessing myself, coming down on my character, or blaming my inner child for our life of tragedy and abandonment. I'm enjoying standing in the middle of the blackout, refusing the trans-ference of light inside or outside of me. I feel good about myself. And I sure as hell feel better about him."

Remi felt her edginess growing; spreading through her veins and spilling out into every organ. She relished in it.

She was saying what she'd been wanting to for years and coming across crystal clear instead of her usual wishy-washy tide pool of mess. For as long as she could remember, she had always held herself to a higher standard than others in her life. She had to prove herself smart enough, capable, flexible, strong, resilient, but also a soft, creamy type woman who'd swoon for the perfect life partner. She wasn't that now. And that poor, timid version of herself would never have enough balls to show her face again- especially not after the baby came. Instinctively, she placed her right hand on her stomach to send a message to the little life inside her that everything was ok now and it would be always.

Remi had herself now.

Remi had a child now too, and together they'd conquer anything and everything that came flying back at them.

She pondered for a moment whether she'd share the news with her now silent and apparently stunned gal pal. Remi would keep it tight to her chest for now but was grateful that her truth was enough to shut up the gift of gabber for at least a moment or two so she could take a deeper look at the snack menu lying on the cafe table in front of her. She was eating for two now, so there was no shame in ordering herself a little mid-day treat before resuming the role of kind, caring, realtor.

The sound of Kay's voice penetrating the surrounding oxygen slowed her breathing. She was curious about what her friend would say now. But after all that, Kay said breezily, "Well, that's great. Should we get a bite here too? Then maybe you can create a plan for me to get back at Ed and get him off my tits for good."

Remi and Kay exchanged a glowing look of appreciation for one another. Their friendship seemed to have just gotten stronger.

Good thing too, Remi could always use another strong-willed, independent, in her back pocket. They ordered two chocolate crescents and a single piece of strawberry shortcake to split. It appeared they were celebrating.

Stella

Stella's lunch hour was jam-packed, there was no wiggle room for dawdling. She skipped packing up her things, knowing that she'd be returning to her on-site office for client meetings in the afternoon. No matter how much she didn't want to get deeper into the scheme with Tom, she had no choice. In the eyes of Tom's not-so-long-ago landlord, she was his legal aide. The lawyer that was cleaning up all the final messy details after Tom's passing. The messiest being that the fucker wasn't actually dead.

Ensuring interactions with Tom, now Ben, with others, was as minimal as possible being the priority. Stella's sole mission for her mid-day work intermission was to complete a final walk-through of his old apartment, making sure there were no more personal assets remaining or permanent damages that needed tending to.

Memories, most happy, few sad, came flooding behind the dom's eyes as she turned the key she'd picked up from the rental office in Tom's apartment door lock. Stella was known to be the strong, not-so-silent type; not a whiner, not a crier. But it took her several seconds to reassure herself of her strength and perseverance before pushing the door open. She let it slam behind her, its sounds echoing throughout the vast empty solitude of space that lie ahead of her.

If they thought it looked barren, or impersonal before, this was an entirely different definition of the word "void". The place was naked of any source of warmth, color, character, style, and...him. There was nothing left of him there. For a minute Stella felt the need to remind herself that the cheating bastard wasn't really dead; though it seemed frighteningly realistic at the moment. Doing everything in her powers besides physically lifting her legs to walk, she drew what she needed to move forward... barely, but she did.

The most obvious place to look was Tom's old living room area. There were some minor scratches in the wall paint here and there and a few scuffs on the floor, but nothing that looked irreversible. All things that would come off with a little janitorial elbow grease. She sure as shit wouldn't be the one doing the clean-up. Then again, it'd look very strange if his lawyer ponied up to the bitch work.

Good.

A final sweep of her eyes convinced her she could move forward to the kitchen, which looked like it had been ravished by a hoard of hungry homeless people. Every cabinet door was flung open, their bottoms covered with crumbs and bits of old food wrappers that had fallen, camouflaged over the years. Again, nothing of value or real damage here. She closed each miniature door after she'd scoured through; as she turned to go to the next open pair, her eye caught something but it disappeared as quickly as they had landed on it.

Had that little red light really been there, or had she imagined it?

Turning her body to face the corner of the tray ceiling she'd seen it come from, she paused and waited, hoping to confirm her sanity by witnessing its warm spark again. Stella hadn't held that still in a long time; she'd never even noticed the elegant and sleek design of the double tray in Tom's apartment before.

There. It flashed again.

An unmistakable red light flashed for a millisecond. Time to climb. But on what? She had an idea. Turning back to the kitchen cupboards, she grabbed the sides of a pair of uppers and pulled herself up to stand on the concrete countertops Tom had installed while they were "dating". If her hunch was right, her outstretched hands would feel a small, thin electrical cord that would guide her to a digital intruder like the ones she'd found in her dungeon. And there it was.

Sliding her hand along the lead and shuffling her feet in unison atop her narrow self-made boardwalk, she came to a small plastic lump and pulled. It detached from the wall with a small Velcro sound. Bringing it down as far as the taught cord systems allowed, she made direct eye contact with it. She'd seen it and whoever she assumed was still watching, saw her.

What a twisted, tainted, pervert. So desperate - where else had he installed these? Had either of the other two women checked their homes for the cameras?

Jumping down from her ledge, she jaunted to his bedroom. Low and behold, tray ceiling once again. Fighting the urge to flip the light switch, she waited, unknowingly holding her breath in the pitch-black space she'd become so familiar with. Her eyes danced along the tops of the walls until, finally, she saw all she needed to. Three small red bleeps of light went off at the same time. Tom was a bona fide, real-life sex addict. Stella had met a few in her after-hours industry, but they were few and far between. What were the chances that she'd be in a relationship with a guy that wasn't just playing the field but was a straight-up predator? Jesus Christ, if this ends up being the case- that'd change everything. She already understood he deserved to lose his life on paper, but if this were true, he'd have deserved to be blind too - if not dead. Her mind was reeling with excuses for him and, of course, herself until it faltered on one ideal she couldn't budge out of her brain... she needed to be tested for STDs.

Why hadn't she thought of this before?

With trembling hands she searched her bag for her cell... this just couldn't wait. But instead of searching for the local clinic's phone number, she dialed Tom. Fighting against her inner urge to hang up, she remained on the line until finally, a gruff-sounding Tom answered.

"Hey babe," Stella stuttered initially, but regained control over her voice, returning to her signature rich tone. "I haven't heard from you for a while and just wanted to check-in. Have you been traveling for work again?" Realizing that she was sounding uncharacteristically caring, she wrote a little dig into her mind to add to the convo, "My pussy's getting so lonely over there that I actually thought about having sex with one of my clients the other night. And you *know* what they are like, so I must be getting desperate. Ever been that desperate Tom that you'd fuck pretty much anyone or anything, whether it's what they were expecting?" Stella tried to roll heat into her voice, promising sultry on the surface and spice underneath- like a rolling smoke that could only be excavated by a spiteful tongue.

Tom seemed to pause; it was obvious he was trying to assess who he was talking to since he could no longer use his eyes as cheaters. "Stella," Tom said her name painfully slow. Again, he was giving her the opportunity to correct him, though things would be very awkward for him if he had to be.

She wasn't sure he'd care if his secret was ousted anymore- his confidence sounded quite shaken. He was over it and she could tell. " So nice to hear from you. No, I haven't been traveling for work... I actually had an accident - well, it's hard to explain, but I've been in and out of the hospital without my phone. I wanted to call you so you could come and visit, but things were very complicated in there... you know, just difficult to make a phone call."

"Oh no, what happened?" Stella tried to balance the sound of surprise and her typical sharp-tongued demeanor so as not to give anything away. It wasn't as hard to do as one might think- the instantaneous evolution back to deceit was a mood killer for Ms. Madsen. She appreciated honesty. She hated being manipulated. Or managed. The knife-edge personality flaw was her strength at moments like this and she was having no issue re-engaging it.

"Well, I won't bore you with the details of how, but essentially, the most important thing to know is that I seem to be permanently blind. Or at least that's what the doctors have told me." Stella's mind tried to wrap itself around the idea that Tom might have gone into a clinic with Rachel's assistance. She knew from her numerous cases involving the medical field that no person could be denied services in an emergency room; whether or not they had health insurance, a physical residential address, or even a first and last name. Before she could dive much further into it, Tom filled the silence with more lies. "Since the incident, I found my apartment extremely challenging and not handicap friendly in the least so... I moved."

What an arrogant lie- a smooth one, but arrogant all the same. He was playing it cautious. Smart. Tom was using the cards he was dealt to paint a completely different picture, to protect himself. He couldn't be sure who was all involved with Remi's scheme, but he knew that she didn't act alone, so everyone was a suspect. And Stella knew his kid-glove handling was because she was still on the list of possibilities. *Probabilities* actually, Stella gleaned to herself. She loved having a secret as long as she had the upper hand and in this scenario; she had use of her eyes yet, so.... winning.

"Well holy shit, their cowboy. That IS a lot of news. I am so sorry to hear about your eyes! I think we are just gonna have to come up with new ways for you to see my ass." Stella needed to play it cool. It's not a secret, she wasn't a compassionate person, or at least not one that got overly concerned about other people's personal shit. And this was a prime example of her definition of personal shit so she needed to continue to keep face. Now for the question, she actually cared about the answer to, "So where did you move to? Can I know, or is it top-secret?"

"Interestingly enough, I haven't found the right place yet so I'm staying with a friend, well more like my caretaker, Rachel, until I find something. I'm actually considering having something built for me out in the countryside more. Completely out of character, I know, but with things the way they are now, I'm thinking a slower pace might be just what I need."

And with what funds? Stella thought to herself.

She knew he had nothing - no access to whatever money might still be remaining in his old account. He had no job...and what the fuck was going on there with Rachel, letting Tom live with her?! That was going way past the call of duty - or the role she'd asked her to fill in for. The two of them staying under the same roof for more than the allotted week she'd gotten the stupid little bitch to agree to was dangerous. A lot of things can come out between roommates. She'd extinguish this wildfire when she got back to the office. She'd gotten the info she was looking for; time to shut things down- Madam Madsen style.

"Well then, I hope you enjoy your time at your *friend* Rachel's place... you know what they say about people in patient care- they know their way around a body. Let me know when we can get together and I will find us a nice, expensive, handicap-accessible place to eat out." That last dig was cold. She knew that. And she loved it. She didn't even let him respond, she just pressed the red phone icon to hang up on him and continued on her way.

Finishing *his final* apartment walk-through because *yes, dearest Tom,* she knew all about it. She did from the start and she was sure as shit going to be there at the end. She'd make sure that Rachel kept the person who hired her, Stella's, identity secret, or else maybe it was time someone came out of the closet by force. Rachel may be on the road to recovery and self-acceptance, but there was no fricken way she'd be ready for the shame storm social media would bring.

Before leaving, Stella remembered she'd hidden a little treasure for her to explore at a later date. Inside Tom's closet, Stella stuck her hand atop the shade of the ceiling light fixture. There in her hand was the padded top book she had found just enough time to sneak out of the position of the stuck drawer the last time she was there. Flipping the cover open, there was a picture of a beautiful blonde girl with blue eyes that seemed to live off the photo paper as their own entity. The young girl was wearing a sundress, hair flowing down her naked shoulders and back. A slim smile on her face and pearls dancing along her neckline, and a matching miniature gracing her dainty little white girl hand. A spoiled little princess, no doubt. Looks like a girl that had everything handed to her in life. Looks like a girl Stella had seen before.

Back at the office, Stella grabbed Rachel by the arm as she passed by her in the most nonchalant manner she could manage.

"So I just got off the phone with Ben. He said you did a great job helping him get back on his feet and is sooooo appreciative of you." Start with something sweet and then finish with the sour. "He also said he was curious about who hired you and that no matter how many times he asked you, you didn't spill the smallest of clues. Which is something I sooooo appreciate. I never want him to think he is any less than or incapable, you know." Stella almost choked on those words as they left her mouth like bats flying out of a ravenous cave. "He did mention that he moved; however, and said that you offered to let him stay at your place until he found something. And in fact, he even took you up on the offer... that's going above and beyond- even for you, don't you think? I mean, I'd hate for him to get the wrong idea about your relationship- I mean you ARE a lesbian for Pete's sake. Have you shared *that* tidbit with him?"

The look on Rachel's face made Stella realize she needed to pedal backward a bit and try again. "I mean, it's just that he's been through so much and you- well, you are too. Truly, I think you might be good for one another right now. With all the learning and growing you are both doing, living together might be like the blind leading the blind. Am I wrong in saying that?" Stella stared blankly at Rachel, waiting for her response with her head tilted- like an inquisitive cat that had just unraveled an entire ball of yarn and was having a hard time comprehending why its owner was upset.

Rachel's mouth finally opened to speak, but the words that came out weren't anything near what Stella had expected to hear. "Ms. Madsen, I'm so sorry but I think our friend Ben is confused. I never offered to let him stay with me, so he's not. I simply helped him for a week- what you asked- and then stopped going there this week."

Huh? What the fuck now?

Someone was lying and Stella was having a hard time deciphering who this time.

Myra

Myra jolted awake; it had been a rough night's sleep and having her wind chime ringtone on blast wasn't the gentlest way for a girl to be woken up. Slightly turning, she stuck her right arm sideways, blindly feeling around for the peace-killing machine. Ah, yup, there it was. She curled her fingers around her phone and brought it to her face without looking to see who was calling.

"Yeah, good morning," Myra mumbled out from behind her recently barricaded mouth.

"Well, good morning to you too, sunshine. I'm back in town from my path to peace tour and I'd love to see you - ha, funny story there. I actually can't see you or anyone, or anything, right now. One of my major senses went on hiatus on the road. But I'd still love to visit with my girl."

Tommy Gun's voice sent a chill down her spine; though he'd had no reason to believe that Myra had anything to do with that evening in his apartment, she, for some reason, had told herself that she'd never hear from him again. And yet, there he was, calling her with a whole new wad of lies.

She was uncomfortable, to say the least, but there was not much else to do at the time than play along with the whole damn thing.

"Oh hey there guy," that didn't sound right and she knew it. Try again. "I've missed you and a lot has happened since the last time we spoke. But honestly, it sounds like you have much more concerning updates than me... what do you mean you can't see? What happened? Are you ok?" Myra was fully sitting up in her bed now and reaching that same right hand out towards her nightstand drawer. If she was going to be forced to have this awkward conversation, she was going to need a little puff-puff pass... it back to herself. Tom started his chalked-full of lies story as she packed her bowl and lit the top.

"Myra, I think it's life leading me down a different path. When I was on the tour we met these guys - the GREATEST guys- one of them played guitar, and the other the flute, and I got a chance to play around on the bongos.. have you ever heard me on the bongos babe?" Tom didn't wait for a response. Evidently, he was too invested in his bullshit to stop the rhythm of his flow. "Well, we jammed together until about midnight; some folks from my crew had gone off into their tents to sleep and these guys asked me if I was lost. Now babe, at first, I was totally confused- completely mind mangled, but they said that they felt my aura was stuck in some bad shit. So you know what I did... I took them up on their offer to try Ayahuasca. Of course, I puked my guts out at first, but then I started having some revelations about some people in my life and just how toxic they are for me."

Myra felt the urge to interrupt him and went with it, "Is one of those people me, Tom?"

"Of course not boo... unless there is something you did while I was away that I don't know about and should know about..." Once more, Tom left no gap for a response so Myra went with another easy 'get out of jail free card. "So after a very insightful trip, I came back in the morning, opened my eyes, and realized I couldn't see anything. The guys I was with said sometimes that can happen to those seeing for the first time with Ayahuasca... like if you see so much so fast that you have seen everything you need to for the rest of your life to live one of higher meaning and enlightenment. No more sensory burden from my eyes. At first, I was a bit upset, but now I see that it's a blessing bestowed on me from the universe. Now I just have to hold up my end of the agreement to myself and eliminate those toxic entities I envisioned."

No matter how big a lie this all was, Myra knew there was some truth to it; specifically, the part where he said he was going to eliminate the toxic people. At her heart's core, Myra knew he was being passive-aggressive with her meaning one hundred percent meant what he said.

Tom was warning her he was about to make war with the one person he *knew* to be at fault for his condition - Remi. And to be fair, it *was her* fault that he was blind. And Remi would have him dead if she would have been successful in her overdosing, poisoning, whatever the hell you'd call what she attempted to do. It wasn't Stella's or her own fault... they were innocent bystanders in that case of vengeance.

Now... the job loss, the homelessness, the poverty, the loss of identity... that *was* on all of them. But did *he* know that?

One thing Myra *was* sure Tom was unaware of was her gallery opening, scheduled for that day at four. And she'd need to keep him in the dark of his own death display throughout the rest of their conversation. And so she did. She expressed her weird empathetic enthusiasm towards his new impairment and actually said the words "I'm happy for you". How fucked up was this entire ordeal going to get if she had to pretend that a man's handicap was a phony blessing from a fake tale he weaved to get out of having a love triangle? Sigh. She ended it by telling him they could get together sometime early the following week, making sure not to leave a hint of scent behind about her art show.

The phone clicked on the other end of the line and almost in perfect unison, so did Myra's lighter.

———————

Only an hour remained before the doors to Expose' were to be unlocked and her artwork unleashed to hungry eyes, she told herself. She was feeling snippy- it was her anxiety kicking in but there was nowhere for her to sneak a smoke, so she just had to push through, accepting she was going to be the little bit of bitch she knew she could be. Those that fell underneath her wrath and actually knew Myra, would best describe this side of her as straight "mood". Strangers interpreted it as snottiness.

Either way, Myra was who she was and there was no changing that. So moving right along, she dove back into her final touches. Obviously, her show was all around losing her lover to cancer- so tons of gloom and doom pottery, paintings, and elaborate staged displays with vintage furniture pieces- some of which were borrowed from friends, but most of them she found by her own apartment's garbage. Someone with some vintage charm had evidently just moved out and gracefully left their thrifted home decor behind for someone who'd be looking for it. Here, she was the someone, and it happened at just the right time too; earlier in the week she saw it almost peering back at her through her studio window- the rich mustards and wheat velours beckoned her to come and see what other treasures were buried underneath their stacked sanctuary. It was fate- that's all there was to it... fricken fate. And here they were making the most realistic, vintage-goth arrangements that mimicked sitting areas and even a bedroom where a sick man could be found dying in his own home. A sick man that no one else would believe was still alive. Since Tom didn't have a social media presence and Myra had always kept her love life on the down-low in order to defy the patriarchy, no one attending would actually know when Tom would have died. It could be months ago, years, shit she was getting to be old enough. It could even have happened a decade ago for all they knew- if they even cared. Doubtful.

With all that being said, her death displays were perfectly recreated, but she wanted to sneak a few of her vaginal creations into them, tucking a potted plant here and there that secretly held the crevice of a lady within its clay body. There were a few clitoral abstracts that hung from the ceiling in between chairs, side tables, and lamps. They were her original works disguised as your everyday canvas hanging on invisible living room walls. Why shouldn't she use this opportunity at max capacity- showcase her genuine passion and talents? Tom was paying for the whole thing and after everything, it just seemed fair. So away she went, continuing to spread her fairy dust to bring her show into full-bodied life. She fluttered about in her serious, take-no-shit, mood when she was abruptly interrupted by a thought...a worry... something none of the three had thought of yet.

What if Rachel showed up with Tom? Aka Ben?! Stella told them that Tom claimed to be living with the in-home nurse temporarily until he found "a home good enough for a man of his stature". It wasn't a direct quote, more like how Myra had translated the foreboding message Stella had passed onto her and Remi on the phone.

Initially, Myra thought little of it, but when Stella continued on to say that Rachel denied the whole damn thing- well, then she was just confused. It sounded like Stella was too -like she didn't know who to believe. Who was telling the truth between the two of them was beside the point, Myra realized, because if Rachel was in with the art crowd in any way- she'd be there tonight. How could she know if Rachel, the apparent dog-woman, was a pottery-head or faint for the paint? And if she was every bit of the kiss-ass Stella described her as this Rachel chick would never imagine leaving her "patient" unattended.

There wasn't time to investigate it, you know, snoop on the web since Myra knew nothing more than the first name. So.... would this be a time she'd have to put her faith in the Universe to not betray her?

Shit, she guessed so.

The clock continued its unromantic duty of clicking down the minutes before bodies of energetic, charismatic, artsy-fartsy types came cruising through the unlocked and beckoning gallery doors. It was really happening- all of it; Myra was starting a new chapter of showcasing her work while tamping down one of the biggest cons she could have ever imagined herself getting tangled up in. Smile. All she needed to do was smile and the night would go however she perceived it to be. She was going to choose *remarkably*.

As the space started flooding with familiar faces, Myra shared disconnected smiles and forced head nods of gratitude for nonverbal and silently mouthed compliments that sailed across the room. Not that she wasn't appreciative of them being there nor was it because she wasn't proud as fuck about all the pieces she'd been able to put together from scratch in such a short time frame- she was simply too concerned about searching out faces that knew what she knew.

Stella. Remi. Michelle. Sam. For fuck's sake, Tom. Secretly, Myra was hoping Remi, Stella, or both would show for moral support - this was kind of their showcase of talents too, come to think of it... it was a metaphorical display of all the hard work the trio had done to make Tom Williams a dead man on paper. And on the internet. And according to the Feds, the bank, and his landlord. The exhibit should have been called, "The Living, Breathing, Murdered", *a visual display of how the cruelties of the heart can leave a man with nothing...not even his sight.*

Was it too late for a redo, she thought half-kiddingly to herself?

The night wore on and no Tom and, she assumed, no Rachel. Around an hour before closing, Myra spotted the stunning brunette that had entranced her from the moment they met. Her eyes locked with the stunning pair of pale turquoise gems staring back at her. Remi had made it too. Myra shifted inside of her own awkwardness. She was excited and about to barf with nerves at the same time. Deep down she really liked Remi- it was almost mystical respect she held for the brown-haired beauty. There was an other-worldly depth to her that seemed to pool in her irises; placing anyone and everyone to catch her glance under a spell. Myra was easy bait for anyone with eyes like hers; she tried to pull away but felt her body moving towards Remi instead, like a magnet getting pulled towards a dainty metal pin in the crowd. Not the other way around. It was the enticement, Myra said, forgiving her skeleton for moving outside of her command.

"Hello stranger, glad you could make it to my big wild night here. Are you enjoying yourself? Like what you see?" Myra tried to contain her unexpected giddiness, but it was quite the task to do when the two women were alone, without the sadist.

"I am. You have a lot of intriguing pieces here tonight, Myra. My friends and I really love how realistic the home-like installations feel around your partner's path to the other side. That must have been a very difficult time for you." Remi played the part of a curious but empathetic supporter perfectly.

"It was one of the most challenging times in my life, but I have been lucky enough to have good friends around me to get me through. Both old and new. You can't take for granted the power of genuine friendship." Myra was getting lost in those dark tide pools again. She couldn't figure out why she was so easily entertained by them- she felt like she would do anything for those eyes- all they had to do was ask. And so they did.

"Speaking of friends, I was wondering if you had seen our bestie, Stella, around yet? I spoke with her earlier and she said she was going to make it out here even if it were for only a bit."

"No, nothing from her. But, I'm sure if she said she was going to come out, then we should see her within the next half an hour or so since we'll be winding things up here." Instinctively, Myra reached for her cell to make sure there weren't any texts or missed calls from the missing partner in crime. There was something- nothing from her- but something.

Tom 4:25 PM: "Hey doll, I know you said you wouldn't be around to get together until early next week but I was wondering if you could find even an ounce of time tonight to help cheer me up? I sure could use a cute little something to bring a smile to my face...*kissy face emoji*"

Tom 4:45 PM: "Babe, you there?"

Tom 5:15 PM: "Don't worry about me. My temporary roomie, Rachel, just got back and offered to tell me a story... strange thing to say but I'm bored enough to take her up on it. Who knows, maybe it will be a real knee-slapper."

Myra, Current Moment "Shit."

She could feel the rise of panic exploding from her pupils as they tried to penetrate through the distraction of Remi's appearance, straight to her brain. If eyes could shout-scream, hers would be loud enough for the entire block to think they needed to evacuate. Remi seemed to understand they were trying to communicate something desperately ugly with her- she didn't know what, but she was about to ask when Stella brushed shoulders with the pair, completing the remaining side of the trio.

"Hello bitches, sorry I'm so late. I had a client book last minute, and it ran longer than expected."

"A paying client or someone that is paying the price?" Remi stated flatly, apparently catching the same scent of gameplay Myra had.

"Hm, well, it's complicated, but it's most definitely not what the two of you are probably thinking. My client and I were just following up across the street at The Pour House; in fact, she's still there waiting for my return. I just wanted to show my face here, you know, make an appearance and such, so... everything going as planned? Any fan mail or buyers, Le Artiste Myra?"

Myra's eyes invisibly rolled. Stella was never one of her favorite people, but over time she was becoming less and less desirable to be around. Stella had this whole feminism thing wrong- she thought that for a woman to be empowered meant she had disempowered others- mostly males, but not conclusively. Instead of lifting other women up around her, she raised herself solely by pushing their faces into the ground for her to stomp across.

Myra was smarter than this.. deep down, underneath the legal pencil skirts, layers of make-up, and hardened smirks of judgment lie this broken little girl who had been run over all her life growing up. She was an over-compensator; Myra typically had compassion for those less pulled together, but there was something tricky about Stella's highly manipulative persona. Something she couldn't quite put her finger on- a sticky stain that only stuck to the soles of her shoes. Hiding, clinging, making things worse for the wearer. Making obnoxious, unsolicited noises along the way which, of course, subsequently called attention to their presence- completely annihilating the whole " I just want to hide, I'm so meek" bullshit they tried to tell the world.

"Yes I think about a dozen pots are going out the door at the end of the night and I have someone interested in purchasing two of my personal vulva abstracts on canvas- so overall, a very successful evening. I feel almost bad about profiting off of Tom's 'death' though. A few conversations got a little awkward when folks started recognizing that this man was real- that he was my boyfriend and that he was dead. I think I maintained myself well enough- it just felt a little, I don't know, wrong, maybe?"

"It's not wrong. Not one bit. After all that bastard did to us, he owed us all something." Remi chimed in. "Myra, a little extra jingle in your pocket and some more followers of your work. I am definitely getting my end of the deal of out this- in fact, I was thinking we could all meet afterward for a celebratory drink? I have some really exciting news and have a limited amount of people I can share it with- I was hoping to spill the beans to you ladies tonight if you're up for it?" Remi seemed to be a glowing, walking-talking invitation for the bright side of crime. She could be a walking, talking felon if she didn't watch herself, Myra thought to herself, but curiosity won in the end as she and Stella agreed to meet for a nightcap.

"Why don't the two of you join me and my client across the street at The Pour House?" Stella added with a wink. Another glory moment for her to try to shine brighter than the rest of them, no doubt. Rich, sadist, bitch. Myra turned to catch a look of disproval on Remi's neat, enunciated face. It was clear she wasn't too impressed by sassy Miss Madsen either. Another tick in the air for team Remi. Myra waved an imaginative finger in the air to the right of her.

The pack broke up without a word slipping about Tom's text. Myra figured there wasn't much to do about it - assuming there was actually something being "shared"- until after the gallery; more realistically the next day even. Nothing more than frustrated panic could come of letting the others know about the suggestive text Tom had sent - they would all probably hear Rachel's knee-slapper of a story firsthand soon enough...

Myra could have never guessed it could have been within a half hour's time.

Waiting for her when she entered the high-end hipster bar was a baffled-looking Remi, a steaming and beaming Stella, and a very unfamiliar nerd-bird of a face.

"Hi, I'm Rachel. Rachel Dobbs," said the stranger as she held her hand out to be shaken.

Myra glanced up at Stella as she clarified, "the Rachel? The one that helped us out with our friend, To... Benjamin?"

Stella nodded yes and went on to brag about how well the two women were getting along. How she would have never seen their connection coming from a mile away. That the two of them had been working on a part of Rachel's journey together, which ultimately pushed Stella down a new pathway of her own. Because of fucking course it did. Stella wins. Stella would always win. Even if she had to lie about it.

"I never realize how attracted I can be to females. Males too still. But women- wow, their bodies can really talk if you let them," Stella brought back her favorite movement of the night and shared a not-so-secretive wink with her gal pal sub, Rachel.

Rachel's face turned tomato-soup red in response. "Stella's really the only woman I've ever been with. Ever allowed myself to be with and to think it all started from a misunderstanding. I mean, when I said I needed to book an appointment for your services after hours, I only meant legal guidance but then you came out in full BDSM gear and I knew I was in for so much more than a letter of recommendation- the one and only thing I was told to ask for."

Stella's head snapped to her side, staring with complete confusion at her submissive unleashed bitch of a client, or whatever the fuck she was supposed to be to her. "What do you mean, you didn't know you were coming for a pay and play in my dungeon?" Now Myra and Remi both felt out of the loop.. what the hell were these two even talking about? "And who told you to get a letter of recommendation? And for what?"

Stella does BDSM? Stella fucks girls? What now?

Rachel nervously fiddled the tips of her hair in her fingers, "Stella, I have to tell you something. Something, I know you aren't going to like but I have grown to really like and care for you so I think it only fair to tell you the truth about that night."

The dog-face girl paused for encouragement to continue. She was either afraid to death of Stella or she was a hell of a good actress- which one, Myra had no clue. She was completely and utterly stumped. If Rachel had been with Stella prior to the bar and Tom claimed to be chatting it up with his temporary roomie- Rachel, what the hell was actually going on here? Who's on first, second, and at home with Tommy Gun? Better yet, what was the "knee-slapper" this stranger was sharing with the ex-boy toy as they speak? Could the prick have just made the entire thing up?

"See, you've always been so mean, on the verge of cruelty, to me and you probably already know this, but I was trying to find my way to the top. Well, after complaining about you to a somewhat new friend of mine, they told me you were the type of person that was created to stand in the way of others' growth. That the only way around you was to topple you first. This friend of mine did some looking into you and found out that you were offering contract legal work after hours- out of your home and outside of the firm. She thought that if I could somehow prove you were doing this in a passive-aggressive way to the partners, then they would fire you and instead spend some of that money to help fund my efforts in getting my law degree. I was coming to you that night to get fake legal advice on a settlement that didn't exist about an unpaid student loan that was sent to collections when I was technically still a minor. All of it was phony- I never went to school. I mean, it's not a lie that I want to go to law school, but the whole charade was, well, just that. By the end of this all, I was hoping for some hand-written legal advice on how to proceed with reopening the law-suit that had been unfairly settled and a typed letter of recommendation to the loan office. But then when I showed up, and I found out there was a miscommunication- you thought I was there as a sub-client for a Dominatrix side-hustle I honestly had no clue you were involved with... well, I just went with it because I didn't know what else to do." Rachel's hands flung out at her sides. "From there, I found out that you would be an integral part of my growth- a more personal... more important side of me that needed tending to. My friend was so wrong about you and looking back, I feel so dumb for even listening to her. I mean, for Pete's sake, we had just met. I was literally taking big, life-altering advice from a pure stranger. Stella, can you forgive me?"

Myra wondered if Stella had heard anything Rachel had said after the part about her trying to con her into a situation that would cost the legal Goddess her career. Stella would have been fired for sure, but the firm could have taken it a step further and taken her to court to strip her of her license to practice. She could have been disbarred if they wanted to take it that far. Myra escaped her internal dialogue to scope out Stella's facial expressions. And the strong, tall, independent, apparent Dominatrix looked pissed to all Hell. Swiveling her head, Myra turned to look at Remi who in return mouthed "she's a DOM?" to her. Myra smiled slightly in a minor effort to lighten the mood and mouthed back, "and a lesbian." She added a wink to seal the end of the silent convo. Then both of their heads swiveled towards the main actress of the show that had been unfolding in front of them- in front of every curious, nosy drunk nearby.

Stella opened her mouth to respond...

Tom

There he sat, blind, technically homeless, hungry, bored, and unforeseeably lonely. What the fuck massacre just swept through his life like a tornado tripping on a roid rage? He went from the King of the Hill to the lowly blind beggar at the outside of the castle gates within a matter of a week. No job, no identity, no money, no pussy, no life. And it was all because of that stupid cunt Remi. True, he got caught in a game that he knew was dangerous, but never in his wildest dreams could have imagined this being his life.

Twiddling his thumbs wasn't his style- he grew up a loser, but he changed all that. He made a name for himself. He created a character that at least fifty percent of the population could fall in love with. He was self-made, nothing he once was, and he could- he WOULD do it all again. But before he started over, he needed to tie up a few loose ends before he could move on to becoming Benjamin, the asshole. Apparently. And the man everyone else thought he really was.

Because, why not? What's wrong with a new name when Tom never seemed to serve him that well over the years? The rain hitting his bedroom window seemed to be the only one that truly loved it. He knew he was strong, but in all reality, his sweet little deal with the Devil was what really pushed him over the wall that had been keeping him from success and self-made happiness. Who knew, maybe a new name, a fresh pad, an extra life would allow him to hide when Satan himself came to collect him?

Before completely jumping into a new skin, he knew he had to carry out everything Remi deserved coming to her. Over the short time he had with the bitch, he'd learned a lot about her but mostly about her insecurities, probably all stemming from being raised by a tone-deaf single dad. Remi had never shared with him where her Mom went, but he always figured she died. There was no fire, no rage driving Remi. She was too bland to be a woman who'd been betrayed by a parent-death wasn't a betrayal, leaving was, but not death. Even if it had been a suicide, it wouldn't have been a knife in Remi's back, just the front side of her Mama's chest.

He'd tried getting Myra to come to get him for a sex sesh- getting back on the horse is what he really needed, but that wasn't just a no-go, it was a no response. She was ghosting him suddenly- very suspicious. Stella, who wasn't always so amicable, had a client scheduled for tonight so she couldn't come or cum for him so... there he sat imagining, devising a plan to destroy Remi- the bitch in a business suit, behind a mask of insecurities. He was going to pluck each one of those fucking head rotting thoughts from her brain and plant them in her heart as he ripped it out from her corpse. She *should* die. It's what she intended for him. Sadly for her, she discovered another thing she sucked at. She didn't have the smarts or the balls to end a life even when they are utterly helpless and lying unconscious on the ground. She didn't know what to do with him- too bad he wasn't able to speak outside his body because he could have walked her through it step by step. No, he never killed anyone before, but he spent the first eighteen years planning out logistics on exterminating his cock-loving roach for a mother. Luckily for him, she was sick and sad enough to kill herself off with the bottle. Fucking flea-bag whore probably has holes bore through her coffin by now from all the bugs finally leaving. Even the parasites have nothing to get from her anymore- she is alone. But so was he.

The sound of the door opening made his ears perk up a bit. Rachel had been a solid enough person to let him stay with her temporarily, but it seemed the gloom and doom version had planted itself firmly because there hadn't been a hint of happiness in her voice since he'd arrived. Sure, she acknowledged him; he could even feel her sitting there staring at him silently from time to time. What she was watching, waiting for, he had not the foggiest, but he imagined she was undressing him with her eyes and that made him feel better.

"Hey Rachel, is that you?" Tom called out into the blackness that was now his world.

"Yup. Just me Ben- no friends with me. It's just me and you in the room. You hungry?" Wow, she hadn't asked that before- she'd always just made food and plunked it down in front of him whether he wanted it. He usually ended up eating it- it smelled decent, and he knew he'd be hungry later if he didn't. None of the meals were anywhere near what he was used to filling his body with. He was kind of a health nut, but beggars can't be choosers.

Taking the opportunity to insert his opinion, he answered politely enough to try and get what he really wanted, "I sure am. You wouldn't happen to have any extra meat lying around that kitchen of yours, would you? I could really go for something hearty tonight if it's not too much trouble?"

"Yeah, I have some steaks I could cook up if you'd fancy." Rachel was being nice- too nice. She hadn't been this accommodating or warm to him in a while- then again, they had only known each other for a little over a week. You don't ever really know someone, let alone know them in a week's time.

"Oh, thank you- that sounds amazing. Do you know what my favorite thing to drink with supper is? It sounds a little..." Rachel cut him off.

"Milk, you like milk with your dinner. It is the one motherly thing that woman ever did for you, so naturally, your inner child feels soothed by drinking milk with your meals."

Holy shit, that was accurate.

"Yeah, how did you know that? Do we know each other from the past somehow?" Tom could sense a new thickness in the air between the two "roomies". Tensions were back to being sky-high.

"Nope. Lucky guess. A lot of men prefer milk with their meals when there's no beer to be had because a lot of men are still hurting little boys inside." Rachel's bitter response led to him think she might be getting out of an ugly relationship. He really didn't want to hear her sob story, but he did really want that steak she'd promised him.

"Bad break-up or just bad luck with men overall?"

"Just with men- there was one really hard break-up, hurtful, but the rest are just egocentric assholes. You aren't though, are you Ben? I can tell you are different... I'm sorry if I came off harsh towards you - I'm just in the middle of dealing with a lot of emotions right now and I'm struggling a bit more than I thought I would." Rachel seemed sincere. Solemnly sincere.

" I try. I guess that's the best I can claim- we are all human you know and make mistakes. I hate to admit it, but I've made at least one big one as of late, and it seems I will pay the price for the rest of my life over it." Now it was Tom's turn to be solemn. It felt sincere, but he had been faking everything for so long it was getting harder and harder for even him to know the true Tom Williams. No, actually Benjamin. Old Benny boy now.

The mood seemed to lighten up a little as Rachel continued, "I feel that. There are so many things I regret doing now- like things I did back when I was a teen and in my early twenties." Rachel gave a low, throaty chuckle. It seemed a bit out of context of the conversation, but mostly out of character. Rachel's laugh had been bubbly light before. Perhaps she was just forcing one out to return to an easy-breezy flow for the night.

Apparently not. "Can I tell you a secret, Ben? Something I have never breathed a word about to another soul?"

Tom was hesitant- how badly did he want this damn steak? Bad. He might even kill for it.

"Of course, I'm all ears, Rachel."

"I did something back in high school, senior year to exact, that I'll never forgive myself for. I can't because she won't let me. At the end of senior year, I found out I was pregnant. I wasn't one hundred percent sure who the father was. I mean, I knew who I wanted the father to be but there was a chance it was someone else's... someone who was taking what they wanted from me against my will. I couldn't stomach the idea of procreating with that monster even though there was a higher likeliness that it wasn't his but my boyfriend's instead. Oh God, I wish I wouldn't have been put in the situation where I had to second guess it from the start, but my mom - she never listened to me. She always took his side in things- it was so unfair." Tom realized that the monster Rachel was referring to was a father figure of some sort. Ew. "Anyway, I did the only thing I thought I should. I had an abortion. A painful, botched one that has left me unable to carry children full term now as an adult. I was so ashamed and embarrassed about everything that had happened and was continuing to happen back at home that I ended up dumping my boyfriend and hiding from the world. I canceled my plans to go to college, my dream of becoming an elementary school teacher- I couldn't face a classroom of innocent children knowing I had killed one. I was at my lowest point for the next couple of years, only to discover rock bottom when I tried inviting someone back into my life. It was a stupid decision but my heart was broken, shattered, bleeding. I needed the one and only person I had ever been able to trust that loved me for me to save me. But they didn't. Instead, they obliterated any last hope I had in humankind. I have been trying to pick myself up by the bootstraps and reinvent myself since, but it's harder to let go of things than you think."

Now it was Tom's turn to be out of character, to himself, that is. He felt for this woman. He actually empathized with her. There was no one else on this planet that he knew besides himself that had been forced to use their pain as cement to fill the cracks that were made in their foundation by years of familiar abandonment and abuse. What was happening to him? Was he getting soft in his thirties? Why the hell was he caring about this woman's story?

"Wow, Rachel. That took a lot of guts to share with me. I know that wasn't easy, but I am being one hundred percent with you when I say that I understand. I too have had to rebuild myself from the ground up. It's hard- there's nothing fucking harder really. I'd be happy to share ideas or offer words of wisdom if and when you want them." This girl needed a friend, but did it need to be him? He needed her for shelter, food, and some money here and there. Welp, guess they were going to be friends then.

"Steaks are done," Rachel chimed in. Her voice seemed light again like she had just lifted and thrown a boulder off her chest. Tom's taste buds were doing a preemptive cha-cha-cha while his salivary glands slicked the runway for food to enter. He heard a plate and some silverware get set down on the kitchen island in front of him. Reaching over, he grabbed his fork and knife and poked around his plate until he made contact with his juicy prize. He earned this. He listened to the sad-sack and now was getting payment.

First bite in, delicious. Different flavor than what he was used to, but delicious all the same. The texture was a bit rubbery here and there, but that could be easily blamed on the age of the steak. He didn't want to know how long they'd been in her freezer so he didn't ask, but he couldn't stop himself from finding out what seasonings she went with to get such a unique, rich flavor.

"This is amazing Rachel! I can't remember the last time I ate something so good. Hats off to the Chef! Can I ask, what seasonings did you use for the steak? It's divine!"

"Well, Tom. I have to admit something else to you- Jesus, I'm just putting you through the wringer of TMI tonight- but that's actually not steak at all. It's not seasonings you are tasting because I didn't use any... I wanted you to have the full experience that you will probably never get the chance to have again." Rachel reached across the countertop, grabbed his hand, lifted and lowered it until it was resting on top of the mystery meat. Tom hadn't breathed a word in response yet. He was trying not to throw up from the memory of the steak-like substance entering his palette and currently being digested. He was trying not to panic when he heard Rachel call him Tom- she'd only ever called him and, to his knowledge, believed him to be Benjamin. Who the fuck was Rachel and what the fuck was his right-hand touching?

"It's placenta Tom. Her placenta... the one that connected me to her before I had it ripped away from me. I thought Daddy should be included in this too... after all these years, it only seemed fair."

"What the fuck are you talking about, Rachel? What's going on here? Who sent you to my apartment a week ago? You need to tell me- you owe it to me. I can't even see to protect myself." He was nothing but a simpering fool now.

"Well, let's get a few things straight here. Your dear friend Stella -not so dear, really. She sent me to you because she felt obligated to help clean up Remi's mess after she fucked up her attempt to kill you. See Stella, Myra, and Remi all know each other now. And I guess depending on how you look at things- I really sent them... to each other. I was the one that planted vengeance in their souls. I was the one that led them to this- to try to and kill you."

"But why? Did I get you pregnant? I don't recall ever hooking up with a Rachel- I think there is a mix-up here." He felt her hand wrap around his wrists. She pulled and he was zip-tied together. Before he could try to stand, she had one of his legs tied to the stool he had been teetering on the last hour. Fuck.

"Well, that's because we didn't just hook up you sleazy piece of shit. You were the one that broke me. But killing you - well, that's going to fix me again and make our dead little girl very happy." Rachel must have read the confused look on his face, "Oh, you sad sack of dumb shit- do you seriously not remember me? You came into my life in high school, abducted my heart, I found out I was pregnant, did what I did without ever telling you, and then drove all the way out to your college to tell you the truth- to ask for you back. But all you did was set me up to embarrass me - to make me out as a whore that wasn't worth hearing out. You never could have handled the truth back then, I see that now, but what did you, how you treated me afterward was unforgivable. I trusted you. I thought I knew you. I believed you when you said you would always love me, no matter what. That you'd always be there for me. All you are is a pathetic loser that painted himself a pretty face for a surgeon to make with a raging hard-on for anything that walks. So when I found you, found out who you were and what you were doing, I knew it was my time. My years of pain and suffering are long gone- you're just the final stop on the gameboard and I almost had them erase you, my little puppets. But a real bitch knows she has to do the hard shit herself. So you understand who I am now, Tom? You know what's about to go down here?"

"Kim? It has to be you, Kim?"

"Yeah, well, now I go by Kay, but you can still call me that for the next hour or so. See, I'm going to make killing you fun... for me. You- well, you're gonna hate it." Kim laughed insanely as she ripped through the front of his shirt. The sound of miniature buttons hitting the floor sprung through his ears. Kim was dragging the tip of his placenta knife across his chest, pushing down just enough to break the skin. He felt slow, warm trickles of blood leaving the long slits she gently carved.

"Kim, Kay. Whatever you like to be called now, I didn't know. I never thought you were pregnant. Why didn't you tell me?" Tom was grasping at straws here. He was desperate to distract her but through his ploy, there was genuine sorrow. He'd loved this girl, this woman; she was the one that broke *him*. Could it be true that neither of them ever stopped loving the other and, at the same time, hating another?

"It was my step-dad. He was molesting me at night- raping me. I told my mother but she didn't believe me, said I was a sick, jealous little brat with daddy issues. She blamed my biological father and said she hoped one day I would just disappear- run off to find him since I was so much like him. Always telling lies. I couldn't tell you about it- I was afraid you wouldn't believe me either and you were all I had. There was a chance the baby was his and at the time I couldn't fathom having to stare at some ugly raper baby every day for the rest of my life. It was the biggest mistake I've ever made besides trusting you as much or as little as I did. And now look at you- you're the predator."

"Whoa, whoa, whoa, I have never raped anyone. Everyone I've ever been with has been more than willing." She tightened the zip ties around his hands with a jerk. They were digging in, threatening to touch bone.

"Yeah, whatever. They are your prey, aren't they? Usually stupid little birds you pick- most independently wealthy- now Myra... she was a bit of shock. She's definitely not your typical girl, is she? That's why you had to try so had to be someone you're not to be with her. But my question for you is, why? Why try so hard to be with someone that you don't really care about? Is it really all just to get in their pants whenever you want? If it were all just about sex, couldn't you just go out to the nightclubs and bars and have one-night stands every night? I mean it is New York City- there are a lot of options out there it's hard to believe you would get through them all. I should know, I watched you fornicate with them on those stupid bizarre little cameras you installed in your home like a genuine sick-fuck; not nearly enough to claim the entire NYC female population. A solid try but another far-off failure. And by the way, next time INVEST some money in the tech you choose - the cheap pieces of melted plastic you bought were hilariously easy to hack - a monkey could do it."

"You're right, not just about cheaping out on the cameras, but about it not just being about sex. It's a game. I felt fooled by you and I guess my gameplay now is to see if I could do the same and for how long until I got caught. I always thought you were the master of pretend- the best actress I had ever met. A wicked one. A pretty one. One that I loved. But now I want to be the one that gets to set the rules, cheat, and win the game. What's so wrong with that? I mean, after you, there was no one worth living for besides myself- a newer, better version of *me*." Kim had picked the knife back up and was doodling with its blade along the top of his panted crotch. He knew he needed to back down again. He'd had practiced playing the Sub with Stella. He just needed to step into that character now- to save his dick from being cut off.

"You were the one playing the game from the start, Tom. Don't you dare lie to me. I did everything for you- including withholding my secrets. They hurt me enough - I didn't want them to hurt you too. I knew that if I told you all the things, there'd be no way you'd grow up to be the man you dreamt of being. You probably would have gone to prison for murdering my stepdad, and your life would have been ruined. I loved you back then. I loved you so much that I wanted to spare you the hurt. But then you didn't care enough about me to do the same, did you? You lied to me; told me anything you thought a silly young teen girl might want to hear just to get in her panties."

"Do you hear yourself right now? You just said that you felt like I would have killed the sick son of a bitch if I would have known the truth about what he was doing to you. And you know what? You're right, I would have. I know that. You knew that. So why wouldn't that be living proof that I loved you? That I was sincere in my feelings for you? It's proof to me- why can't you see that?"

For the first time since Kim had been reintroduced into his life, she seemed to tumble over her own words, "I am, yeah, I guess, well, wait now..."

"No, you just wait there. I lived through a lot of pain, not knowing why you ended things with me- not really. My mind went to some really dark places, Kim- you say I broke you, but you broke me too. You say you loved me and I love you, too. Do you think you might still be in love with me? I mean, why else would you make it your life's business to seek revenge on me if you didn't still care just a little? Huh? Wouldn't seeing me and knowing what I do with those other sluts be enough to break you right there if you didn't still have hope?"

"Hope for what Tom?"

"Hope that we could still make it? Hope that we could have a life together? A family? Jesus Christ Kim, you were the only person I ever imagined having that kinda life with and still are." There was silence between the pair. Tom had let something slip out; something he hadn't even allowed himself to hear in the past decade.

"You mean that Tom? You still would want that life with me?"

"Of fucking course, Kim. No matter what, I know you're my god-damn soulmate; I was a fool in college. I was hurt; devastated by you. But no matter how many bitches I get with, I can't catch feelings for a single one while you- you just keep dancing around in my head. When I fuck them, I pretend I'm fucking you. Not every time, but the times I want it to feel like I mean it... like *it* means something."

"We could never have the life we dreamt of together. I *just* told you, I can't have children anymore."

"There's always adoption..."

"No, I want it to be a part of you and me. Not some stranger's baby."

Tom started piecing together some of the shards he remembered from the night of Remi's attempted murder. She had mentioned a baby... his baby? It had to be. Who the fucks else would it be? Bingo. He just got himself out of a sticky situation from creating another sticky situation up inside Remi's twat.

"Well, good news for us. I have a child on the way and its birth mom is about to die, so..."

A spark of lightness lept across Kim's face. Too bad Tom couldn't see her moment of excitement. "I'm not sure what to do here... I never thought this would be how this conversation or this night was going to go." Tom felt the knife at the sides of his palms as it separated his wrists with one fowl swoop. She was untying him because she still loved him. He was crying because he knew he was going to live. And because deep down, he couldn't help but still love the crazy cunt, too.

Looking down at her finger, Kay admired the pearl ring. Sliding it around on her still thin finger, remembering the day he'd given it to her. It felt like it was only yesterday that he was making a promise to her. All these years and she still had it. She could never will herself enough to hawk it even in times she could have really used the cold, hard cash. Maybe there was hope in her heart after all? Maybe it was buried in the cavity of their unborn child, the one she still carried in her heart of hearts and talked to from time to time?

Trio | Remi, Stella, & Myra

"Who is this friend of yours? She sounds like a complete riot- I'd love to meet her," Stella said with a snort. Now the world knows how the impenetrable Miss Madam Madsen reacts when she is actually shook.

"Well, you kind of already have. I mean, very briefly. But her name is Kay, she's the woman I met at the coffee shop one day and she came back with me to the firm... blonde, a real interesting dresser. Old-fashioned style."

Something clicked inside of Remi's mind, flagging her to question, "Wait a minute. You said her name is Kay. Would she happen to look like this?" Remi pointed at a picture that the gal pals had snapped on her phone that day at the coffee shop. The day Remi had story-vomited for an ego-boost.

"Yeah, that's her. Do you know her too?" Rachel seemed surprised in asking.

"Of fucking course. She works in my building, on the floor above mine. We started hanging out for coffee breaks and outside of work here and there about a year ago when we met. Come to think of it, I divested quite a bit of info with this chick. She's always curious about everything and wants all the dirty details. Of course, she's involved. She is the Queen of 'up to something'." Remi was worried now more than ever about what she shared with her phony-ass friend.

"Well, I have something else to come clean about. Kay had been helping me with taking care of your sick friend, Benjamin, Stella. I'm really sorry. I know you were trusting me to help, and in turn, thought it might be just the thing to help me figure out who I am and who I want to become. But it was a lot of extra hours- I've been going through some stuff right now, as you well know, and Kay offered to take half the shifts off my plate. She said no one would ever need to know, so how could it hurt anything?"

The original trio all turned to stare one another down. Stella was the first to speak, "So Rachel, my friend Ben had mentioned he was staying with you since his apartment fell through and you say he hasn't been. Is there a chance that Ben thinks you and Kay are the same person and he's staying with her?"

"Yeah, I mean I guess. Kay and I decided to not tell your friend that we were two different people- we didn't want to stress or freak him out. But why would Kay let a stranger stay at her place?" Rachel could feel all three women's glares penetrating through the sides of her highly placed cheekbones. "I get it. I don't know her very well, and this all seems pretty fucked up. My bad." Rachel touted.

"Yeah, your bad, huh? Well, Rach... this Kay gal sounds like a shady character who might not have our little friend Benny Boy's best inter-est in mind. So #notagreatfuckingchoice. Let's do better." Stella said snidely, with a full mean-girl, toothy sneer baring the fronts of her lips.

"I wonder how her boyfriend feels about that? Do you know where she lives, Rachel? I think it might be high time for us ladies to pay her a brief visit to see what she's been getting herself into these days." Remi followed, almost completely ignoring the staggering blow Stella had just thrown to the dog-face girl.

Remi felt nauseous. It wasn't because of the unfolding drama, nor was it because she was unnerved by realizing there was another snake in her life. Her nausea came from the hard work her body was doing to build a perfect, innocent little baby inside of her. She would keep it pure. She would salvage it from the damning acts that were sure to ensue the rest of her life. She had made a choice earlier that day that even as the Devil's daughter, she would raise an angel.

Rachel admitted she knew where Kay lived. She had just moved out of an old studio in the arts district to a new two-bedroom apartment where she had said she would expect a little more privacy and a lot less drama.

"She wouldn't have left a lot of her furniture out by some dumpsters; would she have had?" Myra thought to ask. The description of her old place sounded a heck of a lot like the area Myra lived in. Was she using the cunning bitch's old furniture in her exhibit across the street? Would life be that tangled? Could the universe intertwine with strangers so deeply as that?

Remi's call to action brought all their attention back to the mission at hand. "Rachel, you lead the way. Ladies, get ready to go toe to toe with a real cunt?"

The baby inside Remi's womb answered.

" Go and kill him. He's not my daddy, anyway."

Meet Ms. Black

Melanie Black is the author of the "mind-bendingly cringeworthy" novel *Attempted*, the first book in the psychological drama series. Black is also a professional copywriter and content strategist serving clients across the US.

As a little girl clutching her pen and paper on the playground, Melanie knew she was born to be a writer. Her first publication, a poem called *My Reflection*, was in the fifth grade. She couldn't wait to grow up and be a writer. And now she is... and a happy one at that.

Melanie enjoys writing dramas, psychological and fantasy thrillers, historical fiction, and remains an avid poet. She writes her masterpieces from a desk that peers out into the wonders of her own acreage.

Learn more about the author and her future works, including *Rekindled,* the sequel to the book you just read: www.authormelanieblack.com

CPSIA information can be obtained
at www.ICGtesting.com
Printed in the USA
JSHW020727070123
35746JS00005B/54/J